"YOU ARE NOT AFRAID?" DRAKE ASKED HER.

"Not any more than I fear the wind in the trees or the waves on the sea," Eileen answered. "They can cause harm, I know, but I do not fear them for all that."

As for the first time her skin felt the masculine roughness of his, Eileen felt the core of excitement within her burst and spread like wildfire. Her fingers dug into the rippling muscles of his shoulders as he lifted her from the floor to bring her closer. Instinctively, her hips moved closer to his, and the heat of him sent the wildfire blazing higher.

"Oh, God, princess," Drake groaned against her ear. "Let me love you now."

Drake placed her down onto the bed, and then lifted her into the heavens with his kisses. . . .

SILVER
ENCHANTRESS

Patricia Rice

AN ONYX BOOK

NEW AMERICAN LIBRARY

Copyright © 1988 by Patricia Rice

All rights reserved

 Onyx is a trademark of New American Library.

SIGNET, SIGNET CLASSIC, MENTOR, ONYX, PLUME, MERIDIAN
and NAL BOOKS are published by NAL PENGUIN INC.,
1633 Broadway, New York, New York 10019

First Printing, July, 1988

1   2   3   4   5   6   7   8   9

PRINTED IN THE UNITED STATES OF AMERICA

To my children,
who seldom understand, but have the grace to endure

Tell me not here, it needs not saying,
What tune the enchantress plays.
A. E. Houseman, *More Poems*

Prologue

——— ❦ ———

The woman's screams lingered on the evening air long after the men disappeared. The autumn-colored trees shivered with her hysteria, and the trampled ground throbbed with her pain. The screams had long since dwindled to broken sobs and died away with the departure of the masked mob, but the forest still held the vibrations of their violence.

Amid the muddied leaves left littering the forest's floor lay the crumpled body of a large man, his rich, golden hair now caked with a brownish substance that bore no resemblance to the mud below him. His torn clothing and the trampled ground bore the evidence of the strength of his resistance, but one man against many can only fall, as he had been told often enough during his lifetime.

Another leaf drifted from the oak above, adding to the small mound of leaves already forming like a red and brown mantle upon the fallen warrior. No movement disturbed nature's blanket.

Except in one corner of the clearing. Beneath a chestnut sapling, a tiny mound of dark green velvet whimpered and moved faintly. That sound alone brought alertness to the crouching figure hiding in the bushes, gazing fearfully on this scene of carnage.

Terrified, the intruder gave the corpse a wide berth

as she ran across the clearing, her old eyes searching anxiously for the source of the faint sobs. Discovering the velvet-clad bundle on the ground, the old woman knelt beside it and gently lifted a small head in her capable hands. The child whimpered and buried herself deeper into the debris of summers past, but when the woman spoke, a small face turned expectantly toward the sound.

A gasp escaped the old woman's lips as she raised her fingers from the child's copper tresses and stared in horror at the blood staining her palm. The blank gray gaze of the child's eyes briefly reflected the last glimpse of blue in the sky above, then went dark.

Chapter I

—— ❦ ——

England
August, 1735

A thick canopy of oaks blocked out all but the most daring of the sun's rays, holding in the heat of a late summer day. No breeze lifted the damp tendrils of her heavy hair as Ellen stooped to rescue a buttercup from the crude roadway. No carriage could traverse this old grass-covered cart path, but the woodcutter's donkeys with their heavy loads had worn ruts through spring mud and left hardened traces in the baked clay of summer.

The road divided in two paths at this clearing, but Ellen had no interest in following either of them. She foraged among the brambles at the road's edge for berries, but more often than not, dawdled over the beauty of a rich purple violet or the startling flight of a brilliant butterfly. The unusually oppressive heat had no apparent effect on her other than a slight beading of moisture on her childish brow.

The dull thud of hoofbeats startled her from her reverie, but she made no effort to run and hide as her brothers did when strangers intruded upon the forest. The boys were older and wiser in the ways of the world and knew better than to confront imminent danger in the open. Ellen, however, had the unnerving habit of meeting all confrontations fearlessly, though she often felt the stripes of the woodcutter's switch for her obstinacy. The boys called her a dull-witted fool for not learning the sly ways that allowed them to escape their father's ire. Ellen ignored their insults as she ignored all else, tearlessly traipsing through her childhood, accepting whatever life brought.

This day it brought the sight of two elegantly garbed gentlemen on horseback, or rather, one gentleman and one youth. The elder was garbed conservatively in a long waistcoat, knee breeches of rich satin, and bagwig, but the younger had discarded both coat and waistcoat and rode in shirt sleeves, with his lace cravat untied. The boy's golden hair shone like candle flames against the forest's dark backdrop, and his laughing eyes made a mockery of any dignity he might have achieved with his noble mount and wealthy dress.

As the girl stared up at the intruders with curiosity, they returned her regard with equal fascination, for forest sprites were seldom encountered in these mundane times. The child's thick auburn hair gleamed like burnished copper, though no ray of sun broke the gloom to enhance its color. She could be no more than nine or ten, and her slim figure beneath its tattered gown seemed slighter than any elfin creature's. But it was the bold stare of silver eyes that spoke of magic and inflamed the boy's imagination. Like the mirror of a still pond, her eyes captured the clouds and reflected the light, revealing nothing of hidden recesses.

"Have we entered an enchanted forest?" The boy spoke seriously, but his eyes continued to laugh. "Are you the fairy princess who lives here and guards the inhabitants? Are we trespassing?"

The child made no reply, but seemed to consider this question solemnly. With no patience for this foolery, the older man intruded.

"Is there a well around here? A stream? Somewhere we might rest the horses and take a sip of something cool?" he demanded abruptly.

"A morsel of bread or a crumb of cheese would be

appreciated also," the youth laughed. "My belly growls and threatens to eat me alive. Surely fairy princesses can command a feast, if it be only an apple?"

A flicker of something much like laughter lightened those still gray eyes, and the child motioned for them to follow before turning down the right-hand path.

Quicker than his father, the boy gathered her intention and hastened to turn his mount after her. Too hungry to keep the sedate pace required by her small steps, he removed his foot from the stirrup and leaned over to offer his hand to the child.

"Ride with me and point the way, Princess."

A brief flicker of delight lit her eyes before they shadowed and grew cool again. Taking his hand, she lithely placed her foot in the stirrup and allowed him to haul her up in front of him. She rested easily in the curve of the saddle, as if accustomed to riding in such a manner, though her tattered garb told another story.

She led them to a clearing surrounding a small thatched cottage, its barren yard speaking of the poverty of its owners. No flowers bedecked the windowsills, though an exhausted, scraggly garden grew in one corner of the lot. An ancient donkey swished its tail lazily at a nagging fly, and the girl made a face at the sight. Shrugging her shoulders, she gestured to be let down.

Both strangers dismounted, eyeing the dark windows of the poor house with some degree of trepidation. The child's shining eyes and scrubbed cheeks had given the impression of rude health, overriding the simpleness of her crude gown. Something in her gestures had led them to believe she belonged to a wealthier house than this, perhaps as servant or child of caretakers but not daughter to poverty. They exchanged uneasy glances.

The girl took no heed of their discomfort, directing them to the stream trickling through the yard to water their mounts. When they obeyed, she disappeared through the darkness of the gaping cottage door.

In a twinkling she returned, carrying two battered mugs and a jug of cider on a platter, as if she were indeed a princess and serving tea to royalty. The effect was instantly spoiled by the appearance of an unshaven scarecrow of a man, who yelled after the girl.

"What do you mean to do with that jug, girl? Come back here, you little hellion!" He halted at the sight of the gentlemen.

The girl calmly poured the drink and offered it to her guests.

Glancing from the grimy scarecrow to the dignified child, the youth rebelliously put the mug to his lips and drank long and deep. His father gave him an angry glance, but now that the damage was done, he, too, sipped the offered refreshment before speaking to his "host."

"Do not scold the child, man, she only does our bidding. I will pay to replace the jug. We have come far this day and the next inn is farther still. Would you begrudge us a drink on a day such as this?"

The man tucked his filthy hands beneath his armpits and glared at the stranger. "A drink and no more. This ain't no alehouse."

While the men confronted each other angrily, the child slipped away, motioning for the boy to follow. Five or six years her elder, he was caught between the need to hold his place among the adults and the desire of a child to explore. Curiosity and hunger won the battle, and he followed the sprite.

She reappeared bearing a soft pouch of leather that seemed to carry a heavy weight. Keeping it hidden in the folds of her skirt, she surreptitiously passed it to her newfound friend.

Knowing at once its contents from the mischievous gleam of silver eyes, the youth grinned and accepted the package. Keeping one eye on their elders, who continued to argue vociferously, he led the girl back to his horse, where he deposited the pouch and rummaged in the capacious pockets of his coat. In a moment he withdrew a small packet of ribbons.

"My sister has no need for more of these. I daresay even fairy princesses can find use for ribbons. I like the yellow best."

The unexpectedness of this gesture brought an instant's joy to childish lips, but then, hastily remembering her manners, she dropped a clumsy curtsy. The effect of this respectful gesture was quickly lost when she used the moment to hide the packet in her garter, but the youth had no appreciation of respect and more interest in her quickness of wit.

Before he could question her as he longed to do, she gestured toward his father and motioned for him to mount. Her fingers flew in a manner that left no doubt to her message, though she spoke not a word. He mounted and, with a quick gesture of farewell, hastened to follow after his furious parent.

Out of sight of the cottage once more, the older man turned in suspicion at the sound of a crunching apple.

"Where in hell did you steal that?" he demanded irritably.

"The Princess of Apples gave it to me. Would you like one?" He reached in the pouch and produced another, his eyes blue and laughing.

His father glared his confusion at this puzzling offspring of his. The boy had all the makings of a man but the wits of a fool. How did one teach a fool responsibility? He took the apple and bit into it harshly.

"Charm your sister with your fairy tales if you must, but leave girls like that one back there alone. I doubt if Lady Pamela would understand if you are knee-deep in bastards before your vows are said."

His son snorted rudely and took the last bite of his apple. Out of sight, the image of copper and silver glimmered mystically in his imagination, and his father's prosaic warnings provided food for irritation. "One does not bed fairy princesses, Father," he replied mockingly. "I trust Lady Pamela does not consider herself in that category."

Remembering that young lady's haughty demeanor, his father had to give a curt bark of laughter at the aptness of this cut. "She will grow out of it soon enough if she does. You're both too young, for now. There will be time enough to please each other after she comes of age."

The boy looked doubtful, but had the wisdom to remain silent.

Chapter II

England
September, 1740

Elli carried in an armful of firewood and neatly stacked it by the grate, feeding smaller kindling into the flames to revive last night's ashes. She enjoyed watching the small flames licking the dry twigs, growing larger and hungrier until the whole kitchen filled with their warmth.

The coziness of Dulcie's kitchen always attracted her, and she worked willingly to keep it that way. The kettle sang a merry tune as the fire grew strong, and Elli reached for the tin mugs hanging on the hooks on the wall. She brought down the blackened frying pan, too, and sliced a small portion of rashers into it. Dulcie enjoyed waking to the smell of coffee and breakfast cooking. It was one of the reasons she had first allowed Elli to make herself at home there.

Elli's thoughts were far from that past now as she stirred the meat in the pan and sliced a slab of bread and held it above the fire. This day had begun with a frost upon the ground, but the sun promised a lovely day, at last, and she had plans for just such a day.

Dulcie waddled achingly into the tiny kitchen area behind her shop, rubbing the arthritic hip that had kept her awake most of the night. Her scowl softened at the sight of the young girl working over the fire, her fair cheeks ruddy with the heat and her eyes sparkling with anticipation. Dulcie had no idea how the young scamp spent her days, but she appreciated the girl's presence in the morning.

"You're a dear, my girl. What's an old woman to do without a young one about?" She settled comfortably at the old wooden table, inhaling the aroma from the mug Elli set before her.

The girl made no reply, but busily lifted the pan from the fire, sopping the grease onto the toasted bread and producing plates for both of them. She hummed contentedly as she worked.

The old woman sighed and shook her head. She would give a year's earnings to hear the tale that never passed those silent lips. The first time Elli had appeared in the village she had been just a child tagging behind Nan and her assorted brood. Nan had always wanted a girl, instead of that unruly herd of young hooligans. But Nan had sworn she was her sister's child and none knew any better.

Over the years the child had taken to wandering into the village on her own. At first, one or the other of Nan's brood would come to fetch her and take her back, but after a while she came and went on her own. There was no questioning the girl, but the occasional blackening bruise upon her fair wrist or cheek spoke volumes. Her willingness to work had opened doors as well as hearts.

Until the child had become a part of the village, sleeping wherever there was a spare bed, eating wherever there was an extra bowl. One of the men had sought out the girl's family, only to discover them gone from the hut they had occupied for so long. The villagers could have turned her over to the parish, but none seemed willing to agree to that. So the child stayed, adopted by an entire town.

The girl's silence irritated some but was accepted by most. Many thought her a half-wit and laughed at her daydreaming ways, but Dulcie knew better. She had once worked in a house of quality and knew their looks and manners. This changeling child had the high, fine cheekbones and straight, proud nose of an aristocratic lineage. Her long, slender figure was repeated in the fine bones of her hands and feet. By-blow she might be, but witless she was not. Her seemingly mindless wanderings had a purpose, though it differed from the prosaic ones of the villagers. If only the girl could speak, Dulcie was convinced the correctness of her opinion would be proved.

"Fine day today. Off to the woods, are you?" she inquired lightly, watching as the girl bit hungrily into the toast.

Elli nodded eagerly, sketching with her hands in the air as she would with a stub of charcoal later. Her fingers itched to apply autumn colors to the black-and-white sketches she had made earlier. She had learned to coax color from many of the plants in the woods, and the berries should be ripe enough today to make red.

Dulcie nodded in understanding, wishing she had the coins to buy the child real watercolors. But this was a poor village, and the meager living she made at mending and sewing scarcely kept a roof over her head. The others, too, had families to feed and clothe. Elli received what little they had to give, but coins for watercolors none had to spare.

The girl moved with swift grace about the tiled floor, nearly dancing as she scrubbed the last of the grease from the pan and washed the breakfast utensils. Dulcie guessed she must nearly be fifteen years of age by now and sighed again. The skinny child of a year ago was rapidly blossoming into a woman. There were not many boys hereabouts, not since Nan and her brood had left, leastways, but men had a way of searching out unattached young women. This one would be no exception. She wondered how much the child knew about the ways of men but hesitated to broach the subject. Every woman learned soon enough.

Elli gave her friend a peck on the cheek and danced out the door. She stopped at the Clancys' back door and helped the youngest pull up his breeches before following him into the kitchen. The baby wailed for its breakfast while his mother harriedly spooned out gruel for the others. Elli relieved her of the pot and finished the task while Molly gratefully picked up the babe and quieted it with a full breast. For a fifteen-year-old, Elli had learned more about life than many more educated girls.

Molly gave her a hunk of day-old bread and a slab of cheese as she left a while later. Elli smiled, hugged the baby, and wandered on. She had no regrets at losing the home in the woods where she had spent so many years. Nan had tried to love her, but the others never had. They had begrudged every morsel that passed her lips. The boys had been rough with her, knowing she could not cry for help or tell on them. As they grew older, they had been worse than rough, and she did not miss their constant harassment in the least. The village was her home. Its inhabitants were her family. She was as content here as she could be anywhere.

That was not to say she was any angel. When aroused, her anger was violent and rebellious. One of the boys still bore the scars of the red-hot coals she had flung at him. The blacksmith had nearly lost a finger when he made the mistake of touching her in the wrong place while her hands were within easy reach of a knife. Luckily for everyone, her anger stayed well buried for the most part, a hidden demon that haunted her dreams more often than her days.

Elli switched at the long grass beside the road as she wandered away from the village, sketchpad in hand. She had stolen the sketchpad from a drunken soldier who had stayed at the tavern one night. He had no use for it where he was going, and his poor attempts at likenesses had not been worth the waste of the precious paper.

A carriage rolled sedately along the road ahead, approaching the village Elli had just left behind. Carriages were rare in these parts, and this one seemed to have some difficulty adjusting to the rutted cart path. It lurched slowly from side to side, sending up clouds of dust.

Elli delicately stepped from the road into the tall grass, watching with a mixture of amusement and fascination as the unwieldy vehicle hit a bump and the driver cursed loudly. She admired the proud bays working so diligently to haul their heavy load, and her silver gaze reflected her admiration.

The morning sun glittered on auburn tresses caught up in a simple yellow ribbon. She wore a wide-pocketed apron over an old frock of Molly's, taken in and hemmed up until it was good as new. Her fair skin bore a hint of rose from the brisk walk, and her smile beamed as naturally as the morning sun as she watched the carriage's progress.

Elli could see a pale woman garbed in mourning inside the carriage, her hair capped and hidden from view. A man sat on the far side of her, but she could discern little of his figure except the rich blue of his coat. She wished she could squeeze a color such as that from her plants and berries, but so far she had succeeded in only a watered-down version.

The woman glanced out at her as the carriage rolled by, and for one brief moment their eyes met. Elli smiled and waited patiently for the dust to settle so she might walk on. The woman screamed and tugged violently on her husband's coat.

The screams could not be heard over the rattle of wheels and gallop of horses, and Elli continued on her way, unaware of the carriage's slowing pace. The place where the best berries grew was another half a mile into the forest, and she kicked her dusty shoes at a pebble in her way.

Inside the carriage, the woman frantically tugged at her husband's arm as he called for the driver to halt.

"Emily! It was Emily! I swear it! Not her ghost, John! Oh, God, please stop and catch her! John, make him stop!" Her screams grew more frantic with each passing moment as the driver struggled to bring the prancing horses to a halt.

The hapless husband looked harried and worried at the same time, nervously patting his wife's hand and muttering reassuring phrases as he tried to glance down the road behind him. He knew better than to expect to see their dead daughter risen from the grave, but his wife was not normally an excitable woman. Her daughter's untimely death had strained her health, but he never had reason to suspect it had taxed her mind.

The carriage finally came to a halt and a footman leaped to open the door. Sir John attempted to persuade his wife to stay inside, but she insisted on following him into the roadway.

"There she is, going into the woods! Oh, follow her, John, hurry please!"

They had traveled nearly half a mile from where the girl had veered off into the tall grass and strode toward the stand of trees. The man gazed down at his wife in incredulity at her command. Normally a placid man of middle age, he had not run since he was a boy, and he had no intention of taking up the practice now.

He turned to the footman and gestured toward the disappearing figure down the road. "Follow that girl, Quigley. Tell her my wife would like to speak with her, if you please."

The young footman looked mildly astonished, but hastened to do as told.

As the lad ran in pursuit of the girl, the woman wilted against her husband's arm. "Oh, John, am I losing my mind, then? Is this what happens when grief takes its toll? She was so young, John. It just does not seem fair."

Awkwardly, he held her close and patted her shoulder. "Don't cry, Emma. You'll see. It's the hair, I should imagine. The hair is much like Emily's. But she'll be some robust country miss with rotting teeth or crossed eyes or pox marks. Quigley will bring her back and I'll give her a shilling to be on her way. You can't help wishing, my dear. I'd give all I had to bring Emily back for you, but I daresay she's happy where she is. We must remember that, Emma."

His reassuring monologue murmured on as the footman raced down the road in pursuit of his prey. The woman grew quiet, but refused to return to the carriage. She had seen what she had seen, and she refused to believe her eyes had confused a snaggletoothed peasant with her own lovely, delicate daughter.

Quigley followed as best as he could, but this was unfamiliar terrain. As soon as the girl slipped into the shade of the trees, she was lost to him. Brambles tore his clothes and small branches slapped his face as he sought some discernible path to follow, some sight of the mysterious girl who had sent the missus into tears, to no avail.

Elli heard his thrashing and cursing and paused behind a wide oak to discover the source. Unimpressed with the young man in fancy gray livery who had obviously followed her into this lonely place, she slipped away, leaving him to his plight. Men did not rate high on her list of favorite things.

In despair at disappointing the man who had treated him well for so many years, Quigley finally fought his way from the woods back to the waiting carriage. The absence of his quarry told his tale without words, and the lady began to sob quietly. Sir John questioned him with his eyes.

"It weren't no use, sir. There's no sign of a path. I

called, but she didn't answer. Disappeared. she did, like a deer at dawn."

Or a ghost, but Sir John did not put that thought into words. "Thank you, Quigley, you did your best. Make inquiries in the village, will you? She must live hereabouts. I'll take Lady Summerville to the inn and return to help you."

The command was curt and unemotional, but produced an instantaneous response. Quigley made a rapid bow and set off toward the village, and the lady hugged her husband tearfully. Sir John had expected both responses and accepted them as his due.

"Come, Emma. You are overwrought. This journey has been too much for you. We will make you comfortable, then settle this mystery at once."

They climbed into the carriage and rode off, leaving the hapless Quigley to question the suspicious and closemouthed villagers.

By the end of the day, the young footman had resorted to sitting on a stump beside a small tavern, whittling a piece of kindling and watching the world go by. The carriage had not returned and neither had the girl, if she existed at all.

Returning with her sketchpad crammed with colors and leaves, her apron filled with the treasures she had found, Elli spied the young man at his post before she had passed the first house. She turned quickly down an alleyway and entered Molly's kitchen from the rear.

Brown-eyed, dark-haired Molly glanced up in relief at the young girl's entrance. "There you are. There's a gent from one of the fancy houses askin' after you. What've you gone and done now? Stolen more apples from his lordship's trees?"

Elli shrugged her slender shoulders and sampled the stew simmering over the fire. She was aware of doing nothing wrong, though she considered his lordship's apples the same as the leaves on the trees or the chestnuts on the ground, free for the taking. The fancy young man would never find her if she did not wish to be found, and he could prove nothing against her if he did.

Presenting a handful of acorns to the toddler, Elli slipped out into the deepening twilight. Molly knew nothing of interest. Perhaps Dulcie would.

Mischief made her cross the road near enough to the tavern to be seen. The young man looked up in time to catch sight of long auburn hair and a yellow gown disappearing down a side road. He yelled and jumped up and ran after her, but she paid him no heed.

Dulcie gave Elli a look of irritation as the girl entered by the back door. The child was well behaved enough most times, but there was a wayward streak in her that would cause them trouble soon enough. She prayed that time had not yet come.

"What have you been up to now that the swells are looking after you, you naughty heathen?" Dulcie demanded as Elli stopped to warm her fingers at the fire.

A flicker of laughter played in silver eyes as the girl looked up with a smile and a shrug. Even if she could speak, what could she say? She had done nothing.

"Well, there's some gent's man out there askin' questions of you. I'm surprised you didn't see him when you came in. All day he's been out there. Proper grand, he is. Mayhap you ought to see what he wants."

That suggestion struck Elli as ludicrous. She was curious, certainly, but so was the cat who had looked upon the queen.

A pounding at the shop door warned that the footman had begun his rounds again. The old woman and the young girl exchanged glances. Shrugging, Dulcie dragged herself back to the front room.

Elli listened eagerly as the liveried servant inquired after "the young girl in a yellow frock" seen crossing the street in this direction. Knowing she was listening, Dulcie returned the stranger's questions with a question.

"Isn't there enough girls where you come from that you must pester after ours?"

Quigley grasped gratefully at this opening. "No, ma'am, it's not that, you see. It's me mistress. She's been taken ill since her daughter died. And then she sees this girl what looks so much like Miss Emily, she cries and carries on so that Sir John sent me to look for her. He don't mean her no harm. It's just to make the lady happy, you see."

Elli heard desperation pleading in his voice, and she scowled at the gleaming pots on the walls. She had no great amount of faith in her fellow man, but she did not want to cause anyone trouble, either. She intended to go nowhere alone with the eager young man, but she supposed it would do no harm to show she existed.

There was no sense getting Dulcie in trouble. Elli quietly let herself out the back door and walked around to the front. The sun had not yet set. There would be light enough to see the stranger's expression when she walked in on them.

In the distance, she saw a carriage approaching, probably returning for the servant. She had best get this over with quickly. Then she could escape into the woods, if necessary. No one ever found her there.

She opened the shop door and brought the colors of the setting sun into the room with her. Quigley swung around and gaped openly. Dulcie nodded her approval.

"This here's Elli. Be she the one you seek?" Dulcie inquired innocently.

The young man's thin, dark face was a picture of astonishment as his gaze absorbed the thick, nearly red hair sweeping to a waistline of incredible tininess. Delicately boned, expressive features framed wide, light eyes of intense curiosity, and Quigley understood his lady's hysterics. This girl was no ghost, but more flesh and blood than Miss Emily had ever been. Seen hastily, she would easily pass for the dead girl's twin.

"How do you do, Miss . . . Elli?" Even the name had a passing resemblance. By this time Quigley was prepared to accept the supernatural.

Elli made a brief curtsy and wandered into the shop. She was starving, and a hint of mischief brightened her eyes as she produced an apple from her apron and began to munch on it. Dulcie nearly turned purple, but the young man didn't turn a hair.

"Is there a surname you are called by?" Quigley asked nervously. Now that he had found her, he was not at all certain what to do with her, but he was a resourceful man. He would think of something.

"She don't speak," Dulcie informed him generously, relieved that he had shown no recognition of the forbidden apple.

That posed a serious problem, and Quigley pondered it for a while. "Surely she must have a name. Who are her parents?"

The sound of the carriage in the street put an end to this conversation. Quigley swung around and headed for the door to signal his employer. Dulcie and Elli exchanged looks, and Elli began easing nervously toward the back of the shop.

Quigley gulped in dismay as he realized Lady Summerville had not stayed behind. He had hoped Sir John would settle this matter in his usual sensible manner, and that would be an end on it. Lady Summerville was an entirely different dilemma.

Quigley nodded a courteous bow to her ladyship and stepped aside to allow her in, while over her head he attempted to catch Sir John's eye. The baronet was keeping a concerned gaze on his wife, however, and noted his servant only with a brief nod.

"I trust you found her, Quigley. Good work. Apologize for the delay."

His wife's faint cry instantly returned the baronet's attention to the interior. Some rays of sun continued to pierce the growing gloom within, and Sir John followed his wife's gaze with some wonderment.

"Beth?" Lady Summerville held her fingers to her lips and stared at the girl in the shadows.

Sir John's frown grew more anxious at the sound of this name. "Emma, you should not have come. You have over-tired yourself."

"No, John, look. She looks just like Beth at that age. Beth had all the coloring, everybody said. Emily looked more like me. Oh, my God, John, am I truly losing my mind?"

Since his wife's sister, Elizabeth, had died at the hands of Irish highwaymen years ago, John seriously feared this might be so. He turned to study the younger of the two women with more care.

Elli stared back without shyness. In fact, she stepped several paces forward, fascinated by the elegant, pale lady who looked so sad and frightened. The lady was slightly taller and considerably plumper than herself, but her features were small and delicate, and her hair a faded russet beneath the white cap. Threads of gray glinted in the knotted tresses at her nape, but a shade of copper caught the last fading rays of sun. Elli had seen few people with hair like hers, and she lost all fear of this confrontation.

As the girl approached, John gave a sharp gasp of surprise. He had known both Emma and Elizabeth since they were young girls. They had grown up on the estate neighboring his. Elizabeth had been the younger, wilder, and more beautiful sister of the two. He remembered her well, now that he was faced with her image. But the uncanny resemblance was not what had made him gasp. It was the eyes.

He gestured gently toward the young girl. "Come forward, please. We mean no harm. We have only just lost a daughter to smallpox. You resemble her so closely . . ." He noted Dulcie's skeptical look and sent her a pleading glance, indicating his wife's entranced expression with a nod. The shopkeeper's face softened at the sight of Emma's obvious rapture.

"What is your name, child?" John spoke without thinking, his gaze still intent upon the play of silver in the girl's eyes. Elizabeth had never possessed eyes like that. But her Irish husband had.

"She don't speak, sir," Quigley whispered warningly from behind him. "Her name's Elli. That's all I've learned."

Elli. My God, this wasn't possible. He felt a lurching in his stomach. He was too old for this. But hope had already found a place in his heart. He turned to Dulcie.

"You are her mother?" he demanded curtly, knowing the answer without being told.

Dulcie snorted. "Not me, I ain't. Nan's the one you want, but she ain't been heard from this while back. Claimed the girl was her sister's, but nobody's been by looking for her. None but you, leastways."

The girl Elli now stood before Lady Summerville, and child and woman stared at each other with curiosity and fascination. Emma lifted a frail hand to tuck a straying strand of hair behind the girl's ear, and Elli didn't flinch as she was inclined to do when someone touched her.

"Does she go by any other name but Elli?" John inquired politely, striving to hide his excitement.

"Not 'zactly. Nan called her summat like Ellen, but 'round here she's just called Elli, Nan's girl."

Emma seemed to come awake, and her bright, birdlike eyes turned to her husband. "Eileen? Could they mean Eileen? John, surely this cannot be . . . She's dead like Beth."

But the girl's eyes had gone wide at the sound of her name, and she backed away, waiting for them to say it again.

The baronet noticed the movement and gently said the name again. "Eileen? Is that your real name?"

Elli held back the tears that threatened to spill and shifted her gaze from man to wife and back again. She did not know these people, had never seen them in her life, but they spoke a name that echoed in her memory. Nan's husband had sneered it mockingly upon occasion, calling it a popish name, but the memories jarred were older than that. And she was suddenly afraid.

"Emma, I do not want to raise your hopes. We may both be over-reacting. I'll have to send someone out to find the girl's parents or whoever they might be. But those are Richard's eyes or I'll be damned. Too bloody handsome for his own good, your sister's Irishman was. Could be a by-blow of his, but where would he have found another wench just like your sister?"

Sir John turned pensively toward the woman who appeared to be the child's guardian. "Would you consider allowing the child to come to us? I know how it is to become attached to a child, but it would be for the girl's own good, I promise you. You may come with her, if you wish, to see for yourself, but I promise she will be treated better than our own daughter."

Elli's eyes lit with a fiery light as she understood these words. The memory had frightened her, but not these people. She knew instinctively that this elegant gentleman offered new worlds to explore. She had glimpsed that world once. She would see more of it. With swift determination, she flew from the room.

Emma gave a cry of dismay as the child fled. "Oh, John, you've frightened her. What will we do now?"

Dulcie sent a sharp glance after the lass. "That one's frightened of naught. You'd do well to teach her a little fear, if you ask me. I have no hold on her. She comes and goes as she pleases." She turned a wary eye back to the gentry. "But don't be expecting to get your lady daughter back. She's wild as any vixen. Gentle enough most times, but headstrong. She won't tame easy."

John smiled faintly. "Emma, she's just described

your sister. Do you think there could be two of them in the world?"

"Only the original and her daughter." And Emma's sad lips turned up at the corners in anticipation.

When Elli returned, she bore all her worldly possessions wrapped in an old shawl and carried her sketchpad under her arm. Her gaze danced eagerly from one newcomer to the other. Now life could begin.

Chapter III

—— ❦ ——

England
Spring, 1745

Drake Neville, newly styled Lord Sherbourne, smiled
cynically at the panoply of fancifully garbed country
society gathered in the medieval great room of Summer Hall. Sir John loved the past and had meticu-
lously restored this hall to its primitive grandeur,
complete with gold-embroidered arras and battle-axes
above the chimneys, but the restoration was not what
caused Drake's lips to curl. The outrageously hooped
gowns competing with extravagantly flowing, outdated
wigs in countrified attempts to achieve London elegance caused his amusement, and his regret. He had
hoped for just a small, quiet dinner with his father's
friend, but apparently Lady Summerville sought to
entertain the entire county.

If it had not been for his thorough frustration with
the conflicting advice he received daily from his father's men of business and solicitors, Drake would
have made his excuses and slipped away. But determined to turn his feet down the path he meant to
follow henceforth, Drake refused to return to London
without some decision made. He had hoped the idyllic
peace of the countryside and the sober sensibility of
Sir John would guide his thoughts, but it seemed all
the shallow glitter and pomposity of London had followed him here. It would be much too easy to fall

back on the idle days of his past and allow events to happen as they would, but Drake had no intention of being thus distracted any longer. The responsibility for his family now lay firmly on his shoulders.

Sighing inwardly, but flashing the smile for which he was known, Drake joined the company gathered in his honor. Heads twisted as he passed, young girls giggled and stared, young men hailed him affably. His devil-may-care wink brought a blush to more than one pretty face, and several less hearty companions winced beneath the young lord's enthusiastic slap of greeting. He knew his role and played it well, while simultaneously rehearsing his excuses and his escape.

The new Lord Sherbourne attracted the glances of even those who did not know him. His bright golden crop of curls crowned an arrogantly high forehead, an aquiline nose of aristocratic proportions, a strong, square jaw, and a pair of dancing blue eyes that turned many a maid's head. Thinking this to be an informal visit, he still wore only the brown broadcloth coat and breeches he had traveled in, the skirt of the coat slit at the sides to reveal the hilt of his sword, the lace of his shirt only slightly rumpled from the ride. He had disdained wearing a wig, but though his dress was less than elegant, there was no mistaking his heritage. It was for this reason, more than any other, that heads turned as he passed by. In his youth the first Marquess of Sherbourne had earned a wildly romantic reputation for adventuring; his son bore evidence of continuing his father's legend with a bold flourish all his own.

The rumors of Drake's notorious parties and eccentric friends as well as his quixotic habit of rescuing starving artists and harboring brilliant young members of the Opposition had kept tongues rattling for years. Drake himself had never taken his seat in Parliament, chiefly due to his father's support of the king. The same struggle for change and power between prince and king had embittered the relationship between Drake and his father. But now the marquess was dead and the power was all Drake's, and what he would do with it was anyone's conjecture. Since the majestic Stuarts had been forced from their throne and the staid Hanoverians had claimed their inheritance, times had been too dull. The new Marquess of Sherbourne promised to enliven them.

Sir John hurried forward to greet his guest. "Drake! Good to see you, boy. Though you're a boy no longer, I collect." He pounded his friend's son on the back in vigorous welcome, adequately repaying the marquess for his hearty pummels of earlier. "How is your sister? What brings you from the excitements of the city to our humble abode?"

"A need for advice, but the matter can wait." Drake dismissed business amiably. "Diane is as lovely as ever and sends you her greetings. I thought some fresh country air after the stench of London would be beneficial. As it is, I am contemplating telling my father's men of business to go to Hades."

Sir John chuckled and studied his friend's heir with interest. He had scarcely seen the lad these last years since society's sordid glamour had taken the young lord into its embrace. Boys must sow their wild oats, but he judged Neville had reached that stage when he must choose between dissolution and responsibility, particularly now that his father's reins had passed to him. The baronet placed his wagers on a favorable outcome. Drake had never been serious, but he had never been a fool, either.

"If you wish my advice on the subject of solicitors, I recommend your solution wholeheartedly. The lot have hearts of stone and the minds of weasels. Make yourself at home, lad. If chatter does not suit your mood, my table is at your disposal. And if you should stumble across my niece, tell her she neglects her guests. Chatter is not much her style, either."

Drake nodded and accepted the invitation to eat.

Summer Hall was known for the sumptuousness of its spreads, and he was starving after that ride from London. As he chose from a variety of meats, pies oozing with thick gravy, cheeses, an assortment of garden produce, puddings, and sweetmeats, Drake remembered his father speaking of Sir John's odd adoption of a wild girl he claimed was his niece. Drake had never met the child. People claimed the death of their daughter had made the Summervilles a little odd, but he could see no oddity in taking in an orphan. Calling her their "niece" might be a trifle eccentric, but he knew ladies who called their dogs their "baby" and referred to themselves as the dog's "mama." He saw no difference.

With his platter filled, Drake looked around for congenial company. He caught the sound of a mandolin being strummed and he grinned. He would not be adverse to seeing his old friend Theodore. Spying a gathering of young men about the fireside, he strode quickly in that direction. Simpering misses and court gossip would not be the attraction with that group.

As he approached, the crowd parted enough to give him a glimpse of a young maid sitting beside the fire, enraptured by the melody of the mandolin and Theodore's love song. Judging from her lack of powder and simple gown covered by a large white apron, she was a servant, but something familiar about her nagged at Drake's memory. He had never been one to haunt the backstairs in search of easy takings. Where could he have seen that head of shimmering copper before? As he approached, Drake studied with interest the rise of her slim throat from the square-cut neckline, the vulnerable curve of her delicate jaw, and lips with just a hint of amusement even when composed. He could not see her eyes, for they followed Teddy's fingers, but he was willing to wager they were devastating.

The poet, James, made room for him in the tight circle around the girl and the musician. Drake took no note of the exquisite embroidery on the girl's simple gown of primrose silk, but searched his memory for a glimpse of this slender creature of elfin grace with the glorious mane of auburn hair, without success.

Until she turned those silver eyes to meet his with bold curiosity and startled him into a reminiscence of shocking vividness.

"The Princess of Apples!" Drake crowed in astonishment. Setting aside his plate, he elbowed through the circle of young men to greet this childhood memory joyously.

To the amazement of all onlookers, the modest maiden leapt from her seat to fling her arms boldly around the handsome marquess's neck. And to their equal amazement, the young lord returned the hug with enthusiasm. From a man who had an astonishing ability to elude available young misses, this was an unheard-of lapse of caution. The girl in question, too, had never exhibited any enthusiasm for the embraces of young men.

Controlling his inexplicable delight at this reunion with a child he had seen but once, Drake returned the girl to the ground and bowed ceremoniously before her. She curtsied perfectly and continued smiling expectantly while she waited for the explanation he might offer his friends. She was not disappointed.

"You dull fellows have no appreciation of the royalty in your midst!" he roared, laughing at the astounded looks on the faces of his companions.

"Neville, ain't it a trifle early to be in your cups?" one wit inquired dubiously.

Drake's laughing eyes swept from the quiet merriment in the musician's expression to the varying degrees of disbelief and bored eagerness on the faces of the others. Playing to his audience, he declared grandly, "You are blessed to have among you a sprite of the forest, a princess of fairies, a savior of starving lads! Why, without this lovely lady, I would have perished in the cold, cold forest, with none but the wolves to pick at my bones!"

Stifling her giggles at this outrageous lie, since she had a distinct remembrance of the day being one of the hottest she had ever endured, Eileen dove deep into one of her pockets and produced a perfect apple, a shining, ripe example of her uncle's orchards. She offered it in her outstretched palm, and Drake threw her a laughing look of gratitude.

"You see? A veritable Princess of Apples." He took the gift and bit deeply into the crisp flesh of the ripe fruit, his eyes searching hers with amusement and fascination.

Theodore strummed a chord and lifted a thoughtful eyebrow at the look that passed between these two—so different on the surface but so similar where eyes could not see. Like precious metals, silver and gold and copper, they shimmered in the firelight, as much one as any alloy, separate from their flesh and blood companions. Fascinated by this illusion, he failed to note the approach of reality.

"Well, Neville, you never told me you knew my niece. Naughty wench, her aunt's looking for her." Sir John clapped his friend's son on the shoulder and turned to his wayward charge. "You'd best lose that apron, Eileen, before Emma sees you. Lady Duncan has arrived and has asked for you."

Eileen smiled prettily, curtsied, and quietly disappeared into the crowd. Her departure left a noticeable rift in the conversation as well as an air of tension. The spell broken, the others began to wander off, leaving Drake and Sir John to face each other with an audience of a few others, including Theodore.

Now that he had been returned so rudely from the enchanted forest of his imagination, Drake realized the immensity of his faux pas. How could he have known this sprite of his own creation was the baronet's pampered "niece"? And how in hell would he explain his ardent greeting to her doting "uncle"? Taking another bite of the apple, Drake watched the girl's fleeting figure disappear from the hall. He should have noticed the costliness of the primrose sarcenet of her gown, or the artful style of her loose curls, but like a nodcock, he had seen only her welcoming gaze. How would he explain that to her staid and proper uncle?

With a lazy shrug of his elegant shoulders, Drake began, "I apologize, sir, I had no idea she was your niece . . ."

The baronet suddenly tensed and his sharp eyes watched the young lord closely. "You didn't know she was my niece, but you have met before? Where? When? Do not keep anything from me."

Cautiously Drake glanced around and, finding none but friends here, explained, "It was some years ago, sir. I was no more than a boy. My father and I met her in a wooded area somewhere this side of Westbury."

Sir John grew animated, drawing him away from the fire. "Tell me everything. Describe where you found her precisely. We have been searching for years . . ."

His voice trailed off as they wandered away. Only Theodore, the musician, remained by the fire. His fingers plucked idly at his instrument as his gaze wandered around the elegant setting of the ancient great hall. Against the backdrop of towering stone walls and mahogany paneling, the primrose silk of Sir John's young ward reappeared, the simple style splashing daringly amongst the extravagance of her elders. It was an expensive gown for a young girl, but Sir John had the wealth to pamper his ward as he chose.

Theodore grinned, remembering the bulk of the starched white apron. He did not think silks and satins would impress that eccentric miss, no more than they did Drake Neville. 'Twas a pity the girl could not speak and the marquess would not. He would very much like to hear their thoughts on this day's meeting.

*   *   *

From the latticed window of the turret room she had transformed into her studio, Eileen watched the guests depart the next day. In the five years since she had come to live with the Summervilles, whole new worlds had been opened to her, as she had known they would. She had not found herself a stranger in any of them, but swam through her days with the ease of a fish in water. She absorbed the manners and knowledge around her without thought, but she could not find herself a part of this company any more than she had been part of the village.

She turned away as the last of the carriages rolled down the road. She had not seen the storyteller depart. Staring pensively at the canvas on her easel, she contemplated the golden-haired young lord of yesterday. Perhaps because they had never really tried to talk to each other, she had not found herself cut off from this man as she had all others. He dominated the situation, making speech unnecessary. She liked that, but she feared a prolonged encounter would end as so many had, in frustration and disappointment.

With troubled eyes she gazed upon the painted scene that had formed beneath her fingers these past weeks. A beautiful castle glittered on a distant hill, high above a verdant forest of rich shades and enticing darkness. A peaceful stream rippled through one corner of the painting, winding among the trees and losing itself at the base of the castle's hill. The painting had the immediate effect of soothing calmness, something of the enchantment of the storyteller's fairy tales. Only the artist knew that beneath the layers of oiled green lay an ugly spill of dark red, seen now as only specks of blood in the stream's glistening waters.

At dinner that evening, the young marquess entertained his host and hostess with lively tales of the London season. Ignoring gossip, he embroidered anecdotes and wove stories that made the characters of his social set come alive. The baronet and his wife

laughed heartily over the antics of those they knew
well, while their ward bent a small smile at the teller's
recital. She did not need to know these people person-
ally. She saw them through Lord Sherbourne's eyes.

She knew his name now, but no more than that. He
fascinated her, in the same way she fascinated him.
From the corner of her eye she caught his glances,
hidden beneath laughing looks but studying her just
the same. She did not understand why his gaze kept
coming back to her, but she had great difficulty main-
taining her own modest pose. She wanted to stare at
the sparkling hues of his sky-colored eyes, search for
the soul she saw briefly reflected in the shadows, linger on the square cut of his strong jaw with its cleft
chin. She wanted much more than that, but she stared
purposefully at her plate. Looks often lied, and she
sensed the danger of these unknown currents between
them.

After dinner, Eileen withdrew with her aunt to the
cozy parlor at the side of the house rather than opening up one of the formal salons. This was their family
parlor, where they often sat after dinner, Lady Summerville frequently playing the spinet or working on embroidery while Sir John read his newspapers. Eileen
liked it here. She had no need of London's parties and
teas, although she had attended several on occasion. Her
lack of speech set her apart from the others, and her
lack of background removed her from society in the
eyes of most. She had little use for the fashionable
world. After the poverty of her childhood, she had all
the amenities she needed right here.

She picked up her needlepoint and admired the rich
golds of the thread she worked with. Here were the
advantages her new family offered. Colors of every
sort and kind and texture: watercolors, oils, pastels,
threads, and yarns. These she understood more than
the confusing world outside. She often felt suffocated
by her guardians' constant watchful attention, but she

gladly sacrificed freedom for the security of their love and her art. For now.

Eileen looked up as Lord Sherbourne and Sir John entered. Garbed in a long coat of rich blue velvet and matching breeches, his heavily embroidered waistcoat as pristinely white as his cravat, his golden hair neatly bagged in a queue, the marquess appeared every inch the noble gentleman. Whatever the two had been discussing, it had taken the laughter from the young lord's eyes, and his gaze was sober as it found her.

He came to stand beside her, leaning on the mantel as he studied the tapestry of colors beneath her fingers.

"Your uncle tells me you have a talent for drawing, Miss Eileen."

Eileen flicked him a mischievous glance from the corner of her eye. The marquess was supremely experienced in drawing-room small talk, but even he had difficulty in addressing her. She was not a Summerville. If Sir John and Lady Summerville were to be believed, she was a de Lacy, and not just a Miss de Lacy. Her father was supposedly a land-poor nobleman of English title but Irish descent who had once owned large estates in Ireland. So what did that make her? Her aunt insisted Lady Eileen would be correct, but Eileen had a tendency to giggle whenever anyone attempted to apply that term to her. Miss Eileen was more title and name than she had ever possessed before.

Drake's lips crinkled at the corners as he caught her saucy glance. Perhaps it was a good thing for the world that this one could not unleash her tongue upon it. He whispered as much in her ear as he bent to retrieve the tapestry from her hands, holding it out critically before him.

He hid her outraged and amused gasp with a studied commentary on the tapestry's subject matter. "I fancy the unicorn is a trifle walleyed, but the gold mane is extremely well done. One fancies one could tie a red ribbon in it. But for that, the unicorn would have to lay its head in the lady's lap. Is she a princess, by the way?" He slanted a laughing look to her.

Eileen smothered her laughter and sent him a severe look, indicating he should sit himself properly in the chair where he belonged and leave artistic criticism to those who knew art. She did not need to speak a word; he understood her gestures perfectly and laughed out loud as he deciphered the last.

"My sister would enjoy meeting you, Miss Eileen. You are of much the same age, I believe. She dabbles at watercolor and needlework, but like me, her strength lies in her silver tongue. You would get on well, I believe."

The young couple in the corner behaved as if there were no others in the room, momentarily entranced by the discovery of their easy rapport. Sir John watched edgily as the youngsters apparently exchanged insults in mime and twisted phrases. Eileen possessed all the beauty promised when they had first found her, and he remembered only too well the lovely Elizabeth's infectious ways. Eileen would never be her mother; her aloofness and eccentricity bespoke that even had she been able to speak or produce her family tree. But there was something in the electricity dancing between these two that warned the girl retained some vestige of her mother's flirtatious talent.

He cleared his throat and set aside his newspaper, catching the marquess's attention. Eileen studiously broke her thread and reached for a red one.

"You have said nothing of the Lady Pamela this evening, Drake. Has the date for the nuptials been set?"

John had the oddest sensation that the room fell suddenly silent, though no one but himself had actually been speaking. He glanced quickly at his niece, but she was only discarding the red thread and searching for another.

Drake continued to lounge lazily against the mantel, his broad shoulders supporting the carved wood. "Lady Pamela is quite well, as usual. She is quite taken by the London season and is in no hurry to shoulder the responsibility of marriage, and I see no reason to rush her. My father's death has left the estates and the inheritance in some disorder. My solicitors demand my time, and in the interest of my sister and cousins, I must acquiesce to their demands. There is some question of my cousin's inheritance that I wished to speak to you about, when we have the chance."

Sir John wisely allowed the topic to drop, and shortly the two men were discussing the progress of the war in Europe and the growing tensions at home. Even the excitement of war had grown tarnished beneath the ignominious Hanoverian battles that had no glorious cause or purpose, and the English people grew restless for the grandeurs of their undefeated past. Neither man, however, seemed perturbed by the rumors of a French invasion.

"Cumberland will hold them off until everyone grows bored and goes home," Sir John ruminated, laying aside his paper. "Mark my words, it is the Jacobites who will bring this country to its knees if we don't bring our armies home."

"Yes, well, considering my family's reputation, an army or two might be persuasive," Drake commented wryly.

Something in his tone caught Eileen's ear, and she sent him a swift glance, but she could discern nothing but determined levity in their guest's expression.

Lady Summerville rose and excused herself, and Eileen hastily packed her threads and followed her out. She would very much like to hear more about Drake's notorious family, but she owed too much to her guardians to be blatantly rude and remain where she did not belong.

Besides, Lord Sherbourne was a dangerous playmate. She would do well to avoid his company in the future.

Chapter IV

—— 🍎 ——

Voices—loud male voices. Angry. Shouting. Demanding she knew not what. She huddled in the darkness but the voices grew, coming closer. Screams. She could not stop the screaming. Helpless fists grabbed for weapons, and the screams kept on. Ear-piercing. Heart-rending. Utterly futile in their horror.

Fighting the screams, Eileen threw back the covers, her arms and legs kicking and thrashing. Nothing muffled the sound. Moisture ran down her face and she could not see. She could not stop the sounds. The cries came from within as well as without. Choking, sobbing, racking her small frame.

Walking down the candlelit hall, Drake Neville heard both the angry voices and the muted cries. He paused, knowing the nature of the voices but uncertain of the source of the cries. His first thought was of his sister, and anxiously he stopped at her door, finding all quiet there. Breathing easier, he stepped farther down the carpeted corridor to the door of their latest houseguest. Surely, one so silent could not be making these noises.

The sound of angry argument drifted from below, nearly drowning the faint sounds from behind the heavy door. Suddenly realizing her muteness would prevent screams but these choking sounds well might mean the same, Drake tried the knob. It was frightening to know she could not cry for help. She ought to have a maid with her.

The door opened silently, and the sounds became more audible. Drake glanced around quickly, lifting his candle to pierce the darkness. Nothing. His glance found the bed, discovering the long rope of auburn first. Gradually, his eyes adjusting to the darkness, he noted the pale shadow of her long nightdress entangled in the covers. The gown looked too big for her slender frame, and he suspected it belonged to Lady Summerville. Old women might wear night rails, but not young girls like Eileen. He almost smiled, guessing the reason for Lady Summerville's precautions with her precious "niece." The Sherbourne household had a rakish reputation.

The pitiful cries from the bed wiped away his amusement. She appeared asleep, but she fought like a tigress against the covers, guttural noises emanating from her throat. Whatever nightmare haunted her sleep did not surrender easily. Drake set the candleholder on the bedside stand and grabbed the covers from Eileen's grasping fingers, flinging them to the foot of the bed.

She woke then, a small gasp crossing her lips as she gazed up into the masculine features of Lord Sherbourne. The angry voices echoed in her head, but they were not his. The candlelight glinted off a swathe of gold hair falling across his forehead, and Eileen stilled her racing heartbeat, forcing herself to wake. She felt the moisture of tears across her cheeks but she did not raise her hand to wipe them away. Maybe he would leave.

He did not. Instead, Drake held out his hand to her, not daring to do more but not wishing to leave her alone. If it had been Diane, he would have sat upon the bed and drawn her into his arms and comforted her, but this girl was a virtual stranger in his household. She had avoided him assiduously since he had brought her here, and Drake had respected her privacy. But he could not leave her like this.

Grudgingly Eileen accepted his hand and sat up. A dressing robe lay across a nearby chair, and he brought it to her, helping her to put it on.

"Come, we'll find a cup of hot chocolate." Drake helped her to her feet, wondering if she owned slippers or where they might be. She did not seem to notice their lack, and he said nothing. She could not reply if he questioned her, though his mind raced with a thousand questions. Without the full petticoats and panniers and feminine frippery, she seemed frighteningly small, yet he saw no trace of fear in her tear-stained face. What horrors haunted that silent mind of hers? Remembering the girl's brief history that Sir John had related to him, he thought it best he did not know.

Outside the room on the stairway, the argument below once more intruded upon his consciousness, and Drake scowled. The girl beside him halted warily, drawing away from him and closer to the protection of the wall.

"It's only Auguste and Pierre. I'll send them away if they frighten you."

Eileen grasped the wooden banister and determinedly set one foot on the first step. Those were the voices she had heard in her sleep. No others. She would confront them and the dream would go away. She ignored the toweringly masculine man at her side. He belonged to another world and she had no time for him.

Downstairs, they stopped outside the open study door. A fire flickered in the grate, reflecting the shadows of a pacing figure against the walls and sending shivering glimmers of amber through a brandy glass on the desk. Two other shadows lounged in the high-backed chairs set back from the warmth of the fire, brandy glasses dangling from their fingers.

"I tell you, James Stuart is the rightful king! That Hanoverian timekeeper has the blood of merchants in him, not royalty! With Prince Charles to lead us, we can—" The harangue halted as Drake intruded.

"Hang like all the other traitors," Drake concluded. "Go to bed, Pierre. Your shouting has woken Miss Summerville."

As if by magic, a weary footman appeared in the doorway, and Drake turned to order, "See if you can find a cup of hot chocolate, Smythe."

The servant silently disappeared, and Drake turned back to one of the masculine figures in the fireside chairs. "Mind your manners for a change, Auguste. Get up and offer Miss Summerville a chair."

The young man leaped guiltily from his chair and pushed it closer to the fire, turning it so she might enjoy the full force of the heat. Drake saw her comfortably settled, then reached for the brandy decanter, halting momentarily at the sound of the insolent drawl of the third occupant.

"Who in hell is she? Bit young to be one of your doxies, ain't she?" The man in the second chair made no attempt to rise, acting as if a lady had not intruded upon this all-male conference.

"Edmund, one of these days I'll have your tongue cut from your throat. Don't think I'm not aware that you're the one feeding these young fools with dangerous notions. If you haven't even the rudiments of manners with which to greet a guest, I suggest you remove yourself to whatever tavern you frequent now."

Eileen surmised this was the older cousin who had inherited the position of estate manager. Since arriving at Sherbourne, she had been introduced to innumerable Neville cousins and friends, but not to this man. Bits of information she had compiled from various conversations told her she did not want to know him. She curled deeper into her wing chair, out of his sight.

The servant brought the hot chocolate but Edmund had no interest in an insignificant female. He focused his attention on the marquess.

"I'm going but you do yourself no favor by throwing me out. If this estate is going to make money, you will have to learn to deal with me." Edmund lifted his glass to his mouth, draining the last drops of amber liquid.

"You'll get your percentage whether or not you do your job," Drake informed him stiffly. "Just remember, the lands are mine, not yours. What is the meaning of that fence going up across the south field?"

"I'm turning it to pasturage. It should have been done a century ago." Smoothly Edmund set aside his empty glass and rose to leave.

"Pasturage! You intend to herd sheep under Nanny's washlines and through the vicar's garden?" Sherbourne set aside his drink and glared incredulously at his cousin, no longer aware of the room's other occupants.

Edmund shrugged. "The land is ours. They will have to learn to keep within their boundaries."

"Over my dead body!" Drake shouted. Eileen huddled in her corner at the sound, haunted by the ghosts of old arguments that riddled her black dreams.

Unaware of his guest's horror, Drake continued furiously, "Has our income been so depleted that we must take from the poor to replenish our larders?"

"Yours may not, but you will remember mine is only a percentage. It is in everybody's interest that I increase our income in whatever manner is available."

The marquess shook his head in disbelief. "My God, Edmund. You live in my house, eat my food, make free with my stable—what in hell do you need with the money? Would you have me deny my father's will and divide Sherbourne in two to cultivate your greed?"

Edmund strode toward the door, throwing over his

shoulder, "That won't be necessary. I'll manage on my own."

He stalked out, leaving the marquess fuming. When Drake turned on his younger cousins, Eileen knew he had completely forgotten her presence. Not wishing to draw attention to herself, she curled quietly out of sight in the massive chair. Perhaps understanding the arguments would dissolve the nightmares.

"I don't want to hear any more of this nonsense about 'King' James and 'Bonnie Prince Charlie.' " Drake turned his attack on the two young brothers. "The Stuarts abdicated their thrones with their reputations and you would do best to remember it. You're Frenchmen, for God's sake! Stay out of English politics."

"With the Stuarts back on the throne, we could put an end to these incessant wars!" Pierre argued vehemently. "Even our uncle says so, and he is privy to Louis's affairs. And you have said yourself, Drake, that George is a poor excuse for royalty. He's a barbarian pig! He'd slaughter half the continent to hold those pitiful lands at Hanover for his ugly mistresses. If only we could get men and money to Charles—"

"If only pigs had wings! Your illustrious French court has not sent one sou. Why should I?"

Realizing the argument threatened to continue for the remainder of the night, Eileen gazed sleepily into the fire, remembering her arrival amongst this fractious family. She had been resentful at being produced as the latest plaything for Lord Sherbourne's invalid sister, but she could summon that resentment no longer.

At the time, she had stared at the identical golden hair and blue eyes on the feminine features of Drake's sister with something less than grace. Unaccustomed to living among the upper echelons of society, she had felt dowdy and resentful beneath the cool, aristocratic gaze of Lady Diane Neville. Only the oddity of comparing the haunting shadows of the lady's eyes to the laughing blue of Drake's had kept her waiting for the introductions to end.

Those haunted eyes seemed to brighten when Diane finally grasped the meaning of Drake's fanciful introduction. "The Princess of Apples! Oh, they have never captured her, have they? Has the leprechaun army deserted, then?"

Her genuine distress mixed with confusion and laughter matched a chord somewhere in Eileen. She threw Drake a covert look. There was something so genial and vulnerable in his noble features she could not think of him in the same terms as she did most men. From the first, she had thought of him as a friend, one with a tongue lighter than her fingers. She knew a story lay behind his sister's words.

Drake's grin grew wider as he intercepted Eileen's look. He explained laconically, "The leprechaun army never learned proper military procedures. Leprechauns have a tendency to come and go as they please, disappearing before your very eyes, reappearing when least expected. They protect the Princess of Apples from all sorts of evil, but never in a soldierly fashion. They're a mischievous lot, you see. They drop apples on the heads of evil tyrants and tug the stockings off wicked witches."

His grin was irresistible and a smile tugged at the corners of Eileen's mouth as she understood the turn these tales would take. With a gesture of inquiry, she distracted Drake into watching one hand while the other slipped the black ribbon from his queue. As he felt his hair fall free against his neck, Drake made an exclamation of surprise, then peremptorily held out his hand for the purloined ribbon.

Eileen innocently presented both hands and shook her head in beguiling bewilderment. The serene Lady Diane broke into gales of laughter at the staggering look of confusion on her brother's face.

"Oh, yes! Just like that, Eileen. Leprechauns are

very tricky creatures and can steal the lace from a lady's shoe if she is not careful. Or a ribbon from a man's hair!"

In that instant a friendship was formed. Since then, Eileen had found her weeks at Sherbourne distractingly pleasant. She and Diane had got on splendidly since that first meeting, each enchanted by the differences of the other. The sad loveliness of Diane's quiet nature and Eileen's mute liveliness complemented each other. As Drake had predicted, Diane did all the speaking for both of them, and the silences between them were never awkward.

The odd, wheeled contraption in which Diane was forced to spend her days explained much of the pain behind her eyes. Legs rendered useless by the weight of a horse in a jumping accident when she was just a child, Diane had been confined to a narrow world of her family's creation most of her life. Made uncomfortable by the stares and pity of outsiders, she preferred the security of Sherbourne. Eileen made a delightful diversion, as did her brother's other assorted companions.

Sherbourne and its varying inhabitants provided equal diversion for Eileen, but the laughing lord who presided over this menagerie of cousins and itinerant artists kept her intrigued. Once he had seen her safely settled amid his family, he had not intruded again, but Eileen had the feeling that he knew everything she did. She seldom knew when he was at home until he appeared at mealtime, and it seemed there were always more to be fed when he was about. Guests and family alike vied for his attention, and the marquess gave it unconsciously, slighting no one and seemingly enjoying each with equal interest. When Eileen made no attempt to put herself forward, his laughing gaze would seek her out and reassure her of her welcome, but he had never overstepped the unspoken boundaries between them. Until tonight.

Yawning and fighting to keep awake, Eileen tried to follow the argument between Lord Sherbourne and his younger cousins. Drake had been right about needing an army to control his warring family. Edmund Neville was the eldest son of a younger son, older than Drake but not in line for the title since Drake's birth. That made for difficulties enough, but Drake's mother had been of a French Catholic family, creating another series of problems. Her well-placed connections had fought furiously against her choice of the English marquess, but Drake's father had made certain of his choice, and both families had to capitulate when it became obvious their heir would be born out of wedlock otherwise.

The families had maintained a love–hate relationship ever since, but never more so than between the male cousins. The Monsard brothers, Auguste and Pierre, had become a part of the Neville household at an early age, upon the death of their mother. The various Neville cousins had been in and out all their lives as the London season and family fortunes waxed and waned. The endless rounds of politics and personalities created a whirlwind of dissension in the household. It was a wonder the marquess ever got any rest.

By the time Drake had dispatched his contentious cousins to their respective beds, Eileen had drifted off to sleep. Only when he went to extinguish the dying fire did he discover her small form curled in the large chair. Wondering how much of the argument she had heard or understood, Drake hesitated to wake her. She seemed to be sleeping so peacefully, it would be a shame to return the nightmares.

The last light from the fire flickered in fascinating patterns of red and gold through the thick length of Eileen's auburn braid. Catching his breath, Drake noted the shadows of her long, dark lashes against cheeks as smooth and creamy as ivory satin. Usually in perpetual motion, she had the looks of a Dresden figurine in sleep.

With decision, Drake hefted her slender form into his arms. Propping her head against his shoulder, he carried her toward the stairs to bed. She was as light as a child, but as he maneuvered the stairs, he grew very aware that she was more woman than child. Her robe fell open, revealing the full curve of a firm breast beneath the thin linen. His arms tightened about a tiny waist that dipped softly to rounded hip. As he lay her against the sheets, her lips parted in a soft sigh, and Drake nearly surrendered to the overwhelming urge to taste them. The realization that she could not scream her anger increased the temptation, but Drake's sense of honor won out. Pulling up the covers, he left the little princess to her dreams.

Only when Lord Sherbourne was gone did Eileen dare breathe deeply. She could have sworn she felt his kiss brush her forehead. It must have been a strand of hair. Pushing away the offending curl, she snuggled beneath the covers and slept soundly for the remainder of the night.

Several days later, the Marquess of Sherbourne watched from a ridge overlooking the road, as the Summerville carriage drove away with its enchanting occupant. The frail new leaves of the birch grove made a dappled pattern on his shirt sleeves, and he brushed carelessly at a stray lock of hair falling across his wide brow. Something of the day's brilliant promise dimmed now that he could not expect to see that pert grin at his table any longer, but he did not dissect his feelings beyond noting that the visit had been good for Diane. The first damp weeks of spring were always the worst for her, but Eileen had succeeded in bringing the spring breezes in to warm the old halls of Sherbourne. She had even provided him with inspiration, and Drake longed to try his hand at putting the tale to paper.

Not that he had time for such nonsense anymore

since he had inherited the task of riding herd on this obstreperous family of his, Drake observed dryly, noting the progress of Edmund's horse down the drive in the direction of the village. They filled more of his time than the estate and all of his money. He spurred his horse to follow. This very day he would make certain those fences came down.

A light mist chilled her face as Eileen carried her easel down toward the dock. She gathered her ungainly cloak around her and wished for another hand to straighten her bonnet, but otherwise she ignored the inclement weather. The color of the sea and sky today were perfect for what she had in mind, though for June, it was chillier than she liked.

Eileen tapped lightly on the kitchen door of the tavern near the dock. Sir John would have heart failure if he knew of his niece's acquaintance with the tavern keeper's wife, but Eileen did not find the relationship in the least bit odd. On days like this, when the north wind blew, a cup of hot chocolate in the warm kitchen was a welcome respite. The friendship was not the same as the one with Lady Diane, but friendliness never hurt.

Mrs. Drew scolded her visitor as she ushered the girl into the kitchen before the flaming fire. She knew of Eileen's identity, but very few did. Who would think the tiny girl enveloped in old cloaks and shabby bonnets occasionally haunting the docks was a grand lady from one of the great houses? She scarcely believed it herself.

Eileen smiled her gratitude and accepted the steaming cup of chocolate while the woman took her cloak and bustled about the room. Eileen was as at home here as in her studio, or as she could be anywhere. She had learned to adapt to strange places long ago.

"That wind's too chilly for you to be out and about on that dock, Miss Eileen," the plump woman scolded.

" 'Twill turn your fingers blue and blow away your papers and then what would you have gained? I've a much better idea."

She pushed open the kitchen door and gestured toward the large, empty common room overlooking the sea. "There's none about this time of a morn. You can see as well from them great windows as you could with the wind whipping your hair in your face. The old codger won't object, and if any come in for a nip of cider, I'll see to it they leave you be. You set yourself up right there, dearie."

The proposition was nearly as audacious as her frequenting the docks in the first place. If Sir John had known she rode as far as the coast when she went out, he would have forbidden her the stables. As it was, Eileen had to swear Quigley to silence. He had been assigned to accompany her whenever she went out on her painting expeditions. Bored with lying about the woods all day while she quietly sketched and painted, he had agreed to occasionally abandon her to pursue his courtship of a certain young maid on a neighboring estate. Those were the opportunities Eileen used to escape her confining existence.

It did not take long to be persuaded to set up her easel before the huge bay window. She could catch the blend of grays between sea and sky here as well as anywhere, and the framework of the darkened oak window added an interesting contrast. She set out her paints and bent to her work.

Men occasionally wandered in and out of the tavern, but no more so than wandered the dock this time of day. The fishermen were either out in their crafts or home mending their nets on a day like this, and none but idlers had time to concern themselves with her presence. The first few times she had come here, she had been a subject of much speculation and a ribald jest or two, but she had heard it all before. And even when some drunken lout found her lack of attention a challenge, she had defended her privacy in a manner that left no room for doubt. The Drews had taken her under their wing since then, and she had been left blessedly alone.

So she found no harm in sketching quietly in this dockside tavern of dubious reputation.

She had been there an hour or two, long enough to grow conscious of time passing, when the conversation from the bar in the corner began to intrude upon her concentration. She did not turn to observe the speakers, but a frisson of alarm coursed down her spine as their voices grew louder and she recognized one of them. Eavesdropping on Edmund Neville would soon become a habit.

"Now that Bonnie Prince Charlie has arrived, we'll eliminate the whole damned clan. If they don't murder each other on the battlefield, the king will have them hung along with the rest of the seditious lot." Edmund spoke with insolent assurance.

"I don't know that Charlie wouldn't be a damn sight better than that long-nosed German wearing the crown now. With the bloody Neville luck, they'll come back the winners."

"Charlie is a fool, like all the Stuarts," Edmund admonished. "Without money or arms, he hasn't a chance. But I'll not rely on chance. That's where you come in." His voice lowered. "We'd best go elsewhere to talk. What in hell is that chit doing here?"

"She's a dummy. Don't pay her no mind. Even if she could hear or understand you, she couldn't tell nobody. No tongue. Vicious temper, though."

Laughter came from a third, drunken one. "Near took my hand off, that she did. Carries a wicked knife under those cloaks. Ne'er said a word the whole time she was a'hacking at me. Bloody odd, if you ask me."

Edmund apparently relaxed his vigilance and began to speak again. "Well, then. You know what you're to do. Get your message to the Monsards and they'll be off to join the fray in a twinkling. Our noble lord will be right behind them. He's taken this family business seriously and won't allow the fools to get themselves killed. I'll take care of the rest, and we'll all be wealthy by year's end. It will be a damn sight easier to make a profit out of those lands when I hold the title. Sherbourne treats those tenants of his like family. I'll teach them their places shortly."

Anger slowly burned through Eileen's veins as she recognized the treachery of Edmund's plot, but she forced herself to continue painting quietly. She couldn't afford to draw suspicion, but her anger came out in large, tempestuous waves upon the canvas. She would have to wait until the men were gone, but the idea of involving Lord Sherbourne and the volatile Monsards in some dangerous fray to aid a madman's vindictive ambitions made caution difficult. She made little sense of the plot, but Edmund's danger was evident. Evil came easily to men.

The trio continued laughing and drinking, murmuring obscene jokes in low voices after a warning from the tavern keeper. After one such admonition Eileen heard unsteady footsteps behind her, and sensed a tall man peering over her shoulder. He did not smell like a fisherman, and she judged him to be Diane's treacherous cousin. She did not turn to acknowledge his presence.

"Ugly sea you've got there, miss. A man would drown in waves like that." He indicated the fragile ship tossing on her tempestuous ocean.

Eileen gritted her teeth and pretended not to hear. She feared letting him see her face. She did not think he would recognize her, but she could take no chances.

"What's under that ugly bonnet, wench?" he jibed casually, reaching for the encompassing black brim that so successfully hid her small face.

"Watch out, Edmund, she's reaching for the knife!" chortled one of his companions.

"Leave the wench alone!" Mortimer Drew bellowed from behind the bar. Built like an ox, his forearms wider than the legs of most men, he had the power to enforce his commands. Just the sound of his feet trodding the boards behind the bar was sufficient warning to cease and desist.

Eileen breathed a sigh of relief as Edmund retreated. Hastily she packed her paints in their case and folded her easel. No one would suspect she had any cause for departure but the gentleman's attentions. Their laughter followed her out, but her flushed cheeks had naught to do with embarrassment.

In a fury she found her mount and loaded her gear into the saddlebags.

She had known men were vile, had known it all her life, but this encounter had driven the point home.

She did not know what his cousin intended for Lord Sherbourne, but the Monsards and the villagers would suffer for it, she felt certain. And should anything happen to any of them, Diane would be bereft.

Eileen galloped back to the Hall, forgetting Quigley, forgetting her painting, forgetting everything but the necessity to get word to the Nevilles. How could she warn them? Diane might take her seriously, but she had no authority to stop this disaster. Besides, it would not do to worry her. Helpless as she was, Drake's sister was too inclined to fret already.

The marquess was the one she needed, but Eileen had no idea at all where he could be reached. The Nevilles owned dozens of estates, and Drake had friends all over the kingdom. He could be fishing for salmon in Scotland or hunting to hounds in Ireland for all she knew. Someone must know how to reach him.

By the time she reached her studio, Eileen knew she had only one choice. She had learned social etiquette from her aunt and knew it was highly improper for young ladies to exchange letters with men to whom they were not engaged, but etiquette had little to do with practicality. She disliked alarming Diane, but she was the only person who might know where the marquess was. She could not sit idle and wait for disaster to strike.

The note to Lord Sherbourne was brief and to the point, simply outlining the conversation and including his cousin's name. He would know more what to make of it than she.

The cover letter to Diane was a trifle harder. She had to make it urgent enough to convince Diane to send it on immediately, but without describing the danger. Ideally, it would be preferable if she could make the danger sound as if it were to herself instead of the Nevilles. Diane's romantic fantasies would take it from there.

Writing was not an art Eileen had mastered, but she did what she could, sealing Drake's letter carefully before wrapping it inside Diane's. She trusted Diane not to open her brother's mail no matter how much her curiosity stirred her. With a sigh of relief Eileen packaged it neatly and carried it down to the footman responsible for taking the post. It was out of her hands now.

Lady Diane Neville read the missive from her friend with some puzzlement. Ever since Drake had first come home with his nonsensical stories of the Princess of Apples, she had been fascinated with the little girl just her age who spoke only with her eyes. When Drake had come to her last spring and announced he had found his favorite forest sprite in captivity, she had felt sorrow that the sprite had been imprisoned by civilization, but delighted at the prospect of meeting her. Drake's tales had been so close to the truth, that Diane felt as if she had known Eileen before they ever met.

So she felt no surprise at the intensity of her friend's letter. Under her delicate, quiet exterior, Eileen seethed with explosive passions that seldom surfaced except in her painting. No, it was the subject that worried her. What danger could Eileen possibly face in the security of Summer Hall, and how could Drake possibly alleviate it?

Diane frowned and rubbed her useless leg beneath the woolen blanket. Drake had told her Eileen's history, the possibility that she might be half-Irish. Could some shadow from her past have stepped forward? But why would she call on Drake?

It did not matter. With decisiveness Diane reached for her pen and hastily scrawled Drake's address. Her brother enjoyed a challenge, though he certainly had not found one in his current pursuit of Lady Pamela. Diane suspected her brother's fiancée had been conquered many times and by men other than Drake, but she did not dare whisper a word against the lady. The match had been forged long ago and Drake would not dishonor his father's wishes nor a family pledge. Diane felt the lady's wandering ways had left Drake restless and irritable and ready to conquer new mountains.

Rescuing a lady in distress might prove beneficial. Diane rang for a maid.

Chapter V

——— ❦ ———

England–Ireland
Summer, 1745

In the chamber of his London townhouse, garbed only in a satin dressing robe prior to dressing and calling on his fiancée, Drake Neville scowled at the childish scrawl of the missive his secretary had just handed him. He would have thought the message some jest had it not been for the faded yellow ribbon enclosed. The little urchin had anticipated his suspicions.

Unconsciously wrapping the old ribbon about his fingers, Drake cursed as he regarded Eileen's enigmatic scribbling. She had evidently never mastered penmanship, but her words were terse and all too clear. Obviously, the mysterious little imp had been where she didn't belong to overhear such a conversation. He would like to throttle Edmund barehanded, but instead he could only be grateful that Eileen had heard him and had the sense to gather the import of his words. He owed her for that. It gave him time to make plans.

Drake folded the paper carefully and signaled his valet that he was ready to dress, but his mind continued to work hard and fast. He knew too well the "message" Edmund would see delivered to the Monsard brothers. A call to arms from their uncle in France would send the duo flying to join the rebellious Jacobites in Scotland, ready to serve the gloriously romantic cause of England's "true" king—and get themselves killed in the process. Like the other misguided young men forming behind Charles Stuart, they had no money, no arms, and no training. The slaughter, when it came, would be merciless.

The rest of the plot escaped his reasoning. What Edmund hoped to solve by sending Drake on a wild goose chase after the feckless cousins, he could not ascertain. Edmund had always been a problem. While his father led a dissipated life, Edmund had been more or less raised at Sherbourne, and being older than Drake, he had usurped many of the responsibilities and privileges of an older son. The fact that he would not inherit the title or the estate had made him a bitter man, though he had successfully concealed that fact from the old marquess. The new marquess knew it with the pain of experience.

Drake contemplated whipping the meddling traitor within an inch of his life, but that would raise the ire of his father's family and the feud would erupt messily all over the streets of London. What Drake might once have done while his father was head of the family could not be considered now that he himself held that title. There had to be a peaceful means of eliminating Edmund, but he'd be damned if he knew what it was. Once, he had been eager to assume the burden of responsibility, but the yoke lately was becoming uncommonly irritating.

Drake shrugged on the tightly tailored buff coat his valet held for him, and ignored the neatly curled bob wig the man held out. He had hired the man to keep his clothes neat and clean, but he had not the patience or the affectation to linger over details. Grabbing his walking stick, Drake stalked out, leaving the valet to stare in dismay at his unpowdered locks.

Sending his secretary off in the direction of Sherbourne to intercept all messages and issuing urgent ones of his own, Drake proceeded on to his fiancée's home as

originally planned; only his purpose had changed. Lord
Westly might be a remorseless old rake, but he possessed the acumen to keep his head above troubled
waters when all else around him drowned. His advice
was worth the asking.

Lord Westly looked mildly surprised as his daughter's suitor entered the study with a grim look on his
face, but he rose and shook the young man's hand.
While his father had presided over Sherbourne, Drake
had been at loose ends. Sherbourne had refused to
release any of the reins he had handled so well, and
his son had been left too long in the idle life of
London. But it seemed from all reports that the boy
had done well enough and might even outshine the
father one day. Lord Westly decided he had chosen
well for his only child. Their neighboring estates would
be managed properly when he was gone, providing
this marriage came off as planned. The look on Neville's face gave him pause, however.

"Have a seat, Neville. What brings you here when
you should be out driving with my daughter?" Drake
had never once protested the contract binding him to
Lady Pamela, but the betrothal had never been made
public. Since Pamela's first season, neither participant
had showed any interest in forwarding the match. Had
the young marquess come to reject the agreement his
father had made when Drake was still in leading strings?

"I need your advice, sir." Drake met his prospective
father-in-law's gaze with equanimity, guessing the older
man's concerns. Pamela was a loose piece of baggage,
but her father had powerful connections. Drake could
not honorably break the marriage contract his father
had signed, but he'd damned well like to get something of his own in return.

Westly listened to the young lord's tale attentively,
frowning at Drake's refusal to reveal the source of his
information but nodding his head in understanding.

"Wouldn't do to draw swords against your own kin.

Nasty scandal, that. Edmund always was a greedy lad," Westly speculated out loud as he turned over the various aspects of the problem. With instant decision he offered, "Tell you what, Neville. I'll take Edmund off your hands if you'll do something for me. There's not a thing I can do about your mother's relations, but I can occupy Edmund well enough. Give me your word and consider it settled."

Drake took the glass of brandy offered and swallowed gratefully, knowing what was coming. He had known it when he had walked in here, but it was a price that had to be paid sooner or later. If it meant family peace, he would pay it sooner.

"Name your request, sir." He set the glass down and faced the older man squarely.

"You've dawdled with my daughter long enough, Neville. She's a wild piece, I admit, but she needs a husband to keep her from trouble. Set the date, boy, and get her with child posthaste, then maybe she'll settle down. I want a grandson, and I want my daughter happy. Grant me that, and Edmund will be my problem."

Drake made a rueful face, knowing he only traded one problem for another. Still, Lady Pamela had no tendencies toward violence as did Edmund, and he had never intended to renege on his father's promise. He had postponed the inevitable long enough. He had no desire to be shackled to any woman, but it had come time to take a wife and think of heirs. It might as well be Pamela as any other.

"I fear you gain the worst end of the bargain, sir." Drake rose and offered his hand. "I'll consult your daughter and have the announcements made immediately."

Westly stood and accepted Drake's handshake with a grim smile. "I'd be pleased if she were plump when you lead her down the aisle, boy. Take her in hand for me, before someone else does."

Acknowledging that possibility with a cynical quirk of his lips, Drake bowed out. He would make certain it was his own offspring the lady carried when he made those final vows.

Remembering the sprite who had set him on this path, Drake's smile softened. He had watched Eileen with his sister, though neither girl had been aware of his observation. They had graced his gardens with their loveliness, and Eileen had provided an excellent foil to his sister's too serene stillness. With her long limbs and quicksilver grace, she had glided along the garden paths and darted in and out among the flowers, giving the impression of an ethereal spirit of a liveliness Diane needed. He was convinced that, like a druid, she could disappear into trees at will. Perhaps that was how she had heard this particularly useful piece of information.

Patting the pocket carrying Eileen's message, Drake went in search of his fiancée. He would find some way to thank the girl for her warning, but for the nonce he had battle plans to draw.

Eileen heard nothing from Sherbourne, though Diane swore the message had been forwarded. There was no reason for the marquess to write her, after all. She should not have expected more, but the fate of the Monsard brothers worried her.

She took to reading Sir John's newspapers, but the gathering rebellion in the Scottish Highlands provided little news. It was rumored Prince Charles hid in the hills and gathered the Highland clans about him, but she had no means of discerning whether Drake's cousins joined them. Diane wrote nothing of the matter, either, and Eileen did not dare broach it.

Not until July did she discover any news of particular interest to her, and that did not come in the form expected. Among all the announcements of weddings and engagements of people she did not know, a familiar name leapt from the page. The formal announcement of Lord Sherbourne's betrothal to Lady Pamela held her attention so long, even Emma noticed it.

"What is it, child? You're staring at that page as if it were a snake. I could use a bit of news to break the monotony. Is it someone we know?"

Eileen closed the paper and handed it to her aunt. It was no one she knew. Not really. She picked up her embroidery and stabbed it with a needle.

For her birthday, she received a book on sketching from Diane and, enclosed in the same packet, a slender volume of *Tales from the Sublime to the Ridiculous*. She did not recognize the author's name on the cover, one D. Owen Sherbourne, until she opened the front flap. The inscription, "To the Princess of Apples," told her at once the book's giver, which in turn induced her remembrance of his title, Marquess of Sherbourne. Drake had simply made use of his many family names to blur the identity of the real author of these tales. He had probably laughed all the way to the publisher.

She handed the volume to Sir John to inspect. There was nothing in it to indicate anything more than the innocuous relationship of a family friend, which was all they had. Perhaps Drake had found her letter extremely ridiculous. Who, after all, would plot such schemes against a marquess? She hid her vexation as Sir John chuckled.

"Young scalawag. I trust he had the sense to keep his tales innocent. He handled that situation with his cousins very well, from all reports. A bit over-generous with his promises, I suspect, but it stopped an ugly situation. He'll do well one of these days. Lady Pamela will see to that, I wager."

He chuckled again and returned the volume to Eileen. "Generous of him to think of you. Princess of Apples, indeed! Where does the fellow come up with these things?"

Eileen determined to wipe the incident from her mind. It did not sound as if anyone had come to harm, and she had no further concern in the matter. She rose and carried the book from the room.

At Eileen's abrupt departure, John frowned and turned to his wife. "She ought to have a husband, Emma."

His wife of these past many years smiled up at the frown lines on his brow and shook her head. "Where is it said that all women must marry? She is comfortable here. When we are gone, there should still be sufficient wealth to keep her, I daresay. And don't tell me she needs a man to look after her. She seems quite capable of doing that on her own."

"That's not the same." John reached for his pipe. "I cannot imagine my life without you, my dear. When we are gone, Eileen will be all alone. She has been alone too long as it is, I believe. It's not right. She needs friends. And she needs a husband."

Emma nodded thoughtfully. "That will not be easy, John. I know men laugh and claim they wish their wives had no tongues, but what man could live in eternal silence? And with no way of proving her parentage—it cannot be done. Only fortune hunters would consider her."

"Any man would be lucky to have a gem like that!" John announced defiantly. "I'll find one, you'll see."

Unbeknownst to the Summervilles, the little book that had set off this debate had been inscribed some weeks earlier and placed in Diane's competent hands for mailing at the appropriate time. With Edmund off his hands, the author had finally thought of a way to reward the little princess and keep the Monsards safely under his surveillance at the same time. They wanted adventure, he would give them adventure. The three cousins were in Ireland by the time Eileen received her gift.

With only the name of the estate and the approximate location to work with, it had taken some time to locate the barren corner of Ireland governed by the deLacy earldom. The rocky soil was unsuitable for farming, and the timber had been stripped from the land to provide warmth and shelter for the area's few inhabitants. The hovels in the village bespoke the poverty of the region, a poverty that begat poverty. The Catholic inhabitants could not vote for changes and the Protestants had not wealth or numbers to attract the attention of the greedy Parliament in Dublin. Oppressed by the laws and ignored by the government needed to change them, the inhabitants in these hovels had no other choice but poverty.

Perhaps things would have been different if Richard de Lacy had survived to fight for his people and his lands, but the present earl had little interest in his tenants, Drake discovered after long evenings in the local taverns. Peter de Lacy was loved by no one, but feared by all. Few dared speak against him except when well fortified with drink.

The Monsards were the ones to first discover the deLacy family graveyard. Deciding it to be as good a place as any to explore, Drake rode out to take a look at it, discouraged by his inability to come up with any concrete evidence of Eileen's heritage. The road mounted a small hill, and below and off in a distance Drake could see the crumbling ruin of the once proud castle. Few worked there anymore, for the new earl's needs required naught but strong drink and weak women, according to current gossip. Beyond the castle a river ran down toward the sea. Someone had attempted to replenish the missing trees in the landscape and a veritable forest of leaves blew in the breeze along the riverbank. Drake did not trespass on this private paradise but turned his mount to follow the road down the hill. The graves were in an old churchyard where he could not be accused of trespassing.

Only once had Drake seen the new Lord de Lacy

and that had been in a crowd. Black Irish he had been, with no resemblance to Eileen's fair good looks. There had been a trial where the earl had accused one of the villagers of trespassing and poaching. The outcome had been a foregone conclusion, and Drake had turned away in disgust at the satisfied sneer on the earl's dark face as the sentence was read. If that creature were some relation to Eileen, she would be better off not knowing it.

He found the graveyard with ease and, hitching his horse to a weed-grown fence, walked slowly among the long-dead ancestors of the de Lacy family. Many of the stones had dates that were weathered and indecipherable, but these held no interest for him. In a less overgrown corner of the lot he found what he had come for, the mausoleum holding the recent earls. Silently he read the inscriptions on the newest structure, and he knelt to say a prayer for the three members of the de Lacy family stricken dead on the same date fifteen years earlier. Richard, Elizabeth, and Eileen de Lacy lay buried along with the Summerville hopes.

A rustle in the weeds nearby disturbed his thoughts, but Drake did not look up. The summer sun burned his uncapped head as his mind wandered to the tragedy of that day. It seemed so improbable in this peaceful setting to think of thieves and rebels destroying an entire family, a young, noble family, but he had sensed the currents of unrest in this place. Peace would not be found easily here.

The sound became a rusty chuckle as Drake continued with head bowed. He glanced up in annoyance to confront the withered eyes of an old crone. Garbed in rags that had faded to an indistinguishable gray, she stared at him with inexplicable delight.

She pointed a gnarled finger at the smaller of the three tombs and cackled something in Gaelic Drake found hard to decipher. He stood up, thinking to leave

the old woman to her strange chants, but she caught
the sleeve of his coat and would not let go. Patiently
he listened to her jumbled words, picking out the
English and those in Gaelic he recognized, until a
pattern formed that brought a frown to his brow.

He pointed to the small tomb inscribed "LADY EI-
LEEN DE LACY, 1725-1730" and the woman nodded with a
mad smile, cradling her arms as if she held an infant,
stroking the imaginary hair. Then she pointed at the
tomb beside it, the one for Lady Elizabeth, shook her
head, and repeated the same garbled phrases of earlier.

Before Drake could make her repeat it slowly, an
old man in priest's casscck hurried down the weedy
path toward them. He made a gesture of respect in
Drake's direction, but hastily caught the old crone by
the arm and steered her away.

With an apologetic look the priest explained, "She
is not quite right up here, she is not." He touched his
temple lightly. "I am sorry if she has disturbed your
prayers."

Drake could sense the priest's curiosity, but it was
evident that removing the old woman was more important that satisfying curiosity. The priest hurried his
charge away.

It had been a been a long time since Drake had
practiced the religion of his mother, but this encounter
returned strong memories. Britain's penal codes made
the practice of Catholicism a forbidden topic, and the
fraternity of priests was small but closely knit. If anyone knew anything about the de Lacy tragedy, it would
be the family priest, if there were one. Drake suspected, judging by the family plot's location within the
walls of an abandoned abbey, that there very likely
was a family priest somewhere in the background.
And he knew the man to find him.

Charged with a restlessness that could find no outlet, Eileen spent the summer wandering woods she

knew by heart, searching for the peace she had once found there. Peace seemed to have deserted her, replaced by odd longings that could not be assuaged by any of her usual activities. On this day in August, wild roses spilled their perfume into the heady heat, and green leaves formed a canopy of shade for her comfort, but the musky air only enhanced her restlessness. Purposefully she set up her easel.

With brush in hand, the restlessness gradually retreated. She hummed contentedly to herself as the image she saw in her mind formed on the paper. Summer called for oils and the deep hues of greens and yellows. She smiled at the effect as it appeared beneath her fingers.

The shuffle of moist leaves warned her she was not alone, but, thinking Quigley had returned, she ignored it. She would be finished shortly. He could wait. The deserted cottage behind her should keep him cool and comfortable for the duration.

But Quigley always stayed obediently out of sight, and this intruder kept advancing until she could no longer pretend he was not there. She grew still and looked up at the tall, masculine figure intruding upon her haven.

"You were singing," Drake accused as he stepped into the clearing. He mourned the loss of the sweet melody that had guided him here, but he could not hide his curiosity as his gaze swept quickly over the girl he had not seen since spring. These past weeks she had become a fantasy in his mind, a child whose gravestone rested in an Irish churchyard, a figment of his imagination whose history he had tried his best to discover. The quicksilver sprite he knew and the haunted vision of that tragic landscape had merged into one in his dreams, but neither matched the reality before him. Her slight stature still proclaimed her a child, but he knew enough of her depths to see her as the woman she was.

The August sun was too warm for hampering hoops and petticoats, and Eileen had dressed sensibly for her outing. The pale yellow muslin with its tightly cinched waist and low neckline lost in a froth of lace and ribbons appeared as cool as a mountain spring, and Drake felt as if he had discovered some rare new flower. Her discarded bonnet lay among the clutter of painting paraphernalia at her feet, and her auburn hair glowed with golden sunshine and copper highlights. She wore it loose, caught up in ribbons to keep it from her face but falling in a girlish river over her shoulders and back, exposing her slender throat to his view. This unexpected sight held Drake enthralled, and he could scarcely control his stare.

Startled, Eileen had halted her unconscious humming, but the marquess's open curiosity made her smile. She hummed a few bars of a rather naughty ditty she had heard in the Drews' tavern, and Diane's brother recovered enough to grin broadly.

"Thank God, you haven't changed. I thought I'd find you with your hair done up in powder, fluttering a fan, and pouting at me. Has my neglect put me in complete disapprobation?"

Eileen studied Lord Sherbourne's expression. Beneath the golden tangle of hair, blue eyes had grown darker, more shadowed than she remembered, and the cleft Neville jaw had a determined set to it that made her uneasy. But a smile played about his lips as usual, and the warmth of his gaze was difficult to meet. She shook her head in reply.

He regarded her with a bemused expression, as if just discovering she did not speak. "I have never heard you sing before. If you have a voice, there is no reason you cannot talk. Unless, of course . . ."

Suddenly Drake moved closer, his eyes brimming with mischief as he stood before her. Without a word of warning he slid his arm around her waist and covered her lips with his kiss.

Eileen's initial reaction was to resist, as she had done with other men often enough before. But this man's mouth was warm and soft and inviting, and not in the least fearsome. She felt drawn to him in a manner she could not comprehend, and she succumbed to the temptation to learn more of this phenomenon. His chest did not yield beneath her hands; the firm strength of his arms about her waist was secure and reassuring. When Drake pressed his kiss deeper, Eileen bent to his pressure, and his arms tightened to hold her protectively as he took possession of her mouth.

The touch of his tongue reawakened the restlessness Eileen had buried with her work, and a surge of longing opened a chasm wide and deep. As Drake made his claim, his kiss stole along her senses, but her mind leapt to the defense with instant alarm. Hastily Eileen turned her head away, but she continued to cling to his coat, uncertain of her ability to stand on her own any longer.

Knowing he exceeded the bounds of propriety, Drake continued to hold this fairy princess within the circle of his arms. The dreams that had haunted his sleep these past weeks had become flesh and blood reality, and he was reluctant to part with them. Realizing that the scent of wildflowers he had attributed to some hidden blooms in actuality came from the slight female in his arms, Drake saw the danger of this folly.

"How else could a gentleman ask a lady if she had a tongue?" he inquired facetiously, stroking the thick, rich lengths of hair cascading down her back before she could jerk away from him.

Eileen made an angry moue of distaste and attempted to step away, but Drake kept a grasp on her arms. His gaze held hers as he spoke.

"Slap me, if you wish. I deserve it, I know."

With a flash of the same disastrous mischief Drake had exhibited a moment earlier, Eileen turned her

head up to be kissed again. Not questioning this un-
foreseen response, Drake obligingly bent to taste the
sweet wine of her lips once more, luxuriating in their
heady liquor until the sharp point of a knife pierced
the linen of his shirt just below his unbuttoned waistcoat.

He stepped back in astonishment, then reading the
challenge in Eileen's eyes, he shrugged ruefully. "Quite
right, princess. You are not a toy any more than that
thing is."

Drake skillfully caught her slender wrist and dis-
armed her, but only because she offered no resistance.
He feared what would happen should she truly wish to
kill him, she who was so swift in her judgment and her
reactions. Catching a glance over Eileen's shoulder of
an uncertain figure hovering beneath the tree, Drake
fought off a second reprimand. "Don't worry, Quigley,
Miss Eileen has taught me my lesson."

Eileen grinned and held out her hand for the knife.
Drake returned it, though his gaze lingered long on
her seemingly unconcerned expression.

"Are you in the habit of kissing all your beaus in
that manner?" he inquired jealously. The angry flash
of silver eyes forced a hasty retreat. "You're right. It's
no business of mine." Drake buried his inexplicable
anger in coolness. "I've come to ask you to return to
the house with me. I have something I wish to tell Sir
John, and I thought you ought to be there to hear it."

His voice was almost harsh, and Eileen shivered as
she bent to pack the knife in amongst her other be-
longings. She cleaned her brushes as Drake lifted her
painting from the easel and admired it. His words said
nothing of her artwork, however.

"I do not know how you learned the information
you sent me, and I will not ask, but you have saved
my family much grief. You understand why I could
not write to thank you, don't you?"

Eileen looked up, caught his glance, and nodded. A
hard line had formed at the side of Drake's mouth,
and it did not soften as he spoke.

"Edmund is my cousin. I cannot deal with him as he deserves, but thanks to your warning, I have learned to better protect myself and others. There will be no repeat of the incident. I need not tell you the torment Diane would have suffered should she think the lives of her cousins endangered." Drake helped her to lift the canvas bag of utensils and offered his arm so they might return to the house. Eileen made a sign of a question mark in the air and pointed to him.

"And I?" He shrugged. "I am happy if Diane is happy. My cousins are all creditably employed and momentarily out of mischief, and I have made my prospective father-in-law happy by setting the wedding date for spring. My fiancée has decided she wishes to reside in London, and Edmund is quite content with the arrangements that have been made for him, though not for long, I daresay."

Eileen frowned at this information, but who was she to question the decisions of her betters? Yet Edmund had seemed just a trifle more dangerous than Drake pretended.

Once they reached the Hall, Quigley carried away the paints to the studio, and Eileen made Drake wait while she dashed into the parlor and returned with the thin volume of nonsense tales. She turned swiftly to a page detailing a woman garbed in golden passion and laughter and gestured toward his left hand.

Drake took the book and looked at her oddly, his lips quirked in a half smile as he noted the well-turned pages. "No, I do not describe Lady Pamela in these pages. She is not a fantasy of mine, just a fact of life. Did you enjoy the stories?"

Vaguely puzzled that a man who could describe a woman so passionately on paper referred to his intended so nonchalantly, Eileen nodded without smiling. She closed the book gently, and only then did she look up to catch the brief sadness in Drake's eyes.

"You are right. A grown man should have better things to do than write silly tales."

Astounded by this interpretation of her silence, Eileen shook her head violently and held the volume against her heart, but he paid no heed to her theatrics. Briskly Drake guided her toward the study, where Sir John waited.

The sound of music from somewhere near by brought Eileen to a halt. Avoiding Drake's impatient grasp, she threw open the sliding doors to the main salon, and smiled happily at the sight within.

The trio sprawled across the modern French Regency sofas and chairs looked decidedly out of place in this formal habitat, but they leapt gallantly to their feet at her entrance. Theodore held a Spanish guitar that Eileen flew to inspect. The poet, James, burned red with embarrassment as she turned next to him, reaching knowingly for his coat pocket where his latest scribblings were hidden. When she came to the third party in the room, a formidably large but attractive man, Drake offered introductions.

"Miss de Lacy, Mr. Michael Jasper, lately of the Third Cavalry." Eileen threw Drake a quick look at this use of her surname, but Drake remained impassive as Michael bowed politely in acknowledgment of the introduction. As Eileen could not make the usual polite greeting and Michael was too tongue-tied to offer further explanations, they parted on an exchange of tentative smiles.

Not until they were once more out in the hall and heading for the study did Eileen stop to think why Drake had brought along this retinue. Remembering Michael's rather overwhelming stature, strength, and prior occupation, Eileen sent Drake a surreptitious look. Like many gentlemen, Drake and his friends had occupied themselves in learning to protect themselves at swordpoint, and Drake, at least, had developed quite a reputation. Did he still feel called upon to surround himself with bodyguards against any further attacks by his cousin?

She could not question him, but obediently entered the room Drake opened to her. Her uncle looked up from his desk and smiled warmly.

"You found her! Excellent. Now what is this astonishing news that brings you here in such a manner?"

Drake held out a seat for Eileen and waited until she had settled herself before sitting down. His normally expressive face revealed nothing of his thoughts.

"I have had time on my hands lately, an exceedingly dangerous occurrence for someone with my curiosity. I have amused myself at your expense, I am afraid. I trust you will not resent what I have done when you hear what I have to say."

Sir John looked confused. "Come to the point, Sherbourne."

Drake moved his shoulders restlessly within the confines of his tightly tailored coat. He did not wear elaborate frills as many did, yet the simple elegance of his white cravat was all the more striking against his gold coloring. He looked every inch the part of idle gentleman he played, but the stern set of his features now reflected none of his usual gaiety.

"I ask that you keep this to yourself, sir. I do not believe I have done anything dangerous, but . . ." He shrugged his shoulders, letting the sentence dangle. "The military might question my travels to Ireland and France during the present crisis."

Sir John's eyebrows shot up, but he had the wisdom to hold his tongue. The marquess was bound to seek out his own challenges one way or another. It would be better had they been more constructive, under the circumstances. King George was not amused by the young men supporting the Prince. From all reports, Drake was not a political animal, but these journeys would not go unnoticed.

At Sir John's silence Drake continued, "While I was there, I thought to make one or two inquiries on your behalf. I hope you will forgive my presumption."

Eileen's gaze swiftly searched Drake's face. He did not look at her, but her heart beat a little faster. She could think of only one inquiry he could make in Ireland that would affect her. She waited impatiently for him to continue.

"You had told me of your brother-in-law's estates in Ireland. I knew you were concerned about the fate of your wife's sister, so I thought to inquire while I was there."

Drake spoke casually, as if he had stopped at a neighboring home to ask after someone's health. Eileen could scarcely contain her anxiety, and Sir John appeared to be having equal difficulty. When he received no objections, Drake continued.

"I was directed to the churchyard where your in-laws were said to be interred. While I was there, I heard an interesting story from an old crone who visited the de Lacy vault. It could have been the wanderings of an addled mind, but she seemed quite vehement about the stones erected in memory of your sister-in-law and niece. Much of what she said was in Gaelic, but I understood enough to interpret the fact that she believed the graves to be empty."

Sir John sat upright with a bolt and waited impatiently for Drake to continue.

Drake hesitated, choosing his words cautiously. "That part of Ireland is much set off from the rest of the world. It is too poor to offer more than a few votes to their parliamentary greed and thus it is ignored. Highwaymen abound, as you are sorrowfully aware, but this old woman claimed she knew who had rescued your niece from the rogues. What became of the child, or her mother, I could not interpret, and the village priest soon came and hastened her away."

Drake halted, searching for the best words to finish the tale. He threw a concerned glance to Eileen. "I will not go into detail here. Suffice it to say that the priest gave me an idea and I began making other inquiries. Catholics have learned to mind their tongues over there, but I knew an old priest who is a friend of my mother's family. The tale he tells is not a pretty one, but to make a long story short, I have discovered the name of the convent in France that now harbors a woman who was smuggled from Ireland immediately after the attack on the de Lacy family. I have spoken to the mother superior, but since I am not of the family, she will not communicate with me other than to admit that they know the one I am seeking."

Eileen clasped her hands and looked anxiously from her uncle to Drake and back again. She bit her lip as Sir John slammed his hands against the desk and rose from his seat, gratefully holding out his hand to Drake.

"Well done, my boy! By Jupiter, I had no idea you had it in you! I'll not forget this. Tell me where this place is and I will set out at once."

Drake took the offered hand and shook it briefly, but shook his head in disagreement with the baronet's intentions.

"Even if the woman is Elizabeth de Lacy, I do not think you will find it easy to reach her. This order of nuns has taken a vow of silence. The countess would believe her family dead, since she has made no further effort to communicate with you. We might verify she is alive and well, but there is only one way that we might discover if Eileen is truly her daughter. Eileen must go with us."

Hope blazed in Eileen's eyes as she waited for Sir John's response. She had never dared dream that this day might come, but now that it was here, she would never relinquish it. She would go, with or without her uncle's approval. She wanted desperately to know if she had a family and a home, or if she were only someone's cast-off bastard. She did not understand the importance of this knowledge but knew she must have it.

The baronet looked worried. He could not deny the

hope in Eileen's face, but the outcome of such a search might be even more disappointing than never knowing. The dangers of war-torn Europe presented another concern. But he could see no way out of it.

"If this is truly Elizabeth, she has not seen her child for years. She must believe her dead. How could she possibly recognize a daughter she has not seen since the girl was five years old?"

Disappointment spread across Eileen's mobile features. Practical Sir John was right, as usual. She could not even remember her mother's face. How could she possibly expect someone to recognize her after all those years?

Drake did not relent. "You must try or always regret it. The journey is not any more dangerous than any other with the proper precautions. It may come to nothing, but at least you will have tried. None of us can do more than that."

The younger man won. The wrinkles on Sir John's face softened as he read the hope in his ward's eyes. He could deny her nothing. With a slight nod he surrendered. "Go to your aunt, Eileen. I will join you shortly and try to explain what madness has overcome us."

Eileen leapt from her chair, kissed her uncle's cheek, and ran from the room.

Sir John rubbed the spot where she had kissed him. "That is the first spontaneous show of affection I have ever received from the little rascal. She is so reserved, it is frightening."

Drake had the grace to bite his tongue. Eileen's reserve was only skin-deep, as he had every right to know. He suspected it was a defensive barrier against the cruelty of the world she had found herself in for so many years. With time and care, her reserve might dissolve entirely, and lucky would be the man who enjoyed it.

John settled back in his chair and clasped his hands

over his stomach. "Now, tell me what you left out of your story."

The marquess met the older man's gaze steadily. "It is not a pretty tale."

"I did not think it would be. But I have some right to know what to expect when I go over there."

Drake nodded. "I was in no position to tell hearsay from fact. All agreed that de Lacy had been killed by a band of highwaymen, men who had reason to hate authority, even though de Lacy was known to be fair and honest. The rogues found him picnicking with his wife and daughter. If there were servants there, they ran. It was said the earl fought bravely, trying to hold them off so his wife and daughter might escape. But the countess was caught and raped right before his eyes. We'll never know more than that, I fear. There were those who claimed the little girl was murdered while her mother looked on, but it could be just gossip. I could find no two stories alike. One old woman told me wild animals had carried away the little girl's remains. It has been fifteen years, sir. Those old enough to know the truth are scattered and dead. Eileen must not be led to hope too much."

The baronet felt old and gray as he absorbed the force of these words. He remembered the young Elizabeth as a laughing, fiery beauty who fell madly, passionately in love with the visiting Irishman one season and married him the next. They had been insanely happy with each other. To have such bliss end in the degrading agony Drake described was more than he could accept. He closed his eyes and shook his head.

"You are telling me, if Eileen is truly my niece, she witnessed her father's murder and her mother's defiling. I am not certain I wish her to remember that day."

Drake rose and restlessly walked to the window. "I know. I could almost wish she were someone's bastard rather than wish that fate upon her. I don't care to consider what such a sight could do to the mind of a five-year-old." He turned around and stared at Sir John. "But can you imagine what the difference between aristocracy and bastardy must mean to the woman she is now?"

Before Sir John could reply, Drake forged on. "There is one thing we must consider."

The older man looked up sharply at the marquess' tone.

"De Lacy's brother now owns the land and properties and is called earl. Why has he never written you of the rumors I so easily uncovered? Or tried to trace his sister-in-law if the grave lies empty? What kind of man would not turn one stone to discover the truth?"

"If your rumors are true, a thief," Sir John growled, standing abruptly. "But there may be more we do not know. If Elizabeth lives, she will be the one to tell us."

Chapter VI

—— ❦ ——

France
September, 1745

The convent sat nestled between rolling green slopes
and at the foot of a tree-covered mountain. Grape
arbors meandered up one of the gentler slopes, and
neatly patterned vegetable gardens spread across the
valley. As peaceful as the scene appeared, the travel-
ers knew the truth of its security. The path into this
remote countryside was nearly inaccessible. The inhabitants did not encourage strangers.

Leaving the servants in the kitchen, Sir John, Drake,
and Eileen were escorted by a gray-clad novitiate to
the soaring arches of the convent's recéption hall. A
wall of windows overlooked the cloistered inner gardens, and Eileen drifted toward the view while the
men spoke in French to the stern nun awaiting them.

Refusing to hope, refusing even to think of the
woman who had been spirited from her Irish home to
this serene setting after a nightmarish encounter, Eileen stared intently at the tall blue larkspur dancing in
a wayward breeze in the courtyard outside. Trapped
by their earthly roots, they raised their heads to the
skies and dreamed of the wind. How would it feel to
be a larkspur?

A hush settled over the room; Eileen felt the weight
of many gazes upon her, but she made no effort to
turn just yet. She had lived without a mother for most

of her life. She did not really want one now. An emptiness churned in her stomach as she slowly turned to meet the gazes of her companions.

Drake held back a gasp of shock as the two women came face-to-face, one garbed in a postulant's solemn gray, the other in the dusty green traveling gown of a wealthy young lady. Even with the differences in garb and age, the likeness was startling, and Sir John beside him made no effort to hide his own sigh of satisfaction.

The gray-clad older woman stood a few inches shorter, and the color of her hair could only be imagined, but the fair, almost translucent cheeks matched Eileen's delicate skin. Fragile cheekbones, small rounded chins, and delightfully upraised eyebrows reflected each other as if in a mirror. Only the eyes gave evidence these two were not the same.

Drake held his breath as the slight nun lifted her hand to push Eileen's heavy auburn locks from her forehead. With shaking fingers she traced the long, jagged scar from forehead to earlobe, a white ridge that once must have been a gaping, livid wound. A knot formed somewhere in Drake's chest as he realized how close to death that wound must have taken the faerie creature who stood before them now. No wonder she had no fear of death. She had been there already.

Closer to these two than either Sir John or the other nun, Drake could have sworn he heard the whispered word "Mama" from Eileen's lips, but he decided it must be some echo of the wind in this vast chamber. Tears trickled down porcelain cheeks as the older woman made the sign of the cross and turned to regard the intruders upon this private scene.

Her coolness in the face of this discovery astounded Drake, but Sir John gave no notice of it as he hurried forward to greet the reluctant nun.

"Elizabeth! I cannot believe my own eyes. Why did you not tell us where you were? All these years we've thought you dead and buried. Emma will be ecstatic."

Elizabeth stepped backward, avoiding her brother-in-law's exuberant greeting, darting a quick look to her mother superior before gathering up her skirts and turning to leave.

"Wait!" John cried, suddenly unsure of what happened. "Elizabeth, we must talk. Your daughter needs you. Surely you must see that?"

The slight woman halted, gazed rapturously at Eileen's tear-stained face for a fleeting moment longer, then fled.

With a sob of despair, Eileen ran in the opposite direction, leaving the startled men to turn to the older nun for explanations.

The stern nun met the gazes of both men with sympathy. "Elizabeth has chosen to take the vows of silence of this order. When she is ready, she will become one of us, and the wounds of her past will be healed by her love for less worldly things. I am sorry we cannot help you."

Not waiting to hear more of this religious lunacy, Drake strode rapidly in the direction Eileen had taken. A mother who would desert her own child was no saint in his mind. His sympathies lay entirely with the orphaned waif who had been stripped of home and family and left to forge for herself all these years. The tears in those stricken gray eyes scorched his heart, and he had no other thought but to find her.

The kitchen gardeners directed him to the path she had taken, and once outside the convent walls Drake had no difficulty gauging her direction. The wooded mountainside called like a beacon signal to a floundering ship. His long strides took him rapidly over the rough terrain.

He found Eileen facedown in a mossy glade, her

shoulders shaking with the miniature upheavals of her sobs, all the more heartbreaking for their silence. Auburn hair spilled in a cascade over the forest green of her coat, and she seemed as much a part of her surroundings as the trees and the sky. Only his heart heard her all-too-human cries.

Suddenly unsure of himself, Drake knelt beside her weeping figure. He knew Diane cried like this often enough, but never in front of him, never where he must be confronted with her pain. He knew how to make her smile, how to keep the tears from her eyes, but not how to dry them. Eileen's anguish ripped at his soul, leaving him helpless. Drake cursed the world for its cruelty as he lifted her shuddering slightness into his arms.

Eileen turned to him as a child to a nurse, burying her sobs against his broad shoulder, seeking support from the protection of his strong arms. Her slightness frightened him, and he feared the violence of her cries would tear her apart. Holding her close, Drake brushed kisses across the moist wisps of hair about her face, offering what solace he could.

The sight of her mother's loving eyes had released a flood of memories long dammed behind some wound in Eileen's mind. If only she could cling to the pleasant memories, but the vision of her father's laughing, handsome face dissolved beneath the hideous sight of his body crumpled on the forest floor. Demons rose up to shout and slash, and the mocking madness of dark eyes and a cruel mouth threatened her, terrifying and enraging her, sending her flying for safety. The screams returned as if they were yesterday, echoing wildly through the canyons of Eileen's mind, and the anguished tears she had hid for so long could not stop falling.

The pain drove her to seek comfort, for there could be no understanding. It had been too long ago; only the vision and the horror remained. And the tears. She didn't want to remember, didn't want to hear the screams, and she buried her face in Drake's solid embrace, seeking oblivion, while the tears continued to pour unchecked.

Feeling Eileen's heartrending sobs gradually lessening, Drake increased his efforts, rocking her in his arms and plying kisses along her dampened cheeks. As the painful tremors of her frail body slowed, Drake could not help but become aware of the pressure of her breasts against his shirt. The soft scent of her warm hair where it rested beneath his chin wafted up to him, and his kisses took on a new fervency as they lingered against her temple and down her cheek, tasting the salty sweetness of her skin and the dew drops on her lashes.

Mindlessly Eileen lifted her head to this new sensation and met the brush of his kiss with her lips. This butterfly touch reassured her, providing an escape from bitter memories, and she lingered hesitantly, wanting more. He smelled of horses, sweat, and leather, masculine odors she had learned to abhor, but Drake's gentleness confused her, as it always had.

Rewarded by her diminishing sobs, Drake touched Eileen's upturned lips again, and this time the tremor of her response shook him to the depths of his soul.

Wonderingly Eileen clung to the broad shoulders of Drake's coat as his lips closed more demandingly on hers. Excitement shivered through her veins as she discovered the need in him that so matched her own. It could not be so, must not be so, but she gave no heed to logic. All thought lost, Eileen surrendered to Drake's masculine strength, and her hands slid behind his neck so she might meet the delirium of his kiss and erase the pain of the memories that had all too violently returned to her.

With a groan of satisfaction Drake wrapped her in

his arms and loosed the force of his forbidden passion. She responded as hungrily as he, and flaming currents of desire swept through his blood as her small body pressed into his.

The urge to comfort and be comforted had grown well beyond that now, and Eileen's outpourings of grief found surcease in the power of Drake's kisses. She drowned in the intoxicating liquor of his breath entwined with hers, and her lips parted willingly to drink deeper of this heady wine. At the gentle caress of his tongue, a shudder swept through her, and she found no strangeness in the need to fall back upon the soft grass with his arms about her. She could not have remained upright on her own.

Their kisses grew bolder, seeking, exploring, finding those places that brought the most pleasure, that brought them closer together until there was no telling where one began and the other ended. Drake's mouth teased along her earlobe and scorched paths along her throat as Eileen buried her hands in the rich thickness of his hair and urged the return of his kiss to hers.

Obliging, Drake fastened his mouth against the swollen tenderness of Eileen's lips and allowed the eagerness of her kiss to sweep away all restraint. It was as if a star had fallen from the firmament into his hands, and the urge to explore this miracle drove out all logic. His hand found the laces of her bodice and loosened them with a single tug. The flimsy linen of her chemise yielded its protection, and trembling, the hard tips of his fingers surrounded the softness of her breasts.

Eileen gasped at the unexpectedness of this intimate invasion, but Drake's kisses wooed her back to eagerness. The touch of his masculine fingers upon the sensitive peaks of her breasts sent an exquisite pain piercing through her middle and between her thighs. She undersood instinctively where this led, but she could summon no desire to end it.

With joy just within his reach, Drake traced the line of Eileen's delicate cheek with his kisses. Only as he tasted the last traces of salt there did rationality return. Trustingly, the innocent creature in his arms arched into his embrace, eager for the lesson he would teach her. His sex surged impatiently against the tight entrapment of his breeches, waiting to be unleashed to seek the quivering sheath she unknowingly offered. He had no doubt he could have her and without reproach, but he could not steal a treasure like this in a moment of weakness. He knew now his happiness depended on capturing this elusive faerie, but he would have her willing and fully aware of what she did, as she was not now.

Regretfully Drake propped his weight on one elbow and gazed down upon the disheveled loveliness lying beneath him. Auburn tresses spilled across the mossy grass, and the silver wells of her eyes stared up to him boldly as ever. The froth of her lacy chemise had fallen from her shoulders, exposing the fair white skin beneath to the dappled sun of this dusky glade. With a desire he could barely control, Drake teased a rosebud crest between his fingers, watching it harden into a tempting point he longed to take between his teeth.

"Drake?"

The soft murmur of his name seemed to sigh through the trees like the whisper of wind in the leaves, leaving silence behind.

Unable to resist the urge, Drake bent to kiss the rosy nipple before tugging the chemise lace back to cover it. He felt Eileen's shiver of longing and filled his hand with the plump mound of her breast, not wanting to stop here, wanting just a few minutes more of this freedom.

"Please, Drake," she murmured, arching slightly to press against the pleasure his hand offered.

Startled, certain his imagination had gone too far

this time, Drake hastened to close her bodice, tugging the laces securely about the temptation he had little strength to resist.

"I am sorry, princess. I did not mean for this to happen." Regret shadowed the brilliance of his eyes as Drake stared down at her with a longing he made no attempt to conceal.

"I am not sorry."

The words whispered back up to him with a reality that could not be denied. Shaken, unable to conceal the sudden flare of hope, Drake wove his fingers into the thick skeins of her hair and held her face still.

"Say that again," he demanded, almost roughly.

"I am not sorry." The words came a little louder now, a little less hesitantly. A smile formed upon Eileen's lips at the leap of joy and astonishment in Drake's mobile features.

With the greatest of care, Drake lifted her from the grass as if she were a china doll, cradling her in his arms before rising to bring them both to their feet. Still, he did not release her, but held her closely in his embrace while his gaze searched her lovely face.

"I do not know whether to praise the heavens for the content of your words or the context. This is not an enchanted forest, is it?"

Eileen smiled shakily at this idiocy. This past hour had uprooted everything she had been and known, and she still could not deal lightly with the memories that came flooding back. She leaned gratefully against his strength, uncertain of everything.

"It would be if we could stay here," she murmured indistinctly, knowing even now the impossibility of such an event. Once they left these woods, the world would be all too horribly real again, and she had no desire to face it.

Sensing her disquiet, Drake touched her chin with his hand, turning her gaze up to his. "You are remembering something unpleasant." He read the stormy clouds of her eyes with ease.

She met his gaze without flinching. "I remember all."

Still preoccupied with the newness of hearing her speak, Drake smiled at the discovery of the slight Irish lilt in her words.

The seriousness of her regard and her continuing silence forced Drake to realize the full import of her words. "All?" His hand tightened in the hair at the back of her neck, keeping her from turning away. A churning nausea chewed at his stomach as he saw the answer in her eyes without hearing the words. They had never really needed words between them, even less so now.

"My God," he exclaimed in response to what he saw, and the words were as much a prayer as a curse.

Stunned, Drake held her close, pressing her head against his chest as his mind's eye saw what Eileen must have seen as a five-year-old. How much would a five-year-old have understood of what had happened? Or perhaps the blow that had robbed her of her memory and her speech had also robbed her of her consciousness before she had seen the unspeakable?

Remembering the almost frightening aspects of her otherwise fairy-tale paintings, Drake knew unconsciousness had not come soon enough that day. He could feel her shudders against him now as the memory replayed within her. What did she see? Did she see her handsome young father slain by the knives and swords of brigands not worthy of sharing the same earth as he? Would she understand her mother's terrifying screams as one after the other of the miserable rogues defiled her slender body? How could a merciful God have allowed such atrocities? And what had he done to return such horrors to her?

Taking her head between his hands, Drake pleaded,

"Forgive me, princess, for bringing this to you. I could almost wish you silent again than to give you such memories in exchange."

Closing her eyes and drawing on that inner reserve that had been her strength for many long years, Eileen concentrated on the rough touch of his palm against her skin and the musky male scent of him. These things she knew, and inexplicably, they offered no threat, even though she now understood the source of her dislike of all things masculine.

"It is better to know than to fear. Do not be sorry for me. I cannot bear it." Abruptly she stepped away.

About to protest, Drake held his tongue at the faint sounds of shouts in the distance. She had heard them first, he surmised, and he refrained from reaching for her again.

"Your uncle will be worried. What will you tell him?"

Drake watched with sadness as Eileen lifted her hair, and tied it with a ribbon, covering it with the hood of her traveling cloak. In the shadows she seemed lost to him, and a wave of emptiness brought realization of the distance between them that must be bridged before she could ever be his.

"Nothing." She spoke sharply, starting nervously as the sound of voices came closer. "You must promise me that you will say nothing, too."

Drake drew down his eyebrows in perplexity. "Eileen, I own it would be convenient if I admitted nothing of what happened this day, but you must tell your uncle . . ."

"Nothing," she stated firmly. "Should you say I spoke to you, I will behave as if you have taken leave of your wits."

Up until now her words had been soft and childlike, forming in uncertain, short sentences. Emotion strengthened her command, and there was no doubting she meant what she said. Even the vague hint of a Gaelic brogue did nothing to detract from the forcefulness of her demand.

"You are the one who has lost her wits," Drake answered curtly, watching her with no small measure of wariness.

With one tragic look of reproach Eileen replied, "I told you, I remember everything."

And for emphasis, she turned on her heel and fled.

Chapter VII

—— ❦ ——

English Channel
September, 1745

Eileen stared out the rain-soaked window as the two men across from her exchanged dilatory comments on the state of the roads into Calais. The return journey had been without the nervous excitement and anticipation that had carried them in, and everyone showed signs of weariness.

All except Drake, of course. His restlessness had kept him astride his horse and wandering far astray as the cumbersome coach struggled with rutted cart paths and herds of livestock. He found the best inns and taverns and warned the landlords well in advance of their arrival before returning to guide the coach lumbering along behind him.

He rarely spent time inside the carriage, much to Eileen's relief. Only today, this last day before their sailing to England, his horse had acquired a stone, and the drenching downpour had forced him inside with Eileen and her maid and Sir John. The less-than-roomy interior seemed in danger of exploding with the energy emanating from the long-limbed man on the narrow seat.

Clenching her fists in her lap, Eileen attempted to ignore his presence, although it was much like ignoring a mountain in the road ahead. They had not exchanged another word since Sir John had come upon them in the woods that day. She had sensed Drake's anger and disbelief as she ran gratefully, but silently, to hug her uncle, and she had avoided him ever since. Or that was the reason she gave herself.

The other reason for avoiding Drake struggled within her now. She knew the cause of his restlessness, for it echoed her own. Sitting this close to him, she could smell the mixture of horse sweat and leather and masculine musk that was peculiarly Drake's own, and she could not blot out the images the sensation brought to her mind. She had only to look in front of her to see the hands that had so easily roused her to aching desire. If she raised her eyes, she would see the mouth that had kissed her into submission, and she knew her longing for more would be undisguisable. That, she could not have.

The rain-washed landscape seemed preferable to the trap of temptation. She had been on her own so long, it had been easy to allow someone else to take command. Especially now, when the problems looming before her appeared formidable, perhaps unconquerable. She would gladly and with great relief surrender her burdens to someone who seemed so able to shoulder them. She might have done it, too, had not Drake given her time to remember her position.

And an awkward one it was, too. Eileen fidgeted nervously as she contemplated the choices before her. She sensed each time Drake's gaze strayed to her, and she knew he presented only one small portion of the problem. Were it not for Sir John and Lady Summerville, she would take the easy way out. Surrender to Drake would not be in the least difficult. But then, if it were not for her aunt and uncle, she would have no problem at all. For herself, she felt no concern at the pitfalls that lay before her, but the Summervilles had given her family and home and love, and she would die before she saw harm come to them.

Only harm was all she could foresee if she remained

at Summer Hall. While she had remained innocent of her past and without the power to communicate, she had presented no immediate danger to anyone. But if anyone should learn that her memory of that day had returned—Eileen shuddered. She could not bear another such disaster. There must be some way of protecting them.

Feigning sleep, Drake watched the play of emotions across Eileen's pensive face. He had been disgusted at the ease with which she acted out the lie of muteness to Sir John, but not disgusted enough to leave her alone. He had only been offered a glimpse of the fiery joy she could bring him, but that had been sufficient to induce a craving that he had never before experienced. His desire for her now was so strong that it was a wonder she did not fling open the door and run screaming from him. The current of communication between them was such that he did not see how she could fail to recognize his need.

Which gave ample room for thought. From the proud tilt of that tiny chin, Drake gathered she had a good idea of what was passing through his mind. She was too much woman not to. It just mattered how he went about it. Her passion had been too real to be denied long. If he could somehow cut through their differences, she would be willing enough to grace his bed, he surmised. The fact that she had not complained to her uncle of his behavior told him much. But how could he shove aside all the proprieties and her objections to accomplish his goal?

Drake leaned back and closed his eyes completely. There was a way, if he could overcome Eileen's distrust. The society he lived in and centuries of custom had provided outlets for just such a trap as he found himself in. Forced to marry only within their own narrow circle, his fellow nobles had found many ingenious ways to marry to suit society and still be happy with the women of their choice. The number of Stuart bastards in the annals of aristocracy alone proved that point. He had only to decide which path to take and embark upon it.

By the time they boarded the ship in Calais, Eileen had become all too aware that Drake had come to some decision. His strong hands were the first to reach out and lift her from the carriage to the safety of a boarded walk, and it was in the shelter of his protective cloak that she boarded the waiting ship. Even the arrival of the Monsard brothers after their visit with their uncle in Versailles did nothing to dissuade her protector from his post. In fact, Drake nearly scowled at the return of his cousins. It would be nearly impossible to find Eileen alone with those scalawags around. Once he had decided upon his course, he could not be diverted, and he much preferred to accomplish his goals immediately than wait. The Monsards could cause a lengthy delay.

Their jubilant discussion of the beauties of the French court served to distract Sir John's melancholy thoughts, however, and he listened patiently to their youthful boasts. Drake noted dryly that they made no mention of their aristocratic uncle or invitations to return. It seemed he would be given the opportunity to guide them safely into manhood without the aid of their French relations. The fact that Drake was soon to take a wife probably encouraged his mother's family in this assumption, instead of the opposite. What in hell made them think a new bride could handle this motley assortment of cousins?

With relief Drake watched the brothers follow Sir John out of the rain and into a cabin below for a game of cards. He turned to make certain Eileen would not follow, but she had anticipated him and even now wandered along the railing, staring out over the gray sea. Her cloak billowed out behind her in the driving wind, but she seemed oblivious to the elements.

With a firmness she had learned to expect, Drake

captured her hand and led her into the lee of a bulkhead. Eileen almost regretted what she had done in the forest. It had been much easier to deal with his arrogant forcefulness when he had thought of her as a younger sister. Now, as man and woman, they could only fight at each other and both lose.

"I did not really believe you would go through with this charade so thoroughly, princess. Did I dream those words of yours in the forest?"

Drake's tall frame and heavy cloak blocked all traces of the wind and rain as he confronted her. Neatly trapped between the bulkhead and his masculine solidity, Eileen could only stare up into the endless blue of his eyes and wait.

"It was an enchanted forest. We can't return to it, Drake." The wind whipped the sorrow from her words, but it did not matter. He would not listen.

"Eileen, you are too brave, too alive to bury yourself in fear as your mother has done. Whatever happened that day cannot come back to harm you. Your shield of silence serves no purpose." Drake fought for some understanding, but the gray mists of her eyes prevented trespassing. He could not penetrate the hidden interiors. Not now. Not yet.

"It does not serve your purpose, perhaps, but it serves mine. Go away, Drake. Leave me alone. I can be nothing to you, as you are nothing to me."

Drake did not reveal the pain those words struck in him. She was probably right, as he was most certainly wrong, but he had no intention of admitting it. He knew what he wanted as he had not before, and he would tear the walls of her fortress to the ground to get it.

"Your words lie, princess, as your lips do not. Be silent, if you must, but you cannot hide yourself from me."

Drake's hands closed about her waist, propelling her forward whether she willed it or not. The heavy,

humid air filled their nostrils, and the wetness on their
lips and cheeks had little to do with the rain. Drake's
lips drank deeply of the rich nectar of her kiss and he
knew he could take no other course.

Enfolded in his powerful embrace, Eileen had no
will of her own. Her body slipped so naturally into the
shelter of his that she had no thought of denying it.
This was how it was between them, how it was meant
to be, just as the bees buzzed in flowers and leaves fell
to the ground in winter. She belonged in his arms,
with his mouth warm and possessive upon hers. The
touch of his tongue took her breath away, and she
parted her lips willingly to give him entrance, just as
her body would do should he ask. As he would.

Tears rolled down her cheeks as his hand came up
between them to caress her breast. Dripping cloaks
hid them from prying eyes, but there was no escaping
the aching longing this simple touch generated. He
could have undressed her here, for all the world to
see, and it would not matter so long as she pleased
him. Terrible, terrible thought. And Eileen's tears fell
faster.

Satisfied he had proved his point, though certainly
not satisfied in any other way, Drake relented. Wrapping her shivering slightness within his cloak, next to
the heat of his body, he pressed his kisses against her
hair. With the knowledge of experience, he knew better than she the results of this experiment. He had
desired many women before, but not in this way, not
with the tumultuousness of this passion he found in
her arms. Torn between the desire to protect and the
desire to possess, he could find no rational means of
doing both.

"Will you deny what is between us now, Eileen?"
he demanded, almost angrily.

"I never meant to deny it, my lord," she replied
bitterly, her voice muffled against his shoulder.

Drake's smile was grim at the Gaelic subservience

she mimicked. All her Irish ancestry must be warring within her to call him so, but neither could he deny the title. He was an English marquess. She was the daughter of a land-poor Irish nobleman. Her father's title might have had some English authority, but he had been Irish through and through. Drake had learned that much in his travels. Even had her family lived, they could never have traveled in the society that was his. In feudal times, he could have claimed his rights to her, and no man would have dared protest. Those times were past, but he would have his rights just the same. And with all the instincts of a child of nature, she knew it.

"Eileen, you cannot live like your mother, denying the world, or painting one of your own. You must marry sometime, have children, live among the rest of us. I will make it as easy for you as possible."

He was right, of course. She had been childish and immature to think the world could go on as it did now, that Sir John and Lady Summerville would live forever and that she could wander their estates into eternity. Marriage was the ideal solution, but she knew he did not mean to him. He already had his perfect match in the aristocratic Lady Pamela. He merely sought the solace his haughty bride would not know how to give.

Curiosity getting better of wisdom, Eileen lifted her eyes to consider him quizzically. "What are you suggesting?" She omitted the "my lord" pointedly.

Drake caressed her satin cheek, gazing longingly into the impenetrable depths of her eyes. Could he make her understand? Or would it be better to show her? Deciding he had no choice, he explained.

"There is no longer any doubt in Sir John's mind that you are his only heir. By rights, if your mother forsakes the world, her estates become yours also. You are a wealthy woman, my love. Even if we cannot prove your parentage, you will be welcomed into the best circles simply on the basis of your wealth and connections. A husband will be easily obtained. One who desires only access to your pockets and not your bed may be a trifle difficult to uncover, but if you will allow me, I think I can find the right man. Sir John will be content, your husband will be adequately recompensed, and we can be together as much as we like. Diane would love to have you with us. It is not the way I would wish it had circumstances been otherwise . . ."

Eileen cut him off with an angry shake of her head. "No, thank you, my lord. I cannot see sharing you with Lady Pamela and raising all our children under one roof. I am sure in your set it is all very well and proper, but it does not suit me. Marry I must, if only to acquire a protector stronger than myself or Sir John, but such a man as you describe will be of no use to me. Go away, Drake. You have no part in my life."

Boldly Eileen tore from his grasp and almost escaped, but Drake caught her and swung her back into his arms again. Lips pinched in anger, he had all he could do to keep from shaking sense into that stubborn little head.

"Damn you, Eileen, can you not see? I will be your protector. Tell me what you fear, and I will slay it, whether it be man or beast. You need not grace my bed to gain my protection. I offer it freely. Trust me, Eileen."

Drake saw the confusion of emotions reflected back to him through the mirror of her eyes. He wanted to shake her, to make mad, passionate love to her, and to protect her all at the same time. No woman had driven him to such insanity before. Why must it be this one, who evaded him with every word, every motion, disappearing before his very eyes?

"Trust you?" She stared at him as if he had taken leave of his senses, her eyes wide with disbelief. "My father died of trust. So, too, will you, if you do not take care. Trust is for fools. Go away, Drake. I am not for you."

Her voice whispered over the wind, a sweetly lilting melody, but her words struck cold and hard as any knife. Drake searched her face for any reprieve and, finding none, dropped his hold on her.

"I do not give up so easily, my lady," he informed her, even as he freed her from his trap.

For a brief moment, anguish flickered in silver eyes, then they shuttered closed again. "You will destroy us both, then, my lord."

Before he could make another try, Eileen skirted around him and ran for the safety of the cabin, leaving Drake to the wind and weather. He turned his face to the sky and let the wind howl his misery for him. Why her, Lord? Why not wish for the moon and stars? Why place his heart in the hands of a creature who did not exist? A figment of his imagination? An enchantress of the forest?

From his place in the cabin doorway, Sir John caught the last part of this scene with no small amount of relief. At least one of the two had some sense. It did not matter which.

Straightening his shoulders against a tendency to sag, the baronet turned back to the lighted room. He would have to find a husband for her soon. He had no desire to know what had already gone between his niece and the young lord. The palpable tension around them these past days had been sufficient to tell more than he wanted to know. He only knew Eileen had no defense against a man like Drake, and a man like Drake had no defense against a spirit like Eileen's. The war to come was inevitable, the result—a foregone conclusion.

A husband must be found at all costs.

The remainder of the journey was without event. Drake and the Monsards escorted the small expedition to Summer Hall, then departed hastily. Sir John went to break the exciting discovery of her sister's existence to Emma, and Eileen silently climbed the stairway to her studio.

She stared at the unfinished painting of the castle on the hill. Emerald lawns rolled across an enchanted landscape, fed by the color of blood. She now understood so many things. With a slash of her knife she shredded the canvas, loathing the fairy-tale scene she had created. Castles built on blood made hell, not heaven. No enchantment endured there.

Perhaps her mother had the best solution. Why live in a world of murder and woe? She had found the perfect escape, a silent peace. Perhaps she ought to consider the same solution. What kind of blood flowed in her veins that she should wish it on another?

Staring at the blue lines etched beneath the fine white skin of her wrist, Eileen shuddered. If she came from a heritage that could produce one such monster, might she not be the same? Or her children? Perhaps she ought to reconsider her hasty decision to marry. One less line of de Lacy's in this world would not be missed. If only she could murder the other.

Chapter VIII

— ❦ —

England
September–December, 1745

By the end of that September, Charles Stuart held most of Scotland—as much as any one man can hold those rocky hillsides—in the name of his father, King James VIII. Panic flew north and south. With most of the British army still in Flanders fighting George's endless European wars, Charles could march on England with impunity. Northern landowners made a hasty assessment of their loyalties, and rebellious youths scurried northward in steady streams.

The inevitable bloodshed to come held no romance for Eileen. Wars only convinced her more of the inherent evil of men, and once more she retreated to the haven of her woods. Drake had almost convinced her another life might be possible, but that had been a moment of madness. She would belong to no man. If she stayed hidden away here and silent as her mother in her convent, she could harm no one. Ireland was far away. The Irish devil of her nightmares had shown no interest in her in the past. She saw no reason he would seek her out now. Silence was the solution. Not marriage.

Sir John had other ideas. He knew better than to drag his reclusive niece into the crowds of London society. Instead, he drew London society to the countryside. Unknowingly, he had assistance from other quarters, but whatever the source, a steady stream of eligible men flowed through the portals of Summer Hall that autumn.

At first, Eileen did not gather the import of these strangers appearing with increasing regularity at their table. Sir John had many acquaintances in politics and these were troubled times. Not until the gallant bows became a shade too gallant, the polite smiles too eager, the appreciative stares too assessing, did she begin to understand.

Sir John's wealth had the power to produce a parade of men just for her divertissement. The thought at first amused her. Eileen returned their stares boldly, making them fidget and tug their lace jabots or surreptitiously adjust their powdered wigs. When they spoke to her, she smiled blankly and continued smiling until their monologues dwindled to nervous coughs.

But as the autumn wore on, the parade grew stale and more intrusive. Eileen almost gave serious consideration to the older men who ignored her completely and discussed financial arrangements with Sir John, for the younger men persisted in wooing her in the most irritating of manners. Those with a well-turned leg seemed incapable of standing without propping it to the best advantage while discoursing drearily on subjects of no entertainment to the object of their posing, for they seemed to believe she heard nothing they said. The handsome ones preferred to seek her out in dark corners or lonely walks to teach her the wisdom of their kisses, since their words had no effect. Those with pockets to let and titles for sale peered down at her from aristocratic noses, made approving little noises, and offered their names without consideration of what went with them. Eileen learned to stare blankly at them all.

As his niece succeeded in bringing one more young gallant to the state of babbling idiocy, Sir John threw up his hands in vexation. This one she had cowed by the simple expedient of introducing him to her studio—where she had calmly hung all her works upside-down. The fool had attempted to make intelligent comments on trees hanging from the sky and rivers running uphill until the tears of laughter rolling down Eileen's cheeks had given the game away. Needless to say, he did not stop even to inquire the size of her dowry.

Sir John frowned at the laughter coming from the small salon. Drake's ne'er-do-well artistic friends had begun to make Summer Hall a regular overnight stop on their journeys between London and Sherbourne. On any given day he could expect to see musicians draped over the spinet, poets spouting nonsense at the fire grate, or scribblers submerged in his library. These young louts had no difficulty in communicating with Eileen, if the nonsense they spoke could be called communicating. Had he thought any of them capable of managing an estate, he might even consider drafting them into his war against Eileen's spinsterhood, but not one had a head for figures.

Oblivious to her uncle's frustration, Eileen welcomed these intruders as a bridge between herself and Sherbourne—Diane, not Drake. They carried messages and books, new sheet music, the latest oil colors, whatever they came upon in London that might please either of the two girls, and that they exchanged with the familiarity of community property. It offset some small part of the expense of feeding and housing them, for not one among them had a feather to fly on. Drake more or less supported them all, with the increasing, if unwilling, aid of Sir John.

This day, Eileen welcomed a letter from Diane delivered by Michael. Though no artist, he had somehow become part of the tribe that wandered to and fro, too poor to afford London but too well-bred to succeed elsewhere. Drake found him useful as a temporary estate manager now that Edmund had found his niche in London politics, and Diane took advantage of his gentle generosity with impunity. Eileen laughed at the contents of the note and gave it to Michael to read.

The ex-soldier scanned the contents with a chortle and returned it to her. Theodore grabbed the missive from Eileen's hands, and the letter made the rounds of the room's occupants with growing exuberance.

"It seems Lady Diane does not favor a holiday with her prospective in-laws. Will you take up her suggestion, Apple Princess?"

Drake's name for her had stuck, though in many variations depending on the speaker and his mood. Theodore preferred it to her true name and seemed to delight in discovering new variations. He grinned as Eileen threw him a look of exasperation.

"A ball! You must have a ball and invite us all!" The poet, James, blushed at this inadvertent rhyme.

Standing in the room's center, wearing her paint-speckled apron over a gown of dove gray, her copper hair spilling from its pins, Eileen appeared no more than a simple maid of tender years. Yet she succeeded in holding the attention of every man in the room, Sir John noted as he lingered in the doorway. She radiated life, emitted a vivacious energy that held all within her sight spellbound. When she chose to.

With grudging admiration for her strong will, Sir John stalked into the room and appropriated the letter that had apparently become public property.

Eileen smiled and complacently clasped her hands in front of her while her uncle briefly read Diane's plea for escape. She so seldom left Sherbourne that it was a matter of intense pride for anyone to have her request a visit. That she would rather stay at Summer Hall for the holidays than visit Lady Pamela at Westly spoke volumes of that relationship. Sir John shook his head in dismay at the family feud this would engender, but Nevilles had been fighting among themselves for generations. He glanced up to his expectant ward.

"And you think the visit should be celebrated by a ball? Are you certain that is appropriate?"

Without a moment's hesitation Eileen nodded eagerly, then gestured to Theodore for explanations.

The slender musician shoved back a shock of wiry, unwigged blonde hair as Sir John turned his steady gaze to him. "Diane loves music, sir. The guests do not matter so much as the musicians." With an awkward shrug, he added, "Lord Westly detests dancing and there is not a musical instrument in the entire manor."

Sir John bit back a grin at this piece of information. The young scalawags were a useless lot, but he could not deny enjoying a spirited song or two himself. To spend the holidays without so much as an evening around the spinet would be dreary beyond bearing. The least he could do for the young lady was rescue her from such a dismal fate. Drake might have to lie in the bed he'd made, but there was no reason his sister should.

"Very well, send Lady Diane our eager invitation. Perhaps Emma can help you with a guest list for the festivities. We might as well make an occasion of it." With a shrewd look to Theodore, he finished, "And I expect you can find us the musicians Lady Diane requires. Make yourself useful."

As he walked out, the room behind him erupted into joyous chatter, and Sir John smiled smugly. With all her friends around her, Eileen could not pull her deaf-and-dumb act so easily. Surely some young man would fall under her spell and have sense enough to batter down her defenses on such an occasion. He should have thought of it sooner.

Garbed in a new gown of the latest Paris fashion, the rich satin Watteau pleats draped elegantly in a train behind her, Eileen ornamented the great hall in much the same manner as the garlands of holly and pine. In the candlelight of the massive chandeliers she shimmered in silver and emerald skirts, and the parure of emeralds about her throat accented the fair loveliness emerging from the décolletage. Only the rebelliously unpowdered auburn hair set her apart from the other aristocratic lady guests.

Sir John smiled his pleasure at the number of heads turning as his niece drifted through the crowded hall on the arm of Michael Jasper. The ex-soldier had accompanied Lady Diane on her arrival several days ago and had stayed at everyone's insistence, since he had no other family to visit. Eileen appeared comfortable in his company and had shown no signs of recalcitrance as the various guests were introduced to her. As yet she had danced only with her artist friends, but Sir John held out hope that would change. The evening was young yet.

Eileen spread her skirts on the seat beside Diane's wheeled chair and leaned over to listen to her friend's whispered comment on one of the other guests. She laughed at the sight pointed out, a powdered wig slipping from the bald pate of an elderly gentleman who had made his interests clear earlier in the evening. Diane had eagerly joined in Eileen's war against addlepated suitors, much to the amusement of the military man standing guard behind their chairs.

Michael's companionable silence made it easy for the two friends to forget his presence while Diane chattered and Eileen listened. Theodore and James and others of their set drifted in and out of the chairs surrounding them, but very seldom did one succeed in persuading Eileen from her perch. Only Diane's occasional insistence that Eileen enjoy the dances that she could not kept her friend from remaining contentedly a wallflower.

When the musicians struck up another minuet, Eileen shook her head in adamant refusal as a slender young man presented himself before her. The young lordling had been ardent in his attentions throughout the evening. Diane had declared him thoroughly smitten, which made Eileen avoid him all the more. Disappointed by her refusal, he glanced uncertainly at the chairs next to them, and finding them occupied by a strange assortment of wildly gesticulating young men and ladies engaged in an energetic discussion on the abilities of Hogarth as a true artist, he wandered off again. No one paid him any heed.

Not until she glanced up to the foyer stairs and recognized one of the late arrivals did Eileen regret turning the young man away. Garbed in a dusty-blue coat that nearly matched the shade of his companion's elegantly panniered skirts, his golden locks politely powdered and tied in a black riband, Drake seemed to draw all eyes to his presence. The well-endowed lady on his arm, her hair powdered and stacked and adorned with intricate chains of gold, held herself with regal erectness, as if disdaining to descend to the level of the dancers below.

Eileen's nails bit into her palms at this first sight of Lady Pamela. Unprepared for the wild surge of jealousy threatening to shatter her composure, she could only stare. The woman had everything she did not: wealth, title, aristocratic lineage, and the upbringing that allowed her to move with ease and hauteur through Drake's circle of aristocratic friends. That she had also stunning good looks and a voluptuous figure did nothing to allay Eileen's dismay. Why should Drake even look twice at her when he had all that to enjoy?

Unaccustomed to these feelings of inadequacy and the sickening knot of jealousy forming in her stomach, Eileen turned with mute appeal to the stalwart soldier behind her. Michael glanced at the small hand on his with surprise, unaware of the new arrivals but guessing the action required of him.

With a slight bow he enveloped Eileen's small hand in his large one and assisted her from her seat. "I'm not graceful, you know," he muttered as she came to stand beside him.

Diane watched in surprise as her friend smiled and gave a slight shake of her head to indicate she did not care, before leading Michael off to the dance floor. Michael never danced if he could avoid it, and the minuet particularly distressed him. For all that mattered, Eileen detested it, too.

Long-lashed blue eyes swept the antiquated hall for some source of this unusual behavior. She could scarcely overlook her elegant brother descending the staircase with his fiancée on his arm. She had not expected their appearance, but the look on Drake's face enhanced Diane's curiosity. Instead of his usual affable expression, a frown puckered his brow, and he appeared to be chewing the inside of his cheek with suppressed anger. She could not imagine the empty-headed Lady Pamela saying anything to produce more than boredom in Drake's agreeable features. What in heaven's name had set him off?

Seeing no sign of her cousins—the usual cause of Drake's distress—Diane wrinkled her brow in thought. Theodore chattered lazily at her side about the quality of the musicians and the difficulty of the violin piece, but she disregarded his nonsense. Something was not right, but she could not quite put her finger on it. But trapped as she was in this chair, she had all the time in the world to think on it.

Drake greeted Sir John and Lady Summerville and introduced his fiancée, forcing his eyes to focus on his host and hostess rather than straying to the dance floor where he had already spied Eileen with Michael Jasper. Eileen had every right to dance with anyone she chose; he only wished it would be anyone but the stalwart soldier. If he saw anything of that relationship developing, he must nip it in the making.

Lady Pamela fussed and fumed as they joined the throng and discovered no one to her liking among the guests. "Whatever were you about to accept this invitation, my dear? There is no one here but provincials, and I have worn my best gown for naught. I could have worn muslin and no one would have noticed. Look at that over there!" she exclaimed, pointing to the tall soldier awkwardly out of step with his unwigged companion. "Why, she does not even powder her hair! Have you ever seen such a sight! Parisian gowns on a country miss, I'll be bound. I cannot understand your insistence that we . . ."

As the monologue threatened to carry on into eternity, Drake tuned her out and obediently watched where she had pointed. He rather enjoyed the sight of those auburn tresses glittering beneath the candlelight like a bright bow on Christmas wrapping. He caught himself imagining how they might look with the pins out and the wrapping off, and he cursed himself. Duty required that he attend the lady chosen for him, the lady whose virginity he had taken at an early age, knowing they were betrothed to each other since their cradles. The lady who stood at his side now, venting her petulance like a spoiled child. Marry her he must, but damn, he wished she would at least be silent when he tried to make love to her.

With a lurching pang of longing, Drake turned away from that proudly held head of copper hair. There was one who knew the value of silence, even in the discovery of her voice. Squelching that thought, he searched for his sister.

Understanding began to dawn as Diane observed the grim expression on her brother's face as he approached her, while Eileen valiantly avoided Michael's large feet a safe distance away. By the time Drake and Pamela had made their way through the crowd to inquire after her, Diane was fairly bubbling with her discovery. It couldn't be true. It would be disastrous if it were true. But she couldn't help the dazzling smile that escaped at Drake's greeting.

"Why, beloved brother, what brings you here this evening? Surely your concern for me cannot draw you from the delights of Westly Manor?"

Drake's scowl was almost worth the scold he would deliver shortly. Diane continued blithely on, "And Pamela, my dear, how thoughtful of you to come out in the midst of winter to visit among the provincials. It is a pity that cousin Edmund could not be here tonight. I am certain the two of you would spread joy and cheer among the lesser folks in this holiday season. Had he known you would be here, he would most certainly have accepted his invitation, even though it pull him from the chains of Parliament in these perilous times."

Drake looked as if he would gladly smack her, but Lady Pamela looked pleasantly surprised at this effusive welcome from Drake's younger sister.

"Edmund is a most courageous man, my father says. To serve the king at times like these . . ." She hesitated, trying to remember the rest of the phrases she had overheard.

Impatiently, Drake ignored this witless exchange. "You have been up to some mischief, it is evident, little sister. If you cannot keep a civil tongue in your head, I shall be forced to make inquiries." He lifted an eyebrow to Theodore, who listened with unabashed interest. "Well, Teddy, what has she and the elusive princess been about that she fairly wiggles with excitement?"

Pamela's eyebrows shot up eagerly at the mention of a princess, but Teddy's dry reply provided little information.

"I thought, p'raps, you might provide the answer, Neville. They've been the souls of discretion until now."

"Have they now?" Drake turned a sarcastic glance to his beaming sister, but knowing she would speak nothing but nonsense in front of Pamela, he did not pry further. With sudden decision, he glanced about the room for an acquaintance who would be socially acceptable to his fiancée. Finding the lord with the slightly askew wig, he excused himself and Pamela and made his way back into the throng.

As the dance came to an end, Eileen gave a gasp of surprise when hands not Michael's closed over her bare shoulders. With a pretense at breaking off a loose thread from the froth of lace spilling from her bodice, Drake avoided an angry confrontation with her escort. Michael still regarded him suspiciously, however, and Drake felt a slow burn of anger. With inexcusable possessiveness, his hand trailed down Eileen's bare arm before he retreated to a polite distance and formal bow.

"My lady, I convey my gratitude for your graciousness toward my sister. She seems in high spirits this evening." Immaculate buff knee breeches with gleaming gold buttons accented a muscular leg as Drake made a dramatic obeisance before her.

Still quivering from the touch of his heated palm against her skin, Eileen could not summon an appropriate response to this new masquerade. Only Drake had the ability to undermine her defenses and topple her guard like this, sending her spinning in any direction he chose. The smoldering anger she sensed in him set the fuse of her own temper.

Drake made a half turn and gazed quizzically at his large friend. "Ahhh, Michael, I have never seen you on the dance floor before. Could it be our princess has turned your head with dreams of sugarplums?"

Eileen's gasp of outrage did not distract Drake from his study of the soldier's dogged expression. Michael had an extremely well developed sense of honor, one cause for his departure from His Majesty's service. The Duke of Cumberland's cruelty did not sit well with the gentle giant, and he had retired his colors rather than protest the behavior of his superiors. Drake had applauded his decision at the time, but now he wished his friend in hell.

"I don't believe I need give you explanations,

Neville." With a taut smile Michael offered Eileen his arm. "Miss de Lacy?"

Eileen had no understanding of the suddenly explosive tension between the two men, but her fury at Drake's behavior drove her to accept Michael's arm.

As she lifted her fingers to encircle the powerful forearm disguised beneath velvet and lace, Eileen glanced up at a flurry of figures on the staircase. She froze, and her fingers unconsciously dug into the arm beneath them.

Both men turned immediately to the place where her gaze was riveted. Michael had no understanding of anything but the terror he sensed in the pressure of her fingers. Drake, however, cursed vehemently under his breath. His hand automatically sought Eileen's, and her fingers curled tensely in his grasp. He glanced down at her pale, heart-shaped face, and his heart constricted. Wide gray eyes had become a turbulent stormcloud of hurricane proportions, and he could nearly feel the force of the violent winds of her emotions. Because she was silent, many thought she was content, but Drake knew better. Beneath that daintiness breathed a creature of unleashed passions. The suddenness of her violence—or her love—could be breathtaking. It would not do to have those emotions unharnessed now.

On the stairs, next to Drake's cousin Edmund, stood Eileen's Irish uncle, Lord de Lacy.

Chapter IX

———— ❦ ————

December, 1745

"Jasper, tell Diane the wicked witch of the enchanted forest has arrived. Tell her to call out the leprechaun army." Drake waved away Michael's perplexed expression. "She'll understand. Call her maid and have her ready to be wheeled out of here if necessary."

With a firm hand Drake dragged Eileen into the center of the dancers, leaving Michael to follow his enigmatic orders. The country dance involved much leaping about and changing of partners and giggling, but Drake had no mind for the fun. He kept his eye on Eileen's pale face as she sailed by on the arm of her partner, and remained at her elbow when the dance came to a spirited end. He would prefer to talk with her before the confrontation, but he could see there would be no escaping. Sir John had sent a footman weaving through the crowd toward them.

Eileen took Drake's arm with a sweetly blank expression that made him uneasy until he remembered the tales some of his so-called friends had carried back to him. Here was the empty-headed doll they had complained of, and Drake had to hide a wry grin at the comparison. Far from being empty, this doll was a loaded powder keg. The fireworks should be admirable when they went off.

The footman delivered his message to his decep-

tively smiling mistress, and they trailed across the floor
in his wake. As they progressed, various friends appeared from different directions, seemingly without
purpose, falling into animated discussion over their
delight with the evening, the musicians, the dancing,
and the world in general. Eileen's shimmering copper
hair bobbed and bounced as she turned from one to
the other of this honor guard, falling into their inane
antics with hugs and admiring touches, pointing out
the delightful sparkle of one lady's earrings, laughing
at one of Jamie's silly rhymes, and totally ignoring the
impassive figure waiting on the stairway.

Drake remained at her elbow while surreptitiously
studying the man he had only seen at a distance before. Lord de Lacy towered well over six feet in height,
and the expensive cut of his coat revealed broad shoulders and a powerful chest unweakened by years of
decadence. Powder hid the blue-black of his thick
hair, but the ebony shadow along his closely shaved
cheeks gave evidence of his natural coloring. A scar
along the line of his jaw seemed to tighten as he
glanced toward his laughing niece and her escort, but
otherwise his craggy face remained impassive. A formidable opponent indeed, and the smug expression of
the man beside him revealed Edmund's involvement
in this meeting.

Wondering why or how in hell his cousin had come
in contact with this Irish nobleman, Drake remained
cool as the crowd of young people came to a halt near
Sir John and his guests. Drake flicked a gesture of
greeting to his cousin and made a polite bow to his
host while Eileen continued to cling to his arm. From
the brilliant smile on her face, none would detect the
trembling in her fingers.

"There, sir, do you see how like she is to her mother?
Even to the court of admirers trailing after her?" Sir
John chuckled as he took his niece's hand and lifted
her up a step. "Child, this is your other uncle, Lord
de Lacy."

Eileen could hear the hidden concern in his voice, but she revealed none of her own. With a bright, birdlike interest she swiveled her gaze to the overpowering stranger, smiled blankly, and made a pretty curtsy. Then, with complete lack of interest, she turned a questioning gaze back to Sir John.

Somewhat taken aback by this lack of greeting, Lord de Lacy glanced over his niece's head to her companions. Recognizing the authority in Drake's carriage, he made a nod of respect, then turned back to his niece.

"Come, child. Surely you must remember me? I used to dandle you on my knee. We had quite exciting romps, if I remember correctly." Dark, unfathomable eyes watched as Eileen returned her blank gaze to him.

Sir John moved his shoulders uneasily. "She don't talk, de Lacy, as I've told you. We've no notion of what happened, but she seems to have no memory of any of us." Even as he said it, he realized he lied, but he made no effort to explain. Eileen had recognized her mother. He could have sworn to that. But he had no intention of mentioning Elizabeth's existence.

Teddy and Jamie maneuvered Edmund away while their companions giggled and waited expectantly to be introduced. De Lacy made polite nods as names flowed around him, but his hard gaze returned to Drake when they were done.

"Marquess of Sherbourne? I knew your father. I believe your cousin mentioned you are soon to be married?"

A rather subtle reminder that he had no right to offer Eileen his protection, but Drake casually ignored the hint. While Eileen smiled that heartbreakingly bland smile up to him, Drake replied, "My fiancée is somewhere hereabouts. She'll be happy to meet you. Quite kind of Edmund to realize the connection between you and Miss de Lacy. Didn't know he knew her that well."

That caused another twitch along the man's jaw muscles, but other than that, he revealed nothing. "Actually, Sir John had notified me that he had found our niece. Edmund merely acted as my guide. We met only recently in the house of mutual acquaintances."

Appearing bored with this polite conversation, Eileen idly drifted away in the company of her giggling companions. Noting Michael standing guard immediately behind her, Drake relaxed. That meant Diane was safely out of the way, and he had only Eileen to contend with. And Pamela, but Pamela seldom needed his attention. He would be glad to see the last guest gone, for he had no illusion that Eileen's new uncle would give up on her this easily. He would have to squeeze the story out of the little brat before de Lacy got to her again.

After another few minutes of idle talk Drake maneuvered himself from Sir John's company and hastily sized up the situation. He had acted instinctively to protect Diane from any hint of trouble, but he regretted his hastiness. De Lacy was not the type to cause a public scene. But Eileen was another matter entirely. Drake searched the crowd and caught a glimpse of several of her companions disappearing behind one of the arras leading into the old keep. That way led to the turret and Eileen's studio, and his frown returned.

With another quick reconnoiter, he found Pamela happily chattering with Edmund, and judging that to be a gainful occupation for both of them, Drake followed in the direction of the others.

Climbing the old stone steps at a breakneck pace, Drake caught up with Eileen and her companions just as they lighted the sconces in the turret chamber. Eileen paid him no heed as she began tugging the old Turkish rug covering the planked floor. The wide skirts of her satin gown made this chore a hopeless task, and Michael efficiently took the corner of the rug from her grasp, though he had no understanding of her intention. He glanced up at Drake as he flung the carpet back, revealing the outline of a trapdoor below. Putting aside their differences, both men lifted the trap while Eileen darted about the room, removing paintings from the walls and easels.

"What's this about, Neville?" Teddy asked uneasily as the others wandered about, lifting stacks of canvas at random, admiring the works or relinquishing them to Eileen when she reached for them.

Drake grabbed a particularly large piece from Eileen's hands and turned to examine it before lowering it through the trap with the others. He had already noted Eileen's work tended to fall into two categories: the highly detailed, accurate portrayal of the landscapes around her, and the fanciful, impressionistic scenes of a fairy-tale world of her imagination. Although certainly not of the popular style of the day, he preferred the latter, and these were the ones she was depositing in the hidden chamber.

Drake lifted his gaze to meet Eileen's stubborn impenetrable one over the top of the canvas depicting a fallen unicorn in a forest of blood red and vivid gold. A chill settled around his heart as he finally understood the meaning of these crumbling castles and glades of green with their crimson rivers and black shadows. He lowered the canvas through the door and headed for the next one.

"There is no gold at the end of the rainbow and leprechauns don't exist, Teddy. Hide the Irish landscapes."

Glancing at the paintings disappearing through the door and back to the grim mask of Drake's expression, Michael swiftly assessed the situation and followed his friend's lead. Teddy and the others quickly caught on and the room emptied of tapestries and embroideries and canvas depicting a land they thought existed solely in Eileen's imagination. The real world remained hanging on the walls and lying about the floor. Michael picked up a scene of a turbulent sea and propped it neatly on an empty easel.

"The forest in your uncle's study." Drake spoke his thoughts out loud, but caught Eileen's arm before she could flee to hide this one last piece. "It's his favorite. He would miss it if it were gone. If de Lacy doesn't know the artist, how much would it reveal?"

None but Eileen and Drake understood this conversation, but all could read the stricken look upon Eileen's face. The landscape Sir John had chosen was a fairly accurate representation of the glade she remembered from her worst nightmares. Shadows surrounded the dappled greenery, and an incongruous swatch of blue velvet lay crumpled by a streambank, as if someone had shed their clothes and dived into the cool waters. Only the telltale splotches of red-brown stains gave evidence of the true story. Few noticed the stain; Sir John never had; de Lacy certainly would.

"I will get it," Drake announced curtly. "Michael, take Eileen back before she is missed. Stay with her and keep her out of trouble. Teddy, come with me. If we're caught, we'll call it a prank; just keep the painting from de Lacy."

Throwing orders like a general on the field of battle, Drake cleared the room. He still hadn't the opportunity to talk with Eileen, but he was beginning to gain some comprehension of the problem. His own suspicions of de Lacy made it easier to understand, and his fear for Eileen multiplied.

By the time Drake returned to the ancient hall, Pamela and Edmund had disappeared, and Sir John and de Lacy were pulling aside the arras into the keep, while Eileen and Michael danced blithely in the center of the crowd. Drake wondered angrily why he worried over the irresponsible twit, but he made no effort to desert her or seek out his straying fiancée. He waited for the dance to end.

As Michael politely led his partner from the floor,

Drake caught her elbow in a forceful grip and propelled her toward an alcove that had once housed a
Summerville knight.

When Michael tried to protest, Drake turned on
him. "De Lacy is in the studio now. Warn us when he
returns." And with no other explanation than that, he
removed Eileen from the crowded hall into the privacy
of the alcove.

She turned on him with all the fury of the storm he
had predicted earlier. "You are interfering, Drake.
Leave me alone. Keep your family out of this. I have
enough concerns of my own."

"Obviously," he replied dryly. Hand on her shoulder, he gently shoved her into the small velvet sofa
behind her. "Now talk."

Obstinately she crossed her arms and remained silent.

Drake could easily have throttled her slender throat,
but, distracted by the curves revealed by her low-cut
gown, he recognized the wisdom of keeping his hands
to himself. The past weeks had not abated his desire
for her. His hands would not remain long on her
throat.

"Talk, or I will tell Sir John you can. And then I
will show him your hidden paintings and demand explanations from de Lacy."

"You wouldn't!" Eileen hissed, glaring at Drake's
toweringly handsome figure. In his heavily embroidered coat and waistcoat, with his hair powdered like
a gentleman, he was an imposing figure. All trace of
the laughing youth had fled.

"I most certainly would. As you have so frequently
pointed out, you are not my responsibility. I will hand
the facts over to the man who is." The marquess
leaned his broad shoulders against the wall, crossed
his arms, and waited.

"That is extortion!" Eileen angrily clenched and un-
clenched her hands, trying to determine how much she
must say to keep him happy. "What do you want to

hear that you don't already know?" She kept her eyes averted from his piercing gaze.

"All of it. What is it you remember that keeps you silent among friends?"

"My mother," she whispered, so softly as to be almost inaudible. "And my father." This last came out as an involuntary sob.

Immediately Drake dropped to the seat beside her and produced his handkerchief. "Don't cry, Eileen. Not now, not here." Nervously remembering that day in the forest, he knew he could never survive another such scene. If Sir John did not kill him, any number of her suitors gladly would, for he would tear down the alcove draperies and carry her away with him for all the world to see.

"I'm sorry. There is no other way I can tell it." Half-angry, half-accusing eyes peered out from behind the linen of his handkerchief. "I warned you."

Steeling himself against the softer feelings her tear-lashed eyes produced, Drake rose and paced angrily in the narrow space before the sofa. "Then let me try the tale. De Lacy is your father's brother. He inherited the estates and the title when your father died."

"I don't know. It must be assumed." Eileen tore nervously at the ball of linen in her hands and avoided looking at the man filling the space in front of her. A most difficult feat.

A thought struck Drake. "Your father was not Catholic, by some chance? The churchyard where he is buried once belonged to an abbey."

Eileen glanced up in curiosity. "I would not know. We attended chapel. I remember the pretty windows. And my mother now is a nun, or whatever it is called."

"But your aunt is not Catholic. I suspect your mother converted to your father's religion. But he would not have inherited the entire estate or the title if he were a practicing Catholic, the law prevents that. He could not even have worn a sword."

The trace of bitterness in Drake's voice reminded Eileen that his mother had been a Catholic. The revolution of the Catholic prince in the north came a little closer with these words, but Eileen refused to think in those terms. Quietly she answered, "He wore a sword."

"I suspect he professed Anglicanism for the sake of his lands and family. Many do. Your uncle would be in a position to know."

Drake appeared to be talking to himself, but Eileen listened intently. She had never attempted to find a logical basis for her nightmares; she simply lived with the fears. Somehow, the reason for them did not resolve anything.

"I don't know anything of that." Eileen interrupted, her eyes bleak as winter. "I know only that man killed my father and my mother."

Drake stopped his pacing and stared at her as if she had gone berserk. The only thing that came to his tongue, however, was irrefutable fact. "Your mother is alive."

"No, she's not." Eileen threw away the wadded linen and stood up. "He killed my mother. That is not her behind those walls. That is only her shell. She died when my father died, just like everybody says."

She tried to leave, but Drake caught her arm and swung her around. "You were only five years old. You cannot know for a certainty that your uncle was responsible. Your mother would have had him thrown in prison if she had known such a thing."

Eileen stared at him blankly. "My mother is dead, or she would have done just that. I tell you, I saw the whole thing. For my mother's sake, and for the sake of the friends who protected us, I can say nothing. But he knows. Just look in his eyes. He knows. I did not remain dead, and now I have come back to haunt him."

She wrenched away from Drake's grasp, leaving him staring at the swaying curtains after her.

The shock of realization rippled over Drake like an icy waterfall. She had not only seen her father's murder, but she had seen her uncle commit it. The man freely walking these halls now was a murderer and quite likely a rapist. And she would never allow it for long. Drake swore every oath he had ever heard and some that had no source but his own frustrated fury. He had no idea what the little witch had in mind, but he could count on it being unpleasant for all concerned. And he could do nothing.

With a sudden horrifying remembrance of a silver dagger wielded much too swiftly, Drake tore through the curtains into the crowded ballroom. He easily found Michael's tall frame advancing toward him, but Eileen's petite one had been swallowed up in the throng of glittering finery.

He greeted Michael with a curt "Where are they?"

"Edmund and de Lacy are preparing to leave. Sir John has apparently gone to his study to fetch something."

Drake did not linger to inquire into Eileen's whereabouts. Michael would have mentioned her if he had known, and Drake had a sinking feeling he knew already. Eileen's idiot act had been too convincing. He should have known better. He began to elbow his way through the mob toward the front hall.

From this angle, Drake could see Edmund and de Lacy murmuring in low voices near the massive paneled doors to the courtyard while they waited for the return of their host. Drake spied Sir John's stout figure hurrying toward them from the family wing, his speed indicating the degree of his agitation. Drake could surmise the reason for that agitation if he had just come from the study, but Drake had no time to worry over the result of his theft. From this vantage point, he scanned the vaulted entranceway to the rambling Hall. Suits of armor dotted the dimly lighted foyer. At this time of night, no light illuminated the stone walls from the Gothic windows above. A curved staircase led the way to upper levels, and the newer wings of the house meandered off on either side of this ancient entrance. Once, a drawbridge had probably filled those portals, but they had long since been replaced by more civilized paneling. In the shadow of the grotto to one side Drake found the shimmer of silver he had expected.

Boldly Drake ran up the remainder of the stairway and strode into the foyer. Both men looked up in surprise and, in Edmund's case, displeasure.

"Meant to have a word with you before you left, cousin." Drake lifted an ironic brow at Edmund's fur-lined cloak, acknowledging the fact that Edmund had not intended any such meeting.

"You were busy playing games with your latest acquisition, Sherbourne. Far be it from me to interfere, although I should think Lord de Lacy might take some umbrage at your treatment of his niece."

De Lacy scowled at this ploy, but before he could reply, Sir John huffed into the room.

"It is gone. I cannot understand it. Stolen. There are thieves in my house." He wiped his brow in consternation.

As the silver and emerald figure slipped from the shadows, Drake calmly placed himself between her and the formidable Irish lord growling his displeasure. With a quickness that caught Eileen by surprise, Drake caught her wrist between his fingers and held her hand behind her back as he drew her forward.

"Thank you for coming so promptly," he drawled, easily controlling her outraged struggle. "I thought you might wish to say farewell to your uncle. He is just leaving."

Sir John listened in bewilderment to this non-reply to his dramatic announcement. His confusion grew as he recognized the fury in his niece's eyes and the barely controlled temper jerking a muscle in the marquess's cheek. Only his innate good breeding rescued the situation.

"I apologize, de Lacy. I will uncover the prankster before you return. The painting is quite a good one, and I fancy you would enjoy it. You must recognize Eileen is no common miss. Between us, we can present her to society as your brother's daughter, and people might talk, but they would have to accept her."

De Lacy turned to look more fully on his alleged niece. If he recognized the glitter of his brother's fury in the silver of her eyes, he gave no sign of it. The room's shadows prevented seeing much beyond the fairness of her skin and the shimmer of her hair and gown in the torchlight. He raised a thoughtful brow to the golden lord standing so protectively behind her frail figure, and a slight frown creased his forehead.

"I have seen no proof that she is my brother's heir, sir. She is much like your wife and her sister, I agree, but several explanations for that come to mind. We will have to investigate this matter a little more thoroughly before I am convinced."

He made a languid bow and, in a swirl of cloaks, swept out of the door hastily opened by a silent footman. Edmund held his ground a moment longer, but when it became apparent Drake had nothing further to say to him, he turned to follow in the Irishman's path.

The door closed and Sir John turned his controlled anger on the battling couple before him.

"I will have explanations now, please."

Chapter X

Drake's fingers dug into Eileen's wrist, and she had no choice but to be steered into the study where Sir John led them. If she allowed herself full rein of speech, the air would have turned blue with the heat of her resentment, but she was not yet ready to reveal her secret. She wished she could turn the knife in her hand on her captor, but Drake held her too firmly.

The baronet frowned when Drake closed the door but did not release his grip on Eileen. He did not like the looks of any of this evening's odd occurrences, but this did not bode well at all. If his capricious niece had done something to compromise them both, Neville would feel compelled to do the honorable thing, and all hell would break loose. The romantic madness of youth had to be dealt with swiftly, and Sir John stepped in to defuse the situation.

"Neville, I suggest you turn my niece loose and have a seat. I've never seen Eileen's temper roused, but I remember her mother's. It was not a pretty sight, I assure you." Sir John strode to his desk and indicated the high-backed leather chair beside it. Without waiting for his niece to sit, he sank into the desk chair and stared at the couple with the barest patience.

With a quick twist of Eileen's wrist, Drake relieved her of the silver dagger. Her cry of pain brought Sir

John to his feet, but the weapon slapped down in front of him caused the baronet to sink slowly back to his chair. He could scarcely contain his astonishment but stared at the young marquess for explanation.

Drake shook his head and watched grimly as Eileen stalked away to the fire grate. "I believe, sir, your niece has a few facts she has omitted telling you."

Eileen swung on him in fury. She had no intention of endangering her family with her secrets, even if she could speak of them without tears. Which she could not. And she had no intention of offering Drake that opportunity again. She remained silent.

Sir John's eyebrows rose in surprise, but believing this to be some euphemism of Drake's, he watched Eileen for some signal as to how to continue. He could never figure how so much energy could be bundled into so small a package, but he feared she was in danger of exploding at any moment. Those long, graceful fingers of hers had curled into balls of wrath and silver eyes shot stilettos of rage. Sir John began to doubt his first assessment of the situation. This was no ordinary lover's quarrel.

At Eileen's continued silence, Drake lowered himself comfortably into the leather chair and crossed his stockinged leg over his knee and his arms across his chest. He met her fury immovably. "You would rather he heard it from me?"

Trapped, Eileen reached for the set of brandy snifters on the mantel behind her. The thin crystal goblet flew swiftly and accurately at Drake's arrogant head, but he dodged, and it shattered into a million shards against the floor beyond.

"Damn your festering, interfering carcass to the flames of hell, milord!" she screamed, at last, with all the pent-up frustration of years. "Why did you not let me kill him? I told you to leave me alone! Get out of here before I take a rapier to your blue-blooded, worthless, English heart!"

Since a fine pair of elegantly balanced steel rapiers graced the wall just above the brandy snifters, her threat was less than idle, and Drake immediately began to calculate the shortest distance between his seat and the mantel. He could make it with ease, but he would rather not. With gracious aplomb he rose and bowed before his astounded host.

"Her Irish tongue is not yet silver, but certainly swift. Be certain she explains in detail about that villain, de Lacy. Let me extend my apologies for allowing this charade to continue so long as it has. I trust your niece will explain my delay adequately. If not, please do not hesitate to call on me, sir."

With that, Drake bowed himself from the room, leaving Eileen to face her speechless uncle.

With the object of her wrath out of reach, the storm of Eileen's anger swept away, leaving her drained and limp. With nowhere else to turn, she faced her uncle.

"I am sorry," she whispered.

Her head seemed to bend beneath the weight of her heavy auburn tresses, and for the first time Sir John noted the track of one forlorn tear over a pale cheek. He knew better than to be fooled by her momentary regret. One wrong word and that proud chin would tilt dangerously, and she'd be off and running again. He fingered the silver dagger before him with no small amount of disbelief.

"Will you tell me?" he inquired calmly.

"There is nothing to tell. Meeting my mother made me remember." Eileen sank to the sofa. Killing de Lacy would have been just revenge for all the ruined lives he'd taken, but perhaps it was not the best solution. She would have hurt her aunt and uncle immeasurably, but his continued existence would do the same. The dilemma did not resolve easily.

"You remembered how to speak?" the baronet persisted.

"Yes. And I remembered how to hate. I hate him. I have always hated him. And he knows it."

"De Lacy?"

Eileen nodded, not noticing Sir John's gray pallor as she stared at the carpet.

"Why, Eileen? Why do you hate him?"

She looked up then, her eyes blurred with tears and her lips trembling. "You will not believe me. No one will believe me. And he would kill anyone who accused him of it. Do not ask."

"Eileen, he has been a guest under my roof. I cannot deny him access to his only relative without cause. Despite his words tonight, we know you are his niece. Give me reason to deny him."

"That is what I cannot do," she insisted wildly. "If he knows I speak, that I remember, he will destroy us all. Don't you see? That is why my mother hides, to protect me, to protect her friends. Let me go on as I have, and he will suspect nothing and go back from whence he came."

Sir John stared at her delicate, upturned face with incredulity. With her speech returned and her heritage known, she had the beauty and wealth and wit to take anything she wanted from life. And she pleaded with him to regress to a life not unsimilar to the one her mother led. It was impossible. Surely she must know it.

"I have a few more years of experience than you, Eileen. Let me decide for myself what must be done. Tell me, or let me call Drake if you cannot explain."

A flash of anger quickly replaced her plea. "He has interfered enough as it is. Keep him out of this."

The baronet nodded agreement. "Neville does have a tendency to take matters in his own hands, but he comes by that trait naturally. He suffered the same from his father. I see no reason to involve him further. What has de Lacy done to cause your hate?"

Eileen took a deep breath and closed her eyes. "I cannot remember much. I was very small. There was always arguing when he was about. My mother avoided

him, and I learned to do the same. Only he made my
father very angry, and I hated it when they yelled at
each other. Once I took a fire poker and swung it at
his knees to make him stop shouting. He cursed terribly, but my father took me from the room and we
laughed and everything was better again."

Sir John could almost see the scene through a child's
eyes. Elizabeth and Richard had little wealth, but they
had been deliriously happy with each other and their
charming, elfin child. A child would have seen them as
a god and goddess descended from Mt. Olympus, so
radiant had they been. The intrusion of reality in the
form of the dark prince, de Lacy, would have engendered no end of fears.

Eileen gathered her breath and tried once again to
explain the nightmare that had haunted her for so
many years. "I do not understand many things I remember. Strangers would come and my father would
be up late talking and arguing with them. There were
meetings. The villagers smiled on him, but many whispered behind his back. I can remember not understanding this or the warnings my mother whispered in
my ears when I wished to play with the other children.
I remember being lonely except when I was with my
family. My mother loved picnics. We had a special
place, a lovely place, where we went to be together.
No one came there except us. Until that day."

Her voice broke and Sir John writhed with the agony he caused her, but he had to know. All these
years of wondering, puzzling, and now she was about
to shed some light on it. He could not stop her.

"My uncle came on his horse, with others. They had
swords in their hands. They said terrible things about
my father. He tried arguing with them . . ." Eileen
stumbled, trying to keep the picture clear in her head,
desperately trying to make him see what she did not
understand except in its finality. "I don't know . . .
My uncle was holding my mother and she was scream-

ing. And my father drew his sword and someone else screamed. And then they were all around him and my uncle was laughing and my mother was screaming and screaming and I could not bear it. My father fell and I ran out of the bushes and picked up a knife from the basket and I ran at my uncle, yelling at him to help. He was . . ." Eileen halted, her eyes going wide as she understood the import of her recollection. "He held my mother on the ground. He swung at me and I threw the knife at him. Blood went everywhere, all over my mother, and she just kept screaming. And then he picked me up and threw me and . . ." Shivering now, Eileen clasped her arms around herself and rocked slowly back and forth, trying to suppress the pain and anguish that welled up in her, sending cascading waterfalls down her cheeks. The urge to kill returned, but the object was out of her grasp again. She cursed Drake once more, and wished desperately for his return. The pain was too great to bear alone.

Trembling with the emotions her story engendered, Sir John rose and tentatively offered his hand. "I think you had better go to your room, little one. I will send Emma to you with a sleeping draught and make your excuses to the company. You have had enough for one night."

Eileen gratefully accepted this offer, but her eyes pleaded with him for understanding. "You see, don't you? Why I cannot let him know? I do not want to lose you, too."

Sir John choked on his fury and anguish and nodded silently, not daring to say more. When she fled the room, he grabbed the brandy and swallowed a healthy mouthful. He didn't see, he didn't see at all, but how could he tell her that?

With a sigh the baronet had the first glimmer of what Drake had known from the outset—life would be much simpler had Eileen never regained the use of her tongue.

*   *   *

By mid-afternoon of the next day, Eileen had re-solved on the only solution to her dilemma. As much as she would like to, she had not the strength or resources to kill a man like Lord de Lacy. Now that he knew she could speak, Sir John would never allow her to retreat into her own world again. Already she felt his anxious gaze follow her about as she communi-cated silently with her friends. If she were to return to the real world, Drake's world and her uncle's, she must recover her speech. That would bring de Lacy back with a vengeance. She must protect the Summer-villes from that eventuality, and she knew only one way to do it. She must marry and leave Summer Hall.

Gazing silently at the assortment of guests remain-ing, Eileen mentally tabulated the qualities of the male population of her acquaintance. The ideal candidate, of course, would be Drake. He had the power and authority and wealth to protect her family and shield her from de Lacy's inquiring habits. Except not only was he taken, but she and Drake would in all proba-bility kill each other instead of her uncle. Jamie and Teddie and the other itinerant artists she automatically ruled out. They suited her nature best, perhaps, but they would be useless in any confrontation with de Lacy. Which turned her attention to the man who could stand up to a cavalry of soldiers.

Michael Jasper sat beside Diane at the spinet, turn-ing the pages for her songs, joining in on duets. For such a large man he had remarkably agile fingers, and he and Diane played well together. He was not an imaginative man, or a playful one, but his serious mien hid a multitude of virtues. She had found him to be gentle and understanding, and she suspected he would be dutifully faithful and trustworthy. And he would defend her family with his dying breath if they accepted him. And they would.

As soon as a group distracted Diane into a game of

cards, Eileen tugged gently at Michael's coat sleeve and indicated she would like to walk. Drake and Pamela had left early that morning, and there was none to protest as the couple wandered from the company and into the desolation of the prior night's festivities in the great hall.

The December weather made it too uncomfortable outside for a casual stroll, but Summer Hall provided its own entertainment. Michael followed Eileen's lead as she guided him toward the earthy humidity of the plant-laden conservatory. Drake had never provided him with any explanation of last night's events, and Eileen could not, but he understood a cloud threatened her, and he wished to offer what aid he could. He pushed aside a vine and took her hand to assist her down the stairs into the glass-walled plant room.

It seemed more her natural habitat, and Michael watched with amazement as the silent girl at his side transformed into a blithe spirit darting from plant to plant, enraptured by the rich aromas and brilliant colors around her. Her green skirts trailed along behind her, dancing on the whirlwind of her energy as she bent and snipped and reached for the highest fruits on the orange trees. He laughed and easily plucked the topmost fruit for her, and they shared the juice together.

How she arranged it, Michael would never know, but one moment he was using his handkerchief to wipe a drop of juice from the corner of her mouth, and the next he was plying those delectable lips with his own. And she was responding.

He halted as soon as Eileen lay her small hand against his chest in warning, but the damage was already done. Michael had never had the wealth to court a proper lady, never indulged in stolen kisses with one until now. His eyes opened as he realized the possibilities with this one, and his body cried out its need as he stared down into her smiling eyes. Smiling! She did not reject his advances, and his heart skipped another beat.

"Miss de Lacy, Eileen . . . I had not planned this." Unaccustomed to speaking his thoughts aloud, Michael hurried to explain himself. "I do not regret it, though."

A soft smile touched Eileen's lips as she gazed up into the confusion of the big man's eyes. Michael's neatly powdered hair seemed incongruous above his large, square face, but she liked his eyes. They did not have Drake's long lashes, and they did not pierce her to the quick with their stare, but brown and deep, they seemed genuinely astounded at the present state of affairs. She allowed his admiration to fan her sorely wounded vanity.

She touched his cheek in reply, and Michael caught her hand and held it there.

"If I have your uncle's permission, you will allow me to court you?" He concealed his eagerness easily, for he had been frequent audience to the laughter the suit of many others had received at this one's hands. He still could not believe his good fortune in being allowed this close to the elusive wisp others had begun to call the "wicked enchantress."

Eileen curled her hand in the security of his large one and nodded. She had made her choice; now she must abide by it.

Diane glanced up from the card table as the couple wandered back into the room hand in hand, and her heart sunk to a depth she had not thought possible. She had not thought . . . but she had no right to think. Still, she had been so certain Drake and Eileen . . . they were perfect together. With aching fury she threw down a perfectly good hand, much to her partner's dismay. Damn the self-righteous Lady Pamela to her rightful place in hell.

Sir John, too, worried about this new development. He watched the ex-soldier leave his study, then immediately sent for Eileen. He would have been thrilled by the prospect of such a sensible match had it not

been for the revelations of the prior night. Now he
gravely suspected the precipitousness of this courtship.

In Eileen's entrance he saw no sign of the efferves-
cent happiness Elizabeth had displayed upon discovering her Richard. She appeared as calm and lovely as
ever, but he could not persuade himself to believe love
glowed in her eyes. The fact that she had not revealed
her ability to speak to her suitor told the rest of the
tale.

"You have never shown an interest in Michael before, child. Is there some need for this suddenness?"
The baronet came quickly to the point, a tactic he had
learned early with this one.

Eileen did not bother to sit but stood gracefully in
the room's center. "I cannot expect you to keep my
secret from my aunt forever. If I marry, the danger
will be much less, and I should be able to speak more
freely. I think Michael is the best choice. Don't you
agree?" She lifted her chin and sent him an inquiring
look.

"Michael is a fine choice, and I have told him he is
welcome to court you, but I don't understand. Why
would you feel more free to speak married to Michael
than now?" Even as he said it, Sir John felt some
inkling of understanding, and the thought plucked a
string of anguish in his heart.

By this time Eileen was better prepared for the
question, and she hastily smoothed over the obvious.
"I fear Lord de Lacy if he thinks I can speak and
reveal his villainy. He might think you will encourage
me to speak out to regain my father's inheritance. You
have the authority, but Michael does not. You cannot
be with me always, but Michael can. Married, everything I own becomes my husband's, so my uncle will
no longer have reason to fear you. I do not think he
will fear Michael, except for his strength. If we live
quietly and do not intrude upon him, perhaps Lord de
Lacy will be satisfied to leave us alone. I think I would
feel safe to speak then."

Sir John turned away to stare bleakly out the window. Despite her pretty words, he understood she was protecting him and Emma, perhaps rightly so. If a young warrior like Richard had not been able to defend his family against his younger brother, he certainly could not. And he had a feeling if Eileen's tale were repeated to the authorities, he would soon find himself in the position of defending his family. He had never been a coward where just his self was concerned, but Emma and Eileen . . . She was right. Her speech meant danger, and Michael was more suited for the defense than himself. He suddenly felt old and gray.

"I see," he managed to murmur. "And when do you intend to reveal to your suitor that you have been concealing such a secret from him?"

Eileen fidgeted uneasily. She had given Michael little consideration in this decision-making. Sensing some of this, Sir John swung around and pinned her with a stern gaze.

"You will tell him before you marry. I will not have the lad deceived. He is a good, worthy man. You could not have chosen better, and he will be well rewarded. But I will not allow your flummery with him. If he presses his suit, and I believe he will, you will be honest with him. Give me your word on that."

Feeling the door of her cage inexorably closing, Eileen nodded silently. Holding her head high to keep the tears from falling, she turned to leave. Marriage would be a lesser prison than the one she had courted last night.

Chapter XI

—— ❦ ——

March, 1746

With the month of April drawing ever closer, the Neville household had reached a state of chaos in preparation for the wedding. Diane watched with some distaste as still another indignant maid offered to pack her bags if her services were not satisfactory. Drake had nearly snapped the heads off two of them just this morning alone, and she wagered the kitchen had reached a point of mutiny with this latest development. A dinner for half the county on a last-minute notice like this was enough to force mass resignations.

After calming the maid, Diane contemplated calling a footman to wheel her to the kitchen, but the appearance of her brother in the doorway squelched that notion. He seemed more at loose ends now than he had been when their father lived, roaming restlessly about the estate, creating havoc in his footsteps in his search for perfection. He was like a man driven by a madness over which he had no control.

Diane watched warily as Drake strolled into the room without a greeting, going directly to the French doors and staring out upon the gardens. Half a dozen gardeners were busily trimming and raking and planting in preparation for the wedding six weeks hence. Diane wondered if he had decided they must force the bulbs to bloom sooner in time for his latest entertainment, or if he would be content to let nature take its course.

"Are you inviting anyone I might enjoy, or will it be another evening of Lord Westly's dread bores?" Diane spoke more sharply than was her custom, for she had grown quite out of patience with her usually affable brother's recent irritability. If this would be the normal state of affairs after his marriage, she would most certainly retire to the dower house.

Drake continued to stare out the window. Diane heartily wished she could throw something at him to wake him up, but he would more than likely send for a physician, thinking her ill. He seldom laughed anymore, and the only words out of his mouth now were critical ones. She didn't like this side of Drake, but she was at a loss to correct it. She had troubles enough of her own.

"I have invited the Summervilles. That should please you," Drake finally responded, turning back toward the room and wandering to the mantel. He played with the delicate figurines of a shepherd and shepherdess as he spoke.

"Then I trust Michael has been invited also. I have a feeling Eileen will decline unless he is of the party." Diane bent over the spinet as she said this, studying her finger placement rather than give Drake the opportunity to see her expression.

The crook of the shepherd's stick snapped beneath the pressure of Drake's fingers, and he cursed, setting the piece down and roaming to an alcove hung with various stringed instruments.

"Is he still pursuing her? I thought he would be content with the position of estate manager. I cannot squeeze two words in a row from the devil."

Diane cringed as Drake removed a delicate lyre from its rope and plucked it. If he did not marry soon, he would bring the house crumbling down around their heads.

"Why should he be content with a position when he can have a wealthy wife and lands of his own? You know Lady Summerville is offering her lands as dowry. Michael is of good family and deserves better than you offer. I cannot fault him for seeking to better himself, particularly since Eileen encourages him."

These words barely crept past Diane's compressed lips. She could fault Michael for his decision to court Eileen, but she tried not to. After all, what other encouragement had he ever been given? Drake's next words echoed her own thoughts.

"The match would be disastrous. Eileen has an uncontrollable temper and a wayward streak that Michael will never understand. He needs a quiet, domesticated type, someone to look after, not someone he will spend his days looking for. She won't stay put. Can't you warn her she is making a mistake?"

Diane raised her head and stared in amazement at her brother. He continued mutilating the lyre strings and ignored her look. A thousand questions flitted through her mind, but her mood was such that only sarcasm passed her lips.

"When have lovers ever listened to reason? And I should certainly think that if Michael needs the quiet type, he has made the best choice." She slammed down the lid of her instrument and rang the bell attached to her chair, summoning a footman.

Diane's sharpness finally made some dent in Drake's self-absorption, and he glanced up to his sister. He had not taken the time lately to note the state of her unhappiness, and he could not imagine the cause of it now.

"Do I need to call Dr. Goatley? Have the wedding preparations tired you? I'll hire someone to come in and make order of this chaos if the responsibility is too tiring . . ."

There was the Drake she knew, but it was too late

for him now. The wheels of fate were already in motion and there was no stopping them. Diane shook her head furiously.

"It is you who needs the physician! Even a blind man could see Pamela will not make you happy. But for pride and honor, you would see those you love destroyed. Don't expect sympathy from me."

The lute's strings snapped beneath Drake's fingers as the footman wheeled his sister from the room. How could this damned marriage destroy anyone but himself? With frustration Drake flung the offending instrument against the wall and stalked out the garden door. Just the touch of a faerie's lips had made a demented man of him. He would do well to return to the real world.

By the night of the dinner, Drake had other things on his mind than Diane's anger. The rumors of the Duke of Cumberland's march to Scotland had just begun to trickle down from the north, and Drake's thoughts were more on his fractious cousins than his sister's dismal mood. The Monsards were chewing at the bit, swearing all loyal king's men should be rallying behind the Stuart standard in the face of the German usurper. Perhaps he ought to send them back to France until the inevitable disaster was over.

With these and other weighty considerations on his mind, Drake had little patience for Pamela's chatter as they strolled from one salon to another, greeting guests. The card room was already filled and as a small group of musicians began tuning their instruments in the grand salon, more guests began to fill its vast floor. He had very little opportunity to speak with Sir John, and his cousins seemed to be avoiding him. Gritting his teeth, Drake spied Edmund with Lord Westly, and he began to maneuver Pamela toward him. He would locate his elusive cousins a good deal quicker without his fiancée hampering his search.

Left behind with her father, Pamela watched Drake's erect figure rapidly stride away, and a pout began to form on her beautiful face. Turning rebellious eyes to Drake's darker cousin, she met Edmund's look with perfect accord.

As his daughter and his protégé wandered off together, Lord Westly frowned and shook his head. It was a damned good thing the wedding was less than a month away. If his suspicions were correct, his daughter was already increasing. He'd had enough experience with his mistress and her plenitude of pregnancies to know the certain signs of another brat arriving. He damned well hoped it was Drake's or there would be hell to pay later.

Oblivious to his fiancée's fashionable plumpness or his lordship's suspicions, Drake plowed his way through the throng of guests in search of his young cousins. All thoughts of the Monsards fled, however, upon sight of Michael Jasper's ridiculously large stature leaning attentively over Eileen's petite one as he assisted her in blotting a drop of wine from the fine French lace at her elbow. Her stunningly simple gown of gold velvet, adorned with cascades of white lace at throat and sleeve, had a daringly deep décolletage that made Drake chew at his cheek in anger. Jasper was apparently taking full advantage of his height and viewpoint.

Before Drake could proceed in their direction, Eileen lifted her full skirts and disappeared swiftly through the portals to the music room. He would never have followed her path in this crowd had not Michael's height marked it clearly as he kept to her side. Noting their direction for later use, Drake returned to his search for the Monsards.

Once out of the press of company, Eileen slowed to a more ladylike pace, rightly surmising Drake would not try to follow her now. In a crowd as large as this, she could avoid him all night. Gazing wistfully through the French doors to the pampered garden beyond, she lay a pleading hand on Michael's coat sleeve.

"The evening air would be refreshing, but you might take a chill." Having learned something of Eileen's nature these last months, Michael easily interpreted her wishes. He, too, would be glad to breathe night air after the stench of unwashed and heavily perfumed bodies inside, coupled with the scent of thousands of burning candles. Even the massive halls of Sherbourne could not provide draft enough to clear the air in this crowd.

With a determined gleam in her eye, Eileen lifted the lid to the cushion-covered window seat beside the door. She knew this house well enough by now to know her way around without help. Rather than ask the servants to run upstairs every time she felt chilly, Diane kept wraps at hand. The window seat produced a long length of neatly crocheted wool that wrapped around her shoulders and arms, excellent for a chilly evening. Triumphantly engulfing herself in the warm mantilla, Eileen waited for Michael to open the doors.

The ex-soldier could not conceal his grin at her incongruous attire, but he had grown accustomed to Eileen's eccentricities. If she wished to wrap velvets and lace in musty old wool, that was more sensible than fashionably freezing. He just wished she'd at least consent to powdering her hair so they didn't attract quite so many stares. He could not grow accustomed to that much attention.

He held the door and soon they were strolling almost sedately through the courtyard gardens. Eileen had never quite learned the knack of moving slowly, particularly outdoors, but her heavy skirts hampered her somewhat upon this occasion. Taking advantage of this rare occurrence, Michael waited until they were hidden from sight of the house by a tall hedge, then caught Eileen's shoulders and brought her to a halt.

Silver eyes turned up to his expectantly. Michael seldom put himself forward, but she had learned to listen in respect when he did. Good common sense and sound intelligence hid behind his natural uncommunicativeness.

"Eileen, have you had time enough to consider your feelings toward me?" His calm, square face hid any trace of anxiety he might have felt in the question.

Eileen's heart skipped a beat as she realized the moment she had dreaded had finally arrived. Even she could feel the restlessness of spring stirring in her veins, and she knew she could not postpone the moment much longer. Even now the first scents of woodbine had begun to perfume the air, and the feverish urges Drake had taught her made sleep impossible. If she did not consent to Michael's offer, she would of a certainty fall victim to Drake's. Practicality made it imperative that she listen to Michael's plea.

With a finality that deserved the recognition of tolling bells, Eileen nodded her head and reached to gently caress her escort's rough cheek. Needing further assurance, however, Michael chose to ask her formally before giving in to the tendency to rejoice.

"Do I have your permission to ask your uncle for your hand?" His large hands slid persuasively to her waist.

Now was the time, and Eileen took a deep breath. She knew Michael could be trusted, but it came difficultly to her to reveal much of herself. She must begin to learn, however, if she would make this marriage work.

"If you don't mind a wife who holds her tongue too long," Eileen murmured into the night breeze.

Startled, Michael took a step backward, but he did not loose his hold on this capricious sprite. His eyes shone with the same glitter as the stars as he contemplated those inquiring elfin features. He had the vague, uneasy feeling that he might have wandered a trifle out of his path as he met her gaze, but, ever game, he advanced onward.

"You will tell me the story of your silence someday?" More a command than a question, his words were nonetheless gentle.

"Someday," Eileen agreed, and with relief she felt his hands encompass her more securely.

Another painful thought intruded, one that had nagged Michael's sleep too many nights to go unmentioned now that she could answer it. He could find no way of coming directly to the point, however, and came at it obliquely. "Drake knows of your speech?"

"He was responsible for its return," Eileen agreed again, hoping that would satisfy the questions in his eyes.

It did not. Michael frowned. "If society knew you could speak, you could have your choice of any man. Why me?"

Fearing the drift of this conversation, Eileen sought for placating answers. She had never needed a glib way with words before, and she mourned her lack of practice. "Do you see me as a society miss, then?" She returned a question with a question.

"That does not answer, Eileen. Drake has tried to persuade me to stay away from you, but I know that he has encouraged others to ask after your hand. Is there aught between you that I should know?"

Eileen sighed and rested her head against his broad chest. Michael's arms instinctively closed about her as she spoke. "Drake has been more than friend to me, just as Diane is much my sister. With you by my side, it will remain that way. Do you understand?"

Michael heard her soft words with unease, knowing more of a man's nature than she. Drake was not a men easily denied, and he felt certain that brotherhood was not the relation between these two. But every prize has its price, and he was ready to fight for his.

"You will excuse my bluntness, Eileen, but we must understand each other in this. When I take my marriage vows, I will abide by them. I will expect my wife to do no less. If there is any doubt in your mind . . ."

Eileen tilted her face to meet his quizzical gaze fully. "That is why I chose you, Michael."

His square jaw relaxed and a twinkle lightened his eyes. "Does that give me the rights of your future husband, then?"

With a small smile of anticipation, Eileen nodded.

His kiss was warm and tender and achingly hungry. Eileen felt swallowed in his embrace, and she clung to his shoulders as he engulfed all her senses. If she had ever had any doubts that his gentleness hid a lack of manliness, she discarded them now. His hands were firm and sure as they pressed her close and she felt the bulge of hardness through his satin breeches. Here was the man who would salve her curiosity and give her respite from the desire that flowed in her veins. She returned his kiss eagerly.

A voice of barely controlled fury brought an abrupt end to this embrace.

"Bigod, Jasper, at least have the decency to bed her somewhere private and not on the lawn."

Eileen swung around as if stung. Drake's angrily contorted features confronted her. They glared at each other in silence, unmindful of the tall man in the background.

"Miss de Lacy has just agreed to be my wife, Neville." With no intention of being ignored, Michael strived to remain polite to this man who had been his friend.

Drake's golden features paled slightly and an angry tic jumped along the muscle of his jaw. He did not take his gaze from Eileen's wool-shrouded figure, however. "My congratulations, Michael. You have just earned yourself a lifetime of hell in exchange for a few pieces of gold. Why don't you hurry to her uncle and confirm your good fortune? I wish to speak with your fiancée."

From the tension in the man behind her, Eileen gauged the insults had gone too far, and she hurried to intercede. Turning to Michael, she gently touched his cheek.

"I will join you shortly, Michael, I promise. Let us speak alone this once."

"This once" and Drake's angry intake of breath provided satisfaction enough. With a warning look to his friend, Michael bowed over Eileen's hand, then, coming to parade attention, he touched the hilt of his sword protruding beneath the cut of his coat. His words were for Eileen, but his look was for Drake.

"I will seek your uncle, my dear, but if you do not return soon, I will know where to find you." With a curt nod Michael strode down the garden path without a further look back.

Eileen hastily put some distance between Drake and herself, to no avail. He caught her shoulders and flung her around with none of Michael's earlier gentleness.

"Have you taken complete leave of your senses?" he demanded, his fingers bruising the soft flesh beneath the light covering of wool.

"I am not the one who is mad, my lord," Eileen spat out. "You are the one choosing a mate with the brains of a peagoose and the morals of a rabbit."

"And you possess better?" Drake exclaimed furiously. "Only a peagoose would not see that she is condemning herself to a life of stultifying dullness, and I saw the way you kissed him. If that was a chaste kiss, let me show you a real one."

His lips crushed hard and relentlessly against her mouth, while his hands claimed full possession of her

body. Eileen choked and gasped and tried to escape as
his tongue invaded and drew the breath from her
throat, but as his hands threw aside her protective
wrap and took possession of the rising curves beneath,
her struggles grew less. With the knowledge of experience, Drake pushed aside the flimsy trappings of velvet and lace and found the sensitive peak of her breast
pushed up to tempt him by the stiff whalebone of her
bodice. Eileen moaned against his mouth as his fingers
played her desires shamelessly.

His other hand sought out the lacings at her back,
and Eileen felt the front of her gown give way as his
nimble fingers loosened them, but she could not raise
the strength to protest. She realized now that her
response to Michael's kiss had come only from the
need for this one, and she drank hungrily of the eager
warmth of Drake's mouth. His hand now had full
freedom and played haunting games with her breasts,
and a rising tide of heat inflamed her midsection and
spread lower. She came close to understanding the
mystery that had long eluded her, but she knew she
could not solve it here. If she allowed him to continue,
she would end up beneath him on the cold lawn as
Drake had just accused Michael of doing. That thought
frightened her into sensibility.

"Don't, Drake," she whispered against his mouth as
he pressed kisses to the corners of her lips.

"Why not? If we are both mad, let us be mad
together." Drake tightened his arm against her back
and bent to sample the delectable fruit of her flesh. A
heady scent of wildflowers lingered between her breasts,
and he kissed the place where her heart pounded
before moving on to sample more.

For the first time in her life Eileen felt faint. A
liquid languor stole away her senses as he bent her to
his demands. Drake's lips devoured her, but she could
feel herself evolving into something new even as he

consumed what was left of the old. With sudden sureness she knew her place in nature's design, and she had no objection. As Drake raised her hips to press against his, Eileen surrendered to the inevitable, and she instinctively rubbed against him.

"Now, do you understand, princess?" Drake whispered against her ear. The hand that had once caressed her breast now cupped her buttocks and held her firmly where he wanted her.

She had no shame, and she made no attempt to conceal it now. Eileen's hands slid along his broad shoulders and around his neck while she kissed the throbbing tension of his jaw. Her breasts pressed sensuously along the velvet of his coat, and she wiggled against him joyfully.

"I understand Michael will kill us if I do not leave here immediately," she murmured horribly in his ear as she nibbled on the lobe.

Drake nearly laughed out loud at this return of his bold enchantress. He set her gently on her feet again and gazed longingly on the white breasts gleaming in the moonlight before he slowly worked to cover them.

"Then you know why I cannot let you marry him. Let me come to you tonight, and I will break the news gently to him in the morning." His hands caressed her back as he tightened her laces.

A frisson of alarm shivered down Eileen's spine as she realized where her impetuousness had led. "You cannot tell him, Drake. For my aunt and uncle's sake, I must marry him. Please try to understand."

Drake stiffened, and his hands froze on the soft cloth of her bodice. "You mean to marry him anyway?"

Eileen's chin came up and she met his gaze squarely. "You mean to marry Pamela, do you not?"

"That is different, I . . . ."

Eileen cut him off. "You may protect your family's honor, I will protect my family's safety in the only way

I am able. If you cannot accept those terms, then you will find my door barred to you."

Drake's hands left her waist to clench by his sides. "I will not share you, Eileen."

"Fine. Then Pamela may have you to herself." With an anger and pain bordering on tears, Eileen tugged her wrap back around her and fled for the back stairs. She was in no state to confront Michael or anyone else.

Chapter XII

——— ❧ ———

April, 1746

Exhausted after weeks of fruitless search, sick in mind and soul at the tales of the bloodthirsty massacre at Culloden, Drake simply maneuvered his horse into a copse of trees as still another troop of His Majesty's finest rode by in search of some poor devil. Those lads had been of the finest houses, fighting for a cause they thought just. They had fought bravely and honorably—to be cut down like vermin, hunted like so many rabbits in the field. Drake could not bring himself to greet Cumberland's hunters.

Bile boiled up in his throat as Drake thought of his own young cousins caught in that merciless slaughter. He sent a beseeching prayer to the heavens as he returned his horse to the road. Surely, they had not time to return from France to join that final fray. Please, God, let them be safely on their way home now, their dreams demolished but their lives intact.

His own hopes had gradually dwindled to nothing these last weeks, and only his concern for the Monsards kept him clinging to the saddle, galloping for home. Within the week he would be married, and with nothing to stop her, Eileen would do the same. He had thought, somehow, some way, he could prove her uncle's guilt, protect her from the danger, and save her for himself, but that was not to be. De Lacy eluded him, and Culloden brought him home. There would be time for nothing else. It was over. The chance to capture a faerie had flown, as any fantasy must.

His wretched thoughts nearly prevented Drake from seeing the man darting from the bushes into the highway. He was only a few miles from home. The drive was nearly visible from here. He wanted nothing more than to see Sherbourne again, ascertain the Monsards' safety, and collapse in his own bed and sleep for a week. He had no desire to stop as the man frantically gestured for him to do.

Recognizing one of his own servants, Drake wearily brought his mount to a halt and gazed without interest on his footman.

"What is it that cannot wait until I get home, Smythe?"

"Soldiers, my lord." The man jerked his hat from his head and nervously twisted it in his hands. "Lady Diane says to stay away until she sends for you. Sir John's there. He said to watch the road for you in case you came this way."

Puzzled, too tired to understand, Drake stared at the servant. "Soldiers? What soldiers? Where are Auguste and Pierre?"

The man's eyes widened nervously. "His Majesty's, my lord, looking for you. I don't know where them young ones be at; we thought they was with you." His careful speech slipped to its natural origins as he jerked his gaze back and forth down the road.

"Why in hell would soldiers be interested in me? And why shouldn't I see them?" Drake demanded sharply, growing irritated with this nonsense.

That snapped the man's attention back to his master. "They've got a warrant for your lordship's arrest. They say you've been with them traitors at Culloden, my lord."

The curses Drake spewed lacked their usual luster. He had thought he had met the depths of despair. Obviously he was wrong.

"Stand aside, Smythe. I'll put an end to this nonsense. Traitor, bigod! I'll show the bastards traitors!"

A man could only be driven so far. If those gutless excuses for men thought they could keep him from Sherbourne, they did not know who they dealt with. Traitor! The thought so infuriated him, he could scarcely wait to show the fools who was master here. That Diane would have to suffer this humiliation raised his ire to new degrees.

Drake's tired mount gave a spurt of speed as he galloped up the winding drive toward home. Thick chestnuts lined the way, sheltering him from the rain, hiding the first sight of the towering walls of Sherbourne from his hungry gaze. Home. Nevermore would he stray. His place was here, whatever the fates decreed. Even the air seemed softer, more palatable.

The first sharp reports echoed by him without his changing his pace. His mind could scarcely reconcile the sight of red-coated troops pouring from the trees ahead with reality. His body reacted without thought as more bullets whistled by his ear. He reined in his horse and whirled about, dashing for the hedgerow to the south.

Another loud *crack* and his shoulder felt as if it had been smashed with a hard mallet. Slumping in the saddle, Drake gave the horse its head and turned his concentration to outrunning bullets.

The skirts of Eileen's lawn gown swished in wet leaves as she strode restlessly along the forest path. The long cloak she had worn earlier against the drizzle now hung limply in her hand, dragging occasionally in the dirt. She paid it no heed, as she ignored the boiling thunderclouds in the sky above.

The date of Drake's wedding was two days hence, her own two months more. She did not think on it. Other matters made thoughts of marriage less imperative. Diane's frantic letters of these past weeks and the news from Scotland gave evidence of an entire world gone mad.

Eileen struck viciously at a branch in her way, taking her anger and her helplessness out on an inanimate object. She wanted to cry but couldn't, for she had no reason, not yet. Every instinct in her body warned that tragedy had struck, but she could not bear the thought of it, not again. Her whole mind rebelled against the certainty of it.

But no other reason could explain why Drake and the Monsard brothers had disappeared the night of the dinner party. Eileen cursed herself for every type of fool for denying him that night. Had she welcomed him to her bed, he would not have rushed off like that, and even now all might be well. But she held no hope of that now. If Drake were alive, he would have written. Never would he leave Diane to the mercy of Edmund and panic. Michael and Sir John had gone to her yesterday, so great had been their fear for her. Without Drake she was hysterical.

With the news from Scotland, she had every right to be. The rumors of the massacre at Culloden trickled slowly to these parts, but what Eileen had heard was beyond her limited comprehension. No gentleman could have committed those atrocities. How could a prince of the realm? The Duke of Cumberland must have been mad. And Drake and the Monsards, dead.

Striking out at a large limb, Eileen finally gave a wrenching sob of rage. Leaning her head against the massive oak, tears trickled down her cheeks, blending with the wetness of the rain.

None of it made sense. Why would Drake run off to fight a battle he thought lost? And if he followed the Monsards to bring them back, why had he not returned? Remembering Edmund's veiled threats of last fall, Eileen feared the worst in her heart. If he had been murdered, she had sent him to it.

An arm gently covered her shoulders, and Eileen

gave a jerk of fear before recognizing the strength of it. With a cry she turned into his embrace, burying her face against his shoulder as Drake wrapped her in his great cloak.

"Druids shouldn't cry, princess. They will form a lake."

Eileen heard his words as if from a distance, and her heart stopped as she realized she sought comfort from a man weakly leaning against a tree. He swayed to stand as she pushed away, and she gave a gasp of horror at the dark red stain down the front of his waistcoat.

"You're wounded! Let me get you inside and send for a physician. I'll send word . . ."

Drake placed a finger across her lips. "It's not serious. You must tell no one you saw me. I just wanted you to know . . ." It was his turn to let a sentence die. Gazing down into Eileen's rain-drenched face, streaks of tears mingling with the auburn curls plastered to her cheeks, Drake could no more find the words for what he had to say then he could believe them himself. It had all happened much too quickly. "I'm sorry," he whispered.

Years of survival did not fail her now. Whipping on her cloak and pulling up the hood to cover her face, Eileen indicated Drake do the same.

"We'll go in the back way. If anyone sees, they'll think you're Quigley's mother. She often brings me herbs and flowers. Take my basket." She shoved the half-filled wicker into Drake's hands. The pungent scent of leaves passed with it.

"Eileen, I cannot endanger your family like this. There's an army of soldiers somewhere down the road searching for me. You do not understand the danger. I must go."

With one glance at the etched lines of weariness in his face, she shook her head. "No, I don't understand, but there's no time to argue. There's a priest hole in the cellars. Even Uncle John has forgotten it. You can rest while I send Quigley to the coast. I have friends there who will not ask questions.''

"Eileen, I cannot . . .'' But he could, how easily he could. Every muscle ached for surcease after days of hard riding without food or sleep. He had finally surrendered his weary horse to proceed on foot, only to find his trail blocked at every turn. The bitterness he had felt at being denied access to his own home still rankled, and the poison of it wearied him more. For days there had been no time to think, to plan. She offered this and more.

Without waiting to see if he followed, Eileen hurried down the muddy path toward home. Her blood sang through her veins as she lifted her skirts and tripped quickly over the well-worn road. He lived! He lived and he had come to her! Finally, finally and at long last, he understood. If not, she would make him see. Just wait.

As they came to the lawn around the kitchen garden, Eileen turned and motioned Drake to slow down. It would seem odd should Mrs. Quigley move quickly. The old lady never hurried.

Drake was much too large for the part, but if he bent over slightly . . . Again Eileen gestured and Drake complied. They did not need words. They understood each other now as perfectly as they had that first time. With nerve-racking slowness they ambled across the yard.

No one paid any heed as the two dripping figures entered the kitchen door and moved toward the cloak room. Miss Eileen was as at home in the back of the house as the front, and the servants knew she would not disturb them in the midst of dinner preparations.

Cautiously Eileen spied around the corner past the cloak room, then gestured for Drake to follow. The butler used this corridor when he came for the wine, but few traversed it otherwise. The cellar door was closed and the butler nowhere in sight. They moved safely from the light of the upper halls to the chill damp of the cellar stairs.

"This is madness, Eileen. You'll break your neck in those skirts . . ." Drake protested as the cellar door closed and darkness engulfed them.

With the ease of practice, Eileen struck a flint against the stone wall and ignited a torch in the bracket beside the door. She could carry it, too, but Drake's longer grasp reached it first.

She led him through a maze of crumbling stone and timber into the old keep. The path she took seemed surprisingly clean of dust and cobwebs, evidence that the Hall's housekeeping was extraordinarily diligent or someone used this place with some frequency. Giving Eileen a shrewd look, Drake surmised the latter. Her ability to disappear at will became a shade less mysterious.

Eileen came to a halt at a stretch of wall unblocked by old crates and barrels. By pressing her fingers along a line of stones, a crack appeared in the wall, and a moment later the stones swung inward, revealing a dark cavern behind.

With the torch held high, Drake examined the wooden structure that held the stones in place. It seemed safe enough, though he could not wish for Eileen to visit it often. Old timbers often had a way of crumbling to the ground, but these seemed in no immediate danger of doing so.

Eileen waited impatiently as Drake examined the tiny fireplace, the windowless walls, the stark cot, table, and chair. In a prior century a priest may have cowered here, waiting for the stamp of Cromwell's army to pass overhead. Perhaps smugglers had stored their loot here for distribution. Whatever its prior uses, it offered a haven of safety for the nonce.

"The grate opens into the great chimney above. There is no danger in using it." Eileen indicated a small stack of kindling she had gathered against a rainy day. Today's downpour suited the purpose. "Take off those wet clothes and I will try to find you some dry ones."

Eileen moved to the door, avoiding the look on Drake's face. The pain and bitterness she had seen there earlier hurt her to the quick, and she needed time to get used to it. The Drake she knew had the whole world in his hand and laughed about it. This new Drake needed her more, but the feeling made her uneasy, as if looking at the world while hanging upside-down from a tree limb.

Leaning against the wall, Drake watched Eileen's slight figure flit through the opening and disappear. She had lit a small torch on the wall, so the chamber did not fall into complete darkness with the closing of the door. A great weariness made him stagger as he tried to raise himself upright, but he set his jaw and remained standing.

Following her sound advice, he removed his drenched clothing, wincing as the blood-soaked shirt pulled away the clotted blood forming on his wound. Wrapping himself in the old sheet and blanket from the cot, Drake allowed himself the pleasure of sitting before the grate as he set about lighting a fire. Warmth was a luxury he had not learned to appreciate so well as he did now.

By the time Eileen returned, Drake had a small fire crackling nicely while his clothes steamed over the chair and table. The room was beginning to smell of unwashed linen, and she had to smile at this evidence of a man's naïveté of even basic household tasks. She resolved to remove the clothes for laundering when she left.

"I have sent Quigley to the coast to arrange for a boat. There is time for you to eat and get some rest."

From the basket on her arm Eileen produced a small bottle of rum, which Drake accepted gladly. A large gulp produced instantaneous effects. Color began to return to his cold-pinched lips, and he developed more interest in the rest of the contents of the basket.

"I smell chicken. You wouldn't happen to have . . ." As Eileen produced a small roast capon, he sighed happily. "I always knew you were a magic faerie. I'll not inquire into the source of your riches."

Whatever had happened to him, his sense of the ridiculous had not failed, and Eileen smiled her relief. "It is too early in the season for apples. I had to find something else to distract you."

Stepping around the table, Drake gently touched a still-damp curl clinging to her cheek. The silver of her eyes hid her secrets well, but he was not yet ready to penetrate them. It was better to keep a neutral distance, though his fingers ached to continue their journey.

"You have always known how to do that, princess. I'll not return your favors by bringing danger down upon your head. As soon as Quigley returns, I will leave, but I will not forget."

Eileen studied the darkening blue of his eyes for a moment, then nodded evasively. "Sit, and let me wrap that wound."

Drake did as told, sipping on the rum as she sponged the caked blood from his shoulder. The wound was not deep, but it had bled copiously, and the constant use of those muscles had taken its toll. Eileen gently packed the wound with lint and began to wrap the strips of linen around the powerful muscle of his shoulder.

Drake accepted the old shirt of Sir John's she had brought for him, pulling it over his head with difficulty with one arm wrapped tightly. Small hands instantly came to his aid, and he found himself in the odd position of being dressed by a woman. As his head emerged from the linen, he winked at her.

"You are a horrible man, Lord Sherbourne," she informed him calmly. "For what you have done to Diane, you ought to be horsewhipped through the streets. But I'll give you time to polish your story while I return to Aunt Emma for tea."

Before she could escape, Drake caught her by the arm and twisted her around. "What is wrong with Diane?"

Eileen eyed him suspiciously. "What did you think would happen when you disappeared for weeks without a word? She is hysterical."

"I wrote every chance I got. I left her a message . . ." Drake paled and dropped her arm. "Edmund."

"Yes, Edmund. I warned you of trusting too much. It killed my father. At least you're still alive, though I can't imagine how. Eat and rest. I won't be able to return for a while."

This time he let her go. One blow after another, and soon he would not be able to stand on his own two feet. Drake reached for the chair and lowered himself into it. Perhaps with a little food and rest he would be able to make sense of it all, but the gaping sense of loss that had brought him here only grew more hollow with the passage of time.

By the time Eileen returned later that evening, she found Drake fast asleep upon the narrow cot. The fire had warmed the little room, and he had discarded the old shirt. She eyed his broad, muscular shoulders and blanket-covered hips dubiously, but entered and closed the door quietly. The wild thunder and lightning outside could scarcely be heard from within here.

Just her slight movement as she tidied up the remains of his dinner was sufficient to rouse Drake from his troubled slumber. The scent of wildflowers drifted to him, and he knew his visitor without asking. Wrapping the blanket about his loins, he rose from the bed.

Eileen continued clearing the table, ignoring the tall man towering uncertainly behind her. Until he touched her shoulder with a gentle hand.

She swung around then, and the look in his eyes was such that she could not have refused him had he asked for the moon. As he stared down into her delicate face, the small chin quivering as she fought back tears, Drake knew only his need to comfort her. When his arms clasped her in his hold, she melted quickly into them.

He simply held her like that, resting his head on her sweet-smelling tresses, now neatly dried and pinned. She was so slight in his arms, it was akin to holding the wind, except he felt the pounding of her heart in unison with his own. He had only to move his hands to discover her reality, but he did not dare do that. Not any longer.

"Has Quigley returned?" Drake asked, not because he wanted to but because he must. He had to keep reminding himself of the seriousness of the situation. It was much too easy to forget the world existed when she was in his arms.

"No boats can go out tonight." Eileen whispered against his chest. "There will be one waiting as soon as the storm abates."

"Then I had better go. I owe Sir John too much to put his lands and family in jeopardy." Reluctantly Drake moved his arms from around her, but he could not force himself to step away.

Suddenly aware that she rested against the wide expanse of chest of a man who wore nothing but a blanket, Eileen stepped backward and lifted her eyes to his.

"There is no need to stand out in the pouring rain when you can stay warm and dry. There is a trapdoor beneath the cot should this place somehow be discovered. Besides, Uncle John cannot return in this storm. Even if by some remote chance you are found, he can claim innocence. Stay."

"And you?" Blue eyes watched her steadily.

"Come what may, I stay with you." As simple as

that. If she'd had a horse, she would have followed
him after that first meeting when they were children.
Pride had almost caused her to lose him again. She
had learned her lesson well. Pride had naught to do
with happiness.

"I cannot let you do that, princess." Drake turned
toward the fire, stirring it into flame and adding more
kindling. "You don't understand what has happened. I
am a man with a price on my head. Everything I had is
lost."

"Not everything," Eileen murmured from behind
him.

Drake lifted his head to read her meaning, then
shook it sadly. "Yes, little one, everything. I cannot
protect you when I can scarcely protect myself. For
this one night, perhaps, I could have you for a little
while, pretend I have not lost it all. But in the morn I
must leave you to your uncle and Michael. He was the
wisest choice, after all."

Eileen stared at him with unfathomable silver eyes,
memorizing the glint of gold in his hair as the firelight
danced upon it, admiring the jut of high cheekbones in
a lean, square-jawed face. He was no longer the London dandy of his youth, but a man with all the responsibilities and beliefs of his kind. Men looked upon the
world on a grander scale than women, she had learned.
They treasured pride and honor and duty above the
more mundane aspects of life, such as the people who
loved them. He could be no less than a man, no more
than she could be less of a woman. The differences
were foolish, but she was learning to accept them. In
her own way.

With a smile that brought sparkling highlights to her
eyes, Eileen held out her hand to him. "I can protect
myself, my lord."

This time Drake did not question her meaning. The
fire she had kindled in him long ago blazed hungrily,
and he stepped toward her, his eyes smoldering. In the

morning he would be gone, and she could not follow. Tonight he would find what happiness he could. He folded her in his arms again, and his mouth closed demandingly against hers.

Knowing she had won only half the battle, Eileen surrendered, for the moment. There would be time enough later to plan her attack. For now, the world consisted of Drake's mouth on hers and his strong arms holding her close. She parted her lips, and the first stage of conquest was his.

Fearing he would never have this opportunity again, Drake brutally forced his body into control so that he might savor every moment of her promises. As his lips sought each soft curve and tender spot along Eileen's cheek and throat, his hands found the pins of her hair and inexorably removed each one. When the thick, heavy tresses fell in cascading lengths over her shoulders down to her waist, he filled his hands with their riches and smiled down on her.

"Do you have any idea how long I have longed to do that?"

The fire's red glow played along the heavy lengths, and copper shone like satin as it fell about his hands. Eileen touched a finger to his lips, then brought it to her own, savoring the taste of him.

"As long as I have wished to do that, my Lord Sherbourne."

Just that simple touch sent desire raging through his loins, and Drake could barely control the urge to rip through her hampering clothing to the woman beneath. Instead he released her hair and, staring down into her eyes, deliberately unfastened the lace strings of her bodice.

Firelight flickered shadows over the hollows of his cheeks and made smoldering embers of his eyes as Drake bent all his concentration to the slender woman in his hands.

Eileen held herself still as he released her from the

modesty of lawn and lace. She lifted her arms free of
the hampering cloth as he brought the bodice down
around her waist, and she stepped clear of the yards of
petticoats and lawn as these, too, became victims of
Drake's nimble fingers.

She stood before him in only chemise and stockings,
and her flesh tingled under the intensity of his stare.
His hand caressed the lengths of hair from her shoulders, letting it slide down her back so the curve of her
breasts and the valley between had no other veil but
the flimsy chemise. Light from fire and torch gleamed
along fair, unblemished skin and created mysterious
shadows he had yet to explore.

"You are not afraid?" Drake watched her eyes as
his hand filled with the weight of one firm breast.

"Not any more than I fear the wind in the trees or
the waves on the sea. They can cause harm, I know,
but I do not fear them for all that."

The slightly foreign lilt to her voice touched all the
empty places Drake had ignored for so long, and in
that moment he felt the urge to weep. But that habit
had been beaten out of him long ago, and he could
only respond by kissing the lips that warmed him so.

As for the first time her skin felt the masculine
roughness of his, Eileen felt the core of excitement
within her burst and spread like wildfire. Her fingers
dug into the rippling musculature of his shoulders, and
she understood something of his greater strength as
Drake lifted her from the floor to bring her closer.
Her brief chemise slid upward, and she realized with
rising excitement that his blanket had fallen from his
hips. Instinctively her hips moved closer to his, and
the heat of him sent the wildfire blazing higher.

His kisses smothered her murmured urgings, but his
hands respected her desires. Cupping her buttocks
firmly in one large hand, Drake brought her next to
him, and Eileen gasped at the hardness sliding between her thighs. But she raised her legs obediently,
and the wind blew to whip the flames higher.

"Oh, God, princess," Drake groaned against her ear. "I cannot wait much longer. Let me love you now."

"Please." The word was murmured urgently in the heated air of the tiny room.

In an instant Eileen found herself upon the bed, her chemise only a memory somewhere on the floor. She scarcely noticed the roughness of the poor sheets beneath her, for Drake's kisses lifted her from the bed and into the heavens. She cried out his name as his mouth closed over the hardened peak of her breast, and her body became a mass of flames as his hand penetrated the aching flesh between her thighs.

And then he was in her, shoving deeper as the wildfire drove her to him, propelling her hips upward to meet his driving thrust. She felt split asunder, but she could no more resist the pain than the fire could fight the wind. It blazed within her now, melding her flesh to his, reaching heights of cataclysmic proportions.

Until she could no longer feel her own body but only his, and he swept her into a river of fire that seared her to him for always. The pain and joy combined to make one as convulsions racked her body, and Drake's life fluid combined with her own. There could be no parting after this. She was his.

Chapter XIII

Drake smoothed a tendril of copper around the curve of one warm, soft breast and found his attentions met with the questioning stare of silver eyes. He kissed her brow and met her gaze frankly.

"I thought you slept, princess."

"Not tonight." Eileen moved closer to him, absorbing the sensation of his hair-roughened leg against hers. "Will you tell me what happened?"

Drake had no desire to repeat his confusion out loud. What he wanted lay in the bed beside him, but she had been a virgin and he sensed he had caused her pain. She would not be ready for him yet. He turned on his side and ran his hand along her slender length.

"If you insist, I will tell you. Did I hurt you?"

"Not as much as you gave me pleasure. I wanted you to be the one to teach me." And now that she had learned, she knew she could not share that moment with any other man, but now was not the time to tell him that. "Tell me," she repeated.

"I would rather make love to you." Drake persuasively trailed a line of kisses along her cheek.

"I will beat upon your poor shoulder until you desist." Far from beating, her hand caressed the bandages marring his golden skin.

Sighing, Drake took her in his arms so that he could at least feel the pressure of her breasts against his side. One slender leg wrapped about his, and this time he sighed with satisfaction. She might be unbiddable, but she certainly knew how to hold his attention.

"There is little to tell, Eileen. I discovered my cousins used the occasion of my party to head for Charlie. I was prepared for it, or so I thought. I went after them and arranged to have them kidnapped before they could meet up with the troops. They saved face by not having me physically drag them from their comrades, and even if they might suspect I arranged it, they could still return to Sherbourne without accusations. They will be released somewhere in France shortly, supposedly upon my paying their ransom."

It sounded like a rather costly but effective means of ensnaring the adventurous brothers. They would most likely enjoy every minute of it. But that explained nothing. Eileen stroked the dark golden hair upon Drake's chest.

"And Edmund intercepted your messages telling Diane all was well. Why? Surely it did not take you these many weeks to send the Monsards out of the country?"

He knew she'd ask that, but there was no point in revealing the state of his desperation at the time, now that it had come to no conclusion. Drake shrugged and caught her hand, trapping it against his chest.

"I had other business that required a degree of discretion. I did not think it anyone's concern but my own. When I heard what happened at Culloden, I started home to make certain my cousins could not possibly have joined in that disaster. I found soldiers on the road everywhere, beating the bushes for any of the poor fools Cumberland failed to massacre."

The bitterness in his voice grew strong. "When I was nearly within sight of Sherbourne, I met one of my footmen waiting for me with a message from Diane. She said the house was full of soldiers looking for me, that they had a warrant for my arrest, and your uncle advised me to keep out of sight until he could find out more."

Drake abruptly stood up and strode naked across the room to the remains of the bottle of rum. With the fire nearly gone, Eileen could see little but his shadow. His natural grace held her spell-bound, however, and she watched his muscular physique unabashedly as he returned to the bed.

Drake slid in beside her, but his grasp was cold and angry as he caught her next to him. "Do you really want to hear the rest?"

"There is more?"

"Not much." Drake kissed her provokingly, forcing her to respond, then pulled away. "I did not believe the seriousness of the situation. Admittedly, my loyalties to the king may be questionable, but I was nowhere near Scotland. I had nothing to do with those fool Jacobites other than to prevent my cousins from joining their numbers. So I went home to confront the bastards and throw the lot of them out. They began firing on me even before I rode down the drive."

From a distance, the boom of thunder rocked the ancient walls, and Eileen held tight to the man in her arms. She heard his disbelief, could only imagine the immensity of his horror at being fugitive from his own home. She had been too young to mourn the loss of hers for long. Drake's entire life had been stripped away.

"Can it be so difficult to prove that you were not one of the traitors? Surely it can only be some machinations of Edmund that has caused a warrant to be issued?"

Drake began a trail of kisses along the line from her lips to her earlobe, punctuating every few words with a kiss. "I traveled incognito, princess. No one can say where I was these past weeks. And I did some questioning before I took your uncle's advice. A man using my name and arms was known to be among Charlie's army. They've tortured enough poor devils to have lists of traitors. My name is among them."

As his teeth fastened upon her ear, his hand came up to wreak havoc with her breast, and Eileen instinctively moved closer into his embrace. She learned the result of this foolishness quickly. A heated lance seemed to drive between her thighs, making her gasp with surprise.

"You have friends. They will prove your innocence," she managed to murmur as Drake's hands found new territory to explore. She now knew the meaning of the ache rising between her legs, but perversely she fought it.

"But meanwhile, I am a hunted man. I must run as if I truly am a traitor, simply to protect my hide. It could take months, years, Eileen, and I may never prove my innocence. They will take my house, my lands, my title, and then forget about me. It has been done before. I am no friend of the court. I will fight, Eileen, with every breath in my body, but it will not be an easy fight."

Years. He could be years from her, and he thought he would protect her by leaving her behind. That was what he was telling her—with his words, with his hands, with his body. He was saying his farewells. And she would not have it.

Fiercely she gripped his shoulders and molded herself along his length, covering his throat and jaw with her kisses. Drake responded without hesitation, tumbling her back to the bed and covering her with his greater weight. Eileen struggled for dominance, nipping his fingers and writhing away from him. She wanted to show him her strength, her independence, but he would not have it. With the greatest of ease, Drake pinned her to the bed and smothered her protest with kisses. Within minutes he had spread her legs and penetrated that part of her that had been inviolable.

Eileen cried out her despair as his body captured hers with such ease, carrying her where he wanted to go, when he chose. She could offer him no comfort but a target for his anger and bitterness, and, what was worse, she craved more. Even as he carried them both to the brink of ecstasy, she was demanding more. And he complied.

By dawn, exhaustion had taken its toll. Drake slumbered restlessly by her side, holding one hand possessively around her waist. Eileen ached in places she had never known existed, and her face felt bruised and chafed from Drake's fierce kiss. The pleasure he had taken and returned left her drained and longing for more. She finally understood he did not return her love but merely needed a receptacle for his desire. But she could not leave his bed for another man's arms, and while he needed her, she must stay. Whether he allowed it or not.

Meaning only to return to her room for Drake's laundered clothing and those few things she could take with her, Eileen slipped from Drake's arms. It felt odd to be without clothing, odder still to be lying next to this large man who had possessed her more intimately than she had dreamed possible. In the darkness he seemed a stranger, and she rubbed her breasts where he had bruised her so thoroughly.

But simply the act of moving from his side brought Drake to instant wakefulness, and he reached to prevent her leaving. He kissed the tip of each aching breast tenderly, then pressed his lips to hers.

"I must find Quigley," she protested weakly, already feeling the dangerous languor stealing over her.

"Stay here. Let me remember you lying upon the sheets where we shared the night," he murmured against her ear. Drake rose with the tawny grace of a lion, striding about the small cell, stirring the dying embers, lighting candles.

Eileen lay against the sheets, wishing she had the

talent to capture that rippling musculature on canvas. He returned to her side, holding a candle high as he inspected the damage to her delicate skin.

"You may have some difficulty explaining that to your Uncle John." Drake spoke with a hint of amusement as he rubbed his fingers lightly along reddened skin. His gaze shifted lower, finding the lover's bruises upon her throat and breasts. "It is a good thing you need explain nothing to your maid. I am sorry, princess. I did not mean to be so rough with you."

Still, he thought she would stay behind. She must dissuade him of that nonsense, but talk had long ceased to be her strong point. Eileen sat up, holding the sheet between her breasts while her hair hung in long, disheveled tangles over her back and shoulders.

"Let me go with you, Drake." She spoke softly, willing him to understand.

He refused to see. Shaking his head, he turned to find his clothes. "No, princess. What I did last night was barely forgivable. To lead you into the kind of life I must seek in France would be beyond the realms of decency. I wish I could leave you without fear of de Lacy, but Michael will protect you."

Eileen heard the edge in his voice as he said this, and her heart took a leap of joy. He was trying to be a gentleman, but she was not a lady. He would learn that in time.

She swiftly gained her feet and slipped into her small clothes. "Let me find food and your clean linen. You will need your own clothes if you are to seek out your relatives in France."

Drake watched her with suspicion at this easy submission. "I have tarried too long, Eileen. Every moment brings us closer to disaster."

She blithely ignored this gloomy prognosis and wiggled into her bodice and petticoats. "Lace this," she commanded imperiously, "and I will show you the hiding place I spoke of last night."

Drake gladly obliged her with this last intimacy, lingering over the suppleness of her tiny waist and adjusting the modesty piece of her bodice to better suit his tastes. The glimpse of the valley between her breasts made him hunger again, but he resisted the temptation and let her go.

Instantly she was perching on the edge of the cot and tugging a board beneath it. When the board gave, she leaped to the edge and triumphantly pointed to a dark opening revealed by the upward tilt of the loose board.

"The door lifts, but I don't have the strength to lift it far. I suspect they kept their gold there once upon a time. It looks large enough to hold a man. You cannot be any safer than here."

Drake whistled at this ingenious contraption. 'Twas a pity his ancestors had not the forethought to so endow his own home. He could stay in hiding while he fought his battle from inside. As it was, he could not endanger the Summervilles any longer. If he were caught, they'd be charged with sedition and hung as surely as he. The price was much too high.

"I'll stay only until you find Quigley to lead the way to your friends, no longer. Hurry, for I fear we have lingered too long as it is." Drake caught her as she turned to face him, burying his hands in her hair and kissing her hard before parting. "Don't forget me, princess," he whispered pleadingly.

"I would find you even should you be a frog, my lord." Hastily Eileen kissed his cheek and turned to go.

At these words Drake caught her by the shoulder and swung her back around. "Eileen, I am serious. What happened last night was a once-in-a-lifetime thing. You will leave here and go to Michael and forget this moment of madness. He can provide for you and keep you safe. I don't want to see you dressed in rags again. I can give you nothing but the life of a beggar. You have been deprived of your rightful home for too long. I will not deprive you of it again."

Silver eyes flashed fiercely. "Do not condescend to me, my lord. I am not yours to command." She shook loose of his grip.

"Nor am I yours," Drake informed her firmly. "My gratitude does not extend to being weighed down by a capricious sprite while I try to put my life back together again."

She could have smacked him for that, but there was little time for arguing. Eileen swung back to the door. Quigley would be waiting for her. "Don't worry, my lord," she replied sarcastically, "I take care of myself."

With that, she was gone, leaving Drake to curse fiercely at the closed door.

Eileen could hear servants stirring in the kitchen, but the early morning darkness hid the shadows still. She darted up the stairs to her chambers. She could not send a maid for Quigley until she had returned herself to some sort of order.

Coming in through the front door, Sir John was startled to see what appeared to be the apparition of his niece flying up the back stairs at the end of the corridor, her long hair streaming in disgraceful profusion down her back. It had been a long two days. Perhaps he was imagining things, but he was thankful Michael had remained behind to see to the horses.

Eileen barely had time to draw the brush through her hair when a furious pounding echoed through the empty halls below. Shouts and the jingle of harness came from the kitchen gardens at the same time. Heart quaking, she dashed to the upper hall. She could hear Sir John's voice in the foyer and her spirits plummeted to new depths. She had not expected his return so soon. The angry pounding continued, and the significance of the orders being shouted began to dawn. She ran to the stairs and peered down.

A distinctly bemused and half-dressed footman hurried to open the wide front portals under Sir John's baleful glare. A moment later the morning sun streamed through the opening, illuminating the scarlet and gold glory of His Majesty's military finest standing on the doorstep.

Eileen had never known fear for herself, but fear for Drake and her uncle nearly caused her to scream at the sight of so many rapiers. She recovered her composure quickly as Sir John coldly listened to the words of the warrant read by the soldier apparently in command. They meant to search the house, as Drake had predicted. Fiends. She would show them how to search a house.

With a blindingly innocent smile Eileen tripped daintily down the broad front stairs, her disheveled appearance enticing the eye of every male in the foyer.

"Eileen!" Sir John bellowed furiously. "Go back to your room! This is none of your concern."

Even as he said it, John had the sinking feeling he lied. Bigod, she looked just like her mother had after she had eloped with Richard. Those huge eyes blazed with a fiery light that dared any and all to deprive her of her happiness. He recognized the willful set to her lips and nearly groaned out loud. He might sooner talk to the suit of armor beside him. Love made fools of us all.

Eileen continued down the stairs, smiling blindingly at the captain in his scarlet coat and fierce frown. She curtsied prettily to her uncle when she reached the foyer and made a gesture of questioning.

"They think Lord Sherbourne might be somewhere about the premises. There has been some little mix-up and they wish to question him. You have not seen him, have you?" Sir John spoke as if to a simpleton, playing his part well. He knew the truthful answer already. And he knew the one she would give. Lying came easily when it meant only a shake of the head.

Which was what she gave now as she gazed up with

interest at the commanding figure of the captain. Sir John shrugged and explained.

"She does not speak, but she sees everything. If Neville were here, she would know it. You will disturb my wife greatly if you insist on this search. I have never given His Majesty cause to doubt my loyalty. I must register full protest if you carry out these ridiculous orders."

"You have that right, sir, but my orders are to search the premises until Neville is found. You have just come from Sherbourne. You must admit we have some right to suspicion."

"I admit no such thing!" Sir John replied angrily. "Sherbourne is an innocent victim, and I only did my duty by my late friend to see to his daughter in time of trouble. Search if you must, but you damned well better not overset so much as a teacup or I'll have my solicitor writing up charges that will keep us all in court until we die!"

With a small smile of amusement twisting the corner of her lips, Eileen watched this performance with admiration. "The Englishman defending his castle" the charade could be called. Searching Summer Hall could keep an entire army occupied for a week. It needed no defending.

Still, if Edmund had done his work as well as she suspected, these men would tear the place to pieces to find Drake. They couldn't possibly know where he hid, but they could very well know she would be an accomplice. She daren't leave them for a moment.

So she danced along at their sides as the soldiers spread awkwardly through the towering foyer, switching their swords under tapestry-draped tables, jerking back velvet curtains that loosed clouds of dust. She laughed gaily as they peered beneath footstools too small to hide a kitten, and aided the hunt by opening the iron visors of long-dead Summerville knights. Her giggles echoed in the emptiness, and the captain frowned at this mockery.

"Gregory, post men at every exit. If he's here, we'll flush him out. Make certain the men are prepared to deal with an armed and desperate traitor." The captain's stentorian tones sent the hapless Gregory to shoving his men out the door. Exits would be a good deal easier to locate from outside the rambling hall.

The description of Drake made Eileen pout, and she deliberately trod on the captain's boot as she brushed past him, swinging her skirts huffily. The lawn gown she had worn since the day before looked much the worse for its night upon the floor, but the soldier saw only the glory of her copper-tinted hair, and his mouth twisted involuntarily. He liked spirited women, and he had a feeling this one would lead him a merry chase.

A commotion at the door indicated Michael had returned. Eileen ignored it, proceeding grandly into the ancient hall of the keep, flinging the doors wide and bowing like a servant to beckon their entrance. Sir John observed her rebellious performance and decided instantly that Michael had best not be audience to it. The lad had a good head on his shoulders and might easily discern what Sir John already surmised—and feel honor bound to report it.

Sir John left his niece to her theatrics and returned to the main portals and the irate ex-soldier demanding entrance. "Michael, keep an eye on my stable. Don't let any of these rogues near my horses or I'll have their heads!" he roared to his prospective nephew-in-law through the opened doors.

On the other side of the watchdogs at the door, Michael looked grim but noddd obediently. He disappeared without further word, and Sir John sighed with relief. It was a blessing to deal with a man of few words but swift action. If only that was all that was needed to deal with his wayward niece.

Dreading the progress of this search, Sir John followed the remaining soldiers into the cavernous keep. Used only when entertaining, the hall lay cold and dark at this hour of the morning. But Eileen danced in its center as if all the chandeliers were lit and the fires roaring. The little hoyden of the forest was back in full spirit, gliding in and out of the shadows, thoroughly confusing the awkward young soldiers who tried to keep her in sight.

She flitted from corner to corner, pointing up the giant chimney so one young fool walked in and covered himself with soot to search it, darting behind swagged tapestries and laughing as she spun around, entrapping her follower in the folds. She fell to her hands and knees and crawled as swiftly as any crab beneath the long trestle tables and had half the searchers doing the same in a breathless game of follow-the-leader until the furious captain shouted a few choice phrases to return them to their senses.

Shamefaced, they began to move woodenly about the room, ignoring Eileen's light-footed travels as best they could. Bored with this entertainment, she perched upon the giant carved timber that served as mantel, swinging her slippered foot daintily—and whistling. Sir John cringed at this most unladylike habit, wondering where in heaven's name the little heathen had picked up such knowledge, but he'd rather not know. It was enough to see her perched for all the world like some exotic bird upon his mantel. He didn't need to see more.

But her ploy was effective. The unnerving whistling had the soldiers glancing uneasily over their shoulders, hurrying through their tasks, rushing on to the next room where they could hope the noise would not follow.

The noise did not, but their mischievous faerie did. Wherever they went, she was underfoot, laughing, mocking, and generally making them feel foolish as they prodded among elegant French furniture or kitchen pots and pans. The captain attempted to separate his men and send them in different directions, but then he lost all sight of Eileen and that feeling made him even more uncomfortable.

By the time they reached the cellars, half the men were sweating, the other half grinning. It had become more than obvious the Hall would keep its secrets, and the spirit of the Hall dared twit the nose of His Majesty himself, had he been foolish enough to appear.

Only Eileen felt anything akin to nervousness as the captain indicated the door to the cellars. Her bland smile concealed it well, but her heart pounded like thunder and she was terrified someone would hear it. Or see it. She felt certain it leaped from her chest with every thud.

"We've not been through here, sir. Is it unlocked?" The captain watched his host narrowly.

Sir John did not dare meet Eileen's eyes. When she wished to conceal something, her eyes were like twin mirrors. He knew he'd find that expression in them now.

"Of course not, man, use your head. Only my man is allowed down those stairs. They're dangerous at the best of times, and I'll not have some damned fool maid set on a lover's tryst breaking her silly neck. The walls are none too safe, either. I'll not be responsible for anyone fool enough to attempt the place."

"Nevertheless, sir, we must search it. Call for your man and have it unlocked."

Eileen had prayed she would be able to divert them from even noting the cellars, but now that the damage was done, she would have to disarm their suspicions. With her demurest smile she pushed her way to the door and made a lovely curtsy. Then putting her fingers to her lips as if promising them a secret, she stood on her toes and with a grandiose sweep produced the key from a hook beside the door frame.

With any luck at all, they would think her so innocent as to be revealing all Sir John's secrets. With a
conspiratorial smirk she unlocked the door and opened
it only slightly, peering into the blackness with a dramatic gesture of caution. Years of muteness had brought
out the actress in her, if it had done nothing else at all.

With a grand sweep of her hand she opened the
door to give them entrance. Both amused and irritated, the captain quickly stepped forward, only to
find his arm appropriated by a tiny hand. Lifting her
skirt as grandly as any lady, Eileen bestowed a sweet
smile upon him and set her dainty foot on the first step
beside him.

Not knowing how much of the search Drake had
heard or understood, Eileen sought some manner of
warning him. As one of the soldiers lit the remaining
torch, she remembered the crate of empty wine bottles
left lazily upon the bottom stair. It was only a matter
of minutes from thought to action. As the captain
strode determinedly down the last of the steep stairs,
the girl beside him became entangled in his buckled
sword and fell heavily against the crate on the stair's
edge, shattering bottles with a crash that would have
raised skeletons from the dungeons had there been
any.

Sir John anxiously leapt to his niece's elbow, helping her to right herself while red-coated soldiers hovered above and around her, and the embarrassed captain
apologized profusely. Eileen demurely waved away his
apologies, and bravely and pathetically stepped forward on her obviously injured foot.

"Eileen, you must return to your chamber and let
your aunt see to that foot. This has gone on far
enough." Sir John blocked the stairs as he pleaded
with his adamant niece.

"Sir, if you wish, I will carry her back to her room
while my men continue searching. I am most abjectly
sorry that this has happened."

Before Sir John could launch another tirade, Eileen interrupted him by smiling sweetly and laying her hand against the captain's arm, indicating that he continue with his search. Totally unable to determine if she played him for a fool or if she genuinely wished to show him something, the military man hesitated uncertainly, waiting for some decision from the lady's guardian.

By this time Sir John had had time to make the same observations on cleanliness that Drake had made on the prior day and had come to the same conclusions. He would have to change the lock on the cellar door to keep the little brat out of these dangerous passageways in the future. He had not been down here since he was a lad, but he knew the housecleaning improvements to be major. He hoped the captain did not employ the same insight. With a glance to Eileen for assurance, he nodded his permission to continue.

"I suspect she does not wish to miss the fun when you bring one of these crumbling old beams down upon your head," Sir John grumbled as he took Eileen's other arm and led the way.

The baronet knew instantly when they came dangerously close to wherever she had stashed the fugitive, for Eileen's fingernails nearly pierced the thickness of his coat. He prayed her other hand did not do the same as he covertly glanced around, trying to determine where a man as large as Drake could be hidden. The soldiers were busily ripping the lids off crates and barrels and pounding on walls. No hiding place seemed safe.

The captain felt no telltale pressure on his arm as they neared the hidden door. He had become all too aware of the faint scent of wildflowers, however, and he solicitously slowed his pace as his companion hobbled along, allowing his men to go on ahead of him.

When a soldier's rap echoed ominously hollow on an open space amongst the crates and barrels, Eileen was prepared. Ignoring the shouts of excitement from the soldiers, she tugged on the captain's arm and demanded his attention. When he turned to look down upon her, her eyes sparkled with mischief, and she pointed delightedly to his men.

Sir John could feel himself turning ever grayer as he vaguely remembered the old priest's hole, but he bravely set one foot after another in the path of his niece. He did not know what dangerous game she played, but he sincerely hoped she had hidden all traces of the trapdoor well.

Eileen shook the captain's arm angrily as his men pried with swords at the old stones, knocking the mortar between them to the ground. The captain shouted a command, and they stared at him incredulously, but they desisted. They watched with some impatience as the elflike girl on the captain's arm approached and waved them away as if they were useless ornaments. After all, they had been the ones to discover the hidden chamber.

Their amazement increased as a door opened in the wall upon the merest pressure of her slender fingers. And their faces fell as Eileen happily darted into the room and snatched up her basket of leaves and sketching utensils and displayed them to her uncle. She then settled herself quite comfortably in the chair beside the grate and motioned for the soldier with the torch to light the kindling. Propping her "injured" ankle upon the cot, she began gingerly unlacing the shoe. At the realization that the whole pack of soldiers continued to stare eagerly at her dainty ankle, she sat up straight and waved them away furiously.

Sir John gave a guffaw at the bemused expressions around him. "You have uncovered the little cat's nest, captain. I suggest you continue your search while someone sends for her maid. She has shown you the darkest secret she knows. She will not appreciate it if you trespass long." Sir John peremptorily ushered the intruders from his niece's hidden chamber.

Angry at again being deprived of his victim, the captain stalked from the empty room without a second look back. In his heart he knew he would never find a more likely place for the fugitive. If the traitor were not there, he was gone, but he forced his men to spread out and continue the search. Without the elf to shadow their path, the game was not so much fun, and the cellars were quickly searched and discarded.

As soon as all sound of the soldiers disappeared overhead, Eileen dived for the trapdoor and pried it up. The space beneath was empty.

Chapter XIV

Standing in the doorway of the priest hole, Sir John watched his niece's face with anguish as she rose from the edge of the trapdoor. The stricken look in her usually bright eyes confirmed all his suspicions, and his heart wrung with the sorrow of her choice. He cursed Drake heartily for toying with the emotions of a young girl, but in his soul he couldn't blame the man. Eileen had a will of her own, and she was nearly impossible to resist once she made up her mind. Drake had only followed his natural inclinations.

Eileen looked up to find her uncle waiting there, understanding written in his face. Without a word she went to him, and he held her awkwardly, patting the thick, auburn hair trailing down her back.

"There is a tunnel at the bottom of the stairs, little one. It comes out on the road to the coast. I have sent Quigley with a horse to meet him. With any luck, he will reach the coast before these idiots finish searching the Hall."

He was gone. Without her. She had thought he'd understood. The depths of Drake's betrayal brought tears to her eyes, and she desperately tried to think coherently. After all they had done together . . . Eileen set herself free from her uncle's grasp, not daring to think such thoughts in his presence, fearful he would read her mind.

"Let me take you back to your room. At least give some credence to your playacting by limping on the proper foot when we go upstairs. I will be back to talk with you when the men are gone."

John spoke sternly, hoping to recover some of the authority he had lost when this willful child had come into his life. He wished desperately for her to be happy, but Drake would bring her naught but sorrow. If it had been different, had Drake shown the same love for her as the Irish Richard had shown her mother, perhaps he could have forgiven. But this was a love destined for disaster, and he must put an end to it now. The wedding would most certainly have to be moved up. Michael was a good man. With time, he might make Eileen see reason.

Eileen obediently entered her room under her uncle's escort, but her thoughts circled rebelliously. How much of a head start could Drake have? Would she have time to catch up with him if she cut across country? How would she get away with troops swarming all over the house and lawns?

And Michael. Her heart sank. Michael guarded the stables. How had Uncle John got a horse past all those people?

Eileen's mind worked quickly as she searched the room, her hands automatically gathering those things she needed most. Quigley could have slipped away easily on foot. The troops could not possibly be patrolling all the hedges and gardens. There was not enough of them. Producing Drake's freshly laundered clothes from their hiding place, she shoved them and her simplest gowns into the canvas sack she used to carry her painting gear. Petticoats took too much room; she discarded all but one. Her mind worked at the corners of the puzzle. Anything was better than tears and despair.

The back paddock. Quigley's father kept a few of the older animals in the old stables beyond the back paddock. That's where he would get horses without the soldiers noticing. Even if they patrolled the roads, they would have no reason to halt a liveried footman of Quigley's slight stature out moving his master's horses from one paddock to another. Or whatever excuse he gave. If Quigley could do it, so could she.

Excitement chased the tears from Eileen's eyes. She would follow. She would. No one could stop her. Drake would have to take her with him. She would make him understand. She didn't need security, didn't need titles and land and wealth. He offered all she needed—someone to love. And he needed the same. She knew it. It would work. She would make it work.

With her own few clothes packed neatly in the bag, Eileen stopped to calculate what else would be needed. Coins would be helpful. Drake could not have many left by now, and he would find it difficult to pry it from the banks under the circumstances. She had jewelry, but she could not sell Sir John's heirlooms or the brooch Michael had given her as a betrothal gift. They would stay behind. She would have to borrow some of the gold in Sir John's drawer. Someday she would pay it back.

Once inside Sir John's chambers, she had no compunction about appropriating one or two more items. Drake would need clean shirts and cravats. These would be a little large but better than none at all. All fit neatly into her bag, along with the small pouch of coins. Sir John would understand what she had done.

She supposed she ought to write a note, but she had no words for what needed to be said. Besides, time was growing short. Drake would be far ahead of her. She had to get to the coast before the ship sailed.

Eileen changed into a drab dress of rough cotton, bound up her hair, and covered herself in a hooded cloak. The day was yet chilly, and concealment might be necessary. But if the passage beneath the trapdoor led into the woods, she would be free quickly. Those ridiculous toy soldiers would never find her there.

The problem of returning to the cellars was a major one. And she wished there were some way to say farewell to her aunt. Eileen hesitated in her doorway, knowing there was the one person she would hurt most with her departure. Emma had been more than kind in her quiet, unassuming manner. She could have made life considerably more difficult by forcing her niece into the mold her daughter had left behind, but she had given Eileen freedom to be herself. Unaccustomed to displaying affection, Eileen had difficulty in showing her aunt how much she appreciated what had been done for her. This might be her last opportunity.

Knowing each moment took Drake that much farther away from her, Eileen was torn with indecision, but her better self won this battle. Silently she slipped down the hallway to her aunt's sitting room. She knew the habits of her aunt and uncle well. Sir John would never allow the crude world to intrude upon Lady Summerville's peace. She would be sitting in the wide window of her sitting room, sipping her morning tea as usual, while all the world went mad outside her door.

Emma looked up with surprise as her niece entered garbed for a day of painting in the woods and fields. She had thought for certain the little imp would be in the midst of the uproar below, but then, it was just as likely she would seek to escape attention. The child ever eluded her, but her smile warmed Emma's heart. So much of Beth was in that smile, she could refuse her nothing.

Regretting that she had never allowed her aunt to know her secret, Eileen stood awkwardly in the center of the pretty room. How could she say what must be said without words?

"Come in, my love. Have some tea before you go out. Cook has given you a good meal, I trust?"

In truth, she had eaten nothing since the prior night, but Eileen nodded obediently. Food could be found for the looking, but what Lady Summerville offered could not be had for the asking. Here was the family and love and security she had craved all her life. Every time she found a haven of safety, she threw it all away to chase after still another dream. When would she ever find a place she called home?

With tears in her eyes, Eileen bent and kissed her aunt's white brow, much to that lady's surprise. Then, without another word or gesture, she picked up her bag and fled the room, leaving Emma to stare at the closing door with rising panic.

Eileen found the backstairs unguarded and hurried down them into the kitchens. The search party had apparently broken up into several groups. She could hear men clattering about the pantry while Cook scolded. Two of the scullery maids stared wide-eyed at the handsome, uniformed soldiers invading this sacred territory, and scarcely paid any heed as Miss Eileen slipped into the kitchen and helped herself to fresh rolls and bacon. From this point in the enormous kitchen, the soldiers couldn't see her, and Eileen moved quickly down the corridor to the cellars.

She feared someone would be guarding the door, but once searched, the men had no further interest in it. Fools, she concluded, reaching for the hidden key.

It wasn't there. Heart tearing loose from its mooring and pounding erratically somewhere in her chest, Eileen ran her fingers over the entire frame and shook the door with stealthy rage. Locked. Sir John had been smarter than the idiot soldiers.

Frantically Eileen retraced her steps to the kitchen. She had no idea how much time had elapsed since she had left Drake at dawn. He could have left anytime during the hours since. The ship could be on the sea by now. She had not even been given the chance to say farewell. She couldn't let him slip so easily from her grasp.

With swift decision, Eileen boldly strode out into the courtyard, canvas bag in hand. Let them try to stop her.

Two soldiers leaned lazily against the wall of the timbered stable. Michael's tall figure stood straight and proud nearby. Hands in pockets, he apparently conversed with men with whom he might once have shared camps or battles. That thought caused Eileen some little trepidation, but she proceeded boldly onward.

The men glanced up with interest as the dainty girl appeared in the sunlight, dragging a heavy canvas bag behind her. Garbed as she was, the men could not discern her status in this household, but Michael's instant attention brought them to order before any remarks could be made.

"Eileen, what in heaven's name are you about?" Michael strode swiftly toward her, hoping to head off whatever foolishness she planned.

In the presence of others, however, she would not talk, and he gritted his teeth in frustration as she smiled pleasantly, indicated her painting gear, and kept heading toward the stable.

"For heaven's sake, Eileen, you cannot go out alone. The place is swarming with soldiers. Where is Quigley?" Their betrothal had not been long enough for Michael to feel any certainty with this will-o'-the-wisp who had so abruptly brightened his life and who could so easily darken it again. He dared not make a scene before these men who watched with avid interest, but Michael had the desperate feeling he must do something to stop her.

Eileen waved benignly somewhere in the direction of the sloping lawns and the trees beyond, indicating Quigley's location. Michael saw no sign of the loyal servant who acted as the lady's bodyguard, but that was not to say the servant wasn't out there somewhere. He watched with suspicion as Eileen nodded politely to the two soldiers and proceeded grandly into the stables as if she were the queen and they were her footmen.

When she signaled for one of the stable boys to saddle a horse for her, however, the two soldiers began to stir uneasily.

"I say, miss, we can't have nobody taking them horses out without the captain's permission," one ventured politely, nervously glancing askance at Michael.

Eileen turned and smiled at him, gestured to Michael, as if he were to make her reply, and turned back to help the stable boy steady her mount.

Both soldiers turned expectantly to Michael, whom they recognized as a superior officer even if no longer in uniform.

Cursing himself for a fool, Michael explained. "She cannot speak. She carries her sketching pad and paints in that bag and is accustomed to coming and going as she pleases. She never goes beyond the boundaries of the estate. I can see no harm in letting her go. She certainly cannot hide your prey in that bag."

As if sensing their doubt, Eileen eagerly opened her bag and produced the sketchpad on top. With charming innocence she exhibited the sketch of a primrose-lined brook she had drawn the day before. The soldiers crowded around her, eager to see more as she flipped through the small portfolio. A poor attempt at a likeness of Lady Diane made her frown, and she made as if to crumple it, but Michael snatched it from her hands.

"Diane would like that. You should draw people more often. It is quite good."

So many words from the taciturn Michael in one day! Eileen stared at him with astonishment, then smiled. Standing on her toes, she kissed his cheek warmly. Then she returned her sketches to the bag and imperiously gestured for a hand into the saddle.

No one tried to stop her.

With a gay wave Eileen rode off toward the trees, her skirts blowing lightly behind her as the horse broke into a canter. Michael stared after her cloaked figure and fought the sudden urge to ride after her. He would have the entire troop of soldiers following him if he attempted that. And as loyal to his king as he might be, his loyalty to his friend was greater. He could not betray him.

The rush of excitement brought on by outwitting the soldiers quickly gave way to panic as Eileen drove her mare down forest paths. Her mount was swifter, and she knew shortcuts that Quigley and Drake did not, but too much time had elapsed. She knew it instinctively. Drake had almost certainly reached the coast by now, if he had not been caught by troops patrolling the road. The thought of either possibility made her urge the mare to gallop faster. The picture of the ship sailing without her, its huge sails filled with wind, taking Drake a world away, bloomed vividly in her mind. She could not let him go.

But go he would. He had told her he did not want her with him. He had made it clear he wished only the one night with her. His sense of honor, if nothing else, would force him to board that ship and leave her behind. If he loved her, truly loved her, he would damn honor and wait, but how could he know she would follow? He could hang if he waited.

Tears streaming down her face, hair whipping in the wind, Eileen began to pray he had reached the ship and sailed safely. There could be troops all over the coast by now. She would follow as she could, just let him be safe.

Praying insensibly for conflicting desires, Eileen galloped from greenwood to flat land, over scrub fields to coastal lowlands, avoiding the highway. For almost as long as she could remember, she had lived on her own, done as she pleased, without regard to anyone. In some mysterious way Drake had changed all that, and now he was disappearing from her life without giving her a chance to explore the new life she had glimpsed in his arms. For all she knew, it might be a worse one, but how would she know if she didn't explore it? How could she turn back now?

She couldn't. Coming to the top of a rise that would take her down into the coastal village where the Drews lived, Eileen spied the small ship sailing off toward the morning sun, its brave sails whipping smartly in the April wind. All around it, the waters sparkled blue and silver, and gulls screeched happily in its wake. He was gone. He was safe. But she could not turn back.

Tears dry and cold, Eileen guided the winded horse down the rocky path. Her heart weighed in her chest like one of the boulders littering the field, but she had to know. Perhaps he had left some word for her, some place that she might reach him. Surely he had not sailed without leaving some farewell.

A patrol of red-coated soldiers watched as the forlorn figure crept down the side of the hill to the village. Here was no dangerous fugitive fleeing justice and hiding in shadows. No muskets bristled from her saddle. No sword gleamed in the brilliant sunlight. If they wondered over the oddity of a modestly dressed maid on a mount of obvious quality, they gave it little thought. The night had been a long and miserable one. They were drenched to the bone and shivering in the chill breeze. The fire in front of them presented more temptation than the lone rider.

Unmindful of their regard, Eileen rode slowly into the village and down to the pier. She led her horse into the crude shanty beside the tavern, protecting it from the brisk sea breezes. A boy appeared from the shadows and with the promise of a coin began to remove the saddle and rub down the mare. No other horse was in sight. Quigley must already be returning to the Hall. They would be searching for her shortly.

Once on her feet, Eileen moved quickly to the back door of the inn. The Drews would have seen him last. They could tell her how he looked, what he said. Just the prospect of this small shred of news lifted her hopes, and she stepped lightly through the open door.

The sun didn't reach into this windowless cavern, and Eileen hesitated in the entryway with its litter of mops and brooms and discarded pans and bottles. Figures moved in the shadowy interior, and she gave herself time to adjust to the light. The smell of fresh bread mixed with the stench of sour ale and drifted out on the morning breeze. The murmur of voices brought her farther through the small entryway and closer to the inhabited kitchen.

"We can't be waiting much longer. The tide will turn," a man's voice protested, but not loudly.

Eileen heard no reply and hesitated before entering the kitchen. The bulk of Mr. Drew blocked her vision of the long trestle table on the far side of the room. In the dim light of the kitchen's one lantern, Mrs. Drew efficiently pounded dough on the board at the dry sink. The older woman glanced up expectantly as Eileen's slight shadow moved in the doorway. She broke into a broad grin but wisely kept silent as she followed the girl's gaze.

As Mr. Drew moved impatiently away from his visitor, Eileen could see the silhouette of a man staring out the kitchen's one window. Hands in pockets, broad shoulders squared tensely, he appeared to be fighting a desperate battle within himself while the older man looked on. Even in this dim light the golden light of his hair gleamed, tied now in a knot at his nape. Sir John's old coat hung shapelessly on him, but the lace gleaming from the sleeves was snowy white. Biting her lip, Eileen moved into the room as if in a trance.

At an exclamation from the innkeeper, Drake swung around. The new lines above his brow deepened as he noted the bulging satchel in her hand, but he could not control the flash of hope in his eyes as he advanced toward her.

"Eileen, I cannot let you do this," he warned.

In front of the Drews, she could not speak, but she lifted her chin defiantly, her eyes challenging him.

Drake did not need the words; he could read them in her eyes. He could not stop her. If he sailed on this ship, she would follow on the next. He dared not let her know the joy exploding in bursts of fireworks within him.

"Them soldiers are looking this way. We have to move," Mortimer Drew warned from somewhere in the shadows. "The lass will be blamed if we leave her here. Come on with you, now."

With the decision taken from him, Drake grabbed the heavy satchel from Eileen's hands and propelled her toward the door. He would pay the consequences later.

Chapter XV

———— ❦ ————

England–France
April–May, 1746

There was little the miserable patrol of soldiers could
do as the swift sloop glided onto the sparkling waters
without halting at their command. They came running
at a breakneck pace, blasting their muskets at the
gleaming sails and cursing, but without a ship of their
own they were helpless. Drake would have laughed at
their frantic behavior had he not worries of his own.
Someone would receive a proper chastising for not
guarding the sleepy pier instead of sheltering from the
wind, but Eileen's safety concerned him more than the
soldier's plight.

Drake's worries mounted ever higher, but he would
not let Eileen know of it. Closing the door of the tiny
cabin behind him, he caught her slender waist in his
arms and held her close, content to let her slight body
assuage a hundred assorted wounds, easing the pain to
bearable.

"I knew you would come if I waited long enough,"
he whispered against her hair.

"Fool." Eileen wrapped her arms around his back,
clinging to the solidity of him she had thought lost to
her. "What if they had searched the tavern as they did
the Hall? I could have taken another ship." Now that
he was safe, she could scold him freely for doing what

she had prayed he would do. If the whole world be mad, so must she be.

At her words Drake allowed himself a smile. He had known that, too, but she had no knowledge of the world's dangers. He would protect her where he could. Not from knowledge perhaps. That was beyond his capacity with one of her eager curiosity, but from the dangers. He kissed her forehead and wished fervently that things could have been different.

"The crew is short and I have promised to help them. Will you promise to stay below so I need not worry about your being blown overboard?" Drake asked jestingly, but his eyes no longer laughed as he stared down at her. He should never have brought her to this. She was willful, but not strong. Even now he could see smudges beneath the delicate skin of her eyes, and his hand came up to caress the fevered rose of her cheek. She had saved his life. He must take care of hers.

At his tender touch and concerned look, Eileen smiled and traced the hard line of his lips. She just wanted to touch, to look for a while, to be certain her dream had come true, but he was impatient to be off.

"Your shoulder?" she inquired softly.

"Aches like hell, but I'll survive. Get some rest, princess. I should not have been so hard on you last night."

A mischievous light leapt to her eyes, but she refrained from speaking her thought out loud. Instead she answered demurely, "You were just as you should be, my lord."

Drake grinned, reading the thought behind the words. "And you are a saucy wench. Do I have your promise to behave?"

"Just as I should do, of course, my lord," Eileen replied with just the right amount of sauce to indicate the behavior she had in mind.

For answer, Drake caught his fingers firmly in the

thick hair at the nape of her neck and tilted her head to meet his kiss. Her heated response nearly delayed his departure, but with a strength of will as great as her own, he tore away.

"There will be nothing left of us by the time we reach France," he muttered thickly before departing hurriedly to his duties.

Eileen held her fingers to her lips and stared at the door. The power of his need would have been enough to scare her had she allowed herself fear, but she did not. Instead, anticipation flowed through her veins, and even though she felt the soreness of the prior night, her body ached to hold his once again. He was right. They would devour each other before they reached France. There would be nothing left but ashes in the bed.

When he came to her at last, however, Drake was too exhausted to do more than fall into a heavy slumber. The strain of these last days and nights without sleep or proper food coupled with the physical energy required of a healthy sailor, let alone one who sported a wounded shoulder, had taken its toll. Pressed between the cabin wall and Drake's large physique, Eileen lay curled against his side and listened to his breathing, well satisfied to share this much.

Sometime in the early hours of dawn Drake woke to the movement of a soft hip brushing against his. He scarcely recalled collapsing into the bed, but memory returned quickly as his mind conjured up the image of long auburn tresses trailing across a chemise so fine it left every curve outlined like a second skin. Though she might be small in stature, her limbs were long and graceful, and his hands ached to slide along the long curve of her waist from rounded hips to temptingly full breasts. How nature had managed to mold such perfection in so tiny a package was well beyond Drake's ken, but he knew how to appreciate perfection.

Turning on his side, he cradled her small frame within the curve of his. His hand explored the satin texture of her bare arm while his lips sought the sensitive skin behind her shell-like ear. He sensed she woke as his kisses trailed along her throat, but he held her firmly, leisurely enjoying the gift she gave him. His hand traveled from her arm to the supple curve of her breast, caressing the fullness through the thin linen. Her soft buttock snuggled closer, bringing her in contact with his aroused hardness, and Drake groaned slightly as his hunger sent aching waves of desire through his loins. "Eileen, my sweeting, I hope you know what you do." He gasped as her wiggles brought the chemise up above her hips and flesh met flesh with agonizing heat.

Knowing only that she brought him pleasure, Eileen felt the touch of his maleness between her thighs with piercing delight. His fingers played feverishly with the hardened points of her breast, causing her to squirm more, until she felt him touching the chafed opening between her thighs, and it was her turn to moan.

Before she could take advantage of this new position, Drake caught her shoulders and pushed her down against the crude sheet. His kisses burnt like small fires as he plundered her lips and drank deeply of the sweet wine of her mouth. Slowly, intoxicatingly, he slid her chemise above the full curves of her breasts until his mouth could fasten on the erect nipples.

Convulsed by desire, Eileen instinctively wrapped her legs around Drake's powerful hips. In doing so, she recognized her vulnerability, but she was beyond shame now. She opened herself eagerly to his thrust, and he obliged with a power that left her gasping for breath.

His body carried her away to a place that had no beginning, no end, just this swirling center of rising passion that carried them to heights undreamed of even in her vivid imagination.

Long after, Drake's kisses spread butterfly wings across her cheek, and his hand possessively fondled her breast. Eileen felt him stirring once more inside her, and she held her breath to capture the sensation. But sensitive to the damage he had caused, Drake rolled to his side, carrying her with him.

"I never knew one woman could give so much pleasure," Drake's voice murmured huskily against her ear.

"You are in the custom of using two?" Eileen inquired sweetly, jealous of all the other lovers he had taken to his bed, hating the one to whom he was promised.

Drake pinched her buttocks and enjoyed the sensation of hardened nipples pressing against his chest as he drew her closer. She squirmed in protest, but she had already learned the error of those methods. She quieted immediately as his masculinity responded to such provocation.

"You will wish you were two so one can rest if you continue those tactics, princess," Drake promised. "I fear I will cause you some damage if I'm too hasty in enjoying the delights you offer me. Lie still and let us both sleep a while longer."

Mutinously she tried to escape his hold, but Drake had no intention of letting her go. He had her trapped where he wanted her, and his gentle caresses soon tamed her skittish ways. She curled contentedly within his embrace, and he lightly kissed her forehead, but he did not sleep. The problems of exile kept his mind in a turmoil, and not the least of them lay unsuspectingly in his arms.

Their ride from Calais to Versailles was under considerably reduced circumstances from their last trip to France. Eileen's small store of coins were barely sufficient to buy cartfare and put roofs over their head. It was too early in the season even to steal food from the fields, and they lived on porridge and stale bread for much of their journey. Content so long as Drake lay at her side each night, Eileen worried only that Drake's once elegant clothes would be gone before they reached the court. How would they appear before his mother's relations if they came in clothes fit only for beggars?

Drake concerned himself not with his looks, but the best manner in which to plan his attack against Edmund. He needed access to pen and paper and legal counsel. He must find a way to let Diane know he had arrived safely, set up some kind of communication where they could correspond freely without the danger of his letters being intercepted. Once Edmund was exposed as the traitorous bastard he suspected, the lawyers could disentangle the skeins of legal yarn keeping him from his home and bed.

Drake did not try to worry Eileen over these details. The fact that she was here beside him complicated matters greatly. Michael would have managed his estates with some degree of efficiency in his absence, had Eileen not eloped with him. Now he could no longer rely on one of his closest friends, and the estate could be in jeopardy if Edmund returned to take over the reins. He did not resent Eileen for the complication, but worried over the best means of solving it.

Eileen had a vague sense of his withdrawal as the days wore on, but it was not to be expected that Drake would be happy with this present state of affairs. She missed his laughter, and his silly tales dwindled to a halt, but he still held her tight in whatever bed they found for the night. She could ask for nothing more.

They arrived in Versailles in May. Their dusty, travel-weary clothing contrasted sharply with the brilliant, sun-drenched walks and profusion of sweet-smelling flowers. Eileen stared at the glittering splendor of the golden carriage gates and wished desperately to turn around and retrace her steps. She had no experience with courts and palaces. She could scarcely speak the language.

Drake led her to a small inn where they ordered baths with their last four coins. The innkeeper regarded Drake's noble carriage and ill-fitting clothes with suspicion, but he asked no questions. Gentlemen garbed in furs and velvet were as likely to pinch a coin as ones garbed like gypsies. Sooner or later they all appeared with beautiful women on their arms, and this one was scruffy enough to need a bath. Couldn't blame the gentleman there.

Eileen giggled as the last maid scurried from the room with her empty bucket. Drake had already stripped to the waist and eyed the hot water with eagerness. He turned his questioning glare to his companion.

"There is some cause to laugh at the sight of a tub of water? The first tub, I might add, that we have seen in some weeks?"

Silver eyes lifted in merriment to the sunburned expanse of Drake's broad shoulders and neck before rising farther to inspect the matted filth of his golden hair. Boldly she began to unbutton the bodice of her gown, knowing full well the old chemise she wore did little to cover the swell of her breasts.

"My French is very limited, but I think the maids are saying rather naughty things about our intentions to bathe together."

Drake gave a tired grin and eyed the progress of her unbuttoning with a degree of interest. "There might be some truth to their suspicions in that. Are you going to take all day with all those furbelows?"

The plain gown had little to christen a furbelow, but Eileen dutifully unfastened the last hook and squirmed out of the bodice. The whalebone corset hampered her from reaching the laces of her skirt, so she set about untying the worn strings of the corset first.

With one stride Drake was across the room, his

patience worn to a frazzle by the sight of milk-white
breasts pushed to tempting peaks he could not quite
touch until the damned corset was disposed of. The thin
threads snapped beneath his impatience, and the
ties of her skirts and petticoats fared little better. The
frail chemise slithered to the floor, and with satisfaction he lifted her bodily from the floor and dropped
her into the waiting tub.

Eileen stared up in surprise as Drake hovered over
her, hands on narrow hips, blue eyes burning with a
fire she had not yet learned well enough. When he
began to unfasten the buttons of his breeches, her eyes
widened, and she dived for the cake of soap. Whatever he intended, she would have her bath first.

Never before had she seen him like this in the broad
light of day. With a shiver of fascination she watched
Drake surreptitiously as she doused her hair and worked
the soap through it. He paced the room like some
great naked beast, his lithe muscles moving with a
lion's grace as he emptied their bag of clothing to seek
out those reserved for this day. And when he turned
to see if she had completed her bathing yet, Eileen
realized bathing was not all he had on his mind.

She handed him the pitcher and smiled sweetly.
"Would you help me with my hair, please?"

Drake growled something incomprehensible and knelt
beside the tub to pour the cooling water over long
auburn tresses. Her hair slid cleanly through his fingers as he worked out the soap, and the sensation
inspired the urge for further exploration. Her satin
skin slipped just as smoothly through his hands as he
reached for her, but his grip caught sure and firm
around the dripping tininess of her waist when he
lifted her from the tub.

Eileen gave a small shriek of surprise as she found
herself suspended in the warm air of the upper-story
room, but a small laugh of pleasure escaped a moment
later when she found herself seated in Drake's naked

lap with the waters lapping around them. The blaze of his eyes made it apparent she had tested his patience too far, but anything was better than being ignored.

"If you wish me to wash your back, you are turned the wrong way, my lord." Eileen eyed his furred chest dubiously.

"It is not my back so much as your front that interests me, simpleton. Why do woman hide themselves behind those damned contraptions?" Not waiting for a reply, he bent to lick a water droplet from one exposed peak.

"Drake, you cannot!" Eileen protested, tugging his unbound hair. "There is no room and you will splash water all over . . ." The rest of her words turned to squeals as he proved he not only could but would.

Eileen gave a deep sigh of contentment several minutes later as his seed exploded deep inside of her, filling her with a delicious warmth. The first bruises of their lovemaking had faded, but the soothing waters gave this coupling an erotic sensation she had not yet experienced. She leaned her head against his wet chest and lightly kissed his healing shoulder.

"You are a wicked man, my lord."

"And you a wanton woman." With a twitch of guilt Drake lifted her from him, his hands lingering below her breasts. "Dry yourself quickly. We must find my uncle before he departs for the evening."

He watched with regret as she wrapped herself in a length of linen and began drying her hair. Not once had she spoken words of love or marriage, words any other woman in her place would have spouted with increasing frequency. Eileen demanded nothing of him, but Drake's guilt demanded everything for her. He could offer nothing. He should never have allowed her to come. She would be branded a traitor surely as he, barred from her home and decent society, kept from the respectable marriage she could have made. All because of his selfishness.

In time, she would begin to realize what he had done to her, and resentment would surely follow. He must be prepared for that eventuality also. She had spent too many years deprived of her proper home. Somehow he would see her restored to it, even if he could not follow.

Unaware of these preparations for her future, Eileen continued to dry her hair in the warm sun. They had saved their best clothes for this day so they would not appear as the beggars they were. The coat and breeches of Drake's that she had laundered were still in wearable condition, although the bloodied shirt and waistcoat had had to be discarded. But with Sir John's clean linen and lace, he would appear sufficiently respectable. His relations ought to be quite accustomed to seeing him without a wig or powder.

For herself she had brought one good gown of fine silk, almost too fine for cool spring nights, but it traveled well. She had only the one petticoat and no panniers to wear under it so she would appear quite provincial, but that bothered Eileen little. Aware that Drake was now rising from the tub, she had only one qualm, and that was too minor to mention. Men kept mistresses all the time, and these people did not know her family. She did not have to hide what she was.

He came to her after he had dried himself, lifting her from the stool with one arm and turning her around so he could kiss her cheek and chin and all along the edge of her mouth before firmly taking possession of that which was only his to claim. The luxury of kissing her like this, whenever and however he wanted, eased much of the immediate pain of his losses. This was a wealth that could not be stolen from him, and Drake savored it gladly.

Touching her cheek, Drake gazed down into the cloudy gray of her eyes. "Nervous, my love?"

Eileen shook her head, not tearing her eyes from his beautifully sculpted face, the strong cheekbones, the flexible mouth that gave her such pleasure. She wished she possessed the skill to paint portraits or carve figures from rock. A portrait, she decided suddenly, only a portrait would do him justice, capture the magnificent gold of his hair, color the light in his eyes. How she wished she had that talent.

"Will you do me one favor, princess?" Drake drew his thumb lightly down her cheek, knowing if his hand should wander farther they would end up paying a night's lodging.

Eileen gazed at him questioningly, and he smiled at her silence. Old habits died hard. For that reason alone he would ask what he did.

"Will you not hide behind your silence here? Let me protect you, not your silence. I want you to be happy here."

Eileen had not given it much thought. Her response to the world had always been a silent one. There had been no use in speaking to others in this strange country, for she had little use of the language. She had allowed Drake to speak for both of them throughout their journey. Now he asked that she rejoin the world on her own, and a moment's panic swallowed her up.

"I cannot speak the language," she protested faintly. "I can take care of myself. You do not need to worry—"

Drake clamped his hand over her mouth. "My uncle speaks English. You will answer him when he speaks to you. You protect no one with your silence now, and you will most likely draw considerable attention if you continue with it. Is that what you want?"

She understood. Rumors of a mute girl at the French court would most certainly be relayed back to her aunt and uncle by malicious tongues. She had caused them enough grief, she would not cause them that one. Eileen nodded.

Drake smiled with relief and reached for his clothes. "Good. I would not wish to exert my authority by paddling you here. It would confirm all of the maids' naughty suspicions."

With a gasp of outrage Eileen wreaked revenge with a pinch to his bare posterior. At Drake's yelp she dashed to the far side of the room and grabbed up her clothes. "Don't come any closer or I'll run from the room just like this. Then let the naughty maids think what they will."

Drake growled and eyed her with suspicion. "It is not the maids I fear, in that case. You will have more male attention than you will know how to handle. I am a jealous man, princess. You would not ask me to kill half the male population of Versailles before we even make our introductions?"

Eileen regarded him with no small amount of awe as she realized he half meant what he said. The way Lady Pamela played fast and loose, she'd had no idea jealousy was in his nature. Perhaps he jested, but she was in no hurry to find out. She had no desire to see a duel over her.

"If you are going to be a tyrant, I fear I have made a grave mistake," she replied with as much dignity as she could muster while pulling her chemise over her head.

Drake grinned as a cluster of tousled curls popped out from the neckline. With an effort he began tugging on his breeches. She would make it damned difficult for him to remain decent if she continued her teasing ways.

"By the time I return you to your uncle, you will be a well behaved young lady instead of a wild heathen," he countered.

Laughter made unholy lights of her eyes as she observed the reason for his difficulty in donning his breeches. "On the contrary, my lord," she replied loftily, "by the time we return to England, you will be a wild heathen instead of a pompous curmudgeon."

Her laughter chimed through open windows as the

contents of the bed flew at her with all the vigor of an enraged man.

All memory of that temporary respite of laughter fled as an elegantly clad servant ushered them into the presence of Drake's French uncle. After gazing upon the rich red and gold satin of the servant's livery, his curled and powdered wig, and cynically lifted eyebrow, Eileen knew her precautions over her appearance were all for naught. Her simple silk over one rumpled petticoat might as well be a meal sack in the grandeur of this palace. Even Sherbourne did not compare.

To give him credit, Drake's uncle did not so much as lift an eyebrow as he welcomed his nephew warmly and met Eileen's introduction with politeness. Drake's coat and lace were much the worse for the time spent in a satchel, and the harsh lines creasing his brow were new, but the French nobleman made no comment on appearances. The disaster at Culloden had been whispered about widely. If his nephew had chosen to join the fray, he had obviously backed the losing party, rightly or wrongly.

"It is a pleasure to see you, Drake." The comte indicated a seat and poured wine from a decanter, offering it to his guests. "Perhaps you can explain why those two miscreants of my sister's appeared on my doorstep last week babbling of abductions and harrowing escapades with death."

Drake's relief was plain as he accepted the glass. "Then they are safe. I feared they would have found their way back in time to lose themselves in that massacre at Culloden."

The comte's expression was grim. "I take it, then, that you arranged for them to be conveniently away from the scene. I thank you for that. I trust you have not come to tell me you went in their place? As much as I would have liked to see the arrogant fool win, Charles Stuart never had a chance."

"I was not there, no, but there are those prepared to swear I was. Without Lady Eileen's assistance, I could very well be in the Tower by now. She has lost her home and family in aiding me. For her sake, I beg your assistance in seeking justice."

The comte's gaze swept from his nephew to the silent girl trying desperately to disappear into the woodwork. Her slightness and undistinguished garb had left him unimpressed earlier. Now he looked at her more closely, noting the natural grace of her stance, the aristocratic fineness of her features, and the fascinating light-colored eyes that seemed to absorb everything around them. He spoke to her in lightly accented English.

"If what Drake tells me is true, I owe you a debt beyond my ability to pay, my lady. My nephew is very important to me. I will do everything within my power to restore you to your home. Meanwhile, I insist you stay in my humble abode. I will find a maid to assist you while you are here. Is there anything you wish to ask of me, any way in which I can reward you for your services to my nephew?" His gaze was shrewd as he watched Eileen's reactions.

She paled slightly and glanced at Drake, but he had retreated to some remote corner of his soul and did no more than wait patiently for her reply. Eileen felt more alone than she had ever been in her life, but under Drake's stare she managed a reply.

"I ask nothing for myself, thank you, sir." She wondered what the appropriate title of respect would be for this lofty personage, but lacking knowledge of French etiquette, she settled for this one.

The comte made no effort to hide his smile at the innocence of her reply. He rung a bell close at hand and while waiting for the footman to return, commented, "Perhaps you will think of something later.

You look tired. I will have someone show you to your room."

As Eileen silently followed the servant out, Drake sipped his wine and waited for his uncle's usual candid observations. He did not have long to wait. The comte swung on him as soon as the door closed upon Eileen and the servant.

"She could have asked for your hand in marriage and I would have given it to her. Do you intend to tell me you have left her untouched? She is but a child."

Drake met his uncle's gaze calmly. "Eileen has never been a child, unless you wish to call her a child of nature. She does as she pleases. If she had asked for marriage, I would have given it, against my better judgment. I cannot rightly ask Eileen to share my exile. She needs protection more powerful than I can offer if she is to return home. The best I can give her is her freedom."

The comte frowned but took a seat and waited for the full story. Knowing his nephew, he had no doubt it would be a good one.

Several days later, Drake woke to the sunlight peering through the open casement of Eileen's chamber, and he allowed himself a small smile at this evidence of his companion's love of the outdoors. Turning on his side, he gazed admiringly on the flushed, sleeping features of the woman in the bed beside him. Her fingers had curled into fists beside her cheek, and the smooth roundness of her arm hid much of the curve of her breasts as she lay pressed against him. He had taught her the uselessness of nightclothes, and she lay naked to his gaze, only the thick lengths of auburn hair protecting her.

She was the one glorious promise in the ruins that had become his future, but Drake knew better than to think he possessed her. It would be akin to bottling moonlight or sunshine. For whatever reasons, she had chosen to come with him. She could as easily decide to leave. For her own sake, she ought to leave.

Not wishing to contemplate a world without sunshine, Drake bent to brush a soft kiss across her shoulder, then steeled himself for the day ahead. He could not allow his longing for this ephemeral sprite to hamper his fight for what was rightfully his. His passion for Eileen was a personal indulgence and had no part in the political battle he must wage to retrieve his lands and title for the sake of his family. Too many people depended on him to allow his feelings to enter the matter. Without another glance to the sleeping woman in the bed, Drake rose to dress.

He was gone when Eileen awoke. She turned and hugged the still warm pillow until the maid arrived. She knew Drake had returned to the apartment his uncle had provided for him in another wing of the house, but if he thought he were protecting her name, he was fooling only himself. Eileen stretched and wrapped the sheet around her while the maid explored her desolate wardrobe. Without any other occupation to fill their time, the inhabitants of the tight court circle lived on gossip. Even understanding very little of the language, Eileen knew she had been labeled Drake's mistress from the start.

The maid gave a cry of delight and produced a charming day gown of pale green silk and yellow ribbons with matching petticoat. Eileen stared at the finery with bewilderment. It had not been there yesterday, though to be fair, she had not hung up her clothing last night after Drake had come to her room. She would not have seen it if it had been there.

She touched the shimmering silk with admiration, wanting desperately to wear it so Drake would be proud of her. Perhaps he had bought it for her, meaning it as a surprise. But she knew the sorry state of their finances and could not imagine anyone letting him have it on credit. His uncle possibly. She wished

Drake were here. Would he disapprove if she wore a gown he had not provided?

Shrugging, Eileen allowed the maid to dress her. However it had come there, the gown fit perfectly, and she felt better in wearing it. She did not wish to shame Drake with her dowdiness. She prayed he understood. Men were so odd about these things.

She should not have worried. When she entered the downstairs hall, Drake scarcely gave her attire a second look. Deep in serious discussion with one of his uncle's men of business, he gave Eileen a perfunctory kiss on the forehead and wished her good day before disappearing into the mysterious depths of the book-lined study. She could have thrown something at him.

Instead she accepted the arm of a gallant courtier and, with nose in air, proceeded to take the air in the glorious gardens of Versailles.

Chapter XVI

——— ❧ ———

July, 1746
Versailles

The heat of a July day had already built to stifling
proportions in this upper story room, and Eileen fought
a wave of nausea as she turned too swiftly at the
maid's rap. Automatically she reached for the pillow
beside her—to find it empty, again.

Her head hurt and her stomach felt as if last night's
scallops had risen from the grave to dance with crazed
madness through her innards. She should never have
indulged in all that wine, but while Drake spent his
time at the gaming table, she could find little other
entertainment.

Groaning permission for the little maid to enter,
Eileen slowly dragged herself upright. She should not
complain of Drake's occupation with the gaming tables; it was their sole source of income over and above
his uncle's generosity. But she could not live like this
much longer. She had no place here, and neither did
Drake.

It had all been a mistake; she could see that now.
While the maid brushed and untangled her long tresses,
Eileen stared out the window to the emerald lawns of
the palace in the distance, trying to clear her head to
think. In these last months, Drake had grown so
occupied with his legal entanglements and political
maneuvering, he had become a stranger to her, except

in bed. Now even that was coming to an end. Her
complaint of illness earlier this week had prompted
him to return to his own chambers so she might rest.
He had not returned to her bed since then.

Sighing, Eileen stood to allow the corset to be
strapped around her, holding her breath so the maid
could cinch it to the proper size for her new bodice.
She did not know where these new gowns came from
and feared to ask. Drake surely could not have the
coins for the exquisite silks and laces that kept appearing from time to time in her chambers. But whoever
sent them would soon have to allow for more width in
the seams.

Gazing down at the results of the maid's tight lac-
ing, Eileen finally had to acknowledge what she had
tried not to think about these last weeks. Her breasts
had always been full and high, but the valley between
them now had grown narrower and deeper until the
filmy bodice barely covered them with any decency.
They ached, and she certainly could not blame Drake
for that after these last nights alone. The nausea had
little to do with a surfeit of wine and much to do with
her own ignorance. She had known there were ways to
prevent what had happened, but she had not known
the details. Nor was there anyone here she could ask.
By the time Drake had thought to take precautions, it
had obviously been too late.

The gold silk floated softly around her, pulled out in
a train of pleats at the back, fitting snugly in a deep V
in front, her modesty maintained by a stomacher of
fine lace. Staring at herself in the gilt-framed mirror,
Eileen wondered if the change was noticeable to anyone but herself. The maid had dressed her hair in a
simple coronet at the back of her head and adorned it
with a frilly cap of lace and matching ribbon, and she
appeared as much a lady as those elegants below, but
she knew she had no claim to such title. Without even
the dubious claim to her rightful name here, she was

merely the mistress of an exiled English marquess. Without Drake she had not even that position. She had no identity here beyond his. She understood enough of the French court to know without Drake's protection she was fair game to idle courtiers. The time had come to make some decision.

With determined tread her small feet led her down marble stairs and gilded halls to the heat of a July afternoon. The house of Drake's uncle had just begun to stir and no one interfered with her path. She had deliberately chosen to make these hours her own, and she would make the most of them.

Drake had kept her supplied with pencils and papers and what colors he could find. She could thank him for that much courtesy. She had probably much to thank him for, and only herself to blame for following him here. He had told her not to come. He had known she did not belong here, and he had been right. She had no place among these proud peacocks, no common interests to share with them. She had only Drake and her painting.

She had to admit that the spectacular lawns and fountains made magnificent new subjects for her brushes, but their perpetual perfection had already begun to pall. Seeing the treasures hidden away in obscure corners of the palace had been a breathtaking experience, but she had never been allowed the pleasure of exploring the halls alone. Someday she would like to sneak past the guards and prowl those magnificent rooms without the distraction of a thousand laughing, gossiping people around her.

But that time would never come. Setting up her easel with purposeful finality, Eileen faced the triumphant fountain of Apollo for what she hoped would be the last time. Tonight she would speak with Drake, and in the morning she would be gone.

She treasured no romantic notions that he would beg her to stay. Regaining his lands had become an obsession, and she could not blame him for that in the least. What word they had received from Diane had not been reassuring, and the fate of Sherbourne's tenants lay as delicately in balance as Diane's own. The court had allowed Diane to remain in possession of the Hall and had not given Edmund possession of the title—yet. That would come when Drake was tried and found guilty in absentia. His barristers had postponed the trial these past weeks and more, but surely their excuses must be wearing thin. And still no one had come forward to state Drake's innocence. No witnesses could be found, no evidence given.

Eileen had no heart for Apollo rising from the waters. Instead of sunshine and sparkling waters, her fingers ached to paint darkness and shadows. Nothing had turned out as she had thought. She would have been satisfied to live in a cottage and paint leaves for a living, but Drake would never be happy with so simple a role. All his life he had yearned to take on the responsibility of the Sherbourne estates, to carry out those practices he and his father had argued over for so many years. Then just when he had thought to see his dreams come to fruition, they had been torn from his grasp with a violence that would not let him rest easy. He was a man who would fight to the death for what was his, and not measure his losses.

A shadow covered her canvas, and with annoyance Eileen glanced up to the intruder. The Comte d'Avignon stood admiring her handiwork, though she suspected his gaze had only just discovered the subject of her painting. It fell more frequently on her person, and she had devoted much time to discouraging these attentions. She not only found him physically repugnant but intellectually and morally lacking. She was no saint, but the rumors of his debaucheries left Eileen with the desire to cleanse herself whenever she left his presence.

"You are quite talented, *mademoiselle*. I would like

to display some of your efforts at my home in Paris. I am known to a number of artists there who would be interested in seeing your work."

He spoke English with only a slight accent, but Eileen responded in execrable French. "Thank you, *monsieur*, but I paint only for my own pleasure."

Her cold tones did little to discourage his confidence. "You are being modest. It does not become you. You are a beautiful woman with a marvelous talent. In Paris you could exploit your assets to the fullest and enjoy a life of ease and pleasure. Why hide yourself behind modesty?"

"Sir, I resent your intrusion. Please leave me." Eileen refused to so much as look at his sagging, wig-framed face. He was a large man, not corpulent but physically imposing. She suspected corsets kept the rest of him from sagging as his jowls did, but she had no desire to find out. She wished him to hell for disturbing these few moments of privacy.

A cold hand came to rest on her nape and played with a shining wisp of deep auburn that had escaped its pins. "You are not stupid, I think, *ma cherie*. Your *amour* has grown restless and will soon seek greener pastures. I can be of great assistance to you in keeping him or revenging him, as you please."

Cold horror stole along Eileen's spine, and she rose hastily, packing up her paints. "*Au contraire, monsieur*, I can take care of such things without your help."

Before the comte could object, a cold voice of steel cut through the argument.

"I believe the lady has asked you to leave, François. I'd suggest you listen to her in the future."

Eileen swung around. Drake stood with hand on hilt of his sword, his cheek taut with anger as he glared at the older man. Without the laughter, his eyes looked bleak and cold, and he appeared perfectly capable of severing the comte's offending hand. Avignon had a reputation with a sword, but not the hasty anger of a younger man. He nodded arrogantly to the English lord.

"We are discussing art, Sherbourne. I suspect your appreciation is a shallow one. Good day." He strode off, swinging his gold-handled cane, the gold braid of his elegantly tailored coat glittering in the sun.

"The old roué," Drake muttered, releasing his sword. "You should not encourage that bastard, Eileen."

"Encourage!" Eileen swung on this hard-faced stranger with the ferocity of anger and disgust. "The next time I shall take a knife to his corset strings and see if that encourages him! You are a fine one to talk, my lord. You leave me alone to the company of the likes of that one while you dally with the king's mistress, and you tell me not to encourage the bastard! Go to hell, Drake Neville!"

Irrationally leaving her easel but grabbing her bag of paints, Eileen stalked off, ignoring Drake's shout behind her.

Drake glared after her departing figure, refusing to chase after her. He knew full well she could take care of herself, but the sight of Avignon's hands on her had raised his unreasoning anger, one that haunted his nights and swallowed his days. He had to get Eileen out of here before he killed someone.

With more than enough time to think on it, Drake knew what he must do, but persuading the willful brat would not come easily. And he had certainly not stepped out on the right foot this morning. Her temper had grown shorter than his lately, making it nigh impossible to carry on a rational conversation. But he would have to tell her soon.

Watching Eileen's golden skirts disappear from view, Drake felt the ache of loneliness tugging at his heart. The little enchantress had wormed her way into every fiber of his being. Without her he would be an empty shell. To give her up would be akin to carving out his heart, but it had to be done. Neither of them could go on like this much longer. It was only a matter of time before his temper would outrace his reason and he would kill one of those fawning bastards hanging around Eileen like cats around cream. He had not the time nor the patience to protect her, and, in any case, he could not remain here much longer. He could not take her with him where he was going, either. There was only one place he felt safe in leaving her. She would hate him for it, but there was no other choice. The letter had already been sent.

Eileen had sent her own letters long ago and sorely regretted her hastiness now. When it had just been herself to protect, it had seemed the most expedient solution. Now she had this tiny seed growing within her, and the complications impending were overwhelming. Perhaps her letter had never arrived. She had heard no reply nor seen any results. It would be just as well if it had never been sent.

Flinging her bag to the floor of her chamber, she stared at the small writing desk in the corner. Threatening Lord de Lacy had not been an intelligent thing to do at all, but she had been desperate at the time. She did not know for certain if de Lacy could force Edmund to admit Drake's innocence, but she strongly suspected de Lacy could do almost anything given enough reason. Threatening to expose him as a murderer and rapist seemed sufficient reason.

But it had been a stupid, stupid thing to do. She had burned all her bridges behind her. She could never return to Summer Hall now. He would be waiting for her. She had worked too hard to keep the Summervilles out of this to bring ruin upon them now. De Lacy would not find her in Versailles, but she could not stay here any longer. She had to consider what was in the best interests of the child. Drake's child.

Eileen sat down abruptly on the bed, still shaking with the wonder of it. She had vaguely known what

came of lying with a man, but she had given little
thought to the consequences. The idea of having a
child had always interested her, but the reality added
new dimensions. She wished to know more, but she
could talk to no one here if she would keep Drake
from knowing. That she had resolved to do already.
He had too many burdens to carry still another.

She lay back against the pillows and closed her eyes.
Things had been so much easier when she had only
herself to consider. She disliked hurting her aunt and
uncle, but Drake would probably be relieved to see
her go. Perhaps she could find some way to write the
Summervilles after the child was born. They would
worry, elsewise.

Thinking these thoughts, Eileen drifted off to sleep.

Drake found her there a while later. The taut set of
his jaw relaxed as he gazed down into the innocence of
her sleeping features. He missed waking beside her,
turning to find her copper hair spread across the pillows, her soft breath stirring the hairs along his arm as
he reached for her. She always came willingly, even
from the depths of sleep, but he dared not try that
now.

Gently sitting on the bed's edge, Drake bent to
loosen her gown and corset so she might sleep easier.
These late nights must have been taking their toll for
her to sleep during the day. Or perhaps, like himself,
she slept poorly alone. It would not do to linger on
that thought long.

Eileen stirred as the corset came undone, but she
did not wake. It would be so easy to remove her
bodice and wake her to his needs, but Drake kept
stern control over these urges. He had spent weeks
worrying when she showed no sign of her monthly
flux. He had tried to protect her from that fate, but no
method was flawless. So his relief when she had declared herself "ill" had taught him the height of his
foolishness. Now that he knew her to be safe from the

final humiliation, he must send her away. He had no other choice.

Rising from the bed, Drake kept his fists clenched to his side. Someday he would make his cousin pay for this. But before that day came, he must clear his own slate. All trace of youthful merriment fled the tired lines of Drake's face as he strode out the door.

Eileen stood beneath the magnificent ceiling painting in the Salon of Hercules and tried not to crane her neck to look upward in this glittering crowd. As magnificent as Louis's court might be, she could not appreciate it while balancing a glass of champagne in one hand and fending off amorous suitors with another. If somehow she could rid the palace of these multitudes, she might have time to admire the impressive artwork on the walls and ceilings. The works of Veronese in this room Drake had assured her were masterpieces of Venetian art, but she could get no closer to the one over the fireplace without stumbling into a group of bewigged men arguing over whether Charles Stuart had escaped or would return to Paris. The one on the opposite wall hid behind the elaborate and outdated headdress of a marquise. Sighing, Eileen wandered into the banqueting room.

She had not seen Drake since he had escorted her here earlier in the evening. Except for the opportunity to explore the artwork, she would have preferred to be left behind. What purpose had she at a court reception if he did not need her by his side?

Remembering her state of undress when she had woke from her nap, Eileen hurriedly turned to study the small sculpture on the table behind her. Surely only Drake would have dared to unlace her like that, but why had he stopped there? Had she become so little to him that she presented no further temptation? Could what she had mistaken for love die so easily?

It would not do to dwell on it. She must be grateful

she had retained her independence. These poor women who could not exist without a man at their sides must lead hellish lives. With a cynical glance to the king's latest mistress, Jeanne Poisson—now the Marquise de Pompadour—Eileen moved on. The woman had done everything but throw herself at the king's feet just to claim the position of mistress. Perhaps Louis really did love her, but Eileen doubted such an emotion touched the heart of that calculating lady. It would be wise to stay in La Pompadour's good graces.

For herself, she preferred the freedom of the countryside. It would not be easy, but she need only depend on herself. The surge of loneliness that thought engendered prompted Eileen to face the crowd once more.

She regretted the move instantly. The Comte d'Avignon bore down on her, accompanied by a middle-aged man in a long, flowing wig and an air of distraction. Drake did not know what he did when he left her alone like this. She had learned to fend for herself at an early age, perhaps, but not in the polite parlors of society. She had no sophisticated escape from lecherous aristocrats. She wished violently for the jeweled girdles of medieval times so she might keep her dagger at her side. This revealing gown of bronze silk and lace concealed no hiding place.

"Ah, my pet, I have someone here you might wish to meet. Monsieur Boucher, Mademoiselle de Lacy, the young artist of whom I have spoken."

"Ah, *oui*, mademoiselle." Monsieur Boucher bent politely over her hand, but his mind evidently strayed elsewhere. Eileen watched as his gaze searched among the crowds around her.

"You know of Boucher, of course, do you not?" the comte demanded. "His work is well-known in Paris, and he once taught Madame Pompadour. The king may commission him for her portrait."

Of course. That was why the poor man seemed so

totally distracted. A commission from the king would make his reputation. What interest could an artist like Boucher have in her pitiful dabbling when he could be speaking with kings? Eileen frowned haughtily.

"Then by all means, Comte, take Monsieur Boucher to the king, not to me. I can commission him for nothing."

She swung around and nearly collided with the tall, exceptionally handsome man just entering the room from the vestibule of the Staircase of Ambassadors. People around her began to drop into deep curtsies and bows, and instinctively Eileen hastened to do the same.

Kingly in demeanor but oddly reserved in manner, the new arrival accepted his subjects' obeisance only briefly before turning his back on the room and lifting Eileen to meet his gaze.

"And who are you recommending to me for commissioning?" Louis gave a wry smile as he observed the flustered grace of the pretty bird in his hands.

"Monsieur Boucher, Your Majesty," Eileen stammered, managing to catch the drift of his clipped French. She had not been introduced to the king, but she had seen him frequently in large crowds. At the age of thirty-five, he had reigned for thirty years. He possessed a commanding presence but a gentle face, much like a little boy's. His smile was almost shy as he looked her over, but his knowledge of his own authority prevented his gaze from being anything less than assessing.

The comte immediately intruded, introducing Boucher and possessively taking Eileen's arm as he realized the king required introduction here also.

"And why would you recommend Monsieur Boucher to me, *mademoiselle*?" Speaking in a low, husky voice, Louis gave his nobleman a cold look and appropriated Eileen's hand before striding into the banqueting room. The comte quickly took the hint and dropped behind.

"Monsieur le comte recommends him, sire. He is said to be a fine artist."

The artist in question hovered just behind them, listening to their every word. Louis gestured for him to step forward.

"You paint portraits?"

"No, Your Majesty. I mean, yes, for you, Your Majesty."

Louis waved his hand in the direction of the reception room. "Then find Madame la Marquise and enquire as to whether your services would be accepted." With a regal wave he dismissed the man, then turned authoritatively to the nobleman at his side. "Avignon, if you have no further words for Mademoiselle de Lacy, I require her company."

"Of course, sire." The comte made a courtly bow before turning to address Eileen. "I shall see you later, mademoiselle?" The question contained a large dollop of self-assurance.

"I think not," Eileen replied frostily, but from the gleam in Avignon's eye she suspected he did not believe her. No one in the French court said what they meant or behaved as expected. Her forthright "no" seemed to contain nuances she had never dreamed of to these courtiers.

Avignon departed, leaving Eileen conspicuously on the king's arm.

"Your Majesty wished to speak with me?" Eileen prompted nervously. Her French had improved greatly over these last months, but her accent caused the best of listeners to wince.

"No, we merely wished to rid ourselves of sycophants." Louis shrugged, his attention already beginning to wander in search of his mistress.

"Then, I thank you, sir." Irritated, Eileen swept a gallant curtsy and prepared to depart.

Momentarily diverted by her intention of leaving before she was dismissed, the king returned his attention to the pert Englishwoman at his side. For this evening in the palace she had consented to powder her hair, but Louis began to place her now. One of Charlie's Jacobites, if he remembered rightly. An Irish one, with hair the color of a summer sunset. His eyebrow lifted.

"Where is your Lord Sherbourne?" he demanded, refusing to let her go.

Startled, Eileen looked up into a pair of cold eyes. Without thinking, she replied honestly, "At the gaming table earning our keep."

The king laughed and his eyes became friendly once more. "His uncle pleads his case well, but I can do nothing for him, you realize. The Stuarts are a considerable embarrassment to me at this time."

Eileen felt the first twinge of icy fear. If the French king and Drake's noble family could not provide diplomatic persuasion, how would Drake ever win the ear of the English court? She knew Drake too well to deny the answer to that one. He would have to go to London himself.

"He is not a Jacobite, sir," Eileen offered. "He is a victim of treachery, much as my own father was. His family and his tenants suffer for the greed of one man."

"And you?" At Eileen's questioning look Louis expounded, "Do you suffer as a result of this treachery, too?"

Eileen met his gaze boldly. "I gained by it, and will lose for it if he returns to England. But my gain is nothing in the face of his loss."

Louis contemplated this silently. Before he could make any reply, the crowd shifted, and Drake appeared at Eileen's elbow. Golden hair powdered and pulled back in a severe queue, linen and lace immaculate and flowing, he appeared every inch the aristocrat, and his bow held a hint of arrogance as he greeted the king.

"Your Majesty." Cynical eyes swept to the petite figure on the king's arm. "I trust Miss de Lacy has not annoyed you with her pert tongue?"

Louis grinned at the furious look this drew from the Irish temper beside him. "Her French is admittedly abominable, but her tongue is quite sweet. You should have sent her to plead with me in the first place, Sherbourne."

Drake scowled. "That is not why I brought her here."

The king gave him a shrewd look and released Eileen's hand. "I know. I respect you for that. Take her home, Sherbourne. You are welcome to stay in my court if that is your desire, but she does not belong here. Take her home."

With that, the king strode away, leaving Eileen to stare after him and Drake to grip her arm convulsively. When he began to lead her through the crowd, she balked, forcing him to meet her gaze.

"Where are you taking me?"

"Back to my uncle's house." Drake's jaw was rigid with rage as he stared down into the silver pools of her eyes. The rage was more for himself than for her, but the result was the same. His tongue spoke before his thoughts. "The king is right. You have no business here."

Eileen stared at his beloved features with all the pent-up pain of these last few agonizing days. "No, I don't," she replied slowly, searching his drawn face, where all the laughter had fled. "And neither do you."

With that, she tore from his grasp and disappeared into the crowd. Had there been a tree in the room, Drake would have sworn it swallowed her up.

Chapter XVII

———— ❧ ————

Eileen allowed the young maid to help her with her laces and gown, then dismissed her for the evening. She did not need prying eyes for what she did now.

With the maid gone, she swiftly slipped into one of the old gowns she had brought with her. The loose construction needed no binding corset, and she could travel with more ease. Fine silks and satins would only draw attention, and she had no need for that. She knew how to disappear at will, and blending with her surroundings was much of the secret.

Drake had told her to go and go she would. He had no further use for her, so she must look after herself. And the child. Even if de Lacy should trace her to the French court, he would not find where she went now. Let him think she had disappeared from the face of the earth. Let him spend his nights worrying when she would expose him. She could not do it now, but some-day . . .

Eileen dragged out her canvas bag and calmly packed it with those things that belonged to her. The costly gowns would stay behind. The few gold coins Drake had given her for her needs were neatly tied in the corner of a handkerchief. She considered these repayment for what she had taken from Sir John. She needed them now. Pen and ink and paint entered the bag with the coins and the small stack of old clothes. She would leave this life much as she had entered it. Almost.

The sharp rap at her door broke Eileen's concentration. Something much akin to relief flickered across her face. She had no wish to part from Drake in anger. He would understand her need to leave and perhaps lend his aid. Though he could not love her, she hoped he remained her friend. She softly called a welcome and rose from her task to greet him.

The appearance of Avignon in her doorway came as a total shock. She had forgotten his existence. He entered the room and closed the door before she could find her tongue to protest.

"That is not the most becoming of gowns to wear to show your appreciation of my efforts," the comte spoke disapprovingly as he came farther into the chamber. In the candlelight his sagging jowls had a sallow appearance, but his shadow was long and broad as he approached.

"Get out of here!" Enraged, Eileen refused to be backed into a corner but strode boldly forward to meet him.

Avignon's lips curled at the corners at the sight of such a petite pillar of wrath. "Do not be so quick, my lady. You have no secrets from me. I know who you are and where you come from and why you are here. If you grow tired of your first protector, it would do you well to choose an equally strong replacement. Your enemies are not known for their delicacy and finesse."

Eileen blanched at this insinuating threat. How could he know of Lord de Lacy? A petty Irish noble could have no connections in this court of kings. It did not matter. She would not stay and they could not find her.

"And you, my lord, are the misbegotten results of the bestial mating of a jackass and a venomous serpent. Get out before I scream you into deafness."

Avignon appeared momentarily startled by the calmness of this curse, but he recovered rapidly. With a
quick twitch of his hand he grabbed Eileen's wrist and
pulled her against him.

"I like a woman with spirit. Try your worst, witch.
The servants are understanding."

He bent to cover her mouth with his but Eileen spat
in his face and jerked away. With a swiftness that
belied his size, Avignon grabbed her shoulder and
spun her around, smacking her across the mouth with
the back of his hand.

Eileen crumpled to the floor near the grate, her
head reeling with the force of his blow. The shock
blinded her to thought, and she reacted instinctively.
She had been struck before, but then she had been
helpless. Not so now. Her hand wrapped around the
iron poker behind her. Never again, by all that was
Christian, never again.

When Avignon reached to pull her to him, Eileen
swung with all the force of her tiny stature. The poker
found its mark at the back of his head.

The resounding *crack* echoed in the silent chamber.
A moment later, the comte's awkward body fell to the
floor with a look of surprise and pain in rapidly dulling
eyes. By the time Eileen scrambled to her feet, blood
gushed from his scalp as he lay in an unconscious heap
upon the stone grate.

She had killed him. She knew she had. She wished it
could have been de Lacy, but it was too late for futile
wishes. Now she must run and hide of a certainty.

Too late now, panic engulfed her, and Eileen began
to shake all over. Her head throbbed with the pain of
his blow and the salty taste of blood flowed in her
mouth. She felt his disgusting hands upon her and the
bile in her throat turned to vomit. With painful
wretchedness, the king's banquet came up to fill her
chamber pot.

Still aching and terrified by what she had done,

Eileen grabbed her small bag and fled—to the only security she knew.

Drake had taken her to his chambers before. She knew how to find them. She raced along long, dark hallways, her small steps echoing unnaturally loud in the emptiness. He had to be there. She needed him.

With the familiarity of the intimacy they had shared these last months, Eileen flung open Drake's door and darted into the room. She stopped instantly and gave a hoarse cry.

In the flickering light of the bed candle, Drake lay half undressed upon his bed, the golden mat of hair upon his chest shimmering in the pale light while his hands clasped the arms of a dark-haired woman next to him. From the unfastened state of the woman's bodice and her disheveled appearance as she raised her head to glare malevolently at the intruder, Eileen needed no further explanation. She did not even stop to consider the pain in Drake's eyes as he cursed and threw the woman aside. Without a word she turned and fled.

By the time Drake disentangled himself and raced to the corridor, Eileen had gone. Disappeared. He turned back into the room and demanded furiously, "Who sent you?"

The woman rose from the bed and shrugged, making no attempt to cover the bared curves revealed by her open bodice. "What does it matter? She is gone, I am here. Stay, and let me show you . . ."

Drake flung her none too gently back to the bed. Hands on hips, towering over her, he loosed the sharp-edged sword of his fury. "Who sent you?"

Reading the murder in his eyes, the woman hastily replied, "Avignon. He thought if you were occupied . . ."

Cursing, Drake grabbed for his shirt. "Let us hope we find him alive. Come on. I will need you for a witness."

When she did not immediately follow, Drake jerked

her to her feet and dragged her to the door. He had
seen the stark terror in Eileen's eyes. If she had not
killed the bastard, he would try his hand on it.

By dawn, the scandal had been safely averted, but
Drake could not rid himself of the murderous look in
Avignon's eyes when he regained consciousness. They
had a dangerous enemy in that one, but with any luck
at all, they would be gone before the comte recovered
the strength to rise from his bed.

With the first streaks of dawn brightening the summer sky, Drake sought the stables. If Eileen had persuaded one of the stable boys to saddle a horse for
her, she would lead him a good race. Of that he had
no doubt. Her fury would give her the strength of ten
men, and she already had the energy of more than
most. The lead she had gained while he had pacified
the authorities would make this a long day's ride. He
refused to allow the possibility that he would not catch
up to her by day's end.

Drake breathed a sigh of relief after questioning the
stable hands and inspecting the stalls. She had not
taken a horse. She had not taken the gowns he had
worked so hard to win for her, either, and that oddity
irritated him more than anything else she had done.
He had not suspected she had any compunction at all
against helping herself to anything that might aid her
escape. The horse might have been difficult to steal,
but the gowns were hers and worth a goodly sum.
What would she use for money?

With his uncle's blessing, Drake commandeered a
powerful stallion, filled his pack with what wine and
food could be found in the kitchen larder, and set out
after his errant lady. On foot, she could not be far
ahead of him. Then he would see her settled once and
for all.

By the end of that first day, Drake's confidence had
dwindled to tired confusion. He had felt certain she

would set out on the road to Calais, but no one he met would admit to seeing such a one as he described. He circled Versailles, inquiring at all the inns and taverns along the way, stirring no small amount of interest and amusement but discovering nothing. It was impossible to believe that no one had noticed a woman of Eileen's looks traveling alone and on foot. By day's end, Drake had begun to suspect a conspiracy.

His suspicions increased when he returned to the Calais road at sunset and stopped at a farmyard along the way. The peasant woman in the doorway regarded his fine horse and saddle with ingrained distrust and refused to speak when he questioned her. Her husband appeared in the doorway and made negative answers to all Drake's inquiries, but as Drake wearily returned to his saddle, he caught the woman's smug expression of satisfaction. Instinct warned him they lied.

Furious at being tricked in such a way, Drake urged his tired mount down the road until darkness made further search futile; he would not see Eileen if she walked beside him in the road. Cursing women, himself, and the stubborn French, he built a small fire in the field and settled in for the night. In the morning he would be more wary when making his inquiries. She could not be far ahead of him. Wondering where she slept this night, Drake drifted off into exhausted slumber.

The second day was a repeat of the first with the exception that Drake had become sensitive to the lies he was given. In mounting frustration he met with each negative shake of the head, and only common sense prevented him from pulling his sword on these unarmed peasants and demanding the truth. The one who deserved his ire stayed one step ahead of him.

He would wring her neck when he found her. With all the hours of the day to think about it, Drake realized Eileen had been prepared to run before she came upon him, probably even before Avignon had come to her. The white-faced ghost he had seen so briefly in his doorway had not been calm enough to pack bags and change her clothes. That had been done before she slammed an iron poker into the head of one of France's noble aristocrats.

Had she planned to tell him she was leaving or would she have just left, disappearing into the night? What had he done to drive her away? Where did she plan to go? Surely she would not return to Michael? Doubt and anger mixed in wild confusion as Drake searched the roadways and fields and badgered the peasants for some clue to Eileen's path.

Heartsick and weary beyond all imagination, Drake sank into a tavern chair at the end of the day and swallowed a long drink of ale. From behind the curtains separating the public room from the kitchen, a maid peered at this travel-stained stranger. Haggard lines of anxiety and exhaustion marred his handsome features, but blue eyes warily watched all around him. Though obviously tired, he did not relax the proud stance of his broad shoulders, and he held his head high. A small frown puckered the maid's brow as she tried to picture this blond gentleman striking the delicate lady whose bruised face she had seen earlier in the day. She knew men too well and this one did not seem the sort to strike one so much smaller than he. But aristocrats were not to be trusted. She held her tongue.

Drake slept little the second night. Images of Eileen's slender form sleeping in cold fields or threatened by drunken strangers kept him from any semblance of peace. She could be trampled beneath the hooves of cattle, abducted by highwaymen, beaten for what few poor things she carried. Drake pounded his flea-ridden pillow with frustration and rose before the break of day.

Not until nearly noon of that third day did Drake

begin to realize what Eileen was doing. From what hints he received, she was still on this road, making no attempt to hide herself or disguise her path. How she managed to stay ahead of him he could not fathom, but her disguise he finally understood. A British lady of quality traveling alone would attract nothing but suspicion and distrust from these wary peasants, just as he did, and he spoke the language without flaw. Eileen spoke only execrable French, but her mute gestures could communicate in any language. She had retreated into her former silence, passing among the villagers as one of their own kind, or close enough.

Drake's jaw clenched in a fury that would brook no further obstacle. The little brat did not fear the authorities following her, for she knew they would not be searching for a mute peasant. She could travel the public road with impunity in that guise. Only, she must know that sooner or later he would figure it out. Did that mean she wished him to follow or thought he would not?

If the latter, she would be severely disappointed. She had led him a merry chase, but it was almost at an end. And then he would make certain of her before she had the opportunity to do it again. These last days had made that clear enough in Drake's mind. Whatever the future might bring, he would not see this hell repeated. Before he did anything else, he would make his claim permanent. Let the little brat protest as she may, but her days of freedom had finally come to an end.

With caution Drake approached a carter hauling a load of hay behind an ancient mule. The old man had his hat pulled down over his brow to ward off the noon sun, and he munched contentedly on a piece of straw. He glanced up to the gentleman on the valuable steed without curiosity.

"Monsieur, if you would . . ." Drake hauled on his stallion's reins, forcing it to keep pace with the mule as he drew the carter's attention. The man said nothing but flicked him a brief look. "I am looking for someone who may have passed this way. It is most important. She could be harmed traveling alone, and it is all my fault. She is petite, with hair the color of the setting sun. She does not speak. Have you seen her?"

Interest flickered briefly this time as the old man took in the gentleman's anxious features and dust-coated clothing. "What is it to you?" he inquired laconically.

Drake did not dare allow hope to rise. "She is my wife. We quarreled, and she ran away. If you have seen her, you must know it is dangerous for her to be alone. I would give you anything you ask if you could but tell me where to find her."

The carter snorted in disbelief. "Seems to me it would be dangerous for her to travel with a brute who strikes women." He whipped the mule's reins but the idle beast did not increase its pace to any degree.

The leather of the harness cut into Drake's hands as he clenched his fists. Avignon. The darkness had been too deep that night to see Eileen's face with any clarity, but the piece fit. Eileen would never allow any man close enough to rape her, but she would not expect a man to strike her. He did not care to imagine her rage and fear when one did. De Lacy had done that once. She had learned to carry weapons since then.

Drake improvised hastily, "That was not my fist but her father's. That was why we quarreled. Since she cannot use words to stop me, she ran away. You have seen her." He made it a statement, not a question.

The old man threw him a long, shrewd look. He found it distinctly odd that a gentleman in lace and satin would be seeking a wench in simple clothes, but the habits of the gentry were beyond his knowledge. The girl did not have the blackened teeth or rough skin of a working woman, so he did not question the gentleman's claim to her. His right to find her was another matter. The carter spit out his straw.

"I've seen her."

Drake breathed a silent prayer of thanksgiving before speaking again. "She is well?"

"Except for the bruise." The older man stared at Drake now with a lessening of suspicion. That his first concern had been for the girl's welfare spoke to his benefit.

"How far ahead is she?"

The carter glanced at the sky. "She passed me nigh on to half a morning ago."

"Passed you?" Startled, Drake wondered if the man's brains were addled.

"Fine mule she had. Young one." The carter's gaze returned warily to the gentleman.

A mule. Drake didn't know whether to curse from anger or frustration or at himself or Eileen. A mule. Of course. No one counted the dray animals in the field. No one would think to look for her on one. If it were not for his admiration for her cleverness, he would like to shake her until her teeth rattled.

"The mule is yours if I find her. Did she say where she headed?"

This unheard-of generosity brightened the carter's interest considerably. "Told her of some friends of mine in the village ahead. Looked like she could use a bite to eat."

Drake did not allow his relief to show. Anything could happen between now and the village. If there were any forests between here and there, she might turn into a tree. He would count on nothing until he found her.

Ascertaining the direction of the village and the man's friends, Drake spurred his mount into a gallop. He had made no use of the beast's speed until now, thinking he would outdistance Eileen. Now haste made sense. He flew down the dirt road, leaving a trail of dust in the air behind him.

He spied the mule tied to a rail outside the thatched cottage long before he arrived. She could not outrun him now, and Drake made no attempt at caution as he galloped his stallion over the remaining distance. These days of searching had raised his temper to a flaring point, but his heart sung songs of rejoicing.

Flinging himself from the saddle, Drake shoved open the crude cottage door without a rap of warning. He would take no chances on giving her time to think of escape. The faces in the darkened room all turned to him in surprise, but his gaze sought only one.

The bruise had darkened into a dull gray and green, but the disfigurement to the delicate cheekbone made Drake's stomach knot in fury. He strode in without a word and raised his hand to touch the blemish.

Instantly a woman screamed and chairs fell backward as the men leaped to their feet to protect the silent lady in their midst. The commotion died quickly enough as Eileen rose and stepped toward the brash intruder instead of backing away.

"If I had known this, I would have killed him." Drake's fingers whispered along the bruise, searching for other damage.

Eileen stared wonderingly at the anguish in his eyes, the vulnerable curve of his mouth as he touched her, but the memory of his body in another woman's arms had not faded. He might have defended her from Avignon, but he still did not love her. She shook her head, chasing away his protective hand.

Aware of the stares they attracted, Drake closed his fingers around Eileen's elbow and spoke to their audience. "I thank you for your care to my wife. She has nothing more to fear from her father, so I have come to take her home. Monsieur Belote will be arriving soon. I leave the mule as gratitude for his help." He produced a coin from his capacious pocket and handed it to the woman who hovered closest behind Eileen. "Would I had more to give you, madame. I am most grateful to find her well."

Eileen raised a dubious eyebrow at this charade, but she smiled her thanks to the woman who had offered her hospitality and did not attempt to shake off Drake's possessive hold. She suspected it would not take much to set off the fuse of his temper, and she had no desire to involve these people in their private arguments.

Satisfied he had made what reparations he could, Drake dragged his silent companion from the dark hut into the brilliant light of a summer day. Without a word of explanation, he lifted her into the saddle and climbed up to join her.

"Hold tight. I'm tired of traveling at a mule's pace." With this curt admonition Drake gave the stallion its head.

Wrapping her arms around his unyielding waist, Eileen rested her head against the strength of Drake's muscular back and allowed the wind to whip the dizziness from her thoughts. She had no idea why he was here or where he was taking her, but she made no effort to question. These past days of being alone with her thoughts had destroyed any desire to widen the distance between them. She could do it again if it became necessary, but not now.

Trusting Eileen would not recognize the gradual change in their direction, Drake rode until their mount would go no farther. He intended to make the journey a swift one, giving her no chance to change her mind or try to escape. He should have done this from the very start, but pride had made a fool of him. He would not make the same mistake twice. He had no pride left. She was all that he had and he would take no chance again on losing her.

When Drake made it apparent he intended to camp beside the brook where he had tethered the horse, Eileen silently set about gathering the kindling for a fire. The trees along the stream's edge provided an abundance of wood, and she soon had the fire bed arranged.

Drake came forward with his pouch of stale bread and wine and cheese he had purchased the day before. He threw the pouch down beside her and set to work lighting the fire.

"You did not have to come after me. The soldiers would never have found me," Eileen stated flatly, seating herself on the cloak she had arranged on the ground. The day's heat had not yet departed, and she had no need of the cloak's shelter.

"They are not even looking for you." Drake tore off a hunk of bread and handed it to her.

She could not detect the emotion behind his voice. She tried to search his face for clues, but in the firelight she saw only weary shadows. She wished they could go back to the days when they had laughed together, but those days were long gone. They had both grown since then, and life could not be solved by simply producing an apple.

"I didn't kill him?" she inquired softly. The thought of a man's death at her hands had preyed at her mind these past nights.

"Unfortunately not. I suspect it would have been better if you had." Drake drank deeply of his wine, avoiding the sight of copper curls gleaming in the firelight. He knew those eyes of hers would haunt his dreams should he look too closely. He would have to be content with her presence, for now.

Remembering Avignon's threats, Eileen had to agree. If the comte knew de Lacy, then her uncle would soon know of her presence in France. It was not a comfortable thought.

"I was not wearing my knife. I'll not be so incautious again," she informed him coldly.

Drake set the bottle aside and stared at her across the firelight. "You will not need the knife. I will see to your protection from now on."

"You, and the whore you were with?" she demanded angrily.

"Avignon's whore. Don't be a fool. Eileen." Drake answered curtly, too exhausted to delve into this point-less argument.

"No, not any longer. I'll not be any man's fool again." With bitterness she turned her head away. "You did not need to follow me. I can take care of myself."

"You had me believing that for a while. I know better now."

Drake watched with sorrow as she stared into the fire, making no reply. Had her bout with Avignon scared her that much? Or was there something else she did not tell him? He wondered if he would ever know the hidden paths of her mind, but he knew his own. She might hate him for what he did now, but he could do no less and count himself still a man. He waited.

"We are not returning to Versailles?" she finally asked.

"No." The reply was immediate and without qualifi-cation.

That seemed to be all she wanted to know. She rose from the fire, and Drake could hear her washing in the brook behind the bushes. When she returned, she wrapped herself in the cloak and, using her canvas bag as pillow, lay down beside the fire to sleep.

Drake watched as the last embers threw their glow on graceful lashes, accenting the porcelain loveliness of her pale cheeks. He wanted to take her in his arms but knew he could not. Not yet. Not until he had made wrong things right.

As he gathered up his own cloak and made his bed beside her, Drake voiced the one nagging question he could not resolve. "Why did you not take the gowns I gave you?"

Eileen lay curled within her cocoon, sensing his

masculine presence beside her as he lay down. For the first time in over a week they would sleep together, but she felt as if she slept with a stranger. He made no effort to touch her. Regret swept over her as she realized the insult she had given him by not taking the gowns he had provided for her. She should have known they were from Drake, but she had not wanted to acknowledge his right to provide for her. So many misunderstandings had come between them, she could no longer believe even in herself.

"I did not know they were from you. I am sorry," she whispered.

Drake crossed his hands behind his head and stared up at the stars, resisting the temptation to turn over and show her what rights he meant to keep.

"Know it now," he commanded sharply. "And in the future."

With that enigmatic response he grew silent.

Drake was all too aware of her fragile body lying beside him as she grew still and her breathing grew even with sleep. He might as well reach out and try to grasp the stars twinkling above them as think he could ever truly hold Eileen to himself, but these last days had taught him he must try. When first he had made his plans and written that letter, he had thought only to find a safe shelter to hide her. Now he knew he could not leave without grasping the stars and calling her his own. She might scorch his fingers or fade away, but a lifetime without her could no longer be imagined. And if he did not have a lifetime, he would die knowing he had done his best.

As the evening grew cooler, Eileen gravitated toward his warmth. By daybreak she slept soundly within the shelter of his arms, rocked by the security of Drake's even breathing.

Chapter XVIII

—— ❧ ——

France
July, 1746

They moved more rapidly than they had by coach, covering long stretches of fields and woods in a day, choosing straighter paths than the wandering roads. No one marked their passing, Eileen decided with satisfaction, and gave no quarrel to Drake's command.

Not until they reached the foothills to the south did she so much as suspect he did not make the Channel his goal. With growing incomprehension she watched as familiar landmarks flew by and they began to climb. Hope warred with disbelief as they reached the hills overlooking the hidden convent. Why in the name of all that was good and wise did he bring her here?

They rode into the valley a little before sunset, two travel-worn strangers on a single horse. The guard at the gate stared at the bearded gentleman in the dust-encrusted coat and hat when he gave his name and claimed that he was expected. He remembered the fair-haired young man who had visited once before, but this apparition bore only a passing resemblance to that elegant gentleman. Only the hair color of the girl clinging to the saddle convinced him there might be some truth to the statement.

He gave them admittance and Drake rode the weary horse up to the convent steps. There he dismounted and reached to lift Eileen from her seat. He marveled again at her weightlessness as he held her briefly in his hands. She had made no complaint of their wild ride. Indeed, she often rose before he, disappearing into the shrubbery to wash and set herself to rights before their day's journey began. She seemed paler than he remembered and she ate little, but she seemed to possess the stamina of a foot soldier. Still, she leaned weakly against him for a brief moment before they approached the massive doors. "Why here, Drake?" she murmured, too tired to conceal her genuine puzzlement.

"Because I do not think they will allow you to share my cell in the Tower."

It was the first clue she had to his intentions, and he had timed it so that she could not object. The doors in front of them opened, and a silent nun bade them welcome.

Eileen quickly found herself separated from Drake. A gray-clad postulate led her down winding corridors to a bare cell containing cot and washstand. After Versailles, this seemed a virtual prison, but after the days on the road, she was grateful for its cleanliness.

She feared after she had washed and rested and changed into clean clothing that Drake would be gone. He was a man who did not hesitate when he knew where his path lay, and she had sensed that his every move had been a purposeful one since he had found her. If his path lay in the direction of London, he would set out immediately despite her or any protest she might make.

When she entered the reception hall to find Drake standing at the windows overlooking the cloister garden, she breathed a sigh of relief. Whatever his purpose, London was not his immediate goal.

He turned, and she saw that he had shaved the journey's growth of beard. In clean linen and long coat and satin knee breeches, he had been restored to English marquess again. Only the unpowdered hair betrayed any of his rebellious nature. In her unfashionable gown Eileen suddenly felt dowdy in front of him, and she hesitated.

Drake did not. He strode forward and captured her hand, blue eyes searching her face with anxiety.

"Was the ride too difficult, princess? The sisters have scolded me for your exhaustion. If my haste has made you ill . . ."

There was some hint of the Drake she knew, the one whose love and concern had led him to create fairy tales for an invalid sister and who had kidnapped his own cousins to save their foolish prides and lives. The cold stranger from Versailles had already lost his place. Eileen managed a small smile.

"I am not ill, just out of practice. These last months have been idle ones."

Relief flooded his face. "Thank God. I fear I have developed the bad habit of believing my own tales and thinking you invincible. I had forgotten you were not well before we left."

"Do not concern yourself over my health, but ease my mind. What did you mean when you spoke of the Tower?" Eileen held his hand anxiously, watching the expression in his eyes. They grew cloudy, and she despaired.

"Perhaps we had best eat before we have this discussion. I fear dinner may be awaiting our appearance."

Hiding her fears, Eileen nodded acceptance and took his arm. A nun in the doorway led them down the stone corridor to the open room lined with trestle tables and rows of orderly, black-gowned figures. A table at the head of the room contained the older nun Eileen recognized as the one who had greeted them before. Beside her stood a priest and his attendant. They all looked up and greeted their visitors with smiles, but the curiosity in their eyes was too evident. Politely, no questions were asked as introductions were made and everyone found their seats.

In the long rows of dark and gray habits Eileen
could not distinguish her mother, but she felt certain
her gaze followed her as she sat between Drake and
the mother superior. Even when they bowed their
heads for prayers, she felt as if someone were watching. Why had Drake brought her here? She did not
know the silent woman who had once called herself
mother, and she had no desire to disturb the woman's
peace.

During the meal, the priest and the older nun discussed the commonalities involved in running an order
the size of this one, and Drake and Eileen remained
respectfully silent. When the meal neared its end, a
chorus of soft voices sang hymns from an upper loft,
and Eileen glanced up in surprise. The silence until
then had been oppressing.

The mother superior caught her glance and smiled.
"We do have voices, child. It is just that we limit their
uses except in worship of God."

Eileen ventured a question that had bothered her
since their first visit. "Why is it that you speak when
the others do not?"

The nun listened carefully. "I am happy to hear that
your own speech is returned. I can see why ours concerns you. I am not of the order which has taken vows
of silence. We must have some among us to communicate with the outside world. Many of our novitiates
who believe they qualify to worship in silence learn
that life is not for them, but there are still places for
them here among us." She hesitated, as if debating
whether to say more. Apparently deciding to add to
her lesson, she finished, "The novitiates are allowed
an hour a day in which to speak. When they have
overcome their need to use that time, they are ready
for their vows."

Eileen immediately wondered if her mother had yet
taken her vows or could use that hour to speak with
her, but she quickly banished the thought. The only

thing they would have in common to speak about would be their hatred for de Lacy. That did not sound like a respectful topic for this house of worship.

In the mingling confusion after dinner, Eileen found herself somehow separated from Drake again. She sensed the eagerness of the young novitiates crowding around her as she was urged to join them in the large, comfortable commons, but her gaze kept sweeping the room for some sign of Drake, or her mother.

A soft voice spoke shyly next to her, and Eileen realized she was to be given the chance to satisfy her curiosity. This must be the hour of freedom, and again she searched for some sign of her mother. The voice beside her sighed with disappointment, and Eileen hastened to turn back to her companion.

"I am sorry, were you speaking to me?"

The young face brightened perceptibly. "I feared perhaps you still could not speak. Have you come to stay among us?"

At this moment, weary in heart and soul as well as body, Eileen wished heartily this was so. This time of waiting that lay ahead of her would be well spent in peaceful healing and learning the patience she must endure alone. Once she had thought she had the strength to cross to England and disappear into the countryside to start a new life of her own, but these last days with Drake had taught her the foolishness of that. Even if he no longer wanted her, she could not stop what she felt for him. So long as he would allow it, she would follow, just so she might reap the pleasure of his company awhile longer. But that would not be safe for her or the child. Somehow she must gain the strength to give up her foolishness.

The young nuns asked eagerly after the outside world, their curiosity over the pleasures of Versailles nearly overwhelming Eileen's ability to speak, until the hour flew by before she knew it. The pealing of bells for prayers immediately produced an immense silence, and the gray habits dutifully began to disappear from the room.

Uncertain what to do next, Eileen rose from her seat, only to find her way blocked by the priest she had met earlier.

"Miss de Lacy, spare me a moment, if you will?" he asked in slow, patient accents so that she might understand clearly.

Obediently Eileen returned to her seat, though her brow lifted in curiosity. The priest smiled at the familiarity of the expression.

"You are your mother's daughter, there is no doubt. I am sorry I was not present during your last visit."

"My mother is well?" Eileen asked politely, uncertain where this conversation led. She judged this man to be much the same age as the mother superior, very near to ancient, or, at best, older than Sir John. But the lines on his face spoke of kindness, and she had nowhere else to be at this moment.

"Physically, yes. Spiritually, well, that is another story. I have come to pry into your story. Do you like it here?"

"Very much," Eileen replied promptly, remembering the larkspur in the cloister garden. She very much needed her roots in the ground for a while.

The priest appeared mildly surprised but pleased. "Most young people would find the silence unbearable. But you are an unusual case, I understand."

Eileen crossed her hands in her lap and stared at them. "Perhaps, Father. I am much accustomed to being alone, if that is what you mean."

"Ahh, your young man does know you well. Then let me ask you this, and please feel free to be honest in your answer, would you care to stay with us for a while?"

His voice was gentle and kind, but the question caught Eileen by surprise. She had just been thinking in those terms. Did the man read minds?

The priest read the wild blaze of hope and fear in the girl's sad gray eyes, and his heart poured out to her. Such tragedy as this family had suffered, surely somewhere there must be an end to it. He prayed he offered the right solution.

Eileen responded without thought, "I would like that, yes, but . . ."

The priest waved his hand for silence. "First, let me tell you I have had a long talk with Lord Sherbourne. He tells me you have saved his life, and in turn, he fears yours may be in danger. Is there some truth to this?"

Puzzled, Eileen met the man's gaze. "Yes, I suppose, but I had not . . ."

He shook his head. "You will notice I come here without him, to allow you to speak freely. Lord Sherbourne is a kind gentleman, but he has a tendency to be quite . . . how do you say it?"

"Forceful," came the wry reply. "But if it is his idea that he might leave me in safety here, then, yes, I agree with him. My only fear is that his 'forcefulness' may persuade you to do what you will regret later. I am no nun."

The old priest chuckled. "You and your Lord Sherbourne are well matched. I enjoy your honesty. Do not concern yourself over worldliness corrupting the sisters. We will welcome the chance to teach you what your neglected childhood has not, but I promise not to preach. I think the opportunity is well met. Elizabeth must make some decision soon. Your presence here should aid in that decision."

Eileen appeared momentarily alarmed at the swiftness with which events were occurring. Agreeing she would enjoy this respite was not the same as actually staying. There were other things to consider, things Drake knew nothing about. And now to consider her mother, too . . . She shook her head in dismay.

"Father, I do not know. I do not want to be anyone's burden. I do not want to be responsible for anyone's decision. I cannot even make my own right now. Has Drake already gone?" Panic-stricken at this idea, she clasped the priest's hand and followed his expression desperately.

He patted her hand soothingly. "No, of course not, child. I simply wished to talk with you alone awhile. He is being very hard on himself at the moment, and I wished to be certain we were doing the right thing. I think we are. You will be free to come and go from here as you please, paint as you wish. But if it is rest and safety you desire, we offer that, too."

Eileen relaxed and leaned against the ladder-backed chair. How much had Drake told this man? How much did she dare say? It would be easier to risk this one man's horror and disgust than to suffer it later from the convent's entire population. She could not hide her burden for long.

"I do not know how much Lord Sherbourne has told you, Father, but there are some things even he does not know. If I stay here for any length of time, the services of a midwife will be required. Are you certain you can tolerate that much corruption?"

A worried frown appeared between the old man's eyes as he gazed upon Eileen's resigned expression. But she had her eyes closed and did not see his concern.

"I think that Lord Sherbourne's suggestion is an excellent one in that case, my dear. No one will have to know the exact date of your wedding vows and the child will be born into secure respectability."

Eileen's eyes shot open and she turned to face the priest with incredulity. "Wedding vows?"

"Of course," the priest replied mildly, rising from his chair. "Lord Sherbourne has asked me to perform the ceremony on the morrow. I will leave it to you to break the news of his heir. He should be quite pleased."

Stunned beyond comprehension, Eileen remained

where she was as the priest hurried to fetch the impatient bridegroom. She had never contemplated marriage. Had Drake given up all thought of returning to England, then? It had not sounded so earlier. Why, then, would he want to marry her? He had a fiancée waiting for him, one who would make a much more respectable marchioness than she. Whatever on earth could he be thinking of?

From the doorway Drake could see Eileen's frozen features and his heart lurched violently. She meant to say him nay. How could he force her to his will? The old priest had seemed quite confident that all was well, but·he did not know Eileen as Drake did. He could read the stubborn tilt of her chin now, see the storm warnings in her eyes, taste the sweetness of those parted lips. On that final thought he entered the room.

Eileen watched him suspiciously as he crossed the room. He had discarded coat and waistcoat in the evening's warmth, and candlelight danced in the unpowdered gilt of his queued hair. He no longer looked the part of marquess but of a man determined to have his way. Why should she deny him?

Drake took her hand and firmly drew her from the chair, taking her in his arms when she came to stand before him. "Father Chardin tells me he has been precipitous in asking you what I should have asked long ago. I would hear your answer for myself. Eileen, will you marry me?"

She hid her wild-eyed panic against his chest, absorbing the comforting security of his hold as he pressed her close. If she thought this was what he truly wanted, she would give an exuberant affirmative and ignore her doubts, but he offered only out of obligation. She shook her head in sorrow.

"Don't, Drake. We owe each other nothing. I do not require legalities for what we have been to each other. Thank you for bringing me here, but you may leave with clear conscience without marrying me."

Drake slid his hand into the thick knot of hair at her nape and pried her head away from the pillow of his chest so he might see her eyes. "I won't leave unless you marry me."

A quirk of amusement turned the corners of her mouth. "Whatever would the poor sisters do with you constantly lurking about? A man such as you would give the young ones second thoughts about a life of maidenhood. I think they would be forced to have you thrown out."

A matching wry smile tilted Drake's lips upward. "Then marry me and the only maidenhood spoiled will be your own."

"Drake, I cannot . . ."

He crossed her lips with his fingers. "Do not tell me no, princess. My reasons are selfish as always. You are all that I have in this world now. If I should lose you, I would have no reason to return, no reason why they should not hang me by the neck if that is how the decision goes. Give me this one hope, princess."

He meant to return to England and take up the fight in person. Eileen stared at his lean features in dismay, noting the new, harsh lines beside his mouth where once there had only been merriment. She touched his lips wonderingly, smoothed a stray wisp of hair back from his temple, and still he stared, willing her to agree.

"You know I can never be a marchioness, Drake. If it is your wish I will wait for you here. If you must return to France, I will marry you then. I need no more than a roof over my head. We can live in a cottage and I will draw pictures for the stories you write. That's all I want, Drake." Tears rimmed her eyes as Eileen stared up into the deepening wells of Drake's eyes, feeling his resistance. "Won't my promise be enough?"

He might never have another chance. He had not come this far to let her slip away so easily. Drake's grip on her waist tightened.

"No, princess, I trust in the fates no longer. Marry me now and let me leave with some confidence that a future awaits me. I will not go without your solemn vow."

What he asked was madness, every instinct cried alarm, but she could not deny him. He did not love her. He could not take her back to England and pretend she was a noble lady. But those were problems for the future. For now, she loved him too much to let him go without consenting to his one request. May the heavens forgive her, she belonged to him.

Eileen's hands tightened behind his neck as she met Drake's gaze. "I should say 'no' and make you stay," she whispered tauntingly.

A gleam of hope leapt to Drake's eyes. "I will make your life a living hell," he warned.

"I know." Sighing, Eileen stood on tiptoe and pressed a kiss to the corner of his hard lips. "For that reason alone I give my consent."

"Witch," he muttered before capturing her mouth with his, sealing the indictment.

Chapter XIX

———— ❦ ————

Excitement seemed to pour from the convent tucked among the hills, taking flight in exuberant song and winging through the air on laughter. Never before had a wedding been performed in the jewel-like chapel; never before had two such handsome young people graced these walls. The charisma of love enveloped the cold stone walls and filled the cloister with warmth and sunshine.

That the bride was the daughter to one of the inhabitants had no small part in this miracle. Most of the sisters had dedicated their lives at a young age and knew nothing of the outside world. Sister Elizabeth carried with her an aura of mystique, and the marriage of her daughter in the chapel set her even farther apart.

She appeared soundlessly in Eileen's small cell shortly before the ceremony. The happy humming and twittering that had accompanied the impromptu fitting came abruptly to a halt, and the two younger novitiates quickly disappeared, leaving mother and daughter alone.

Elizabeth caressed the mantilla of lace draped over Eileen's loosely flowng hair and smiled at the ivory satin hastily retrieved from some long-locked trunk. The gown's style was of another era, if it had ever

possessed style at all. Heavy ruchings of lace filled the
bodice and spilled over into wrist-length sleeves. The
material itself clung simply to Eileen's slender waist
and fell in a waterfall of heavy satin to her feet. The
hem had been hastily basted so she did not trip over
the yards of material, but the long train behind her
remained untouched. The ancient elegance suited Eileen's classic beauty, and her mother nodded her
appreciation.

There was so much she needed to say, so much she
wished to know, but no words came to Eileen's tongue
as she met her mother's emerald gaze. She found
approval there and acceptance. That would have to be
enough.

"You have met Drake?" Eileen spoke swiftly, in
hushed tones, as if she were the one who should not
speak.

Elizabeth smiled and nodded, her eyes lighting with
laughter as she gestured to indicate his height and
broad shoulders.

Eileen understood this universal woman's language
and grinned her agreement. "Yes, he is very handsome. And strong. And when he laughs, bells ring and
there is music everywhere. And when he scowls, clouds
form in the distance. He is a man, for all that, and I
love him."

Elizabeth gave a firm nod of approval and touched
her daughter's cheek. Upon discovering the trace of
moisture there, she gave a cry of distress and wrapped
Eileen in her embrace. With a whispered "Your father
would approve," she fled the room.

That was all the reassurance Eileen needed to carry
her to the lovely chapel, where an ancient organ echoed
its mellow tones in welcome. A choir of angels filled
the air in accompaniment, and the rich perfumes of
dozens of roses permeated the coolness of the darkened walls as she entered. The sun glittered and
danced through the breathtaking stains of indigo and

crimson in the windows, and Eileen could barely turn her fascinated gaze from this display to the altar.

But when she found the man waiting at the end of the long aisle, Eileen could not turn her eyes away. All her life had led her to this moment and to this man. Whatever may come of the future, this moment was right.

The rich blue velvet of Drake's coat had been brushed and pressed until it glowed much as the windows above, but no more so than his eyes when Eileen entered. He stood quietly upright as Eileen approached, not moving, his gaze following her progress to the exclusion of all else. No smile bent his lips, but the admiration and joy in his eyes produced the same effect. A whisper of happiness rustled through the chapel at the sight.

When she reached the altar, his hand firmly closed around hers. A streak of light from the rose window over the nave caught in his neatly queued hair and glimmered gold. Eileen wished she could capture it, but already the priest had begun his prayers. They knelt on the velvet cushions, and the priest's blessings fell upon their heads. Eileen knew only the strength of the man's hand clasping hers, and the familiarity of the masculine arm rubbing against her shoulder. The ceremony became just a part of the spell that bound her to him.

When they rose to take their vows, Eileen's gaze met Drake's, and her heart leapt to her throat, making it almost impossible to speak. The blue of his eyes had darkened with some emotion that made it almost possible to believe he meant the promises he was speaking. In a low, nearly inaudible, voice Eileen repeated the vow to "love, honor, and obey," and the spark of laughter that appeared briefly in Drake's eyes almost decimated what composure she still retained.

Before she was even aware of what he was doing, Drake lifted her hand and slid his signet ring over her third finger. It hung loosely on her small hand, and he closed her fingers into her palm to hold it in place. Hands clasped, they made their final promises, and the priest sealed their vows with the sign of the cross.

Gently Drake touched Eileen's cheek, turning her gaze upward. His kiss was soft and tender, just brushing the edges of her lips, not daring more before this audience. Eileen could feel his breath upon her skin, and a tremor swept through her. Now his possession was complete.

The desire just this brief touch stirred bound them in a manner more forceful than the words they had just uttered. Drake pulled her arm through the crook of his, keeping her close as he led her down the aisle. Aware of the way his long legs moved, of the strength of the arm holding her, of the way these things felt when he took her to his bed, Eileen could concentrate on nothing. She was his. Finally and irrevocably his.

It would not do to ponder on the complexities of her new status. With a brief smile Eileen met the hugs and kisses and congratulations of these people she scarcely knew. Even when the priest brought her mother forward, she felt detached from this scene. Drake gallantly murmured praise and gratitude, bringing a touch of rose to Elizabeth's cheeks, but the confusion in Eileen's mind prevented hearing this chatter distinctly.

As they moved toward the dining hall to celebrate the occasion with feasting, Eileen's head began to swim, and she clung desperately to Drake's coat sleeve, bringing the procession to a halt. Drake darted a quick look to her pale face and swept her up in his arms before she could fall.

White with fear at the helplessness of this slight being in his arms, Drake demanded, "Where can I take her?"

In a flurry of consternation and suggestions the older nun hurried forward to direct Drake to the gardener's cottage that had been cleaned to welcome the bridal couple. In a few strides Drake was laying his bride on the sweet-smelling sheets that was to be their marriage bed, and the crowd was left outside. Only the priest and the nun and Elizabeth entered the room.

"Eileen?" Anxiously Drake knelt beside the bed, his eyes clouded with concern as his hand touched her cheek, searching for some sign of fever.

Dizzy, Eileen tried to sit, and eager arms lifted her gently to arrange pillows behind her. She held her head, trying to shake away the unsteadiness. "I feel so foolish. I am sorry, Drake. Do not let the festivities stop because of me."

"What is it, princess?" Drake's voice was deep with concern as he poured a cup of wine from the bottle the priest produced and handed it to her. "Shall I send for a physician? You look so pale . . ."

Eileen sipped reluctantly at the wine. "I am fine. It's just the crowd . . . I feel a little dizzy. Please, Drake, go on and do not let me keep everyone from their meal."

Behind Drake, the little priest frowned slightly, but he laid a hand on Drake's shoulder and urged, "I will send the apothecary to look after her. Perhaps it would be best if we left the women alone. It is not odd for a new bride to faint from emotion on her wedding day."

Murmuring assurances, he led Drake from the cottage, leaving Sister Agnes Marie and Eileen's mother behind. With a stern look of admonition the older nun commanded, "Your daughter will be in your charge while she is here, Elizabeth. I will leave it up to you to see to her now."

With the stiff scrape of her coarse habit against the planked floor, she departed. Nervously Elizabeth glanced to the closing door, then back again to the frail figure of her daughter upon the bed. Eileen's wide, gray eyes had closed, but she did not sleep.

Feeling the mattress sag with her mother's slight weight, Eileen opened her eyes again. The emerald eyes that met hers were clouded with indecision and uncertainty, and a nervous hand reached to touch her cheek.

"Do not worry, Mother." Eileen smiled as she found herself in the position of reassuring her parent rather than the other way around. "I am not fevered, only *enceinte*, as the French say it."

Elizabeth gasped and brought her hand to her mouth in a characteristic gesture. And then a small light began to gleam behind her eyes as she saw Eileen's shy pride in the fact.

"It seems your husband follows in his father's footsteps." The words were whispered with a ripple of laughter. "If I remember rightly, Drake was born only five months after the wedding. I was quite young then, but the scandal was fabulous."

Eileen's lips turned upward at this piece of gossip. "In that case, we are being quite discreet. A six-month baby is not entirely unheard of."

Elizabeth's laughter quickly turned to anxiety. "You are so young. It seems so sudden . . ." Suddenly frowning, she finished, "You have not told your husband."

Eileen sank back into the pillows. "Nor will I. He would not leave me if he knew."

Elizabeth shook her head in puzzlement. "That is bad?"

"I don't know," Eileen whispered in distress. "If he stays, he will lose everything—his family, his home, his good name. If he returns to England, he may well lose his life. How can I make that decision for him?"

"Holy Mother of a merciful God." Elizabeth clasped her daughter's hands within her own, feeling the old pain return, seeping into her bones and filling her heart with anguish. For so many years she had questioned God and then accepted Him. Now he hurled thunderbolts again. Only this time, it was her daughter who suffered. To find peace again, she would have to deny her love, and staring into Eileen's anguished face, she could not do it.

Bowing her head in acceptance, Elizabeth spoke firmly. "You cannot. Your husband must fight for what he believes, just as your father did. To ask them to do less would be to ask them to be less than men. You have made the right choice."

"Thank you." Wearily Eileen closed her eyes and slept.

When she woke, the sun had shifted to the west, filling the cottage's mullioned window with light, illuminating the dancing dust motes in the air. It gleamed along copper tresses strewn across lace-edged pillows and glimmered in the folds of rich satin wound around her.

With wonder and delight Eileen stared up into the streaming shards of light, until a slight movement in the room diverted her attention.

"You look just like a fairy-tale princess come to life, my love." Drake entered the stream of sunshine, catching the brilliant rays in his hair as he bent over her with an anxious gaze. "How do you feel?"

Impulsively she reached out to him, forcing him to sit beside her so she might reach the anxious lines on his brow. "I feel lovely. And happy. And other things." Her smile erased the lines on his face, and her touch wandered boldly to his temples.

Drake grinned and removed the mantilla from her hair. "Have you no word for those 'other things'?"

"You are the one with words, my lord. Shall I paint you a picture?" Teasingly she traced the outline of his lips with her finger.

Drake hesitated, wanting to believe she was well, but fearful he might harm her. His fingers threaded their way into her hair and he cupped her delicate jaw in his palm.

"Even you could not paint a picture such as the one

I see now. You are beautiful, Lady Sherbourne, and I would not hurt you for the world. Perhaps we should postpone our wedding night until you are stronger."

Sliding both slender hands behind his neck, Eileen applied gentle pressure, forcing him to bend lower until she could lift herself to meet him halfway. With a sigh she touched her lips to his and felt the eagerness of his response. She drew away tauntingly, kissing the corners of his mouth and all along his jaw, everywhere but where he wanted.

"Have you tired of me so easily, then?" she whispered in his ear, knowing by the way his arms tightened behind her back that she mocked the truth.

"I will never tire of you, princess," Drake murmured as he bent a kiss to the sensitive hollow behind her ear. "But I must protect and cherish you so the years ahead of us will be many. I am no greedy child needing all my wealth today."

The heat of his breath along her skin sent shivers of anticipation through Eileen, and she pressed her plea, winding her hands in his hair and tracing kisses down his jaw.

"Like good silver, I improve with age and use. You have been neglecting me. Have I lost my shine?"

Drake laughed out loud, pulling her fully into his arms and crushing her against his chest. "Your Irish tongue will find its own with practice, my sweet, and I can assure you, you will never lack for polishing." He bent to kiss the nape of her neck, then nibbled a path to her earlobe. "The day is still bright. Would you not prefer to walk amongst the flowers first?"

Heart pounding erratically as his kisses made jelly of her spine, Eileen shook her head in emphatic "no." "I fear I will have months of flowers and only hours of you. Don't deny me what precious time remains."

"No, my love, I shall never deny you anything. I only wish to be certain I have not forced you to a decision you may regret. If a child should come of what we do now, he may be born into this world a fatherless pauper. Are you willing to chance such a burden?"

Eileen laughed, suddenly freed of the fear that he had tired of her. He only protected her, as usual. Grateful for his poor male ignorance, she showered kisses upon him. "Our child will be born a man of letters and a singer of songs. Love me and let me prove the truth of it."

"You are a heartless twit, my dear," Drake murmured outrageously as his hand moved to the tiny row of buttons at her back. "Did you know twins run in the family?"

Eileen giggled as his other hand tugged at the hem of her skirt and insinuated itself along the length of her stockinged calf. "You lie. There are no twins in your family."

The back of her bodice gaped open and Drake triumphantly ran his hand up and down her bare back. She wore no chemise, no corset, and his gaze took on a wicked gleam as he stared down at her flushed cheek.

"That shows how little you know of family history, my dear. Shall I begin your instructions now? The Monsards' mother was my mother's twin. I have two uncles who reside in London you have yet to meet. They, too, are twins, on my father's side. Then there is grandfather Neville . . ."

Eileen laughed and gasped as the satin of her bodice suddenly fell to her waist and at the same time he tumbled her back against the covers. "You are telling stories, Drake!" she protested as his hand slid farther up her leg, finding no impediment to his progress.

Leering wickedly, Drake pinched her tender bottom. "And you have dressed with me in mind, wanton woman! You will see where this leads you when you have two squalling brats at your breast."

Eileen squealed as he bent to give her an example

of her dire fate, his teeth sinking gently into the tender flesh of her breast. When she wriggled in protest, she discovered his trap. With one hand beneath her, she could go neither forward nor back without enmeshing herself further in his eager hold. She shuddered as his teeth tugged at a sensitive nipple while his fingers slid along the moist cleft between her thighs.

Drake chuckled as she pulled helplessly at his hair. "You will be well polished before this day is done, my silver enchantress. Come, rid me of these damned clothes."

Their garments melted to the floor in rich profusion. The sunlight from the window played along the golden hairs of Drake's skin as he bent over her. Eileen sank her fingers deep into the powerful muscles of his back as he kneeled between her thighs, pulling him down until their breaths mingled and his tongue robbed her of all resistance. In rich, golden contentment they came together, and the sunshine vibrated with their love.

Afterward, lying in Drake's arms and staring out the window, Eileen could still feel his seed warm inside her, and the enormity of what they had done over-whelmed her. Sitting with his back propped against the head of the bed, Drake contented himself with exploring the curves and valleys that were now his alone to touch. Only Eileen knew that his child—or children, as he would have it—had already begun to grow beneath those places where his hand strayed. In the coupling they had done without thought or planning, a child had been created, a child that might never know his father or his home.

Even with the warm sunlight pouring over her from the window, Eileen shivered. Instantly Drake reached for the light blanket that had fallen to the floor in their lovemaking.

Eileen stopped his hand and settled herself more comfortably against his side, enjoying the liberty of touching and seeing without fear or darkness. Her hand strayed to the powerful muscles of his chest and played in the golden mat of hair there.

"When will you go?" she whispered, needing to know, dreading it.

Drake's hand wound itself in thick lengths of copper. "If you are well, it must be soon. The barristers have pleaded postponement one more time, promising that I will appear to testify. But I cannot leave you here unless I know you will be well and happy."

Eileen turned to watch his eyes and touch a finger to the small dent in his chin. "I will be more comfortable here than in Versailles. You know me too well. But what will you tell the court that the barristers cannot say for you? Why must you give yourself up to prison to prove your innocence?"

Drake could not read behind the silver of her eyes. Instead he concentrated on the enchanting rosebud of her breast, admiring the way it tightened beneath his touch. In these last months she had grown from a slim wisp of a girl to the full curves of a woman, and his desire for her had grown apace. The temptation to stay and make love to her, to surrender his claims to land and title rather than risk losing the one thing of value he possessed, was a strong one. But others relied upon him and he could not do it.

"I traveled under an assumed name. Witnesses can only testify that they saw me hundreds of miles from Culloden if they can identify me in court. I must go, my love."

"Where were you that you must travel under an assumed name?" This piece of knowledge had eluded her, but Eileen felt daring enough to broach it now.

Drake hesitated, then with a sigh admitted, "In Ireland."

Eileen sat up and turned to confront him with astonishment. "Ireland? Before your wedding? You must be mad."

Drake contemplated the sight she presented with a wry grin. The fall of auburn tresses did little to conceal the full breasts or tiny waist beneath, but she seemed totally oblivious to the effect her nudity had on him. Perhaps druids felt more at ease without clothes.

Lifting his gaze to meet hers honestly, he answered, "Crazed, admittedly. I could not let you marry Michael, so I thought to find evidence to have your uncle imprisoned. Then you would need not marry at all."

Eileen's eyes widened and a sinking feeling entered the pit of her stomach. "And what did you find?"

"That your parents practiced Catholicism and lived in danger of losing their lands and rights. That your uncle, when in his cups, often threatened to expose them. That the woman who was your nurse disappeared the day after your father's murder. She might possibly have witnessed it, but I had no time to trace her. I returned to England after receiving word of the battle at Culloden."

Drake watched the shadow of her eyes with sorrow. He had meant to help but had only harmed. He did not think she yet understood that he could not reveal his whereabouts without arousing de Lacy's alarm and endangering her. He had spent these months stalling for time not only for his sake, but for hers. His barristers had hired men to scout for the evidence he had not been able to obtain. If they had not gathered enough evidence to imprison de Lacy, he could not reveal his whereabouts in court without endangering Eileen. But not to reveal his whereabouts would be to endanger Diane and his tenants. The line he walked was a slender one, but he would not have her know it.

The cloudy blue of his eyes stared out from beneath his square, wide brow, and Eileen touched the obstinate cut of his jaw, feeling the tension there. "Thank you."

Drake had expected anything but that. She should have railed at him for his foolishness, cursed him for interfering where he had no right, but she did none of these. Drake studied her small, heart-shaped face with wonder and the first stirrings of realization that he had married rightly for all the wrong reasons.

But the words that came to his tongue he swallowed. He had no right to put a claim on her emotions when he might not return to hold them. Let her think all that went between them was this physical attraction, and she would less likely be hurt in the end.

So the words she most wanted to hear went unsaid except in the whisper of his kisses.

As Drake's mouth closed possessively over hers and she felt his body quicken, Eileen accepted this token, for now. If the future ever came, she would have more or none at all. The price of freedom was high.

And as his body took hers, she responded with all the passion she possessed, sealing this moment into every pore, every cell, every inch of their minds and bodies, until they became as much one as the child growing within her.

Chapter XX

——— ❦ ———

France
July–October, 1746

Wearing a leather jerkin over a cotton shirt and rough homespun breeches borrowed from the gardener, Drake pressed a parting kiss against Eileen's forehead. Her eyes fluttered open, and she gazed upon his odd attire and golden hair tied severely in a queue and knew the moment had come. She reached to caress the rigid cheek hovering above her, and once laughing eyes grew darker with pain.

"I hate to leave you. Are you certain you are well?" Drake murmured, sitting on the bed's edge as he traced the delicate line of her jaw with his fingers.

If she made no quick movement, the morning nausea stayed calm, and Eileen responded in all truthfulness, "I am well, and you leave me in good hands. Do not concern yourself with me now, but with your future."

"I promise, whatever the verdict, I will find some way to return to you. In the event that we must be parted long, should I send Sir John to you?"

This was his only admission that he might not triumph, that he might be locked behind bars or worse, and Eileen met his gaze bravely. "It might be safer for him if he does not know. If you have the chance, beg my apologies and assure him I am well."

"Surely de Lacy does not have the power to trace

266

you through your letters? There can be no harm in writing." Drake frowned, not understanding her continued reluctance to put pen to paper.

He did not need to know what she had done, the danger she had brought upon herself by revealing her secrets. She would take care of herself and the child somehow. He must concentrate on winning his own life. Eileen hid her grief behind a smile.

"Perhaps you are right, but I would know that the Summervilles forgive what I have done before intruding upon them again. You must do as you think best when the time comes."

Drake bent a quick kiss to her pale lips, not daring more lest he throw their future to the winds and remain here. "All will be well, my love. I will return and we will begin on those twins I promised you."

Eileen laughed, running her hand over his powerful shoulder and down his arm, memorizing this feel of him. "Twins, then, my lord. One for you and one for Diane. Send her my love, if you can."

"I will." Catching her up in his arms, Drake plied her mouth with one long, sweet kiss. Then setting her gently back against the pillows, he strode out without looking back.

Eileen turned her face into the pillow and wept the tears she had so bravely held from him. But for her own foolishness she could have followed. She had only herself to blame, and the knowledge did not ease her anguish. He was gone.

By September Eileen's pregnancy had become obvious to all the inhabitants of the small world behind brick walls, and they fluttered protectively around her wherever she went. If she wished to paint on the hillside, several of the younger novices would find a need to search for herbs among the trees. If she set up her easel in some hidden corner of the garden, an older nun would find a sunny spot nearby to do her mending. Their concern was touching, and Eileen learned to accept it as she had accepted Quigley's surveillance. They meant well, and she had nowhere else to go.

Upon occasion her mother appeared as bodyguard. For the most part she remained silent as required, but her anxiety for her daughter frequently overrode her good intentions. Finding Eileen sitting idly on a bench beside the dying bed of larkspur, Elizabeth frowned and appropriated the space beside her.

"What is wrong?"

Eileen glanced quickly around the cloistered garden but no one was there to observe them. She turned inquiring eyes to this near-stranger who was her mother. "How is it that you speak when the others do not?"

A mischievous grin flirted at the corners of Elizabeth's mouth. "Because they are very, very good, and I am not. Sister Agnes Marie despairs of me. That is the reason I am not yet one of them. She doubts my dedication."

In the sunlight, the lines around her mother's eyes could be seen, but otherwise she still appeared as lovely and youthful as Eileen had remembered. Despite the silence between them, the bond was still strong, and Eileen felt no oddity in sharing secrets.

"Perhaps you ought to return to the outside world."

Elizabeth looked mildly startled by this thought, then, smiling, shook her head. "There is naught for me out there but trouble and woe. It is better here."

Eileen heard a hint of doubt, but she understood. Outside these walls they must contend with de Lacy and the trouble he could wreak on them and their loved ones. Eileen had not yet come to terms with the time she must part from the safety of these walls. She was more vulnerable now than ever before.

"If you were to go to the authorities—" Eileen began to suggest, but her mother's emphatic shake of the head silenced her.

"You were too young to understand. I cannot live through that again. It is best forgotten for all concerned. I am only grateful that I have been given this chance to be with you. Your husband is kind to think of leaving you here."

Eileen played with a fading blue flower. "Drake knows me too well. He thinks to protect me from myself as well as others. But the child grows more real with each passing day. I can feel his movement, and, too soon, he must become part of the world. I cannot hide him here forever. Somehow, I must deal with de Lacy."

Elizabeth closed her eyes and bent her head, and Eileen thought perhaps she prayed for guidance, but a moment later she shook her head vigorously. "No. That is for your husband to do. When his lands and title are returned, he must go to the authorities. Once Peter is behind bars, witnesses will come forward, I promise. Then you and the child will be safe."

That solution came too easily, and Eileen had learned long ago that nothing came easily. Still, she did not need to worry her mother. The sun had lost its warmth, however, and Eileen rose, smoothing her gown over the small mound of her belly. The growing weight reassured her, bringing her closer to Drake somehow.

Elizabeth observed her daughter's growing pear-shaped figure with curiosity. "When is the baby due?"

"Not until long after Christmas." If Drake did not return soon, the babe would be born behind convent walls. In another month or two she would not be able to travel at all.

Elizabeth looked dubious. "You are much too small to be carrying so great a weight already. Could you possibly have your dates confused?"

Eileen smiled and patted the mound proudly. "Culloden was in April, Mother. You are free to count for yourself. I shall have to make a Jacobite of him if they do not free Drake soon."

A small knot of jealousy formed in Elizabeth's breast at the obvious pride and love her daughter had for her new husband, but the feeling dissipated as quickly as it came. She had known a man's love once. That should be enough.

"You should hear from him soon, should you not?" she inquired anxiously.

Eileen lied and gave the easiest answer. "He will write when all is well."

All was not well at all. For the first time in the months since the massive doors of the Tower had closed behind him, Drake had a visitor other than his lawyer. He met Sir John's cold gaze without emotion and accepted the older man's refusal to shake his hand with equanimity.

He gestured toward the hard cot and the straight-backed chair beside it. "Have a seat, sir. I regret that I cannot send for refreshments."

Sir John remained standing. The bitterness in the young marquess's voice was new but understandable. Still, he felt no softening of emotion as he observed Drake's vitality forced to find outlet in leaning against the wall, flexing his unused muscles.

"Where is she, Sherbourne?" The baronet relied on his usual direct tactics to work with this man as well as with his niece.

"I left her well and safe. As I wrote you, she sends her apologies, but it is mine that must be extended. I cannot expect you to forgive what I have done." Drake wished heartily for the freedom to pace the floor, but Sir John's large frame limited the small space to a few steps.

"I do not need apologies. I need my niece. Her aunt has been distraught since she left. Women always fear the worst, but you must admit her fears are justified. Just tell me where to find her."

With time enough to consider his answer to the

question he knew would come, Drake did not hesitate in his reply. He preferred to leave Eileen in safety until he could come for her, but the chances of that grew slimmer with each passing day. The choice now lay with her uncle.

"She is with her mother. My barristers have assured me that all charges of aiding my escape have been dismissed against her, so it should be safe for her to return if that is what you think best. I fear my reputation will make her persona non grata in society, though." Drake crossed his arms and continued leaning against the wall. He knew that ultimately Eileen would be the one to decide what she wished to do, but he would not keep her uncle from her any longer.

Sir John made a curt nod that might have passed for gratitude for this information. "I will go to her directly. You will understand why I cannot express my thanks for your doing the honorable thing by her."

In the shadows Drake's gaze grew bleak. "Marriage to a proclaimed traitor is certainly not the fate I wished for her."

Sir John strode to the tiny cell window overlooking the Thames and stared out. "For that reason alone I will do all in my power to see your name cleared. For that, and your sister. But in the meantime I have told no one of the marriage. I must protect Eileen in any way I can."

Drake nodded his understanding, but the pain in his heart did not acknowledge logic. He wanted the world to know she was his, wanted to bring her home to his family, but he must hide behind this mask of civilization and deny what was his. It went against the grain, but as long as he was behind bars and Sir John was not, he had no other choice.

Hearing the sound of a key unlocking the door at the end of the corridor, Drake straightened and walked to the cell door. He was the last of the Jacobite traitors in this wing, so the visitor would be for him. All the other prisoners had been hung and were long past expecting anyone.

The guard opened the door at the end of the corridor, swinging his chain of keys and gesticulating to this second distinguished visitor. Edmund's bob wig and sedate brown frock coat created an aura of aristocratic elegance as he entered, swinging his walking stick at his side. Drake grimaced but continued to block the cell door.

"Ahhh, my dear cousin. How considerate is our monarch to allow the condemned traitor these last few minutes with his family." Edmund's arrogant smile belied the content of his words.

"Don't count your traitors till they're hung, Edmund." Drake waited. Edmund had not come here out of the kindness of his heart.

"Oh, have no fear of that, cuz. I have an ally who is prepared to testify you were on the moon, should I ask. He rather resents the interest you have taken in his past. Just what did you think you would gain by angering a man like de Lacy?"

Drake laughed to cover the gasp from behind him. Edmund would speak more freely if he thought he were alone.

"Amusement, dear Edmund. But surely even Lord de Lacy would not perjure himself for amusement. You go too far."

"No, I don't think so," Edmund replied in all seriousness. "You had to be confident of your position to come back here. And de Lacy has as much an interest in seeing you out of the way as I do, I gather. That niece of his is a thorn in his side, and your unseemly interest in her has not been helpful. Quite foolish of you to think you could hide yourself in de Lacy's territories. There is much I could learn from that man."

The admiration in Edmund's voice bordered on the infatuated, and Drake gave his cousin a look of disgust. "De Lacy is a villain, but you are only a fool. Why couldn't you be satisfied with Pamela and politics? Why do you need it all?"

Edmund shrugged gracefully. "Pamela is a bit of a bore. I can understand your disenchantment. But she bears the next heir to Sherbourne, and it will be much more convenient if I hold that title instead of you. And with you out of the way, de Lacy is free to remove that niece of his without interference, so we will all live happily ever after. Except you. And the girl. Who does that make a fool?"

Drake's fingers wrapped painfully around the bars of his cell as if he would rip them from the stone walls to get at Edmund. Eyes blazing with the fury of a summer storm, Drake swore, "If you touch one hair of Eileen's head, I will see to it that you and de Lacy are drawn and quartered, Edmund. This I swear."

Edmund turned slightly green and stepped back a pace as he bore the brunt of Drake's fury, but the metal door between them gave him courage.

"You will have to do it from the grave, cuz. You'll swing before you see her again."

With a jaunty grin he lifted his walking stick in salute and strode out, leaving Drake to writhe in agony and frustration behind locked bars.

He had all but forgotten the man hidden behind him until Sir John coughed and took a tentative step forward.

"I think we had better go to Eileen quickly, Sherbourne. De Lacy is not a man to act hastily unless forced. I rather suspect Eileen is providing the force."

Drake's jaw muscle twitched with anger, but his eyes were bleak with the helplessness of his situation. "You had better have Michael gather some of his friends and go to her. I will find some way out of this hole, but I fear it will not be in time."

Sir John met the younger man's gaze grimly. "After what I have just heard, you will be a free man before the next session. Give me the name of your barristers."

Sitting among the fallen leaves of red and gold, Eileen read the letter of warning sent by Drake's uncle in Versailles. If, as the letter said, de Lacy had joined his friend, Avignon, no good could come of it. The comte had carried out his threats to reveal her presence in France. If de Lacy wished to put an end to the threat she posed, Avignon would make an admirable accomplice.

Staring at the peaceful setting below her, the convent walls slumbering in the October sunlight, Eileen felt the icy chill of premonition. Drake had found her mother so easily. What would keep de Lacy from doing the same? De Lacy, of all people, must know Elizabeth was not dead. It would take only an elementary step of logic to trace the daughter through the mother.

The sharp kick of small feet inside Eileen's distended belly warned of the difficulty of escape. No longer could she disappear at will among the leafy trees or hidden passages. Just walking from place to place grew more awkward with each passing day. Running and hiding would not save her from danger this time.

The lack of word from Drake was the deciding factor. If the court convicted him, he would never tell her. She would read the condolences from his solicitors before she ever knew of his peril. No word at all meant he had no good news to relate. She had promised to remain here, but what if he could not make good his escape? The Tower was a formidable place. Perhaps he had only promised return to ease her fears. He lied more easily than she.

Crumpling the letter, Eileen began to make her way down the hillside. The little novitiate with her watched her progress anxiously but knew better than to offer aid. As quiet as the lady had grown these past weeks, she still had a sharp tongue for those who intruded upon her privacy. It was the pregnancy, some said, but judging from the letter's fate, the young nun suspected worse. When they reached the convent wall, she hurried to find Elizabeth.

Eileen exhibited no surprise when her mother appeared shortly after she returned to her room. For a community without words, news traveled fast. With studied care she continued sewing Drake's ring into the hem of her cloak.

"What are you doing?" Elizabeth lost no time in quibbling over her use of speech. Where her daughter was concerned, the convent's rules no longer applied.

"I have no chain to hang it on and I do not wish to lose it," Eileen replied calmly.

"There is little chance anyone would steal it here. You need not hide it."

"I cannot stay here. De Lacy is in Paris." Eileen knotted the thread and broke it with her teeth. Then laying the cloak aside, she began removing the small store of clothing she had accumulated these past months.

"For the love of heaven, child, where else can you go? Do you intend to live in the woods for the winter? Or ride out of here on muleback in your condition?"

Eileen ignored her mother's sarcasm, knowing it came of fear rather than anger. "The good father has a carriage, and he has promised to allow me to go anytime I desire. He cannot deny me now."

Elizabeth saw the stubborn tilt of her daughter's jaw and despaired. At moments like these, she saw Richard's gifts to his daughter: stubborn pride and the will of a monarch. There would be no dissuading her short of chains.

"You cannot go alone," she declared firmly.

"I can do anything I want to do." Eileen shoved the garments in her canvas pack.

"Mother of God, you are even worse than your

father! You cannot leave until morning at the very least. Father Chardin will not go down into the village until then. That will give me time to pack my bags and say my farewells. When you give birth to my grand-child, I intend to be there."

With the firm stride of a vigorous woman, Elizabeth left her startled daughter staring at the door closing behind her.

Chapter XXI

England–France
October, 1746

"Michael, I'm frightened."

Michael swung from the window and sat down in the chair facing Diane's, taking her hand reassuringly. "You have been strong through all of this. It will only be a little longer."

She glanced up, her face paler than usual and her eyes anxious. "I don't understand why all of you must go to bring Eileen back. Why cannot just Sir John go? Or you? What is it you are keeping from me?"

She was much too perceptive, and Michael moved his shoulders uneasily beneath his hampering coat. Sir John had grown grim and taciturn these last days and even Michael did not know all his thoughts.

"Drake wishes it. I do not know more than that. We are leaving Auguste with you. I cannot believe Edmund would do anything rash while we are gone. There is nothing to fear."

"Yes, there is, but you will not tell me! Can you not see how much worse it is when I do not know? My irresponsible brother should have no say in the matter! Would I could go to London and tell him what I thought of him. Had he not insisted on keeping his precious word and marrying Pamela, none of this would have happened. He is a fool."

"He bought family peace with his foolishness," Michael reminded her quietly. "It is the one thing he did that your father approved and was not easily undone. Then when Lord Westly offered to take Edmund off his hands, Drake had no choice. You cannot understand these things. Drake may occasionally be impetuous, but his family has always come first. You should know that."

Diane stared at her fingers. She should be ashamed of herself. She knew Drake had agreed to her father's wishes to keep her from fretting over their continual arguments. He had answered her every whim, protected her from reality, and she complained because he could not give her the impossible. Now her brother sat in prison for a crime that was not his, and she could do nothing.

"I'm sorry, Michael. I should not have said that. I do not understand why he has not married Pamela yet. The child is due any day. I am glad I do not go out in society. I do not think I could hold my head up long. Just enduring Edmund is wearing me down. I cannot blame you if you will not take Eileen back, but it would make Drake's plight easier, I should think."

Michael stared at her bent blond head with aching longing, then rose from his seat and paced back to the window. "If it will ease any of your burden, I will pretend these last months never happened."

The misery in Diane's face did not lessen, but she nodded agreement. "That might be best. Drake tells me he hopes to have his name cleared shortly. Perhaps then he will feel free to marry Pamela."

Knowing little more about Drake's present plight than she, Michael had to agree.

Unaware that others planned her future, Eileen rode silently beside her mother in the carriage taking them from the valley. Their leave-taking had been tearful, and even now her mother looked uncomfortable in the simple woolen gown that had been provided for her.

But Eileen could not deny her relief at having this companionship. Carrying this child was frightening enough. To carry it alone and on a journey such as this would be petrifying. Eileen squeezed her mother's hand gratefully.

The priest had insisted on leaving them with friends who could carry them by coach to another town and to another coach and another friend of the church who would see them safely to Calais. The weather had not yet grown chilly, and the journey promised to be a smooth one, if only she could make the horses go twice the speed.

Eileen stared out the window at the passing landscape and wished for the faith that had her mother counting prayers on her rosary. If only she knew how Drake fared, it might ease this band of steel crushing her chest. She might have the ability to do anything she wanted as she had told her mother, but without Drake she wanted nothing.

A frown puckered the bridge over her nose as Eileen caught a glimpse of the road ahead from around a curve. She caught at Father Chardin's cassock to warn him, but the coachman had already spied the obstruction. The carriage began to slow for the tree blocking the only passage out of these hills.

A spate of rapid French ensued between the priest and the driver. As the coach drew to a halt, the old man reassured them, "There are men already working on the problem. The delay should only be minor."

Eileen's frown did not relax. What men would be out in this desolate area working on a tree that had so conveniently crossed the road? There had been no storm, no wind. She did not like this at all, but she was chained to the seat by the responsibilities she had somehow acquired. The babe in her womb responded to the tension with a fusillade of kicks that made her wince, and she looked up to find her mother's sympathetic eyes watching her. No, there would be no running away this time. She was fairly trapped.

When Peter de Lacy opened the carriage door, Eileen was prepared for him. She had counted the numbers of men in the woods surrounding them and knew there was nothing one old priest and two women could do to fight them. She met her uncle's cold gaze with the defiant tilt of her chin.

"Uncle Peter! You have come just in time to rescue us. Father Chardin, this is my uncle, Lord de Lacy."

Eileen clenched her mother's hand so tightly her nails bit into the fine skin, and she shielded Elizabeth's terrified face from the two men as well as she could. She prayed her mother would have the good sense to follow her lead.

Peter de Lacy met his niece's gray-eyed stare with a grim smile of acknowledgment. "How fortunate that we arrived when we did, or we would have missed you." His quick gaze caught the hidden figure against the far wall, and his voice lost some of its smoothness. "Sister Elizabeth. What a pleasant surprise. I had not expected both of you. Father, I must thank you for caring for my family so well, but now that I have found them, I will relieve you of the burden."

Father Chardin frowned anxiously, not at all certain he liked the circumstances of this meeting. He glanced quickly to Elizabeth, but she retained a serene pose, and the little girl's smile was quite bright as she turned to him.

"It may take them the better part of the day to remove that tree, Father. Why don't you return to the convent while we go with my uncle? I will tell them in the village of the delay and perhaps they can send more men to help."

De Lacy suppressed a frown but his jaw muscle jerked angrily at this ploy. Still, even he had compunctions about killing a priest if it was not necessary.

"Perhaps you are right, my dear, but I hate to be parted from you so abruptly." The priest hesitated expectantly, waiting for an invitation from the dark

Englishman in the doorway. When none was forth-coming, he chose the wiser course. "I will expect you to write and tell us you arrived safely. Go with God's blessing, my dears."

With a flutter of gowns and caps and kisses, the two women disembarked from one carriage and silently walked around the fallen tree to the other. De Lacy solicitously walked at their elbows, steadying their prog-ress with a firm hand, while his men began to pick up their tools and gather their horses.

The band of steel became suffocating as Eileen heard the old coach slowly maneuver around the clearing to return to the convent. She may have led a frivolous and useless life until now, but she felt certain she had just saved the lives of two men. Would that she could do the same for her own.

Eyeing Eileen's increasing figure as he handed her into the carriage, de Lacy commented caustically, "I see you have gained more than your tongue since we last met."

Bitterly he remembered how the brat had almost fooled him that night, and when she ignored him now, he turned a jaded eye to the frail woman who still appeared a nun even without the habit. "Ahhh, Eliza-beth. Have you decided you have gone long enough without a man? You did not used to be so prudish, I remember."

Eileen watched her mother's face grow gray and panicky as de Lacy held her arm in a most insinuating manner, and the band of tension snapped with her anger.

"Leave her alone or I will scream until even the nuns in the hills hear us. They will know who to blame, and you will not escape so easily this time."

De Lacy could not fail to recognize his brother's eyes this time as Eileen leaned out of the carriage and jerked her mother's arm from his grasp. The gray had grown as cold and hard as steel, and it was almost as if

Richard's ghost spoke through her words. He released Elizabeth and met the girl's gaze with interest.

"Now that you have so cleverly bandied my name about, I suppose you think you are safe from my wrath?"

Eileen made room for her mother to enter the carriage, but she did not tear her gaze from her uncle's. "I am no fool. Leave my mother alone and I will be as silent and simple as you can desire. Touch her again, and I will scar more than your jaw."

De Lacy's hand instinctively went to the jagged gash that he had received at a five-year-old's hands and contemplated the damage she might do as a grown woman, even a pregnant one. She would have the temerity to try, of that he had no doubt. He did not get where he was now by underestimating his enemies.

With cynical respect he bowed agreement. "If you play the part as well as the night we met, we shall go along smoothly."

He strode away, leaving one of his men to close the carriage door.

White-faced, the two women stared at each other while the carriage lurched into movement. They had only to look out the window to see the precariousness of their position. Half a dozen men rode on either side of the carriage, rough men with the bearing of soldiers. It had been an Irish army that had beaten back the English on the field of battle only two years ago. These men looked to be of much the same caliber.

"How can you speak so calmly to him?" Elizabeth gritted out from between clenched teeth. "I want to rip his entrails out through his nose. If he had a heart, I would eat it."

A wan trace of amusement crossed Eileen's face at this vehement outburst from a woman who had once thought to take holy vows.

"He intends to kill us. The longer we delay, the

more chances we have of escaping. It would pay to keep our wits about us."

Eileen boldly put her words into action. De Lacy made the mistake of thinking a silent woman a noncommunicative one, but both Eileen and her mother had years of experience in communicating without words. Perhaps the innkeepers and their patrons did not quite understand the distress these two silent women spoke of with their hands and eyes, but a trail of suspicion grew and murmured behind them wherever they went. None dared actually defy de Lacy and his bodyguards, but all remembered him.

As they traveled, word spread in advance of their arrival. The Englishman was treated with less and less respect while the two women became objects of some reverence. Eileen did not know what rumor had grown around them, but she found herself treated with awe and respect, her every wish anticipated except the one she most craved. Freedom they could not provide.

Irked by the accommodations he found himself lowered to at one small village, de Lacy appeared in the doorway of the spacious chamber where Eileen and Elizabeth made themselves at home. He glanced around at the linen-covered feather mattresses, the bathing tub, and porcelain washbowl and pitcher, and snarled. "I've half a mind to move in here with you. Or throw the two of you in the stable they offer me."

"Your gallantry exceeds your morality, my lord," Eileen replied sarcastically. In de Lacy's presence Elizabeth retreated into a frozen shell, and Eileen felt compelled to fill the gap. "Only you may find a small rebellion on your hands. From what little I understand of the language, there appears to be some tale circulating that my mother is a saint. You don't deal harshly with saints in these lands."

"Bahhh, it is that religious whining that has brought you to this in the first place. Not that I hold you guilty of such pious leanings, my dear niece." He gave Eileen's swollen figure a sardonic look. " 'Tis a pity you cannot be less like your father and more like me. As it is, I certainly don't need another brat claiming my lands. Your days of luxury will soon be at an end."

Elizabeth remained motionless in a far corner of the room, her cap still covering her hair and her cloak unfastened. Eileen knew she must drive her uncle from the room to ease her mother's fears, but she wished dearly to understand what emotion had worked to destroy all their lives.

With a slight lift of her inquiring brows she asked, "What did my father ever do to you that you must destroy all trace of him?"

De Lacy looked visibly startled. Then, with a shrug, he excused himself. "He always got everything I wanted, and then did not have the sense to keep it."

He strode out, slamming the door behind him.

From the corner Elizabeth spoke. "He coveted everything your father ever possessed. He resented Richard's being the eldest son. He swears their parents loved Richard more. He even craved the same women and horses. Your father bent over backward trying to offer Peter whatever he wanted. If Peter wished to court one of the village girls, Richard bowed out. If Peter wished to own the horse Richard bought, Richard would sell him. The only two things Richard never gave him were the lands and me. So Peter took them both."

She spoke as if she read the words from a book, but Eileen heard the emotion hidden behind them. For the first time she had some glimmer of understanding of what had happened that day.

"You do not need to speak of it," Eileen answered softly, wishing to spare her the pain.

"I will not speak of it again, but before we die, you must at least understand why. After he killed your father, he spent days raving his imagined misfortunes to me. He is perfectly sane in all else, but he is utterly mad when it comes to Richard. In the six short years of our marriage Richard came to realize this, too. It was one of the reasons he decided to declare his religion openly. He began selling off his lands to provide a school for the Catholic children in the county. It meant we would have little to live on but my dowry, but it also meant we could leave Peter behind and get away to some corner of the world where we could live in peace. His decision was the final blow to what wall of sanity remained in Peter."

Elizabeth rose and began to remove her cap and cloak. Eileen hesitated, uncertain if this meant the tale was complete. She could piece together many of the pieces from this knowledge, but she felt a gap remained.

The last piece fell in place as Elizabeth turned to her daughter and finished the tale. "There are always those who resent change and covet power. Peter had cultivated these types for years. The news that Richard practiced his religion and meant to protect it drew fury from the upper echelons of society. His decision to sell his lands drew fear and anger from every level. Peter had no difficulty in finding his band of assassins, I'm certain. I doubt that they had in mind killing women and children, but Peter chose that role for himself. I honestly don't believe he rode in with the intention of killing us, but his madness led him to worse. When you attacked him, he saw only Richard and a chance to destroy him. After that, he knew he could never hold me. We both thought he had killed you. It took days before the servants could get him drunk enough to pass out. By then I was barely conscious. I do not even remember being transported to the convent. When the fever ran its course, the physician told me what Peter had done to me would keep me from ever having children again. After that, I saw no reason to leave. I knew Peter had been told I was dead, so I did nothing to dispel the rumor, not even to write my sister. Without you and Richard, I wanted no further part of the world."

Utterly drained, Elizabeth completed her undressing and fell into the bed. Within minutes she was sound asleep.

Eileen continued to sit and watch her, unable to seek that blessed state of oblivion. She tried not to imagine what that madman below could have done to her frail mother in those few days, but her imagination had always been too vivid. De Lacy was a large, powerful man even now. Fifteen years ago he would have been in the prime of manhood. The images played through her mind in painful detail. Drake had never been anything but gentle with her, yet she often found herself bruised and sore after an evening of lovemaking. How much worse might it be were the act done with vengeance and hatred?

The steely inner strength she had drawn on these last few days was almost exhausted. Trapped in this cage de Lacy had built around her, Eileen had tried not to tire herself with useless protests, but the tension had taken its toll. Had it only been herself, she might have held out longer, but the terror of what might happen to her mother and the babe ate at the fabric of her soul. The tale she had just heard gave her the renewed strength of fury, but that was a surface strength at best. She had nothing left to fall back on. How would they ever escape this fiend's hold?

De Lacy's warning that they had only a few days of luxury left confirmed Eileen's worst fears. In a few days they would be in Calais and on a ship that de Lacy commanded. She doubted if they would ever see the other shore.

Michael watched Sir John grow old before his eyes as the small priest recited his tale with much gesticulation and anxiety. Michael understood little of what was being said, but he understood Eileen's absence and the name de Lacy. It did not take long to put two and two together. He wished desperately to ask where and when and be gone after her, but he curbed his impatience and awaited Sir John's word.

Not until they were outside the convent's walls again did the baronet find the strength to speak what must be told. The small band of friends and ex-soldiers Michael had so hastily assembled lingered politely with the horses as Sir John gripped Michael's shoulder for support before speaking. Only Pierre Monsard hurried forward, anxious to learn why Eileen did not accompany them. The older men took little heed of his presence.

"De Lacy was a week ahead of us. He has taken both of them."

Michael flinched. An entire week. It would not pay to dwell on what could be done in a week.

But Sir John was not through. His lined face an ashen gray, he lifted his blurred eyes to meet Michael's stern ones. "Eileen is near seven months gone with Drake's child."

Beside them, Drake's young cousin blanched. "*Mon Dieu*," he whispered to no one in particular.

Chapter XXII

———— ❧ ————

London—Calais
November, 1746

Drake leaned lazily against the cell door listening to
Edmund's bragging. As long as his cousin felt secure
in the iron bars between them, he dared speak as he
had never done before. Drake clenched his teeth until
the muscle in his jaw twitched, but Edmund was too
engrossed in himself to note the poised tension of an
animal prepared to strike.

Not until he uttered Eileen's name did Edmund
realize the extent of his danger. The supposedly locked
door flew open and Drake leapt to grab his cousin by
the cravat.

"When? When did you hear from de Lacy?" Drake
shook Edmund so brutally the silent men lurking in
the darkened cell behind him stepped in to interfere.

Edmund grew white at the stately appearance of
these members of His Majesty's cabinet, but the hand
at his throat presented more immediate peril.

"A week . . . a week ago." Edmund gasped. "He'll
have her by now. There's nothing you can do."

Drake's other hand closed around his cousin's wind-
pipe. "How does he know where she is?"

"Avignon . . ." Edmund gasped for breath until
Drake loosened his grip enough to allow air to pass.
"Avignon had you traced, and de Lacy knew of the
convent. He has men outside all the walls. She has

288

only to set foot outside the doors and she is his. It's too late, cuz."

Even in his capture Edmund could not disguise his triumph. At long last he had found Drake's weakness.

As Edmund began to turn blue, Lord Westly stepped from behind the other witnesses to lay a hand on Drake's shoulder.

"We have heard enough, Sherbourne. I am sorry for my part in this, but Edmund is my responsibility now. Go to Miss de Lacy. We will not stop you."

With a cry of anger and despair Drake flung Edmund across the floor and fled down the corridor. The door at the end barely swung forward in time as he shoved through the opening and raced down the stairs. Not enough time. There would never be enough time.

Outside, he spied a rangy stallion of promising strength and grabbed the reins from the startled attendant. They could hang him for a horse thief. The convent was more than a week away, and Eileen would never stay within the walls for more than a day at a time.

Eileen stared out the upper-story window to the ships bobbing in the bay below, their sails tightly furled and all signs of life swept away by the torrents of rain pouring from leaden skies. Rain ran in rivers down the warped and dingy glass, making it impossible to open the window to allow in even the slightest breath of air. Confinement to these narrow chambers these last days had given her a taste of the tomb, and the need to scream and flee kept her fingers clinging to the windowsill.

The child within her weighed heavier than usual, and she could not stand for long. Lowering herself to the window seat, Eileen glanced at her mother. Elizabeth de Lacy sat calmly in the room's only chair, counting her rosary ceaselessly from morning to night.

Whatever assistance she sought from the heavens above did not seem to be forthcoming.

De Lacy entered the room without knocking, an irritating habit he had developed these past days. Eileen threw him a look of annoyance and returned to staring out the window. Elizabeth did not stop counting even to acknowledge his presence.

"We sail when the tide turns. I've had enough of this delay," he announced without preliminaries.

"Besides, if our bodies by some mischance are washed up to shore, it will be easy to blame the storm." Eileen spoke without inflection, without so much as looking at her captor.

Before de Lacy could make an angry reply, Elizabeth rose from her chair and distracted him. In the gloomy light none of the lovely copper shone in her hair, but even the few wisps of gray did nothing to detract from her glowing beauty. De Lacy watched with suspicion as she approached him. She had not spoken two words to him throughout the journey.

"Let Eileen and her child go free. She cannot be a threat to you." She spoke softly, without a hint of plea in her voice.

De Lacy leaned back against the door jamb and studied his brother's wife with malevolent interest. He disdained powder and wigs while traveling, and his own black locks framed his dark, sardonic face.

"She has already threatened me. As long as she lives, I can expect a knife in my back at any time. I don't like being threatened, Elizabeth." His gaze traveled over her slender length, stripping away the layers of modest clothing to the woman he had possessed so thoroughly for too short a time.

Eileen turned back into the room and spoke sharply. "Don't plead for me, Mother. I have no fear of dying. It will be better than spending my life waiting for him to turn his back so I may plunge a knife into it."

Elizabeth ignored her taunt and de Lacy's sharp bark of laughter. "She is young and does not understand the finality of death. Let me be hostage against her good behavior."

Eileen gasped and opened her mouth to protest, but one look at her mother convinced her it would be foolish. The woman she remembered from so long ago stood there now, her emerald eyes blazing, her stance proud and haughty. She could not rob her mother of this chance to return to life, however briefly. The look in de Lacy's eyes would have withered a flower, and Eileen had to bite her tongue to keep from crying out.

"That is an interesting proposition." The earl kept his arms crossed over his chest as he eyed his opponent speculatively. "After all these years without a man, you must be more than eager to so readily offer your services to me."

Elizabeth's lips grew pale and pinched, but she did not retreat. "If that is what I must do, God will forgive me. Let Eileen go."

"No, Mother!" Eileen cried in dismay, coming to her feet, but the two combatants took no notice.

De Lacy's mouth bent in an anticipatory grin. "I cannot allow her to return home, but it would be easy enough to sell her into service in the colonies. After fifteen years of indenture she may give up the foolish notion of revenge. A wench like that will likely find a husband to father her bastard and settle there. That's the best I can offer, Elizabeth."

Eileen saw her mother's silent nod of agreement and, stunned, fell back into the window seat. Hope licked at her heart. She might have days, even weeks to make her escape. But the horror of what her mother offered in exchange for this small reprieve was revolting to every sentiment she possessed.

Trying to hide the tremor in her voice, Eileen intruded, "You had best delay payment until you are assured of my arrival in the colonies, Mother. The opportunity to drop me in an even larger sea will have already occurred to our charming host."

Elizabeth sent her a weak, grateful smile. De Lacy scowled.

"I will cut your tongue out one of these days and make you truly silent." Turning his black gaze back to Elizabeth, he declared, "You have until we arrive at my home to make your decision."

He turned on his heel and strode out.

Eileen held her hand to the place where Drake's child kicked restlessly, and her eyes lifted to meet her mother's.

"For the babe," Elizabeth whispered, emerald eyes wide with the fear and loathing of her encounter. "He will come for you. I know it."

Eileen nodded, but an icy chill crept through her bones. Drake would come, if they did not hang him. And even then, how many weeks, how many months would it be before he found her? Her mother would surely die in the hands of a man like de Lacy, but she—and her unborn child—would die if she refused. The choice was no choice at all.

A small break in the clouds overhead let them pass from the inn to the waiting ship without being drenched. Eileen pushed back the hood of her cloak and breathed deeply of the cold, damp air. A glimmer of sunshine slipped through the clouds to send a shimmer of copper down the long braid her mother had plaited for her. She preferred the simple style for this weather, not realizing how the childlike effect framed her delicate, heart-shaped face into a portrait of innocence. More than one turned to stare as she walked slowly to meet her fate.

Out in the bay, a ship flying an English flag tacked dangerously in the stormy wind in an attempt to reach shore. Eileen turned a pensive stare to the billowing sails and wished for some way to stow herself aboard this new arrival. Had it not been for her ungainly shape, she could easily have slipped away from de Lacy's men in these narrow streets. But she could not run fast enough any longer, or climb over fences or under boxes as before. There would be no seeking safety on another ship. De Lacy's vessel awaited.

Sir John's lips tightened grimly as he listened to the tale told eagerly by the village innkeeper. He gave the man a gold coin for his kindness to the two "saints" who had resided in his upper room for a night, and thanked him for his information. He strode out with the firmness of a young man, but his face beneath the unpowdered gray hair was lined and old.

Saints indeed, he muttered to himself as he approached the small band of horsemen waiting for him. If de Lacy had made saints of those two miscreants, he should thank the man. If they ever caught up with him.

He met Michael's anxious gaze with a shake of his head. "They are well and still two days ahead of us. Calais is another day's ride. We will have to search every inn in the town and pray they did not board ship immediately."

The other members of the party looked glum at this news. Except for Michael and Pierre, the others were only casually acquainted with Eileen and had never known her mother, but they had become as involved in this quest as her uncle. The idea of two helpless females in the hands of a mercenary villain like de Lacy enraged their sense of justice, and it had become a matter of soldierly pride to catch the bastard. To a man, they followed Michael's gallop down the road to Calais with grim speed and murderous intent.

They arrived in the port city just before dusk. Storm clouds had settled thickly on the horizon again, and a

cold wind whipped their cloaks about their ankles as
they sped through the mud to the waterfront. Soaked
to the skin, besplattered with their week's journey,
they made a sorry sight as they dismounted in front of
a low-slung, rough stone tavern.

With a determined set to his jaw Michael gave the
orders. "We'll divide in half. Pierre can speak the
language. Three of us will follow him and begin questioning down the road to the right. Sir John will take
the rest of you and go to the left. Fire two shots in the
air if you find anything."

"If nothing else, that will test our gunpowder," Pierre
grumbled as he removed his once jaunty tricorne and
shook the water from it. But he swaggered proudly
down the road directed with the knowledge that he
had some value in this adventure.

Cursing the tide that delayed their arrival, Drake
trained his spyglass on the harbor ahead. He could not
hope to see anything except empty streets, but the
frustration of being this close and unable to get closer
made him restless.

The foul weather had driven all signs of life from
the ships lined near the shore but one. Drake trained
his glass in that direction with idle interest. Braving
the rough weather, men scuttled up and down the
rigging, releasing the battened sails to catch the air.
Someone must be in a hurry to chance these winds,
but the tide would soon be in their favor. It would
make for a speedy journey.

Just as he moved to turn the glass on the houses
along the shore, Drake caught a glimpse of movement
that did not appear natural to a ship's deck. He adjusted the focus and searched the stern, locating the
whipping black cloak that had caught his eye. Few
sailors wore cloaks. Even fewer stood as small and
delicate as this. The wind caught the cloak's hood and

flung it back, revealing a long, shining strand of copper hidden beneath.

Drake yelled and the sailors standing nearby scrambled to attention, but the silent figure on that distant ship could not hear. His fingers crushed the glass's barrel as he fought to bring the still figure closer, but the mist in his eyes prevented certain focusing.

It was Eileen; it had to be. What other female would stand in this gale without even the protection of her hood? But even as he watched, a towering, masculine figure approached her and led her firmly from the deck to somewhere in the ship's interior. Drake could not even glimpse her face as she went without protest. That seemed odd, but so did her movements. Eileen had always darted about with the grace and agility of a butterfly. This woman moved slowly and heavily.

Drake cursed and flung the glass to the nearest sailor before running to the helm. It had to be Eileen, and if de Lacy had harmed her in any way, he would murder the villain with his bare hands. In the meantime they had to keep that ship from leaving the harbor.

As the captain maneuvered his frail craft to intercept the right-of-way of the larger, Drake borrowed the captain's glass to study the deck moving in closer now. Things had changed since his last glimpse, and his heart took a sudden leap of hope. In the gathering gloom of dusk there appeared to be a struggle of some sort on the gangplank. A sword was brandished, catching the last rays of sun, and a puff of smoke from a firearm caught in the wind.

Drake groaned as more sailors poured from the hatch at this first signal of trouble, but they found an obstacle in their way. From over the side of the ship a six-foot giant leapt with gun in hand, shortly to be joined by three others bearing swords and muskets. In the ensuing battle Drake could identify only the familiar figure. Michael.

There was no time to allow jealousy to interfere. As his ship scraped against the side of the larger one, Drake raced to the bow and helped heave the grappling hooks over the side. Before anyone could stop him, he had the rope in his hands, pulling himself aboard. Eager to join the fray, the men behind followed his lead.

From her cabin below deck, Eileen heard the first shot with a start of alarm. Cautiously she peered out into the corridor and, seeing no one, opened the door across from hers. The minuscule officer's quarters had room for only one bunk and a trunk, and she and her mother had each been assigned their own. Elizabeth glanced up in fear as her daughter entered.

Another shot rang out and they could hear the pounding of feet racing across the deck overhead. Memories of a day long ago when shots and screams had destroyed their world swept through their thoughts, and they grabbed each other's hands.

But not for long. Wild, searing hope flashed through Eileen's eyes as the sound of swords clashing rang down the hatchway. It could only mean help had arrived, and she would do all she could to aid it. With a swirl of long skirts she raced down the corridor to the stairs to the upper deck, Elizabeth close behind her.

Eileen's thick, auburn braid caught in the wind as her head rose above the hatchway, and her breath was nearly swept away at the sight her eyes encountered. Men swore and fought and tumbled about, falling over lengths of hemp, rolling about the deck with knives flashing, and slashing the air with steel swords. Those with pistols and muskets had flung them aside without reloading after the first shot, leaping into the fray with fists and knives and whatever weapons came to hand. She gasped as she recognized the younger Monsard

brother rolling about the deck with a lad much his
size, fists flying furiously, but her gaze was quickly
distracted by another sight.

"Drake!" she screamed, watching with horror as a
burly sailor raised a barrel stave behind Drake's head
while Drake fought off one of de Lacy's guards with
his sword.

With a powerful riposte and a quick step Drake
threw off the other's sword and turned to slash his
cowardly attacker. The sailor fell, and the clash of
swords rang out again as the guard regained his footing. Eileen crawled up out of the stairwell and grabbed
a water barrel. With her mother's help they turned the
container on its side and shoved until it rolled across
the deck, directly toward the guard's legs.

With a laugh of triumph Drake leapt out of the way
just as the barrel collided with his opponent, throwing
the other man off balance and into the waters below.
In a single stride he crossed the space to Eileen and
caught her by the waist, planting a resounding kiss
upon her cheek.

"Well done, princess!" And then with a proud grin
to the burden she carried, he boasted, "Twins! I told
you!"

There was not further time to exchange pleasant-
ries. Drake glanced in concern as Eileen's mother
pulled a knife from the hand of a fallen sailor and
hurried down the deck. Hugging Eileen close and pulling her back into the shelter of the bulkhead, he
glanced around for a familiar face.

Spying Michael's large frame bearing down on them,
Drake shouted and signaled. Catching Eileen by surprise, Drake shoved her into his friend's arms.

"Get her to my ship and tell the captain to get the
hell out of here. This isn't the Barbary coast and
pirates aren't welcome. We'll have the gendarmes on
us soon, and I'll not have the brat born in this hole."

With this terse message Drake raced after Elizabeth, leaving Eileen to Michael's care.

Too shocked to protest, Eileen found herself lifted up in Michael's powerful hold and carried unceremoniously to the side of the ship, where she was handed in a most unseemly fashion to arms waiting below.

Before she thoroughly realized what had happened, grappling hooks were removed, anchors weighed, and sails unfurled. Drake's ship caught the ebbing tide, and the stormy breeze blew them out to sea.

Chapter XXIII

———— ❧ ————

England
November, 1746

Eileen leaned against the cabin wall and watched the last of the previous day's storm clouds disappear over the horizon. After these past weeks of tension she felt too drained to even attempt to make sense of yesterday's battle. All she knew was that Drake was alive and the babe was safe. To question further would just cause grief and worry she did not feel prepared to handle.

She gave Michael a smile as he fought the cold wind to reach her sheltered position. There had been no time to talk before. They had watched only until they had seen that Drake's crew had control of de Lacy's craft before Eileen had been swept off to her cabin. Perhaps now a few questions would be answered, although the worried concern in Michael's eyes warned his first words would be the usual cautionary ones.

"You should not be out here in this cold," Michael admonished, coming to stand before her. Without his wig, his short-cropped fair hair provided little frame for his broad, square face, but his eyes were gentle and saved his features from plainness.

Eileen smiled at her own astuteness in judging his greeting, but she made no effort to follow his advice. "It is too good to be alive to complain of a little cold.

Tell me, how will the others return if we have taken Drake's ship?"

Michael frowned and shoved his hands in the deep pockets of his coat. "I daresay they will purloin de Lacy's craft, if they can, but Sir John had made arrangements, too. That is not a matter of concern."

Eileen pulled her cloak around her and studied Michael intently. He seemed more distant than she remembered, more reluctant to speak openly. Had she misjudged his feelings that badly when she ran off with Drake? She had not thought there was any more than affection between them, but even that seemed less than she remembered.

"There is some other matter of concern?" she asked lightly, silver eyes hiding her true feelings.

Michael shifted his weight uneasily. He had misunderstood Eileen's character from the very first, blinded by his gratitude and eagerness for the opportunity she offered. He still did not understand her completely, but he saw her more clearly now. She was no silent, compliant child who needed his protection, but a woman with a will and a mind of her own. He did not object to that, but it did not make his task less difficult.

"You," he finally blurted out. "And Drake," he amended, with a touch of anger.

Eileen raised her eyebrows inquisitively. "Unless de Lacy escapes, I am safe now. I fail to see how I may be a matter of concern. Is Drake still in trouble? Are you telling me he cannot return after us?"

"Oh, hell, Eileen!" Michael exploded, pacing up and down rather than meet her fearless gaze. "The last I heard, Edmund was under suspicion, and Drake needed only the formalities for the charges against him to be dropped. That's not my concern, and you know it."

Bewildered, Eileen watched his frustrated pacing with increasing anxiety. "Then, what is it? If it is the loss of my dowry that worries you, I am certain Drake

will find some means of making it up to you. I regret
what we have done to you in return for all your
kindnesses, but . . ."

Michael threw up his hands in surrender and met
her gaze frankly. "Diane and I have agreed that it
would be best if our betrothal remained unbroken and
the weddings went on as planned before. Drake cannot marry you both. I was not convinced you would
agree, but now that there is a child in question . . ."
He faltered, then boldly took the plunge. "Tongues
will wag when both brides walk to the altar as moth-
ers, but there is some small justification that yours could
be mine. Drake will have to claim Lady Pamela's."

Just minutes before, the sky had appeared clear and
blue, but clouds had come from nowhere to obscure
the sun. Eileen fought the shiver that turned her lips
to blue and her legs to jelly. Lady Pamela. How easily
she had forgotten the grand Lady Pamela. Of course,
that child would be Drake's, the product of centuries
of noble breeding and aristocratic heritage. The Lady
Pamela would make a perfect marchioness and raise
well-bred little lords and ladies. The child kicking within
Eileen's womb was the product of an eccentric Irishman
and the hoyden daughter of a country squire. The only
lineage she knew of was a mad uncle and Catholic
grandparents. She had learned no manners or etiquette, knew nothing of Drake's society or entertaining. Her children would most likely be rebellious brats
unacceptable to any level of society. Drake had married her out of desperation only. Now everything had
changed.

Refusing to reveal the sharp pangs of grief and
despair ravaging her soul, Eileen lifted her chin proudly.
The fact that Drake had told no one, not even Diane,
of his marriage spoke all she needed to know. "Thank
you, Michael, but I will not ask you to honor our
betrothal. I know now that we would not suit. Tell

me, how is Diane? How has she come through this upheaval?"

Left floundering by this reaction to his noble offer, Michael attempted to find an even keel again. "She is worried about both of you. Drake should think of these things before he cavorts off on these mad escapades. She is not well at all, and I lay the blame on him."

Startled by this unusual vehemence, Eileen set aside her own concerns and contemplated this new development. Michael appeared more animated than usual, and a flicker of something in his eyes caught her interest.

"Diane's health has never been a problem. You are saying she is worrying herself ill?"

Michael ran his hand through his hair, and anxiety lined his face. "She is so helpless. I think it eats at her soul not to be able to take things into her own hands and make them right. She can only sit and pray someone will listen. I wanted to tear Edmund into mincemeat when he began erecting those damned fences, but I had no right to do anything. Diane had to listen to the villagers' complaints and make promises she could not keep. Edmund listened to nothing she said. He even threatened to fire me, but Drake had drawn up a contract so tight he could not touch it. All he could do was ignore all my suggestions. Diane cried when he had the commons plowed under and, damn it all, I could do nothing!"

Eileen's eyes grew wide with wonder at this revelation from hitherto so taciturn a man. A small hint of a smile played about her lips as she recognized some of the symptoms.

"You love her, don't you?" Eileen put her hands in her pockets and let the wind whip back her cloak as she contemplated Michael's reaction to her question. He scowled.

"That is not to the point. The point is that Drake

has much to account for. If it were not for Diane, I would call him out. As it is, I think we had best marry quickly and discreetly before he returns. Once Diane knows you are both safe, she will come around."

Eileen smiled more broadly at this innocence. "Michael, you are a very good man, and I love you dearly—as a friend. Is there any chance that Diane might love you as something more?"

Michael began to look irritated. "Do you listen to nothing I say? How do I know how Diane feels? What difference would it make? Any man would be lucky to have a woman like that, but, fool that she is, she thinks she cannot be a wife unless she is a 'whole' woman, whatever that might be. You have two legs, but I'm not certain you have half a head. Does that make you less a woman?"

The need to laugh was overwhelming. She was alive and Drake was alive and their child was strong and kicking. Perhaps everything had not turned out as planned, but Eileen held too much respect for life to allow its blows to keep her down.

"Did you know you are very cute when you are angry?" Eileen asked outrageously. Before he could murder her, she added hastily, "Michael, I am listening to you. I am listening with a heart that loves as surely as does your own. I must follow my heart and so must you. Diane is of age. She needs no one's permission to marry. As her husband you will have the right to protect her from the Edmunds of this world. And the Drakes, if necessary."

Mildly bemused, Michael stared at Eileen's upturned face for confirmation of what he had heard. Arched eyebrows held a hint of amusement, but the soft glow of her eyes gave all the evidence he needed. He would have to kill Drake, after all.

"Sir John cannot exert the same influence as Lord Westly. Drake cannot marry you, Eileen," he argued with concern.

That was scarcely her problem, but the less said about their hasty marriage, the better. If Drake wished to seek a quiet annulment, she would not stand in his way. She knew her own faults as well as any. Eileen shrugged.

"Perhaps I am not meant for marriage. It does not worry me as it ought. But you and Diane are of a different sort. I think she needs you, Michael."

Michael looked uncomfortable. "Perhaps so, but not as a husband. She has made it quite clear that she does not intend to marry. I am a man, Eileen, with a man's normal desires, but I would not even ask that of her if I thought she would have me. But she is too proud to accept my offer or any man's."

Eileen touched his face gently, then took his arm, indicating she wished to return to her cabin. He protected her from the worst of the wind with his bulk as he led her down the deck.

"Diane is angry that she cannot walk or ride or run with any children that she might have, but it is not her inability to bear children that keeps her from marrying. It is only her legs that are damaged, not the rest of her." Eileen spoke quietly, not facing him, giving him time to absorb what she said without embarrassment.

"You can't be certain of that." Michael stalled, unwilling to believe what she offered.

"I cannot be certain the sun will rise tomorrow, either. I only know what Diane has told me. She has badgered her doctors for years with questions they cannot answer, but that is one they can, however unwillingly. They have hemmed and hawed and spoke of difficulties, but they all agree, physically she is capable of having children. That is not the part that worries Diane."

Michael grew quiet, understanding they traversed upon a delicate subject that they should rightly not be discussing at all. But the glimpse of happiness she had handed him made him eager for more.

"You are telling me I must convince her that her useless legs mean nothing to the way I feel for her. That is not easily done. I am not a man of wealth. She may think I say what I do simply for the money she represents."

Eileen stopped at the door of her cabin and turned to face him with a light smile. "Tell her you will take a position with my uncle and she must learn to live on an estate manager's income. If she loves you, she will take you anyway. Just take good care of her, Michael, or I will regret telling you all of this."

Michael caught her hand and prevented her from escaping. "I still cannot desert you like this. Your child needs a name. If Drake will not provide . . ."

Eileen shook her hand free. "The child has a name, Michael. I cannot marry you. I am already married."

Without any other explanation, she disappeared into her room and closed the door.

Fog covered the coast as the ship anchored in the bay. A small dory carried them to land and to the tavern, where they warmed themselves before the blazing fire while Mortimer Drew hastily ordered a carriage to carry them on the remainder of their journey. The cold November night held no hospitality, but Eileen was eager to leave by the time the carriage drew up to the tavern door. She had had plenty of time to make her plans. Now she need only carry them out.

Mortimer Drew drove the ancient equipage, leaving Michael and Eileen to sit in silence in the carriage's musty interior. Eileen had refused to reveal any more to him than she already had, and no other topics crossed their minds. As Summer Hall grew visible around the bend, Michael took Eileen's hand.

"Eileen, do not let me do something that is less than

honorable. Sir John has placed his trust in me. Tell me truthfully, have I reason to call Drake out?"

Men and honor. Eileen sighed, not understanding their code. Life had little to do with honor and much to do with living. Honor was a pleasant thing to have, but dueling seldom encouraged it. She lied without a qualm.

"Drake has naught to do with anything. I ran away and I married. All Drake did was see to my comfort. Now go to Diane and tell her we are both well and happy and ask if she will join you in becoming the babe's godparents."

Michael kissed her hand as the carriage drew to a halt outside the Hall. "I doubt that I can believe a word you say, but if Sir John accepts it, it is all for the best. I mean to ride on tonight. Wish me luck."

Eileen caressed his cheek. "I want to be the first to hear the news. Be quick."

And still she lied, for she had no intention of being here when the news arrived.

Lady Summerville crowed with delight at Eileen's return, but by the time her niece had finished her tale, her pretty features had grown pale and thoughtful. Her hand lingered on Eileen's hair as her niece curled up on the small stool beside her bed, but she made no attempt to hold her back.

"I am so very sorry that I cannot be the daughter you want me to be," Eileen finished miserably.

The miracle of actually hearing Eileen speak had taken away much of the pain of her words. After all these years of guessing what the child must be thinking, Emma felt mostly relief at actually hearing Eileen's thoughts. That she could not totally agree with their content was irrelevant.

"You are a grown woman now, Eileen. You must act as you think best. I would not want you to be any other way." She sighed and poured a small glass of sherry for each of them. "I could dearly wish to be with you in your lying-in. You should have some family with you at such a time."

"There are months before that must be considered. Perhaps all will be resolved by then."

"Months?" Emma lifted an inquiring eyebrow to her niece's already unwieldy size. "I am surprised the child was not born aboard ship. Drake must be mad to send you off like that without a woman to tend to you."

"Drake can count, Aunt Emma." Eileen smiled. "This is only the end of November. The babe is not due until late in January. There is plenty of time."

Emma looked dubious but had to accept the facts of the calendar. "I still do not think you ought to be traveling. There must be some easier way."

"I'm not looking for an easy way. Drake must make a choice. I know of no other way to give it to him."

"I suppose, in your own odd way, you are right, but things were never done that way in my time. I will have difficulty explaining it to your uncle."

With a grin and a quick kiss to her understanding aunt's cheek, Eileen replied, "I would advise explaining nothing. Men just don't understand these things."

Emma laughed and met her niece's dancing gaze with love. "Just don't stay away so long this time. Now that we can talk, I will miss you more than ever."

"You will have my mother to gossip with. Just think of all the years that must be caught up on." With a hasty hug Eileen left the room. It was always better to end farewells with laughter. She would be gone well before her aunt woke in the morning.

Quigley did not understand in the least why miss should arrive one night and leave the next morning, particularly in her delicate condition. He understood even less the reason for letting her out of the carriage in the middle of nowhere with no more than a small satchel to her name. It would seem she was the traitor the soldiers sought and not Lord Sherbourne.

Eileen read her faithful bodyguard's scowl with ease,

but she could offer him little reassurance. She merely thanked him for rising so early and pressed a coin in his palm to remind him of the need for his silence.

"If Sir John asks, I got to tell him, miss," Quigley protested.

"Tell him you are only following Lady Summerville's orders, Quigley. That will send him scurrying back to the house quick enough. But if even Lady Summerville insists, then I suppose you must tell. It will not matter so greatly."

Here, on her own territory, she could hide easily enough, even if she could not move so quickly as before. Strangers could be seen for some distance. She would have sufficient warning to disappear. No, Quigley could tell Sir John without harming a thing, now that she was home again.

Eileen smiled and waved as the carriage rattled away. Taking the short cut through his lordship's orchards, where a few culls still clung to the trees, and through the woods of his lordship's game preserve, she soon strode quickly down the hill to the awakening village, whistling happily and munching on her breakfast of apples.

Chapter XXIV

———— 🍎 ————

England
December, 1746

Horse and rider were well lathered by the time they came to a prancing halt at the foot of the long stairway to Sherbourne, but the jubilant grin on the rider's face spoke of a race well run. He swung eagerly from the saddle and took the steps two at a time, nearly beating the footman to the door.

Flinging off hat and gloves and throwing them to the equally beaming servant, Drake demanded, "Where is my wife?"

The footman's smile died of incomprehension, but Drake scarcely noticed as he heard sounds of laughter drifting from the music room. She would be with Diane, of course, and he strode rapidly down the hallway to the pair of broad, paneled doors.

Throwing them wide with the triumphant gesture of a king returned to his palace, Drake came to an abrupt halt before he had taken two paces into the room.

"What in hell . . .!" He glared at the two figures half reclining on the sofa.

Michael leapt to his feet at once, but Diane continued to lie lazily against the rolled arm, a mischievous light brightening her usually serene face to glowing beauty. She met her brother's gaze with defiance.

"Welcome home, Ulysses," she murmured dryly as the two men attempted to kill each other with looks.

"I demand some explanation, Jasper." Drake's hand did not go to the hilt of his sword but clenched in a threatening fist.

"I had thought to tell you at a more propitious time, but if you must break down closed doors, do not expect courtesy in return. Diane and I are to be married. We were just discussing the date."

Stunned, Drake glanced to his sister for confirmation, then back to his old friend. The grim determination in Michael's eyes warned angry denials would be useless, but Drake's own joy softened this blow. With a laugh he realized Michael had stolen no less than he—one sister for one fiancée.

"I think a brotherly discussion might be called for, but I am in no mood for it at the moment." Drake dismissed the occasion hurriedly. "Where is Eileen?"

Michael and Diane's expressions went swiftly from relief to bewilderment.

"Eileen?" Diane asked cautiously, struggling to regain a sitting position. Michael instantly leapt to her aid, catching her skirts and helping her swing her legs over the chair's edge.

A flicker of suspicion made Drake suddenly wary. "Eileen," he repeated firmly. "Where is my wife?"

"Wife?" Both repeated blankly.

"Since when has this room acquired an echo?" he demanded furiously. "Or is this some new game to mock me? Haven't I endured enough? *Where is my wife*?"

"Lady Pamela, you mean," Diane ventured, not daring to allow the sudden hope burgeoning in her heart.

"Pamela?" Drake stared at her in incredulity. "You mean Edmund hasn't married the poor twit yet? Even from behind bars he could manage one last gesture of decency."

Michael had a fleeting glimpse of doom and sat quite abruptly on the sofa. "Edmund?"

Deciding love had scrambled their brains, Drake recited patiently, "My cousin, Edmund, and my former fiancée, Pamela. They are still expecting a child, are they not? Although"—he counted swiftly on his fingers—"it seems to me the child ought to be well on its way into the world by now. Surely you did not think I was fool enough to believe the bastard to be mine?"

Michael and Diane exchanged guilty glances, and Drake experienced an incredible impression of sinking. "You thought the child was mine?" he asked in disbelief. When they nodded, he groaned. "And you told Eileen?" The words came through his clenched teeth in torment.

"I did not know . . . She said nothing of being your wife. I only meant to protect her," Michael offered lamely, cringing as he remembered what Eileen had given him in return.

"Protect her," Drake groaned. "Why did you not just slap her in the face?"

"That's enough, Drake," Diane spoke sharply. "It is your own fault for being so closemouthed about everything. You could at least have had the decency to tell me you were wed. Here I have been worrying myself sick that if His Majesty did not hang you, Lord Westly would shoot you and Sir John horsewhip your remains. Surely you must have some idea where Eileen could have gone. Is she not with Sir John?"

"We just came from Summer Hall. When she was not there, I simply assumed . . ." Drake swung around as he heard whistling in the hall. The voices that followed, however, were male, and his face composed itself into a polite mask.

Auguste and Pierre rambled in, gesticulating wildly as they caught each other up on the past weeks at the same time. Following behind in resigned amusement came Teddy and James.

Drake brightened. "Good, just the men I need. Auguste, Pierre, ride back to Summer Hall and see if you can find out Eileen's whereabouts from anyone there."

Pierre's face fell nearly to the ground. He had just run the wildest race of his life in Drake's trail and had been without sleep for nearly twenty-four hours prior to that. To turn around and go back again? He shook his head in bewilderment.

"Drake, you are not thinking clearly," Michael interrupted. "Go upstairs, get some rest, let me ride to Sir John. I left her with her aunt. Surely she would not disappear without some word."

Drake strode impatiently through the room to stare at the gathering clouds on the horizon. "It's going to snow. There isn't much time. Michael, you've seen her. My God, what if she is out there in the woods somewhere, living off stolen apples and berries? You don't know the little monster. I can't just sit here and wait. My heir could be born in a snowdrift."

At this mention of an heir, the newcomers glanced around expectantly for enlightenment. Only Diane understood their predicament, and she filled in the gaps in a whisper while Drake and Michael argued.

"Eileen might be headstrong, but she is no fool. Let me go to Sir John and enlist his help. If she cannot be found at Summer Hall, we're likely to find her sooner if there is a number of us."

Drake nodded agreement to this sensibile suggestion, though in his heart he knew logic did not apply to Eileen. If she wanted to hide, they would never find her. His only consolation lay in the fact that she had always left a trail if any cared to follow. But this time it had been well over a fortnight. The trail might be more than cold by now.

Diane intruded as Michael hurriedly left the room, leaving the others restlessly milling about. "What of Lord de Lacy, Drake? He will not represent any further danger, will he?"

Drake gave a reluctant grin as he turned to face his

audience again. "That is the reason it has taken us so long to return. It seems Eileen comes by her temper honestly. Her good mother—and you must realize, Lady de Lacy is even tinier than Eileen—went after the earl with a dagger. She only nicked him, of course, but then she found a bottle, and when he meant to throttle her, she broke it over his head. A damned good wallop she gave him. He fell like an unmanned fortress. That caused all manner of rioting among his men and we had a time of it for a while, until the gendarmes appeared. Then it seemed nobody could find his noble lordship's remains."

Drake's tale-telling drew a gasp from Diane, and the rest of his audience appeared intrigued, all except Pierre, who already knew the ending. He scowled at having his own story up-staged.

"So the scoundrel's still on the loose?" Auguste asked impatiently.

"No. It appears some of my men got a little hasty about clearing the decks when the law came upon us. They flung everything that wasn't moving into the tide, which was going out. Rapidly. De Lacy wasn't moving."

"Oh, my." Diane held her fingers to her mouth and stared at her brother in horror. "That means he could still be alive. He could have woke when he hit that cold water and swum to shore."

"Which he undoubtedly did." Drake shrugged complacently. "We spent weeks explaining to the French what happened and looking for some trace of de Lacy. Lady de Lacy was in near hysterics when she realized she may not have killed him. She led the search and would have carried a sword if I had not persuaded her there were none available in her size. 'Tis a pity we did not find him first. I would have enjoyed watching her wallop the bastard again. She stole a frying pan from the inn kitchen."

A chorus of "bravos" went up from the male portion of the audience, but Diane waited with impatience for her brother to complete the tale.

"Unfortunately, his lordship fell into less gentle hands than Lady de Lacy's. You should not be hearing the rest of this, Diane."

Diane calmly lifted one eyebrow in a gesture characteristic of her brother. "Do you want me to change the subject? Shall I ask just exactly when you persuaded Eileen to marry an annoying fellow like yourself?"

Drake ignored the broad grins of his audience and hurried on. "Just don't tell Michael I told you this. De Lacy apparently made it to shore but was in no state to go far. He was discovered by a number of the less-than-gentle tribe who walk the waterfront. He was rolled for what he had and when he attempted to protest, a few others apparently joined in for entertainment. His last moments were less than pleasant, I venture to say. By the time the incident was reported to us, we could only identify the description they gave us. We were allowed to leave then, but I don't believe any of us will be welcome in Calais for a good long while."

Drake bowed to the applause of his audience, but his eyes wore a haunted look as he straightened and moved toward the doorway. "Wake me when Michael returns."

"Drake!"

Diane caught his attention, and he swung around patiently to listen.

"She loves you, you know." Diane waited, watching her brother's face.

"I forced her to marry me. How can you know that?" Drake demanded wearily. The weight of that knowledge sat heavy on his heart. He had given her no choice. She must have known she was carrying his child even then. She'd had no choice at all.

Diane smiled as she recognized the despair of thwarted love on her brother's handsome face. It was high time he realized he was not God but mortal like all else. "She told Michael she loved her husband. There would not be more than one, would there?"

A familiar light leapt to blue eyes as Drake considered this piece of knowledge. "Twins. It may be twins. You can all be godparents."

With this utterly incomprehensible reply Drake left the room, his step a trifle jauntier than a moment before.

Michael arrived by dinnertime and it was all the small party could do to keep Drake from setting out the instant Michael made his report. Not only was Eileen not at Summer Hall, but her mother had disappeared shortly after her arrival also.

"Damn and blast it to bloody hell!" Drake swore, pacing up and down in front of the fire in the study. "Did you search all the hiding places in the cellars? The cottages in the woods?"

Michael sank wearily into a high-backed chair beside the fire and rested his frozen boots upon the grate. "We tore the place apart. Lady Summerville does not seem exceedingly worried, so I venture to say they are safe somewhere, but more than a little angry with you. I explained my error, and she was a trifle disturbed about that, but I don't think she really knows where they are. We can only hope they try to communicate with her sometime."

"Eileen? Communicate? You nearly have to bludgeon the little fool to get information out of her. Did you search Lady Summerville's estate, the one she offered as dowry? What about the Drews' tavern?"

Michael shook his head. "There was not enough time for all that. I knew you were anxious, and I came straight back. I don't think there's any real need for concern. She's safe, somewhere."

"Safe? Do you have any idea what she considers safe? Remind me to tell you sometime how she hid me

from His Majesty's finest. You are talking about a
woman who crossed half of France, alone, on a mule.
She could be in Ireland by now. I'm trusting she has
enough sense not to set out for the colonies in her
condition, or I wouldn't doubt she'd try that. For all I
know, she has a tree house somewhere and intends to
spend the winter living off apples."

Drake abruptly halted his pacing as the force of his
words struck home. Apples and trees. Not a tree house,
but a castle for a princess. She had gone home.

"You've thought of something?" Michael watched
him narrowly.

"The enchanted forest. Tell Diane to send out the
leprechaun army to search those other places I've
named, but I am going to the enchanted forest. Send
Diane any messages. If you do not find Eileen anywhere else, follow me. It may take an army to flush
the vixen from her den."

Drake practically sprang to the study door in his
haste to set out and was halfway into the hall before
Michael gathered his wits to yell after him.

"You want me to send someone to Ireland?" he
asked incredulously.

"Pierre and Auguste know the way. Let them toss a
coin," Drake yelled back, before disappearing in the
direction of the stable.

Snow had already begun to fall by the time Drake
set out. Diane had called him a fool for leaving in the
dark, but she had promised to send a carriage after
him in the morning. He'd had to wait until she scribbled a hasty note to Eileen and the cook had prepared
a feast for the new marchioness and the entire staff
came forward to offer their aid in the search. If he did
not find Eileen tonight, she would be the subject of a
search the likes England had never seen by morning.

Drake prayed it wouldn't come to that. Perhaps he
had done a lot of things wrong, but he had done them
for the right reasons. Surely she would understand

that. Perhaps he shouldn't have forced her to marry him, but there had not been time to tear away that defensive barrier she always wore. And if there were any chance she felt the same as he did . . . Their marriage could not be wrong. Even if she did not love him, it could not be wrong. He could never have let his child wear the name of bastard.

By the time the sky showed promise of growing light, Drake had worked himself into a frenzy of anger and despair. Snow had begun to blow in dry piles across the road, but it did not come down fast enough to accumulate. The bitter cold made him frantic for Eileen's safety, and anxiety heightened his anger. She should never have endangered herself and their child by disappearing in weather like this.

The enchanted forest where he had first met Eileen hid any promise of daylight, and Drake maneuvered the rutted cart paths with care. The woodcutter's cottage he remembered now lay in gutted ruins, but he stopped his horse and explored the remains just the same. Dawn gave just enough light to turn the fallen thatch and rotting timbers to dull gray, but not silver. She had not returned here.

That left no other choice. Sir John had told him of the village where he had found her. Drake knew the place, built on the remains of some medieval town adjoining the estate of a rather formidable earl who lived in London. The family would most likely be at home for the Christmas holidays, but Drake had no intention of calling upon their services unless necessary. He would search the village himself first. If she did not come out of hiding, he might resort to more desperate measures.

Smoke already rose from most of the chimneys in the village by the time Drake made his way out of the woods and onto the hill overlooking the tiny cottages. From this distance the low-lying buildings appeared to be a fairy-tale sketch from a childhood storybook. One or two of the larger houses sported slate tiles for roof, but most had neatly piled thatch. Cobbed walls sparkled with recent whitewash in the dawn's light, blending in with the patches of clear snow blowing across the hard-packed dirt road. The snow had all but given up, and the first rays of sun glittered on narrow windows.

Drake dismounted on the hill and carefully tethered his horse. Deliberately spreading a woolen blanket upon the frozen grass, he sat and made his breakfast from the meal packed in the saddle pouch. His gaze never left the village as he followed every movement. He would give her time to come to him.

An hour later, his patience had grown thin. The blacksmith had thrown open the forge doors and already worked at his day's task. An unusually well dressed tribe of children yelled and screamed and threw handfuls of loose snow at each other in the street. A tall, black-haired woman hung her wash out to freeze, and a stout, crippled old lady waddled over to keep her entertained. If Eileen were anywhere in that village, she knew of his presence by now, and she had not come out.

He could take that as a sign she did not wish to see him, but Drake had no intention whatever of heeding that wish. Whether she liked it or not, they were married, for better or worse, and it was about time the little heathen recognized the fact. She could not spend the rest of her life running away, or running after something that existed only in her imagination. She would have to accept him as he was, with all his faults and foibles. It was time the druid became a mortal just like him.

By the time Drake had pounded on half the doors in the village, his anger had worked to a boiling point. He knew she was here; there were signs of her everywhere, even if the deliberately blank stares and evasive answers he received were not evidence enough.

Sketches that could come only from Eileen's talented fingers graced the walls of half the rooms he had seen. The pinafores on the girls tumbling in the streets were decorated in gay embroidery with pictures of unicorns and laughing flowers. Even the boys carried small wooden shields painted in fanciful coats of arms as they played some game that called for fire-breathing dragons and damsels in distress. She was here, and he would tear the damned town down to find her.

Drake beat furiously upon the wooden door under a sign denoting a seamstress. He remembered Sir John mentioning a seamstress, and God only knew, Eileen had learned to make those delicate stitches somewhere. She had certainly spent little time with proper teachers. No one answered his knock, but before he could try the latch, one of the small girls in the street apparently became victim to a fire-breathing dragon. In her effort to escape, she tumbled at Drake's feet, tearing a great hole in her woolen gown and scraping her knee on the cobblestone path.

The child's anguished cries brought Drake to his knees beside her. Feeling utterly helpless, he lifted the sobbing child into his arms and muttered soothing words and promises until the girl's cries diminished to tearful gulps. She peered up at the golden-haired man bending over her with suspicion and a hint of coquetry.

"Are you a handsome prince?" Her lips quivered slightly as the painful scrape reminded her of her downfall.

Drake grinned. "No, I'm just the frog. I'm looking for my princess. Will you help me find her?"

"Is she beautiful?" The child's eyes went wide and a finger popped contemplatively in her mouth.

"More beautiful than the sun and the moon. She is an enchanted princess, you see. She can turn apples into dreams and gold into moonlight." Drake smoothed the child's long pinafore and pointed to the neatly stitched stars and rainbows. "She can make stars and rainbows just like these."

A smile grew around her grubby finger. "Oh, you mean Elli. She's standing behind you."

With a giggle the child leapt from Drake's lap and ran off to rejoin the play, leaving Drake to rise slowly and stare at the vision miraculously appearing in the now open doorway.

"Would the frog like a kiss?" Auburn hair gleamed in the dawn's light as she looked up at him through laughing silver eyes, and a mischievous dimple appeared at one corner of her lips as she popped a finger in her mouth, making it totally impossible to steal even a taste of what she offered.

Chapter XXV

━━━ ❧ ━━━

Drake stood in blank amazement a moment longer, devouring her with his eyes. Caught in braids around her head, copper hair gleamed as if polished, and lips of rose laughed temptingly, but the full swell of her rounding belly beneath the simple apron held his gaze longest.

When finally Drake recovered his senses sufficiently to catch her by the waist and move her back into the room so he might close the door on their audience, the laughter had disappeared from her eyes. Slowly Eileen backed from his grasp and deeper into the cottage's interior.

"If it is just the child you want, you cannot have it," Eileen informed him firmly.

"The child?" Bewildered, Drake finally took her meaning, and his anger returned with a rush. "And you think you are capable of raising a child yourself? You do not even have the sense to stay where the child will be warm and safe. Did you intend to raise him on roots and berries?"

"I have told you often enough, I can take care of myself. I do not need much, and I have been offered more than that for some of my sketches. So you need not worry about the child starving." His anger tore at her heart, and Eileen responded scathingly, hiding the hurt. But she could not hide the one bitterness between them. She flung it at him with fury. "I am certain Lady Pamela must have produced your heir by now. You do not need what is mine."

"Yours?" Drake roared. "You are mine and that child is mine and I am taking you both home where you belong."

Eileen gaped at him in astonishment but continued to back away. She had spent these last weeks in varying degrees of despair and anxiety, but once she knew Drake was alive and well, other fears had taken their place. She had never dreamed he would insist on taking her back to Sherbourne. She could not do it. Not like this. Not now.

"No, Drake. I told you I am no marchioness. Go back to Lady Pamela and leave me be. This is my home. This is how I was raised. You cannot expect me to act the part that Lady Pamela fills."

"Damn Pam to hell and back! Damn this hovel and everything in it! I have not risked my neck to bring you home only to pretend our vows were never made. Whether you like it or not, Lady Sherbourne, you are my wife and you belong in my bed, where I am taking you immediately."

Eileen paled as Drake stepped closer, trapping her in a corner against a chair. She knew better than he that she would travel nowhere this day, but she struggled to hide the pain. She would know where she stood with him before surrendering to the helplessness of childbirth.

"You cannot take me anywhere against my will. I am not without friends," she replied with as much dignity as she could muster. He stood so close, she could feel the heat of his breath against her face and the tension in the powerful muscles at his side.

"This is nonsense, Eileen," Drake cried in frustration. He could take her nowhere until the carriage arrived, but he would prefer not having to carry her out kicking and screaming when it came. "I want my child born in my house with a physician and a nurse and all the other proprieties to assure his safety and yours. Why would you have him born in a hovel?"

"Because this is my hovel and this is my child and no one is going to take them away from me! Take Lady Pamela to your bed if you must. I am certain she will appreciate your proprieties more than I."

Drake rolled his eyes heavenward as if pleading for guidance, then grabbed Eileen's shoulders as if he would shake her, pulling her close in hopes of forcing her to see reason. "Lady Pamela is Edmund's problem, not mine. Did you think I would have taken you with me had I thought there was any possibility Pam carried a child of mine? What do you take me for, Eileen?"

The shock of those words vibrated every nerve in Eileen's body. The implications were too great to absorb all at once, and she had no mind for it now. The pain contracting her belly came more forcefully this time, making it nigh on to impossible to stand. Growing pale with the effort to stay upright, her fingers clutched tightly at Drake's coat.

"Eileen?" Terrified by her sudden silence and look of distress, Drake caught her in his arms and glanced desperately around for help. The cottage seemed to have no other inhabitants and the wooden furniture offered no comfort. "Eileen? What is it? Is it the baby? My God, is there no one here to call?"

As the pain dissipated, Eileen straightened and tried to struggle free, but Drake would have none of it. He held her firmly.

"Your child will be born here and there is nothing you can say that will stop him." Eileen gave up the physical struggle but not the argument.

Drake cursed and glanced anxiously out the window. No sign of a carriage, but dark clouds were slowly filling the sky. The chances of getting Eileen to

Sherbourne before the snow fell were next to nil. He
groaned his dismay.

"Where is your mother? You ought to be in bed.
Does this blasted village even lay claim to a midwife?
Where in hell is the bed?" Frantically Drake glanced
around, hoping to conjure up an army of staff to help
in this desperate situation, spying only a doorway that
might conceal a bedroom.

As he caught Eileen's waist in preparation for carrying her off to bed, Eileen wiggled from his grasp.
"I am not ready. It is not time. The others will come
when you leave. You need not worry about me. I can
take care of myself."

"Eileen, I may have to throttle you," Drake fumed.
"That child is going to be born any minute now and
I'm not going anywhere until it is. So you had best call
your women now or it will be born with only me in
attendance."

Eileen obstinately lowered herself into the chair and
crossed her arms. "The child won't be born for hours
and I'll not be fussed over."

Drake took one look at her defiant expression and
strode purposefully to the door. Instead of going out,
however, he began to shout, to Eileen's dismay, "Lady
de Lacy!" to the empty street.

"Stop that, Drake!" Eileen struggled from the chair
and rushed to close the door. "I'll not be made a fool
of."

Drake slammed the door and turned to glare at her.
"You've already done a proper job of that, my lady.
You didn't trust me to come for you. You didn't want
to hear my side of the story. And now you are going
to whelp that brat right on the floor with no one in
attendance because you're too damn stubborn to admit
you're wrong."

Before Eileen could reply, another pain nearly bent
her in two. With a cry of mixed despair and disgust

Drake caught her and swept her from the floor. There had to be a bed somewhere in this damn house.

As he strode toward the darkened doorway, Eileen fought for her freedom. "Put me down, Drake! It is not time yet!"

Ignoring her pleas, Drake entered the darkened chamber and nearly stumbled over the carved bedstead filling the small room. From the gray light creeping through the tiny windows he could discern enough of the bed to decide it might be suitable for his wife and child. Gently he lay Eileen against the pillows.

Immediately she struggled to sit up and fling her legs over the side. "Go back to Sherbourne and leave me be, Drake! You'll find another Lady Pamela soon enough."

"I don't want another Lady Pamela! I have you and I have that child and I don't want any other. What do I have to do to convince you?" Drake firmly planted himself in front of her, forcing her to remain where she was.

"I want my own home and my own life. I don't want to be a marchioness. I don't want to be mistress of Sherbourne. I'll never be the kind of wife you want, Drake, so go away and pretend this never happened."

Even as she spoke, another pain struck and tears leapt to Eileen's eyes as she struggled to remain sitting, fighting the contractions that would soon render her helpless. Why couldn't he have come another day later? But even while she thought this, she grasped gratefully at Drake's outstretched hand.

Drake eased her back against the pillows once more, his hands trembling as he sought to unfasten all the feminine buttons and laces that confined her. Where in hell were all the damned women?

"I'll give you your own home if that is what you want, Eileen. You can have any home you like. I'll find a cottage in the village near Sherbourne if you want. I can't take away the title, but you don't have to use it. Eileen, for God's sake, will you lie still and let me get this gown off you?"

Eileen couldn't help but giggle at his nervousness. The mighty marquess had lost much of his self-assurance and fumbled like a schoolboy in trying to remove her clothing. Meekly she helped him remove the bodice and breathed easier for its absence.

"Do you mean that? Will you really let me have my own home? And keep the child with me?" she added hastily.

Drake would have promised her the moon if necessary to keep her in bed while he sought assistance. Anxiously he nodded agreement. "You can ask for Whitehall and I will find some way to give it to you. Just let me go find your mother."

Eileen grabbed his hand and struggled to sit up against the pillows. "Not yet. Tell me what happened. Have the charges against you been dropped?"

"I don't know, love. Our argument may have been for naught if they have not. I only know that they opened my cell long enough for me to flee. If you will hurry and get this business of bearing our brat over, we can go home and find out."

When Drake made as if to rise, Eileen held him back, her gaze anxiously searching his face. "Drake, are you certain you want to do this? I can stay here and no one will have to know we are married. You can go on as before and none will be the wiser. You may come and go as you wish. I will not keep you from the child."

Drake stared at her in exasperation. "Accept it, Eileen. You are my wife and I do not intend to give you up. I will do whatever is necessary to make you happy, but what is mine, I keep." His voice softened as dismay filled her eyes. "Will being my wife be such a terrible thing, princess?"

It would if he did not love her. It would if he were ashamed of her. It would be even worse if he found someone like Lady Pamela who would be so much more suitable. But how could she tell him this? He was the one with words, not she.

"I never wanted this." Tears coursed down her cheeks as another contraction claimed her, and she could not explain. She had only wanted his love and had married him in hopes of winning it. When he was without home or title or family, there had been a chance. Now there was none. All she would have was mansions and money, without hope.

Drake heard only her words and not her thoughts and the anguish they caused was nearly unbearable. He had trapped her, as he had never intended to do. Better than any, he knew she was a free spirit, not to be held against her will but to be admired in flight. He wanted to keep her, to proclaim to all the world that she was his, but the joy of this possession came only with her willingness. Without that he had nothing.

He held her hand until the pain passed, then sadly, he rose from the bed. "I will find your mother, my love. You need a woman with you at a time like this."

This time Eileen did not protest as he moved to leave. She could not bear to let him see her tears. The pain in her heart was greater than the one in her abdomen. To bear Drake's child was a pain she would welcome. Not to bear his love was a burden she could not carry.

Lady de Lacy appeared almost as soon as Drake stepped outside the door. She frowned at the expression on his face and entered the cottage without a word, followed shortly by Dulcie and Molly. The carriage arrived not long after that and Drake cursed as he recognized the only passenger: Diane. Well, she would have to resign herself to a long stay. He needed the carriage and men for other things.

Diane had no objections to being carried into the cottage. Drake sent one footman and his horse back to Sherbourne with messages, and the carriage and driver

on to London for a physician. He'd be damned if his
child would be born into this world without the best.
Eileen was small and the child was coming too soon.
He paced nervously up and down the street once his
duty was done.

The women wouldn't allow him to return to Eileen,
and he finally sought shelter from the sleet in a nearby
tavern. The occupants had never met a marquess before, but word had already spread that this was Elli's
husband, and curiosity and sympathy made them
friendly. As they toasted the father-to-be, the results
of Drake's messages slowly trickled in.

Michael appeared first, and after being thrown from
the cottage with Diane's approval, he found his way to
Drake's side. James and Theodore arrived next with
word that Auguste and Pierre had already departed
for Ireland. After a few drinks to warm their frozen
fingers, Theodore began to strum his mandolin and
James entertained himself with a woeful ballad that
others soon joined.

By the time Sir John and Lady Summerville arrived,
the small tavern rocked with lusty song that could be
heard into the street. After escorting his wife inside
Dulcie's cottage to be with her sister and niece, Sir
John went in search of Eileen's rakehell husband. He
had little doubt where he would find him.

Surprisingly, the usually laughing young lord was
staring morosely into his mug of ale while all around
him regaled his ears with riotous sound. The other
men made room for Sir John as he shoved his way to
the seat next to Drake, but above the uproar he could
not make himself heard. Drake raised his mug in
greeting, then tilted his head back and downed it all.
From the look on the tavernkeeper's face, this was not
the first to disappear in such a manner. He hurried
forward with another.

Deeming it wisest if the young lord were still able to
stand when his child entered the world, Sir John ges-

tured toward the door. Drake followed without protest, mug still in hand. Unfortunately, half the crowd in the tavern also chose to tag along.

Outside, with the noise level at a minimum, it was possible to speak. Drake noted that the carriage had returned and glanced up to the lowering sky. Already mid-afternoon. The sleet had turned to snow.

"The physician has arrived?" He spoke with only a slight slur to his words.

"He's with Eileen now," Sir John assured him. "The first one always takes a long time."

Worriedly Drake lurched toward the cottage. "I want to see her."

Sir John yelled a warning. "You cannot go in there now! There is barely room for her mother and the midwife."

Drake ignored the warning, intent on making Eileen understand. She had to understand. His thoughts went no further than that.

At Sir John's yell Michael loped to the front of the crowd, blocking Drake's path. He caught his friend's shoulder to restrain him, but, remembering other grievances, Drake took this interference without patience. He swung his fist hard and fast at Michael's jaw.

Michael staggered backward, but with his own complaints to air, he quickly found his footing and came forward swinging.

Within minutes a circle had formed around the combatants and the remainder of the tavern crowd poured out into the street as the two gentlemen doffed their coats and rolled up the cuffs of their sleeves. Knowing something of the prowess of both men at fisticuffs, the perpetually penniless Theodore and James casually accepted several wagers as the odds were measured by the growing crowd.

Inside the darkened bedroom, the yells and cheers of the crowd sounded muffled, and it was some moments before Eileen noticed the change in the din outside. Pain erased all clear thought except in those brief moments when one wave passed and the next had not begun. Silently she pulled on the lengths of cloth her mother had fastened to the bed until the contraction ended, then she caught her mother's eye.

"What is happening?" she whispered between dry lips.

Molly hurried to wet a cloth while Elizabeth attempted to peer around the corner of the cottage to the street.

"I can only see some small boys jumping up and down and yelling. Whatever they are watching is in front of the house."

Eileen groaned as the pain tore through her insides, worse than all the others before. The doctor spoke sharply and both women hurried to return to their tasks.

Eileen's piercing screams caught Drake's ears just before he swung, and he faltered, giving Michael time to land the final blow before he, too, heard the sound. Drake went sprawling in the dust, much to the dismay of his backers. Shaking his head and rubbing his jaw, the marquess attempted to rise, Eileen's screams penetrating his stupor with growing urgency. Michael grabbed his arm and helped him to stagger to his feet again.

"She'll kill me when she sees that face of yours," Michael muttered worriedly as, arms around each other, they stumbled through the crowd and back to the cottage, leaving Teddy and James to dispute the fight's outcome or forfeit coins they did not possess.

"That's all right, my mother-in-law will break a bottle over my head when she sees us. You don't happen to have one on you, do you?" Holding his jaw, Drake caught his hand on the door jamb as he made the transfer from daylight to dim interior.

Eileen's scream died abruptly, and Drake went deathly pale, staggering forward in the direction of the bedchamber until Sir John halted his progress.

"My God, man, get out of my way!" Drake caught the baronet's shoulders and attempted to physically lift him from his path.

Observing the dust-covered, bruised, and battered specimens of manhood entering the cottage, Diane opened her mouth, but the occasion was too much for speech. Her lips compressed into a fearful frown that warned Michael to keep his distance from this fray. Drake did not notice as he frantically tried to reach his wife.

The tiny wail of a newborn stole through the sudden silence between cottage walls, and all the occupants froze.

Chapter XXVI

Sir John braced the young marquess as he sagged momentarily against him, and then as the wails of an outraged infant continued, Drake straightened his shoulders and dropped his hold on the baronet.

"I want to see Eileen," Drake spoke stiffly but politely, waiting for his wife's guardian to step from his path.

Sir John gave Drake's expression a quick glance, then, nodding approval of what he found there, he stepped aside. He had feared Drake had chosen the path of his idle, rakehell ways, but the man of honor and courage John had known he could be shone quietly from that bruised face. Eileen had the husband she needed, and her uncle relinquished the burden of his protection to the younger man. He sat down beside his wife and Emma patted his hand.

Without hesitation Drake entered the room. The chords of Theodore's guitar entered with him, and Eileen's tired eyes turned to him immediately. Her eyebrows rose slightly at the sight of his swelling jaw and blackened eye, but she could not resist a proud smile as she lifted the tiny bundle in her arms.

"A girl, my lord. Isn't she beautiful?"

The physician frowned as the battered marquess entered the room, but having some experience of the

Neville family, he held his tongue. The old marquess had been an exasperating curmudgeon, but this new one held some promise of being relatively reasonable. The look of awe in Drake's eyes as he pulled back the blanket around his daughter's face satisfied any other qualms the physician had had upon discovering the ignoble location of this birthing.

"She has your hair," Drake whispered in wonderment as he stared into the cherubic features of his firstborn. "Have you thought of a name yet?" There had been no time for such thoughts before, but he suddenly had the desire to see that this tiny human being be given the best of everything, including a name.

Eileen touched the tiny curled finger of her sleeping daughter and glanced hesitantly at the husband she had scarcely had time to know. "Would you mind if we call her Emily?"

"Emily?" Drake tasted the name on his tongue, and then, remembering the daughter the Summervilles had lost, he nodded approvingly. "Emily it is." He glanced at Lady de Lacy bustling silently about the far end of the room. She felt his glance and looked up. "My grandmother's name was Elizabeth, too. Would you mind?"

Lady de Lacy looked vaguely pleased and smiled. "Emily Elizabeth is a lovely name. Emma will like it."

Smiling at how quickly Drake had won her mother's favor, Eileen held Emily Elizabeth up to be taken by her father as another pain warned all was not over. She would have him gone before it began again.

Drake struggled awkwardly with folds of blankets and floppy limbs until he had his daughter safely tucked in the curve of his arm. The bemused look upon his face as he held this helpless being for the first time brought a loud cough from the physician and a laugh from Molly.

"Introduce her to her family, Drake," Eileen whispered, struggling to hide the wave of pain building again.

Desperately clutching the bundle threatening to escape his arms, Drake gave Eileen a look of concern. He wanted to talk to her, to be assured everything was well, but the roomful of people prevented intimacy. He bent to press a kiss against her brow and murmur, "Thank you, my love," before Molly chased him from the room.

In the outer room, a cheer rocked the walls as Drake entered proudly bearing his offspring. James immediately demanded the name so he might dedicate the poem he had scribbled, and the Summervilles smiled tearfully as Drake presented his daughter.

"Lady Emily Elizabeth Neville, sir, madam." He held the sleeping infant so that Lady Summerville might take her, and then he froze again.

Another wail echoed thinly through the closed chamber door.

"My God!" Drake nearly dropped Emily Elizabeth as he turned abruptly toward the source of the ear-piercing sound. Lady Summerville rescued the infant while the shocked word "Twins!" escaped Drake's bruised lips.

In the corner, Michael and Diane began to laugh quietly at the marquess's stunned expression as he moved uncertainly toward the bedroom. Ever arrogant and self-assured, his lordship had been brought to public confusion by a slip of a female and a babe. His usual casual elegance had deteriorated to rags. His handsome face had swollen into a purple knot on one side and his golden hair escaped its neat queue, but his attention focused solely on the wooden door and the rising wail behind it. The moment was too rare to waste. As the laughter grew, the guitar's tune grew bolder, and Drake disappeared once more behind the closed door.

This time Eileen's eyes were closed as he entered,

and the women still worked busily to clean the squalling infant. Drake glanced anxiously to his wife's motionless form lying so small beneath the sheets, then shot a glance to the physician, who calmly bathed his hands in the washbowl.

"My wife?" Drake's face was pale beneath the disheveled hair, and blue eyes burned with anxiety.

"She is weak but will recover," the physician answered grumpily. Twins. To a marquess. In a hovel. Damn, but why couldn't these Nevilles ever do anything properly? The sound of laughter and music from outside the room soured his humor further. You'd think they were gypsies.

Drake took no heed of the medical man's disgruntlement and dropped to his knees beside the bed so he might be on a level with Eileen. He took her hand and was rewarded with the flicker of long lashes.

"Eileen?" he pleaded, not caring who heard.

She turned her head to the sound of his voice and smiled as her eyes opened to meet his. "Twins, as promised," she whispered.

Shakily Drake pressed her hand to his mouth, searing it with his kiss, willing her to understand. Before he could speak, Molly laid the infant between them.

"A boy, my lord," she announced proudly, pleased to be given the honor of introducing the heir.

Drake stared blankly at the red-faced, squalling, kicking creature who would bear the title of earl once christened, and then he glanced up to meet the splendid silver eyes of his wife.

"Richard?" he inquired softly, and at the tears moistening her lashes, he knew he had chosen rightly. "Richard, Lord Neville, he shall be."

"He will look like his father," Eileen proclaimed, leaving no room for doubt.

When she closed her eyes and seemed to sleep, Drake lifted his son from the covers and rose to his full height and usual noble bearing. Catching both

Lady de Lacy and the physician with his glare, he questioned, "When may I take them home?"

Lady de Lacy pursed her lips in contemplation of this question, but the doctor grunted his relief.

"When she says she feels well enough to travel, take her home. She won't rest here with all this noise, and you'll not find a nurse willing to live like this. Take her home, by all means." The physician shrugged on his coat and stomped out.

Elizabeth de Lacy watched how Drake cuddled his son against his chest, calming the child's fearful cries even as he turned his glare on her, and she nodded. "You have won this round, my lord. She is yours. Take care of her."

Drake relaxed. "You will come with her?"

Elizabeth considered this proposal. "For a time, perhaps. The babies will cause an uproar for a while. But there are other matters I must see to when everything calms down."

"You know you can call on me for anything you need," Drake reminded her.

She nodded acknowledgment, but her eyes were on her sleeping daughter. "Let her sleep while she can. There will be no peace once the babes grow hungry."

Taking this as dismissal, Drake returned to the outer room to introduce his heir to the world. The resounding cheer this introduction produced disturbed the infant into wild cries of protest at once.

Within days, Eileen found herself ensconced among fur rugs and pillows in a carriage traveling very carefully and slowly along the road to Sherbourne. In the seat across from her, Drake watched closely to be certain she did not tire or weaken. The nurse beside him held Richard, and occasionally he turned a proud glance to the sleeping infants in her arms and Lady de Lacy's across from him, but mostly he watched Eileen.

She seemed paler than he ever remembered her, and black smudges ringed eyes of fragile gray. She had insisted that she felt well enough to travel, but Drake suspected his constant presence in the cramped cottage had much to do with that decision. He had left her only long enough to prepare for her homecoming, fearful she would fade away or disappear entirely were he not there to watch her.

Nervous under Drake's constant regard, Eileen stared out the window for some sight of the cottage he had promised her. She had never learned to manage servants, knew little about planning proper meals, and knew less about entertaining society. She could never manage the elegant halls of Sherbourne, but a cottage would be just her size. Many wives lived apart from their husbands. It would certainly not be any more shameful than his original proposal when he was still affianced to Pamela.

That thought made her restless, and Eileen threw her husband a quick look. If he did not intend to be faithful to Pamela, he certainly would not consider keeping his vows to her. The cottage was the best solution for everyone. She could cling to some small part of her pride, and he could go about his life much as before.

Drake could only interpret her glance as curiosity, and he gestured toward the village street they now traversed. "It is just ahead, set back from the road. You should see it well in a moment."

Eileen nodded and hid her pain. He had played the part of attentive husband these past days, but the casual deliberateness of his tone now suggested he had tired of it. He would be glad to be home and rid of her, but his gentlemanliness prevented showing any sign of it.

She stared out the window again and watched with curiosity as a brick wall half hidden under sheltering trees appeared in view. The carriage slowed and she glimpsed the timbered gables of a tiled roof behind the trees. Her eyes widened as the brick wall opened out on an iron carriage gate and she could glance up the drive to the towering Tudor mansion set in amongst a jungle of trees and overgrown shrubs. The house appeared empty and neglected, but seemed to beg for occupancy. It was magnificent. And enormous.

She turned an incredulous stare to her husband. "That is not a cottage. Is there some smaller building behind that I cannot see?"

Cautiously Drake denied it. "No, this is the place. Don't you like it?"

As the carriage continued down the street, Eileen craned her neck to look behind for another glimpse. "The trees are magnificent, but it is a mansion, Drake! I did not mean for you to spend so much money." Suddenly realizing the carriage had passed all possible entrances to the house, she turned back to face him. "Why aren't we stopping?"

Drake sensed Lady de Lacy's quiet interest in this conversation, and with the nurse avidly taking in every word, he could not explain fully. But neither could Eileen protest his answer.

"The cost was negligible, but considerable repairs are needed. I have started workmen on it, and when you are well enough, you can come oversee what you want done."

Their gazes met and clashed, one willful and proud, the other thoughtful and waiting. Words that could not be said out loud were communicated silently, and Eileen stiffened. They would be going to Sherbourne.

"You do not play fair, my lord," she informed him quietly.

"I do not play at all, my love. The house is yours, as are all my others. For now, Sherbourne will be most comfortable." Drake crossed his arms and waited for the explosion he expected.

It did not come. Glancing thoughtfully at Drake's firm expression, Eileen turned away to lift a whimpering Emily Elizabeth from her mother's arms. She did not understand Drake's reasoning, but her heart pounded wildly with renewed hope. She could not put her hopes to words. Too many times they had been dashed. She would play his game and wait and see.

Lady de Lacy gave her son-in-law a swift look of approval as her daughter offered no protest to this diversion of his promises. She had not known her daughter long but she knew her well, for she was just like her father. And her mother. It would take a strong man to protect her, and a patient one to keep her at all. What she needed now was a loving one to keep her happy. Lady de Lacy reserved judgment on this last point, but the light in Drake's eyes as his gaze rested on the sight of wife and child gave hope for the future. She smiled contentedly.

Several days later, Eileen found herself ensconced in the master bedroom at Sherbourne. The towering, velvet-curtained bed held the warmth of the crackling fire from the grate, and weak December sunlight crept through the wall of mullioned windows. Heavy, masculine furniture dominated the chamber, but traces of femininity could be detected everywhere already. A lacy night shift had been laid upon the bachelor's chest in preparation for the night's ablutions. A pale yellow dressing gown had been flung over the back of one of the wing chairs. Eileen's ivory combs and brushes lay upon the dresser, and gift boxes of perfumes, fans, parasols, and other nonsense spilled across the chaise longue beneath the windows. Drake had lost no time in indulging his desire to provide her with everything she could ever need.

Eileen smiled at the sight of the other stack of boxes spilling over with pairs of christening gowns, tiny slippers, frilled caps, brightly colored wood beads, and anything else that had caught the eyes of the entire household these last days. Even the maids had brought a pair of toys that vaguely resembled ridiculous monkeys, which they had obviously spent a night stuffing and sewing themselves. The twins would be spoiled beyond redemption before their first birthday.

Propping herself on one elbow, she gazed adoringly at their angelic faces as they lay sleeping among the pillows beside her. Emily's auburn curls lay plastered against her nearly translucent cheek, while Richard's golden locks stood on end in the single curl she had teased it into. She could see evidence of their father in Richard's wide brow and square jaw and the dimple in Emily's chin. Drake's children could never be less than beautiful.

Halting in the doorway, Drake felt the shock of discovery all over again as he gazed upon this tableau. Eileen's long auburn tresses trailed across her frail gown as she bent over the babes, drawing his attention to the creamy satin of her throat and shoulders, and the shadowed valley lightly hidden beneath the bodice. He knew when she looked up, silver eyes would taunt and tease as they had for nights untold since first they met. Still she eluded him.

"They have grown at least a foot this past week," he observed proudly as he entered.

"And be full grown by next, or at least walking," Eileen scoffed. "Your tales grow more farfetched with each telling. You should write them down for your children to read, say, by the week after next. They are slow learners."

Drake chortled, taking his daughter's chubby fist in his large hand. "This one looks as if she could write her own. Why should I spoil her fun?"

Eileen studied the strong lines of his face, noting some of the tension had faded, though not all. She wished he would share his thoughts with her, but their separation had been too long.

"Diane says you have never written down your children's tales. I wish you would. I'd like to hear the one about the leprechaun army."

Drake looked up sharply, but amusement played

about his lips. "You would have me writing nursery tales instead of tending to business?"

"I would have writing tales be your business," Eileen said vehemently, surprising even herself. "Every time you receive one of those letters from London, your face crinkles up in a frown and you get all grumpy and slam the doors. There is no chance they will return you to the Tower, is there?"

At her worried look, Drake caressed her cheek and cursed himself for the foolishness that had taken advantage of such beauty without truly appreciating it. Somehow he would have to make it up to her, if she would ever give him the chance.

"No, princess, I have sworn my loyalty and been released on my own name, such as it is. The trial should be cut and dried. But sooner or later I shall have to go up to London, and that is why I frown."

The knock of the children's nurse interrupted any further elaboration on the subject. A footman with a message for Drake, and the Monsard brothers eager for a lark, followed, and the chance for further privacy was lost to the day's activities. Gradually Eileen was learning the price she must pay for gaining the man she wanted. She was not alone in her demands for his attention.

By Christmas Eve the physician agreed Eileen might be allowed from her bed if she did not overexert herself. Drake took this to mean he might carry her downstairs for the evening's celebration, and despite Eileen's protests that she could very well do it herself, Drake scooped up her velvet-robed figure and carried her out. The entire family had gathered before the traditional yule log, and the chorus of "God Rest Ye Merry Gentlemen" grew exuberantly louder at the appearance of the marquess and his new bride. The harpsichord had been moved in to this larger room, and Diane struck the last few chords of the song with a trill much like laughter.

Drake found Eileen a comfortable seat by the fire, and everyone began talking at once, making it difficult to follow their chatter. Tears sprang to her eyes as Drake's warm hand squeezed her shoulder. Outside the heavy curtains a light snow fell; inside, the firelight and candleglow illuminated the faces of all those she knew and loved. If she could allow this fantasy of happiness to seem real, she would—at long last—be home. Only experience had taught her how illusory happiness could be.

The Summervilles joined them for the festivities, and Sir John sat quietly with his brandy glass, listening to the old songs pouring from Diane's talented fingers. Lady Summerville sat next to her sister on the small sofa, both women with their heads together and chattering excitedly, their glances occasionally straying proudly to the young couple by the fire. The Monsards had sipped more than their fair share of the wassail, and leaned over the harpsichord, encouraging Diane into more spirited tunes, while Michael sat at her side, calmly turning the pages of the music and occasionally joining in the song with his booming baritone. Whatever the future might bring, this was a far cry from that last unhappy Christmas when Lord de Lacy had appeared and all had gone awry. Eileen squeezed Drake's hand and rubbed it against her cheek. He had fought long and hard to bring this about; she must find some way to thank him. The firelight shadowed the gold colors of her robe and sent shimmers of copper through auburn tresses tied loosely by ribbons. Drake could not resist caressing the creamy hollow of her throat, the thrill of publicly being allowed this intimacy not having faded yet. He knew better than to expect she would ever be entirely his, but he also knew enough to recognize the strength of the ties that bound them. Even if she should disappear into the trees, he would find her.

As the first haunting refrain of "Good King Wenceslaus'' rang out, Drake bent to whisper in Eileen's ear, "Let me hear you sing something besides tavern songs, princess. I want to hear your voice."

Eileen's eyes laughed as she glanced up to her handsome husband and the blue of his eyes reminded her of the occasion of which he spoke. Still, she was unaccustomed to singing, and she waited for him to join in the tune before making the first tentative notes.

As she grew more sure of herself, the words became stronger, and Drake's hand squeezed hers with delight at the sound. Gradually the others in the room grew aware of her voice and its meaning, and their voices softened until Eileen's clear, bell-like tones rang melodiously through the room, filling it with excitement. For the first time since childhood, Eileen could join in and raise her voice in chorus with others, and by song's end, tears blurred the eyes of most of the room's occupants. The mute waif had disappeared, replaced by a young lady with a voice to equal any.

That night, when Drake carried her to the bed she had slept in these last weeks, he did not leave her alone as he had in the past. Laying Eileen between the turned-down covers, he went back and closed the chamber door, then proceeded to snuff out the candles one by one.

Eileen watched in silence as her husband discarded his formal long coat and began to unwrap his cravat. This was his bed and she could not deny it to him, but neither could she act as wife to him. It was much too soon; surely he knew that. She gulped as the last candle threw its shadows over the sculptured torso emerging from the folds of linen. She wished desperately to be held in those strong arms again, but would he be content with that?

Drake blew out the last candle before removing the remainder of his clothing. In the ensuing darkness he could hear the whisper of Eileen's robe falling to the floor, and his heart pounded louder. He knew better than to test his self-control in this manner, but it was Christmas and he wanted his wife in the bed beside him.

He came between the covers and found Eileen's slight, silk-draped figure with ease. She fit so naturally into his arms; it was as if he had gone all these weeks and months with a part of him missing. He kissed her forehead, her eyelids, and willed his hungry body into submission.

"You do accept that I have the right to share your bed, even if it is only to hold you?" Drake murmured.

"I have never denied you that," Eileen agreed with more than a little relief. After this beautiful evening she could not have denied him anything. Even though she knew she was out of place, Drake made her feel as if she had come home, at last, and she clung tenaciously to her hopes. Perhaps she could still teach him love.

At her side, Drake chuckled. "I must admit, I have had no reason for complaint on that subject. You are a wanton creature, my love."

Sleepily Eileen kissed his chest and snuggled closer. "If you think I'll give you reason to return to your harlots in London, you have a maggot in your brain, my lord."

Drake laughed, but once he felt her breathing even into that of sleep, he grew silent. He had no desire for any other woman but this one. Only he could not risk her life or that of their children by staying here. Edmund's enmity made his proximity too dangerous. Until he found some way to rid himself of his cousin, he must leave Sherbourne. Word had come that Edmund would be released from the Tower within the week.

Chapter XXVII

—— 🍒 ——

Christmas, 1746

Eileen woke to the tickle of warm kisses trailing down her throat and the wail of a hungry infant outside the door.

"Drake?" she murmured sleepily as a strong arm circled her, pulling her over so that his mouth could capture hers. Beneath the hungry pressure of his kiss, Eileen woke fully and joyfully her arms slipped about him. A sharp rap at the door warned of the fleetingness of this moment.

"I fear you will have to wait, my lord. Another's demands must come first."

Drake growled something irascible against her mouth, then, caressing the swollen tip of her breast through the filmy material of her gown, he raised himself up on one elbow and stared down at her.

"My jealousy is such that I would keep you locked away from the sight of all others, but I bow to my son's right to come first, for now. Merry Christmas, my love." He bent and pressed a kiss against her cheek.

Eileen caught her hands in his hair and persuaded a more satisfactory kiss from him before wiggling from his grasp and sitting up. Drake admired the auburn fall of hair over her thin bodice but resisted the temptation to touch it. Swinging his legs over the side of the bed, he rose and went in search of a dressing gown.

Naked, he strode in masculine self-assurance across the room, and Eileen gave a sigh of admiration. It had been months since he had held her like that, and it would be weeks more before she could entice him to her bed again. Never had she given thought to turning him away. Her young body already felt the effects of their separation, and she did not doubt he suffered similarly. Even the cold chill of dawn did not weaken the evidence of his ardor.

As Drake disappeared into the adjoining room, Eileen called out permission for the nursery maid to enter. Another maid scurried in behind to add coals to the fire and warm the room as the first placed the wailing infant into his mother's arms. Eileen slipped aside her gown, and tiny fingers beat against her breast as her son's greedy mouth groped toward the nipple brushing his cheek. Eileen winced as he found what he sought and pulled eagerly, but she settled comfortably against the pillows as he drank his fill.

When Drake re-entered in his dressing gown, the maids scattered at once, leaving the young couple alone with their nursing son. Somewhat in awe of the picture before him, Drake scarcely remembered the package in his hand as he seated himself at the bed's edge. With wonder he watched the infant's hands knead the ivory satin of Eileen's breast. Together they had created this tiny living being. He had taken her to his bed, stripped her of her innocence, and planted his seed within her womb. It seemed incredible that so brief a pleasure could have such impact on their lives, but he would not forgo a moment of it.

Engrossed in the special bond that grows between mother and child at times like these, Eileen did not notice her husband's expression until Richard was nearly satisfied. Glancing up, she caught Drake's look, and her heart leapt an extra beat. His slow smile as their eyes met sent warm shivers through her.

"Have I ever told you how much I love you?" Drake asked softly, disentangling a strand of auburn hair from a little fist before taking the sleepy infant into his arms. But his eyes were fastened only on the brilliant silver playing beneath long lashes.

The words took Eileen's breath away, and, flustered, she ducked her head as she arranged the square of soft linen over Drake's dressing gown and beneath their son's burbling hiccups. When Richard was well in hand, she adjusted her nightgown slowly before glancing up to see if his words still hung in the air between them.

Drake's proud blue eyes questioned her silently. A brilliant smile slowly formed upon Eileen's lips.

"I have only hoped that what I felt was returned, my lord."

Pride and love swelled Drake's heart as his gaze caught hers. She still shied from words, but her thoughts expressed themselves beautifully in her face. Holding his son, Drake leaned to press a kiss upon her forehead, and to present her with the elegantly wrapped package he finally remembered in his hand.

"You will forgive my blindness in not seeing that love is more important than pride?"

So he did understand. Feeling completely at one with this man for the first time since they were reunited, Eileen smiled softly and began to unwrap her gift. Inside a velvet box, embedded in satin, lay a gold ring set with diamonds. Eileen gasped and raised her eyes to meet Drake's.

Carefully he removed the band from its box and slid it on her finger. "So all the world will know you're mine," he murmured.

Rendered speechless, Eileen clenched the expensive gift with both hands, finally understanding the completeness of Drake's possession. She was irrevocably his, as the world would soon know. Stunned, she tried to utter words of love and gratitude, but they did not come with ease. So many things still stood in the way of happiness. How would she ever make him see them?

An interruption prevented any words at all.

Drake cursed at the knock. "What do we have to do to earn some privacy around this place?"

"It will be the maid with Emily. I'll send her back to the wet nurse," Eileen assured him hastily before calling permission to enter. The ring was a symbol she must learn to accept. She was no longer free of responsibilities, but neither was she alone. At the moment, she was ready to consider no burden too great to shoulder if she just might keep Drake at her side.

A harassed-looking footman opened the door, visibly sighing with relief at discovering his lordship's presence. "It's Lord Westly, my lord. He is most insistent that he speak with you."

Drake frowned. "Westly? I'd thought he'd gone to the Continent." He glanced at Eileen, reluctant to leave her side but realizing business must again take the place of pleasure.

Eileen looked resigned, but before she could utter the words releasing him, Lord Westly pushed aside the footman and entered. Grayer and thinner, with deep lines ravaging his jaw, the older man made a quick bow before the young marquess and his lady.

"Sorry to interrupt, Sherbourne, but I need to talk with both of you. This young cur wouldn't listen." He glared at the frightened footman.

Puzzled but hiding his curiosity, Drake dismissed the servant to find the nurse and indicated one of the armchairs. By the time Westly had settled himself beside the fire, the nurse had hurried in to remove the babe and a maid had helped Eileen into her dressing robe.

Westly watched these attentions with sad interest and gestured to be given a look at the new heir to Sherbourne. Satisfied with the babe's healthy, sleeping features and unmistakable Neville jaw, he nodded approval, and the nurse disappeared with the child.

"Fine lad, Drake. And a daughter, too, I hear."
Lord Westly leaned on his walking stick and gazed at
the young couple upon the bed. Drake sat protectively
at the bed's edge, his arm behind the frail delicacy of
his lovely wife. Those oddly light eyes of the lady
made him stir uneasily.

"Twins," Drake agreed carefully. "And Pamela?"

Eileen watched with sorrow as the old man seemed
to turn in upon himself and wither before their eyes.

"Dead. Childbed fever. She did not last out the
week." Westly turned away from the healthy picture
of happiness on the bed and stared into the fire.

Eileen spoke before Drake could recover from his
stunned silence. "And the child?"

The old lord looked up at once at the demanding
tone of her voice. Their eyes met with immediate
understanding. Amazing, how words could be spoken
without tongues. No wonder Drake had fallen for this
enchanting creature. He spoke directly to Eileen.

"A healthy boy. After all the damned girls I've
begotten, to have a grandson who is a bastard . . ."
Indignation trailed off into the querulousness of despair.

"I am sorry, sir." Drake rose and opened one of the
wardrobes to produce a flask, handing it to his friend.
"The way Edmund talked, I felt certain he meant to
marry Pamela."

Westly drank deeply of the liquor and waved away
Drake's apologies. "Regrets will not bring her back. I
spoiled her. I never provided her with the guidance a
child needs. That is why I am here. I'll not have my
only grandson grow up like his mother. Nor his father.
I can't raise him. I can't see Edmund raising him. He's
a Neville, whether you like it or not, Drake. I want to
come to terms with you."

Drake frowned, but Eileen answered unhesitatingly,
"Bring the child here, my lord. The nursery is well
staffed. You know he will be brought up as our own."

Drake exploded. "Now wait one minute! I'll not

have my son endure what I have. Edmund's brat is likely to turn out a bigger bully than Edmund. He is already some months older than Richard. I'll not have my son . . ."

Westly pounded the floor with his ebony cane. "Hear me out, damn you! Don't you think I've thought of all that?"

Eileen tugged fiercely at Drake's robe, forcing him to turn his glare toward her. "You will know better than your father did. It does not have to be the same. Would you have your own kin raised by strangers?"

"Eileen, you do not understand. . ." Drake began to protest, but Westly gave him no time to argue.

"I understand, Sherbourne. A bastard can't inherit titles and estates. But I think we can repair that. The king is sympathetic to tales of ungrateful children, and he owes me a favor or two in dealing with that brat of his. We need only persuade Edmund to legitimize the boy, and the king will see that my title and lands pass to my grandson. He will grow up knowing my estate is his; I will see to that. That should relieve the worst of the competition, shouldn't it?"

Drake paced uneasily beside the bed, but Eileen's penetrating gaze prevented easy thought. He finally halted and turned to meet her eyes.

"I would not have any child raised as I was, Drake," she stated calmly, without the need to plead. She knew he could not deny his own kin, no matter how much his mind might say he must.

Drake ran his hand through his hair and smiled ruefully at the confidence in her eyes. How could he deny his better nature when she behaved as if he had no other? "Does this mean you will stay here?" he demanded, finding an answer to his greatest fear in the unflinching agreement of silver eyes. There were ties that could bind her, and victoriously, he captured her hand and turned back to his neighbor.

"I think I can help you in persuading Edmund to

acknowledge the child. If you are willing to take responsibility for teaching him his heritage when he grows older, I am willing to raise him with my own."

Lord Westly took a deep breath and rose from the chair to extend his hand to Drake. "I'm damned sorry to lose you for a son-in-law, Sherbourne, but I'll rest easier knowing the boy is in good hands."

Gnarled hands clutching hat and walking stick, he turned slowly to Eileen. His powdered wig was long and full in a slightly outdated style, and his clocked stockings and red heels also bespoke an earlier age, but his eyes reflected the youthfulness of his mind as he met her gaze admiringly.

"I remember your mother well, child. If you are as much like her as you appear, every male who meets you will love you. I could not ask for more for my grandson."

Eileen laughed at this blatant flattery. "And if your grandson resembles you, my lord, he will turn my head with pretty phrases and grow up quite spoiled. Try your attentions on my mother. She should be below somewhere and will enjoy reminiscences. Bring your grandson as soon as he may travel. I am eager to make his acquaintance."

The old man's eyes glowed with pleasure and he bowed himself out. Drake immediately dropped to the bed beside Eileen and pushed her down into the mattress.

"You are a devilishly wicked brat, my lady," he murmured without wrath.

"And you are too handsome to be allowed out of the house," Eileen returned serenely, sliding her hands about his shoulders. "And I love you quite insanely."

"Quite," he agreed, before pressing his kiss upon her until she writhed with ecstasy and begged for more.

Drake took his leave of her reluctantly some days later. Perhaps with Westly's aid Edmund could be removed to the continent or given an appointment in the colonies. He had to return to London for that reason alone, although there were numerous other pressing matters he must settle while he was there. Still, they had been separated much too long once. He was not eager for a repeat of that estrangement, not with the uncertainty of Eileen's happiness still between them.

"Lord Westly's grandson will be arriving soon. Must you leave now?" Eileen, too, was reluctant for this parting. Something in Drake's restlessness made her uneasy, but she still did not feel confident about inquiring into his concerns. She would like to know how long this trip might take. Since he did not offer the information, she could not bring herself to ask it of him. He was a man with needs she could not ease. She feared learning the worst if she pressed too hard.

Dressed in a flowing gown of brown velvet with gold lace and inserts, Eileen had moved from bed to chair where she could look out upon the chilly gardens below. She had insisted on dressing this morning, but she had been forbidden to walk further than her chambers.

Drake noted the paleness of her usually pink cheeks and his heart jerked erratically. The physicians had sworn she was well and recovering nicely, but he could not help feeling guilty of her illness. He caressed her cheek, forcing those immense eyes to turn up to him.

"If I do not go now, the weather may prevent my leaving later. You will be safe here with Michael and Diane and your mother, and I will return as soon as I may be permitted. I have plans . . . but you must recover first."

Interest flared and she caught his hand. "What plans? Will you tell me?"

Drake smiled and kissed her forehead. "Many plans. Some you will not like, but must endure. Others, I will need your help in. Think of the cottage you wanted, but reconcile yourself to enjoying it only a few months of the year. I am considering taking my place in the House."

Eileen bit her lip and considered the enormity of this undertaking, It would mean living without him or living in London much of the year. She wished to do neither, but vaguely, she comprehended his need to press for changes. Even her mother had spoken harshly of the unjust laws preventing Catholics from owning land or voting. Drake would want his say in such a matter and many others. It was evidence of the large gap between their learnings, but she said nothing of this to him. She could never become the hostess his position in London would require, but teasingly, she asked, "Can we build a cottage in London?"

Drake laughed, as much with relief as enjoyment at her quickness. He had feared her reaction to his wishes, but it seemed she had finally accepted her position as his wife. "I shall begin looking for land while I am there, but I will not promise trees," he warned.

"Promise to introduce me to Hogarth and we have a deal," Eileen responded with deceptive sweetness.

"A deal it is."

He kissed her and was gone, leaving her to watch his departure with trepidation. For all his light-heartedness, she knew something troubled him. If she were well, she would ride after him, but she could not do such things any longer. She had responsiblities of her own now, and the simple days of freedom had disappeared. The wail of two babes reminded her of that should she ever forget.

Chapter XXVIII

—— ❦ ——

March, and Drake still had not returned home, but his letters overflowed with thoughts and plans and love as he described the people and events around him in vivid detail. Eileen clung to the pages of closely spaced writing and read and reread his words with constant delight, unable to believe he could reveal so much of himself with just the scratch of a pen. She could not doubt his faithfulness as he described the pain of his lonely bed and his desire to be with her. His words too exactly duplicated her own feelings.

Diane ran through a complicated drill on the harpsichord, asserting her presence as Eileen perused the letter for the third time.

Eileen glanced up and laughed at the expression on her sister-in-law's face. "I am being selfish. I believe these pages are meant for you as much as for me." She handed over the pages describing his interview with the Duke of Newcastle and his argument over the current conditions of agriculture. The pages describing Drake's search for a suitable site for a cottage and his loneliness she kept to herself.

Diane only glanced at the pages, preferring to ask rather than read. "Does he say anything of Michael? I know we do not need Drake's permission, but it would be so much easier . . ." Her voice dropped wistfully.

"Has Michael actually asked Drake's permission, then?" Too wrapped in her own affairs these last weeks, she had not taken heed of others. That Michael and Diane were very much in love and would soon marry, she had taken for granted.

"They have spoken of it, I know." Remembering the brawl during the birth of the twins, Diane had no confidence in the matter being mentioned since. Her fingers produced a melancholy tune as she spoke.

Eileen watched Diane's face with interest. Normally serene golden features had taken on a hint of rose and a sparkle of excitement that had not been there last spring. Diane's caustic tongue had mellowed, too, and just the mention of Michael's name brought a glow to her eyes. That she was tied to a wheelchair seemed to be no barrier to love, but Eileen still felt a few qualms about it. The birth of the twins had much to do with the path of her thoughts.

"You and Michael have spoken of children?" Eileen inquired cautiously.

Diane reddened further. "Rather more than that."

A bubble of laughter escaped her lips as Eileen contemplated Diane's averted face. "I don't suppose I dare inquire too closely into the meaning of that statement?"

At the sound of her friend's laughter, Diane glanced up and smiled with relief at the indulgent expression on Eileen's face. "Not if you write every word we share to Drake."

Eileen shook her head vigorously. "Never. I have no talent with pens and too much respect for silence. You want children, then?"

Diane smiled with relief at being able to speak of what was so close to her heart. "Yes, I want Michael's child. He worries. He has some idea of what you went through, but I have convinced him it is because you are much smaller than I and because you carried twins. He's a skeptic and has talked with my physician, but I think we have convinced him."

Mischief leapt to Diane's eyes as she spoke these words, and the happy grin on her lips said the rest. Eileen returned the grin with unmitigated delight. She wanted her friends to be as happy as she, and Michael and Diane deserved the best.

"He has been to your room, hasn't he?" Eileen accused delightedly. At Diane's embarrassed nod she whooped, "Drake will kill him!"

Diane managed to laugh and look worried at the same time. "I had to know it would be all right," she insisted. "I didn't want Michael shackled to a crippled, useless wife for the rest of his life."

"Useless? My word, Diane! You have a thousand more uses than I ever did! You run this entire household, you deal with the tenants and the servants, you play beautifully and your accomplishments keep everyone entertained. There is no end to your talents. Michael would be glad for any one of them." At this recitation Eileen grew worried. "Does this mean Michael will take you away from here? Please tell me it will not or I'll have to discourage this match immediately."

Diane laughed at the earnest expression on Eileen's face. "Then I do not dare tell you such a thing. I have been totally compromised and must marry him." She quieted and regarded her friend more seriously. "I would think, though, that you would rather be mistress of your own household. I have thought about moving to the dower house when Drake returns. You will want to make changes, and I don't want to hinder you."

These past weeks Eileen had given considerable thought to her uneasy position as marchioness. Drake and Diane made it seem quite simple, but she was not as yet receiving guests. What would happen when all Drake's noble friends and relatives arrived to look over his improbable new wife? She had never felt so fettered in her life, but she hid her discomfort behind laughter.

"Changes! May the heavens preserve us! I wouldn't even know what to change. Do you wish Drake to think me a total incompetent? I know you and Michael might prefer a place of your own, but I beg you not to leave for my sake. I will learn if I must . . ."

"But you would much rather paint and play with the children!" Diane laughed, understanding Eileen's discomfiture. "I must admit to relief. I love Sherbourne, and Michael is very proud. If we had to leave, he would make me live on his wages. This way, I can convince him I'm earning our keep while we live in comfort. Is that so very selfish?"

Eileen breathed a small sigh of relief as this one obstacle dissolved. "Supremely practical, as I see it. Michael enjoys managing the estate and Drake scarcely has time for it as it is. And while you're managing the household, I can be your legs. I can run after the children and visit the tenants and go to the village and all those things that are difficult for you. I think it is perfect!"

With the excitement of their futures to discuss, neither woman noticed the entrance of Lady de Lacy until the crackle of the letter in her hand caught their attention.

Eileen glanced up lovingly and indicated the seat beside her. "Join us, Mother. You have received another of those letters from Ireland, haven't you?"

Elizabeth de Lacy unconsciously folded and unfolded the pages between her fingers as she sat beside her daughter. Her eyes had the faraway look that had haunted them these last weeks.

"Yes, another letter," she murmured unhurriedly, searching for the words she needed. "While you two are discussing your futures, I must think of my own. Does his lordship mention when he will return?" She turned her gaze to Eileen.

"Your future is here, with us, of course," Eileen replied, perplexed. "Drake does not give the date of his return, but you know he welcomes you here. And if the noise of the children annoys you, Aunt Emma will be happy . . ."

Elizabeth shook her head firmly. "The children are a delight and I adore them, but I cannot live what remains of my life through you. Now that Peter cannot interfere, I must return to Ireland. I have friends there who risked their lives for me. And Richard's home awaits me."

The happiness in her mother's face prevented Eileen's objections. "You will live there alone?" she inquired softly.

Elizabeth unfolded the letter again. "There is some question as to the legality of my inheriting the estate, but I intend to fight for it. It means claiming Anglicanism, but that does not bother me. God is God, however He is worshiped. It is the result that matters. Richard had plans for those lands and I wish to see them carried out. Now that you have no need of them, I can see no obstacle."

Eileen opened her eyes wide. "You mean to sell the land and build a school?"

"I do. What better way can I thank those who helped us than by helping their children?"

That "us" grated uncomfortably on Eileen's nerves. How had she been helped by being left, unwanted, in poverty, to raise herself as best she might? Her expression revealed something of her thoughts as she asked, "You have learned how I came to be in England?"

Well able to see through her daughter's cautious words, Elizabeth smiled sadly and patted her hand. "You must not blame Meg too harshly, my love. She was old and not quite sound of mind. If she had not found you, you may have bled to death before any others came for you. As it was, they were never quite certain what became of you. Meg was quite out of her senses by the time the priest found her. Her wanderings gave him reason to wonder, but he could never be certain."

Eileen shook her head in bewilderment. "I do not understand. Why did this Meg not take me to the priest or someone who would help me? How did I come to be with Nan?"

"It can only be conjecture, but Meg had two daughters. One worked at a neighboring estate and all I knew of the other was that she had married and gone to live with her husband in Cornwall. I have asked that inquiries be made, but so far all that is known is that the unmarried daughter left Ireland shortly after—" she hesitated, then catching herself, continued—"your father died. The servants who worked with her heard that she died some time after reaching England. I suspect that Nan is the married daughter and never knew who you were, other than that you were her sister's child. She raised you as one of her own. It was the best she could do."

Eileen entwined her fingers in her lap and stared at them. She had contrived to forget those years as much as possible, but she understood now more than she had as a child. Nan had tried to raise a mute, unloving little hoyden even when she had little enough for her own. Nan's only fault lay in marrying the wrong man. There were no recriminations to be made. Someday, perhaps she could find Nan and offer her gratitude.

A sharp rap at the door diverted everyone's attention from sad thoughts, and they all looked eagerly to the portals. Every visitor could mean a message from Drake and London. Diane bade the footman enter.

The liveried servant appeared nervous as he drew open the double doors to announce their guest. "Mr. Edmund to see Lady Sherbourne."

Diane gasped and Eileen's fingers flew to her lips. Surely, it could not be . . . But it was. Edmund loomed dark and forbidding just behind the frightened footman.

He shoved the door open farther and entered. Garbed

respectably in long waistcoat and buff overcoat, his
knee boots polished to a black gleam, his hair neatly
queued and powdered, he carried with him the air of a
respectable gentleman. Only the inscrutable depth of
his dark eyes gave cause for uneasiness—and prior
knowledge of his treachery.

Edmund bowed politely as the servant silently closed
the door behind him. "My ladies." His eyebrow rose
inquisitively in the direction of Elizabeth. "I do not
believe I have had the pleasure."

Without the power to bodily remove the traitor,
Eileen had no choice but to make the introductions.
Perhaps he had learned his lesson and was here to
make amends. She would have to pray for the best.

"Mama, this is Drake's cousin, Edmund Neville.
My mother, Lady de Lacy."

The name "de Lacy" hung heavily in the air, and
Edmund's self-assurance momentarily faltered. He recovered quickly, however, and made a gallant bow.
"My pleasure, my lady." With aplomb he quickly
skirted the matter of identities and turned to Eileen.
"I have been told my son is here. Would it be too
much to ask that I might see him?"

Eileen's heart froze. Despite his air of aristocratic
elegance, Edmund was not to be trusted. He had
every right to see his son, but not like this, not without the protection of Drake and Michael and Lord
Westly. He had timed his arrival too well, when there
was none to obstruct him.

She smiled lightly and gestured for him to have a
seat. "The children are with my aunt and uncle at the
moment. Let me call for some tea and perhaps they
will have returned by the time we're done."

Diane and Elizabeth glanced at her with surprise
but held their tongues. The Summervilles had not
been there for a fortnight, and the babes were all
soundly asleep in their beds upstairs. What Eileen had
in mind they could not ascertain but would not interfere.

Eileen rose and slipped out the door, ostensibly to call for tea although just a signal from the bell on Diane's chair would have brought servants running. She prayed Edmund would not think of that. As soon as the door closed behind her, she lifted her skirts and ran up the wide stairway to the upper-story bedrooms and nursery.

Before she reached the top, she heard the salon doors sliding open again, and she knew Edmund watched from the hall below. It was too late to care; she flew along paneled corridors to the nursery.

She burst in breathlessly on the startled nursemaids. "Get the babies out of here. Hide them and send someone to bring Mr. Jasper home. Hurry!"

The slow-witted wet nurse Lord Westly had hired for his grandson began to protest, but the young girl from the village quickly gathered up Lord Richard and quieted his sleepy protest before reaching for Lady Emily. Eileen grabbed the bouncing six-month-old Lord Westly had named George in honor of the king, but time had run out. Edmund quietly entered the nursery behind her.

"That was cruel, my lady, but I should have known Drake would not marry a simpleton." He stepped forward to examine the infants now clutched in three sets of arms. He chortled as he came to the dark-haired, heavyset toddler in Eileen's arms. The twins had been dangerously small at birth and had only now gained the size George had been when he was born. The differences between their fair tininess and George's husky darkness was marked in the extreme.

"There is no difficulty in telling which is mine. The old man must have paid a hefty sum to persuade Drake to accept him. I cannot see my cousin taking in my progeny willingly."

Instead of taking George, Edmund turned to the young nurse holding Richard. Swaddled in layers of blankets, he was no more than a bundle of cloth that

Edmund removed with ease from the girl's arms. Eileen started forward, but Edmund shook his head, holding the babe at a careless angle.

"Stay back, my lady. You have interfered enough as it is." He gestured at the young nurse. "Take my son from the lady."

As Eileen reluctantly surrendered the wide-awake infant to the nurse, she stared at Edmund in bewilderment. "What do you want? Why have you come here?"

Dark eyes regarded her with hatred. "I have come for my son. And to keep you from interfering, I will take yours also. I will remind you how easily an infant can be injured, even killed, if carelessly handled. Do not give me reason to act hastily."

Cold hands of fear ripped at Eileen's insides, but she held herself with icy control. "I do not understand." She felt the nursemaids staring at her with terror but they would not move without her direction. With Richard dangling from Edmund's hand, she did not dare act incautiously. "We have no intention of harming your son. Had you come here with Lord Westly, I would gladly have surrendered him to you. I only sought to protect him," she pleaded with deliberate misunderstanding.

"That is not likely to happen and we both know it; that is why I'm taking matters in my own hands. Westly will have to deal with me while I hold his precious grandson, and I venture to say my cousin will be eager to persuade him should I hold his son and heir. Stay out of my way and do not interfere and the darling cherubs will be back in your nursery shortly."

Three-month-old Richard stared silently from his cocoon of blankets as Edmund wrapped his hand tighter in the swaddling clothes. Eileen felt her heart being torn from her chest as Edmund signaled to the maid to leave first and turned in the direction of the door. She could not let the child from her sight, but she dared not stop him.

She teetered on the brink of indecision. If she should scream or attack him, it would be so easy for Edmund to swing his tender burden against a wall or drop him down a stairway. But if she kept silent and did nothing, she might never see the child again. She could not live with herself if she did nothing and lost her son. Her fingernails bit into her palms as Edmund marched his hostages out the door.

Elizabeth stood at the bottom of the stairs, her hands resting on the wheelchair in which Diane sat, both their gazes turned upward to the scene unfolding before them. Edmund shifted his tiny burden into the crook of his arm and held it out over the railing as he proceeded downward, the nursemaid and his son before him.

"I'll take leave of you, ladies. Follow Lady Sherbourne's example and do not interfere and all will be well. I'd recommend not sending anyone after us. The brats will be fine as long as I have my way."

Elizabeth pulled Diane from his path and Edmund passed them by. A footman came scurrying to open the door, his eyes wide with fear, but a glance to Eileen at the top of the stairs warned him to silence. She stood white and frozen, clinging to the handrail as the door opened and Edmund's little procession stepped out.

The door swung closed, and they were gone.

Chapter XXIX

Instantly, Eileen became a whirlwind of motion. Racing down the stairs, she ordered servants to find Michael, saddle horses, and send for Drake. Without breaking stride, she grabbed a cloak and flew out the side entrance toward the stable. She could not allow Edmund to know she followed, but follow she would.

The stable boys had only succeeded in bridling a horse by the time she arrived, and Eileen had no patience for waiting. She could hear Edmund's carriage bolting down the drive to the front gates. She must know which way he turned when he reached the road. Without hesitation she grabbed the back hem of her skirt and pulled it between her legs to tuck into her waistband. Without a saddle she would have to ride astride.

The astonished stable hand protested as Eileen demanded to be lifted to the horse's back, but unaccustomed to disobeying commands, he finally surrendered. She had not been on horseback in nearly a year and was in no physical condition for it now, but she gave these things little consideration. The two babes in Edmund's treacherous hands possessed her every thought.

Vaguely she heard yells of protest from the front of the house as she kicked the tall mare into a gallop, but she didn't linger to argue. The horse responded eagerly, and they tore down the front drive after the carriage.

She reached the road just in time to see Edmund's vehicle disappear around the bend to the right. It was easy enough to keep in the shadows of the trees bordering the front lawns of the estate, but when she came to the first of the fields, Eileen had to hold back her mount until the carriage rattled around the next bend.

In this manner—hiding behind trees and curves and hills—she followed the escaping carriage for miles and hours. She had no knowledge of the surrounding countryside, had never strayed farther than the Neville estates when she had visited before, and could not tell where Edmund headed other than west. She wished for some means of leaving a trail for Michael and the others to follow, but she had none. She could only pray that the occasional passerby would heed her cry and forward word to Sherbourne.

As the sun began to descend, Eileen shivered with the cold. She wore a furlined cloak but had wasted no time searching for hat or gloves. Her fingers were red and raw from the chapping effects of wind and cold and she felt certain her nose had turned to icicles. Still, the carriage ahead rolled on, and she doggedly followed it. She dared to come closer as darkness obscured the landscape. Signs of civilization indicated a village lay just ahead, and the carriage slowed.

As the lumbering vehicle turned into the yard of the local inn, Eileen cautiously took an alley down a side road. From this angle behind the inn stable, she could watch the occupants without being seen. The driver climbed down and rubbed his gloved hands together to warm them, then wandered in the direction of the welcoming tavern light. Eileen held impatiently to her restive mount, waiting for someone to step from the carriage.

No one came to open the door. No one stepped out.

Furious tears leapt to Eileen's eyes as she realized what Edmund had done. Somewhere back there in those long stretches of open field when she could not come close, he had directed the carriage to stop and hastened his hostages into hiding. By the time Eileen had been able to ride down the road out of sight of the carriage, they had gone.

Anger and dismay warred within her as she turned her mind back to the miles of road they had traversed this day. Every muscle of her body ached. The wind had torn her hair loose from its pins and it whipped at her frozen face. She had only just begun to recover her strength and this ride had drained what little she possessed. Her hands could barely bend to hold the reins any longer. How could she go on?

She knew she should turn back to Sherbourne. There she could wait for Drake's arrival and tell him the direction Edmund had taken. But Drake might not arrive for days and Michael would already be out searching. She was the only one with any knowledge of where the babes might be. She could not desert them.

With harsh will Eileen turned her horse back down the way they had come. There were several places Edmund might have chosen to go into hiding, but the one by the wooden bridge seemed most likely. She had waited for what seemed like eternity behind a hill until the carriage had crossed the river and disappeared down a crossroads. It would have been easy to hide horses down the river bank. Edmund could not have walked away with a nurse and two infants. There had to be horses waiting. Tracing their path from the bridge would be the hard part.

Her breasts ached for the twins' hungry suck, and Eileen knew the infants would be crying from hunger by now. The young wet nurse she had hired to help with the twins would not have enough milk for both

those hungry boys. Edmund had chosen the wrong
nurse to take with him. She had to find them. It did
not bear thinking what would happen when the infants' incessant crying began to anger their abductor.

The cold had numbed her fingers and toes until
Eileen no longer knew they existed. Her teeth chattered and her legs ached so that she feared she would
not be able to stand should she ever manage to get off
the horse. She had given no thought to her own meals,
but the pain in her stomach came and went after a
while. She had survived hunger before.

Tears began to run down her cheeks as she reached
the bridge and had no idea in which direction to turn.
She had followed the carriage to the left at the crossroads, but they could have taken either of the other
two directions or followed the river and cut across
country. Waves of weariness swept over her, and she
wanted only to climb from the horse and curl up on
the warm planks of the sheltered bridge.

She knew she could not go on any longer, but stubborn courage made her turn the horse down the rutted
path leading toward a copse of trees in the valley. A
hint of light shone through the bare branches, signal-
ing a farmhouse of some sort. She would seek shelter
there and set out again in the morning.

The path grew tangled and full of briars as she tried
to follow it in darkness. At times she lost it altogether,
but kept the horse turned toward the light. Once inside the copse of trees even this signal became obscured, but she had come too far to turn back now.
Uneasiness began to gnaw at the corners of her mind.

No dogs yapped a warning as she approached the
squat, square shape of someone's abandoned hunting
lodge. A candle glimmered somewhere deep in the
interior, but no other signs of life welcomed her. No
hearty fire roared in the chimneys. No voices called to
each other. Thick, despairing silence reigned. Until
the sound of an infant's wail broke the stillness.

Weary exultation warmed her. She had found them. She knew it. With caution, Eileen halted her mount near a fallen tree and painfully eased herself down. She ached in places she had not known could ache. Her legs nearly crumpled beneath her, but she clung to the tree until she steadied herself. The bark tore at her frozen hands, but it no longer mattered. She had found her son.

Eileen inched carefully near the house, searching for other signs of life and means of entry. Bleak eyes of darkness stared at her from blank windows, and she eased around the corner to the next side. The mortar between the stones had begun to crumble from the wall on this side, and a small avalanche of stones had made a mound of rubble beneath one window. Still, she could not find the source of light.

Her small slippers tripped over another stone and Eileen barely managed to muffle her cry of pain. Her toe throbbed from the stumble, but she had reached the corner of the house facing the rear. The smell of a fire burning reached her nose, and a pattern of light spread across the hard-packed dirt of the kitchen yard. This was where the inhabitants had gathered—in the kitchen.

Holding her breath, Eileen stood on tiptoe to peer in the rear window. At first glance, she could see nothing but a crude, weathered board table and the remains of a fire in a wide, crumbling fireplace. The infant still cried somewhere in the distant rooms, but for one brief, hopeful minute, she thought Edmund may have left them alone. That hope was shattered an instant later when he came through a doorway and poked at the fire's embers.

And then rough hands covered her mouth and grabbed her by the waist and carried her kicking and screaming in the back door.

Edmund scowled as his driver dumped his furious captive on the cold flagstone floor. The rotund man in

the tricorne and swarthy face merely spit in his rough
palms and rubbed them together as he observed his
prisoner.

"She be peering in the glass, sirrah. I'll be back to
my horses now." With a brief doff of his hat, the
driver shuffled out the door.

"You damned, interfering bitch!" Edmund glared as
Eileen slowly lifted herself from the floor, her numb
hands pushing her skirts to straighten them. Auburn
hair hung in tangled knots about her pale face, and if
it were not for his lack of superstition, he would swear
those silver eyes cursed him. "You've ruined everything!"

Eileen rested a hand on the table, balancing her
unsteadiness as she returned Edmund's glare. "Where
is my son?" she demanded.

Incredulous, Edmund stared at her. "You don't have
any idea what you have done, do you?"

"And I don't care." In that moment, she meant it.
She knew Richard's cry and she wanted only to answer
it. The tall stranger blocking her way had no meaning
to her other than an obstruction. Only the fury in his
dark eyes and the width of his broad frame compelled
her to listen.

It began to dawn on Edmund why de Lacy had
wished to rid himself of this single-minded brat. She
gave no thought to the proprieties or conventions or
even herself. She seemingly had no fear. She was too
small to be a formidable enemy physically, but even
the tiniest of terriers could worry a stag to the ground.
And this damned, interfering wench was Drake's wife.

A malevolent smile slowly formed on Edmund's lips
as the impact of this realization reached him. Not only
Drake's son, but his beloved wife, his one major weakness. He could ask for the moon and get it now.

With a grave bow Edmund indicated the door through
which he had just entered. "Your son is in there,
madam. I recommend you join him."

*   *   *

Rage and fear whipped through Drake as he read the brief message from Sherbourne. It could not be. They had seen Edmund off on a ship to Plymouth nearly a week ago. He should be well on his way to the colonies by now. He could not be at Sherbourne.

But he knew as surely as he held this sheet of paper in his hand that Edmund had found some way to disembark before the ship left England. Cold blue eyes raised sightlessly to the messenger who had delivered this news, and the lad shivered and stepped backward, fearful his lordship meant to rip him limb from limb. The marquess had always been a good employer, but his was a temper to match the wrath of the gods when roused. As it most certainly was now.

"Order my horse," Drake commanded curtly, turning abruptly from the messenger and back into his chambers. The one tangible bond he had relied on to hold Eileen to him had been stolen. To lose those children would be to lose his wife. He could spare neither.

He should have returned home as soon as he had seen Edmund off. But there had been the final papers to be drawn on the land he meant to purchase for Eileen's cottage, and the surprise he meant to give her, and while he waited, the interview with the Duke of Newcastle. It had seemed reasonable to wait until he had the deed in his pocket and Hogarth's sketch in his hands before returning home to the joyous welcome he expected there. Not once had his thoughts turned to disaster.

Drake strapped on the brace of pistols he had won in a card game some years ago and removed his sword and scabbard from the wall. This time he would have to kill the bastard.

Chapter XXX

❦

Auguste Monsard gave a cry of relief as Drake strode into the study shortly before midnight. The cry died on his lips, however, as he read the stormy blue of his cousin's eyes and noted the weapons of war his generally easygoing cousin never wore. The lamp flickered on the desk, throwing shadows over the exhausted circles of Drake's eyes and the grim line of his mouth. Had he been Edmund, Auguste would have fainted of fear.

"What news?" Drake demanded without preliminaries.

"We know what direction they took. We've traced the carriage," Auguste offered hopefully. Then, with greater hesitation, he produced the carefully folded vellum lying on the desk. "Michael says there may be just enough in the bank if we withhold payment of some of the bills, sell some of the West Indies stock, and persuade a loan from the banker for the difference. It is an amount beyond my ability to imagine."

Drake ripped the letter from Auguste's hand and scanned it quickly. A ransom note. Edmund must have taken leave of his senses. They had found him a respectable position in the colonies, offered him a reasonable allowance, and he threw it in their faces like this. The amount was truly astronomical. He would have to mortgage Sherbourne to operate until the

371

crops came in next year. But then, Edmund had a very good notion of what Sherbourne was worth. He would have to pay it. Eileen would never forgive him if he tried anything else.

Drake's tired eyes lingered over the odd wording of the message. Why did he refer to "their" safe return? Surely Edmund did not mean to ransom his own son?

"Has Lord Westly received one of these?" Drake waved the missive angrily before flinging it to the desk.

"He's gone to London to confer with his bankers already. He promised to be back on the morrow." Auguste clung anxiously to the desktop, waiting warily for the explosion he sensed building inside his older cousin.

"Did Eileen go with him?" It seemed unusual that she would not be here, waiting anxiously for some news. The only logical conclusion was that she could not wait idly but had taken matters in her own hands and gone to London.

Auguste's eyes widened and he sat with a sudden thump in the leather desk chair. It had not occurred to him that Drake did not know . . . But the message had gone out before any of them had realized what Eileen meant to do.

He stammered and nervously reached for the decanter of wine. "No . . . I thought you knew. Let me take you to Michael . . . We were just waiting . . ."

Drake's eyes fastened him to the chair with their steely gaze. "Thought I knew what? Where is Eileen!" With awful, dreadful certainty, he already knew, but he had to hear it for himself. She would never have waited idly. He had been right about that.

"She went after them," Auguste whispered, prepared to duck the blow he feared would come from those powerful fists at Drake's side.

"And?" Drake demanded menacingly.

"She has not returned."

Drake swung and slammed his fist into the tapestry-covered wall behind him. Had it not been for the heavy cloth and the pocket of air behind it, he would have shattered half the bones in his hand. As it was, he merely tore the hanging loose from its mooring and bruised his knuckles on the oak paneling beneath. His rage continued unabated. The stream of invectives he laid upon the cloth, the wall, his cousin, and his wife welled from an imagination and vocabulary of brilliant capacity. Auguste cringed but breathed easier. The explosion had come without harm. Now the real work could begin.

Lady de Lacy waited on the stairway as the two men left the study. Her petite figure wrapped in a velvet dressing gown borrowed from her daughter, her auburn hair gleaming in the light of the bed candle she held, she created a ghostly image in the darkness that nearly stunned Drake into silence. Recovering quickly, he advanced courteously toward his wife's mother.

Waving away any polite phrases he might utter, Elizabeth demanded, "I do not know your cousin Edmund. What kind of man is he? Will he hurt them?" Her gaze focused intently on the tall, young lord who had married her daughter but left her exposed to danger. Her anger did not relent as she heard the pain beneath the proud steel of his voice.

"Edmund is too clever to get himself hung. He will not hurt them, no." He answered her question but did not give her the entire truth. Edmund would never do what he could persuade others to do for him. The lady was too overwrought to be told that. "My sister?" he inquired, distracting her, "is she sleeping?"

"The physicians have given her laudanum. She blames herself for not thinking more quickly, and for not being able to act, I believe. But there is nothing she could have done."

Drake heard the accusation in her voice and acknowledged it. He should have been the one to protect them. She could not blame him any more than he blamed himself.

His fury rung clearly in his reply. "Tell Diane I have gone to bring them home."

Swinging on his heels, he strode out, leaving Elizabeth to stare after him. She had thought Eileen had married a man much like her father. Now she realized that was not so. Richard had been a gentle-tempered man who fought only when all was lost, who preferred a peaceful solution to dissension. The glimmer she had just seen in Lord Sherbourne's eyes warned that was not the case here. There would be no peaceful outcome to this misadventure. Drake meant murder, and Elizabeth was not at all certain that her daughter might come in for some share of the lord's fury.

She turned and hurried back up the stairs.

Eileen waited until the house was still and dark. The young nursemaid slept peacefully with the two infants beside her on the large bed in the upstairs room they had been given. The day had been a nerve-racking one simply because she could do nothing but pace the floor. Now that night had arrived again, Eileen prepared her first move.

Throughout the day, she had seen only the two men: the swarthy driver and Edmund. They both carried weapons and their physical stature made it unlikely that she could escape without harm. But they had to sleep sometime.

The old lodge creaked as she eased out into the upper corridor. The dry wood seemed to stretch and crackle like an old man rising from a nap. Stripped of most of their furniture and hangings, the walls and floors echoed every noise. Eileen's soft shoes made less sound than the boards she walked on.

Her muscles still ached abominably from the prior night's ride, and her hands still burned from the rawness of chapping, but these inconveniences were minor compared to the danger Edmund posed. She had not liked the way he gloated whenever she came into his presence, and his callous disregard to the comfort of the infants made her extremely wary of his intentions. She knew he meant to extort money from Drake and Lord Westly for their return. She feared what he intended once he got it.

The stairs creaked protestingly as she edged down them, carefully seeking the less worn places in hopes they would not be so loud. She wasn't quite certain what she would do should she find her guards asleep. To go back up and wake the babes would be dangerous. To leave and ride for help seemed cowardly. She acted on instinct alone.

She had never seen the front door opened, and she glanced at it as she came down the stairs. Made of heavy, hand-hewn timbers, it appeared to be lodged firmly in its frame. Not even a draft of cold night air stirred around it. The heavy wooden bar across it would have to be removed completely before it could be opened. Eileen suspected the old wood would be warped and unmovable, which was why her captors used the rear.

Moving silently as she had learned to do in childhood, Eileen crept toward the kitchen. The downstairs held only these two rooms. The driver must sleep in the stable with the horses. She hoped Edmund had found repose in the other upstairs chamber. She had heard him there earlier, but it was difficult to keep up with him when two hungry infants wailed for their dinners. She prayed quietly as she reached the kitchen doorway.

No lamp or fire burned in the flagstone-and-timber room. Other than a few embers in the ashes, complete darkness obscured all but the lighter gray of the windows. Eileen hesitated, trying to remember the exact position of the tables and chairs she had seen earlier. The door would be somewhere between the two windows.

She edged into the room, reaching ahead with her fingers to find the table's solidity to guide her. Her toe bumped a chair leg, and she muffled an exclamation of surprise more than pain.

A second later a flint struck between the two windows, and Edmund's face appeared in the glare as he lit a candle wick. The contours appeared even more evil in these shadows than during the day, with only his bodiless visage illuminated. Eileen controlled her gasp, but her fingers bit painfully into the splintery wood of the table.

"Sleepwalking, my dear?" Edmund inquired softly, wickedly. "It's a dangerous practice. I do not recommend it."

Boldly Eileen lied, "I was hungry. I am not accustomed to living on the slovenly gruel you serve as food."

Edmund laughed sharply. "You will have to endure with the rest of us until your husband comes forth with his gold. Go back to bed and don't try this again."

As the candle flame grew stronger, Eileen could see that Edmund sat firmly in a chair propped against the room's only escape. She would have to shoot him and climb over his body to get out. The likelihood of that seemed very slim.

"Will you let us go, then?" She had to ask, had to judge the desperation of the situation by his answer. She would not trust his words so much as the way in which they were said.

Edmund eyed her dubiously. The soft woolen gown she had worn on her wild ride was much the worse for its inappropriate use, and, petticoats crushed, it hung in bedraggled wrinkles from her slender waist. She had made some effort to pin up her thick hair, but there was nothing elegant or stately in its disarray. His cousin had married a puny tatterdemalion who disgraced the title she wore. Edmund snorted at her question.

"I would be doing Drake a favor to give you to the gypsies in the woods beyond, but the fool probably will not see it that way. I am still debating. You are a complication I had not counted on."

"But the babies? Surely you will return them?" Eileen inquired anxiously. If there were truly gypsies in the woods, she would not put it past this monster to sell the babies.

"It will be convenient to have my son called Lord Westly. If you had simply let me have him when I requested it, you would have been spared this inconvenience. Now I will have to forego my negotiations with Westly and go to the Continent after all. Drake would never allow me to remain here after this. That's a problem I have yet to resolve. Go to bed and don't anger me by trying any more of your tricks."

His tone was curt bordering on abusive. Eileen swiftly turned and left him there, her heart pounding with fear. It did not sound as if he meant to release her or Richard. His hatred of Drake would force him to cause as much pain as he could. She did not think cold-blooded murder quite his style, but the threat of the gypsies would be. He would sell her son and she might never see him again. If he were not quite so clever, he would sell her, too, but the rape that would most certainly mean would not keep her from escaping with Richard. Drake would follow him to the ends of the earth if he did that. No, he would have to leave Drake in uncertainty. Eileen could not imagine what path that would take.

She slept little that night and dawn brought the certainty that she would have to disarm Edmund if they were to escape. If it had not been winter, she could have invented some excuse to go out in the overgrown yard. She doubted if she would be so lucky as to find nightshade there, but henbane perhaps, if the kitchen garden had ever grown medicinal herbs. Only the seeds would be usable this time of year. They would be difficult to disguise in Edmund's food, but he might ingest enough to render him ill. But she had no conviction she would recognize the plant without the leaves.

It was a start, though. There had to be some weapon she could use if she just kept her wits about her. With no other plan than that in mind, Eileen lifted her squalling son from the nursemaid's arms and sat in the chair by the window to nurse him. He quieted quickly, but her mind raced from possibility to possibility as he drank his fill. Her love for this infant in her arms was stronger than any man could ever be. She would defeat Edmund, sooner or later.

By the end of the day, her store of weapons consisted of a hefty rock hidden in her skirts after a trip to the privy, a dull knife lifted from the kitchen when she prepared their coarse meal of cheese and bread, and a goose feather she had found lodged between kitchen wall and floor. They did not make a formidable array, but Eileen refused to be discouraged. Drake would be searching for them by now. She need only find some way to signal him, or disarm Edmund so she could run for help.

One or the other seemed imperative when Edmund invited Eileen to join him for the evening meal. His confidence could only mean that he expected the ransom to be paid soon. She had heard the driver ride out earlier. His horse was back in the yard now. He had heard something, but Eileen could not venture to guess what.

She sipped slowly at the ghastly concoction Edmund called tea and listened with only half an ear as he droned on about his plans to travel in Italy. Perhaps if Drake had found him a position in Italy instead of the colonies, Edmund would not have felt compelled to carry out these mad plans. He seemed to have an abhorrence for the "savages" in the Americas. But he would have found some other excuse, she thought idly.

Lack of sleep these past nights made her lids heavy, and Eileen fought to stay awake. She had to learn what his plans were, what he had found out today, but she was unable to force her tongue to turn the conversation. It took all her strength just to hold her head up. Edmund's monotone made it worse. Lord, but he was the most boring conversationalist she had ever heard. Could he speak of naught but himself?

She wished for a glass of cool spring water instead of this muck he forced upon her. Her tongue felt like sandpaper, and she pushed the cup away with distaste. Instantly, Edmund was bending solicitously over her, offering more.

"You do not look well. Let me add a little brandy to your tea and see if that does not make you stronger." He produced a flask from his pocket and poured a thimbleful of the liquor into her cup before shoving it back to her.

Eileen stared at the cup, then dragged her gaze back to Edmund's unfathomable dark eyes. "You have heard from Drake?" She managed to speak the words with care.

Satisfaction flickered somewhere in the depths of his eyes as he watched her. "We will retrieve the gold on the morrow. It was a pity I couldn't demand enough to break him, but I needed it immediately, and it would have taken him too much time to gather more."

"And us? You will leave us here for Drake to find?" That would be easiest, but even her sleep-blurred mind knew Edmund had no inclination for simplicity.

His smile grew a trifle wider, giving him an even more evil look. "The nurse and my son, yes. They will go back to Westly. As I've told you before, you present more of a problem. Drake will not be content to let me live in peace in Italy after this. I need insurance, and you will be it. It will drive him mad with rage, but he will not be able to get me without going through you. Who knows? Perhaps you will learn to prefer my company to his. So many things can happen in a day's time, and we will have weeks. Perhaps months. Until Drake agrees to leave me alone."

Her head seemed to buzz oddly, and Eileen was not quite certain she heard him rightly, but she shook her head in what she meant to be vehemence. "Never. I will not go with you. I will scream. Someone will hear."

Edmund chuckled and pressed her hands around the tea cup. "Have another drink, my dear."

When she resisted, he forced the cup to Eileen's lips until the warm liquid slid from the corners of her mouth and trickled down her throat and she discovered no strength with which to fight him. Groggily she twisted her head, trying to avoid whatever poison the tea contained, but gradually the remainder of the tea poured down her throat and chin, and she sagged limply, with only Edmund's arm to hold her upright.

He lifted her in his arms as he would a rag doll, and she felt the crisp wool of his coat rub her cheek. His voice vibrated through her head from somewhere inside his chest as he spoke.

"Hear me now, my lady. You will fit quite nicely in the trunk I will have delivered to my cabin. No one will see you. No one will hear you. As you have already seen, I can keep the drug down you for as long as is necessary for us to get away. If you learn to behave, we can travel more comfortably. The choice is yours."

Eileen's small hand came up restlessly to paw the satin of his waistcoat, but her motion scarcely disturbed his stride. Within minutes he had deposited her on a bed she did not recognize, in a room that did not contain her son. The door closed, and she could not raise her head to scream.

Chapter XXXI

The sound of guitar music brought pleasant dreams. Drake's eyes hovered over her, laughing, loving. She reached out to him, wanting to touch the strong muscle of his jaw. It had been so long, so terribly long since she had lain in his arms and felt his kisses. She yearned for the hard pressure of his chest against hers, the whispered words that made her soul rise and her body hunger. His laughter turned diabolical, and she cringed, knowing her inadequacy. A marchioness! She had dared think she could be a marchioness! Her head filled with the laughter and she twisted restlessly against the pillows, fighting it, striving to escape, to run, to find the home and safety she had never known. Always it was just over the next hill, and her legs were so tired, she could hardly lift them. She needed sleep, so sleepy. If she could just sleep a while longer . . .

Again the strains of guitar lifted her from the lethargy. Did Edmund play a guitar? Startled, Eileen's dreams fled, leaving her drained and aching. She could not move, but her thoughts tumbled. Perhaps the drug had not been so strong as Edmund anticipated, or he had spilled more than he thought. She opened her mouth to test her ability to scream but thought better of it. He would come with more of that filthy tea and she would not be able to fight him. Perhaps it was later than she thought. Had he gone to find his gold then? Was that why he drugged her?

The possibility that Edmund might have left the house roused Eileen's confused mind more thoroughly than a splash of cold water. She had to find the babies.

With great effort, she found her feet. They slid unwillingly to the side of the bed. Her head felt as if someone had installed an anvil in it and was beating upon it regularly with an iron mallet. She could not lift the anvil, and the mallet was pure torture. Perhaps if she sat upright . . .

She swayed dizzily on the bed's edge, and all her senses warned her to lie back down and go to sleep until this went away. But the thought of her son kept her upright and gave her willpower. She rose from the bed and felt as if she would tilt and hit the floor from the weight of the anvil on her shoulders, but she made one foot move. And then the other. Right. Left. Until she reached the door.

Breathing a sigh of relief as the door handle turned, Eileen hung onto it as she eased the door open. The balancing act of standing and opening seemed beyond her, but, clinging to door and frame, she managed it. Unable to think beyond her next step, she ceased to worry about Edmund's whereabouts.

The door across the hall opened with just as much difficulty, but this time, the young nursemaid was there to help. With quiet exclamations she ran to catch Eileen and lead her to the bed, managing the difficulty of opening and closing the door with surprising ease.

The guitar music was louder here, filling the air with quiet ripples of sound. Eileen looked up questioningly to the village girl, her braided flaxen hair framing a pointed face of quick intelligence. She pointed to the window and whispered, "Gypsies."

Gypsies. Come to buy Richard. Eileen staggered to her feet again and leaned against the window. It took awhile before her foggy eyes could decipher shapes

and shadows. The underbrush had grown into thickets
and brambles all around the lodge, creating a nearly
impenetrable barrier. Gradually, she discerned a man's
shape leaning against a tree just beyond the perimeter
of the overgrown yard. He seemed small for a gypsy.
Not as fearsome as she had expected.

Was it possible? Could she turn this stranger from
foe to friend? No others strayed this far from the road.
It might be her last chance to communicate with the
world.

Knowing she was not thinking clearly but thankful
she was thinking at all, Eileen motioned for the maid
to bring her the writing box that had been left on the
dresser. She had examined it earlier and found the ink
long since dried and all paper gone but a scrap at the
bottom, but she had the goose quill now. Maybe . . .

Carefully trickling a few drops of water from the
washbasin into the inkpot and shaking it, Eileen prayed
it would produce some sort of color. She pushed the
quill into the wet mixture and laboriously transferred
it to the corner of vellum. She had no idea what to
say. Words failed her at the best of times, and this was
certainly not the best of times. Only Drake's name
came to mind. Desperately she wanted him here with
her, and the words to bring him came quickly to mind.

"Bring Lord Sherbourne. Reward." It just fit on the
scrap of paper, though her shaky penmanship left much
to be desired. She prayed the gypsy could read.

Still fighting the lethargy threatening to claim her,
Eileen did not try to rise again but gestured for the girl
to bring her the rock. Tearing a strip of lace from her
petticoat, she knotted the message to the rock. So far,
so good.

Now she had to catch the attention of the man out
in the woods. She did not know if he was even aware
of their existence. Eileen stared at the heavy rock in
her hand and back up to the window. The effort it
would take to coordinate rising from the bed, opening

the window, and heaving the rock seemed more than she could bear.

As Eileen staggered upright once more, the nurse-maid finally understood her goal. Relieving the lady of the rock, she hefted the warped and ancient window, rocking its leaden weights in ominous echoes until they held their breaths in fear. Gradually, between them, they shoved the unwieldy window to a height sufficient for the maid to lean out.

"I'm good at throwin', milady," the maid whispered. "You want me to hit him?"

"Catch his attention," Eileen said, nodding vaguely.

The heavy missile struck the unsuspecting musician on the shoulder blade, and they could hear his curse as he swung around to find his attacker.

Eileen gasped as a shred of moonlight caught his face. Teddy! Wigged in improbable black and garbed in leather jerkin and loose blouse, but still unmistakably the fey musician who followed Drake about like a wandering minstrel. Not finding an immediate assailant, he glanced up to the window where she stood. She could not divine whether he saw her or not, but he seemed to make a small salute before turning to retrieve the rock and trotting out of sight.

Galvanized by the realization that Drake must be near, Eileen shook off enough of her stupor to take the next step. The babies must be out of the house before Drake could come in. They were much too easy a target. She turned and caught at the sheet on the bed, shifting the sleeping infants to the bare mattress as she pulled the covers from beneath them.

Not quite understanding Eileen's intentions but grasping what needed to be done, the maid helped rip and tear the old sheet into wide strips. The infants didn't weigh much. With careful construction the old sheet tied to the blanket might make a safe cradle to lower them.

No one came to investigate the noise they were

making. Vaguely Eileen realized she ought to descend the stairs to see if Edmund had left, but she doubted her ability to do so. One small task at a time kept her awake; the drug had not yet left her system. She moved slowly, with much difficulty, and her head hurt too much to think clearly at all. Her hands ripped and knotted the sheets of their own accord.

With that task complete, Eileen felt the urge to collapse beside the soundly sleeping babes and give in to the waves of sleep washing over her. Drake would come and all would be fine. She need only rest her head for a little while.

A sharp whistle beneath the window warned her task was not yet finished. Cautiously she peered into the darkness, searching for the barely discernible shapes in the underbrush. They all looked like gypsies. She could see dark hair, the occasional glitter of gold, the flash of white sleeves as they crept under the window. One wearing a red bandana around his hair stared intently upward, obviously commanding the others. Eileen sagged with relief against the window frame as she recognized the square cut of his jaw with its deep cleft. Drake.

No flashing smile greeted her this time as she leaned out to signal him. He waited grimly for her to return as she turned back into the room and motioned for the maid to bring the infants. He was angry and Eileen knew she should be fearful, but she could not summon the emotion.

As the two women began to lower their precious burdens from the window, Drake understood at once what they did. Frantically he signaled two of the other figures hidden in the trees to come forward. It was a reckless, mad thing they did. Edmund could come upon them at any moment. The ropes could break. The babies could tilt or tumble. Drake cursed viciously and without thought as he anxiously watched the makeshift cradle lower to within arm's reach.

He grabbed the first infant as soon as he could reach it. Richard. The infant gave a surprised cry as his father hugged him with passionate relief. From above, Eileen watched this reunion with strange detachment. The look on Drake's face as his child reached out to tap his nose should have brought tears of joy to her eyes. Instead, she felt only the isolation of loneliness.

Drake passed his son on to the man behind him and waited for the second child to be lowered. George was larger and more active, and the nursemaid had to tie him into the blanket to be certain he would not roll over and tumble out. When Drake caught him, they threw the shredded sheets to the ground.

With the babies safely out of reach, the major need for caution was gone, and Eileen sagged against the windowsill with a weariness too heavy to bear. Drake had to whistle again to catch her attention.

"How many are there?" His whisper carried softly on the night breeze.

Strange, even now she understood him without questioning. She could not see the concern in his eyes as she slowly held up her fingers to indicate two. Her son was safe; nothing else mattered. Her eyelids drooped heavily, but there was still one more message to be passed on.

"Go in the rear," she whispered, before falling forward and collapsing in the arms of the sturdy nursemaid.

"Eileen!" Drake's quiet cry brought more of the "gypsies" frantically from the bushes, but the lady had disappeared from view.

The frightened maid reappeared in the window. "She said to go in the rear," she called out softly, knowing her mistress's last words had not carried beyond her ears. "Hurry, I cannot wake her."

Drake needed no further urging. Sword drawn, he signaled the band of friends, relatives, tenants, and even a few real gypsies to surround the lodge. It had not been difficult to trace Edmund's driver to this neighborhood, and the discovery of the gypsies had been pure luck. They knew everything that went on in the area surrounding their encampment and had been persuaded to part with the information for relatively few coins. Undoubtedly they joined in the fray in hopes of further reward, but Drake had no quarrel with that. He only wanted Eileen safely in his arms again.

A small party stood behind Drake as he kicked open the rear door and entered. The lamp wick on the table had almost extinguished itself, but there was sufficient light for the startled driver to wake and see the grim expressions on the faces of the intruders. Groggily he tried to stand and back away, but Drake had no patience for menials. He shoved the servant into the hands of the man behind him and strode swiftly to the next room. In the confusion the hired guard's pistol fell to the floor and there was a hasty scuffle to recover it. Someone knocked over the lamp, spilling the oil, but another was quickly lit. Drake paid no heed.

Edmund had already woken from the first sound sleep he had allowed himself in days. With Eileen drugged and the gold promised, he had felt confident enough to take a well-earned rest. The sound of the door crashing in the far room brought him instantly to his feet. Without hesitation he raced toward the stairs and the hostages who would protect him.

Drake hurled a curse after his cousin as he caught sight of Edmund fleeing to the upstairs rooms. The remainder of the search party followed his voice and boiled into the front room, but only a few could fit on the narrow steps. The others stayed behind to bind the driver and put out the fire slowly kindling in the spilled lamp oil.

Crashing through the door of the chamber where he had left Eileen, Edmund came to a wrathful halt at the discovery of her absence. She could not be gone! It took only a split second to dive for the second door in the upper hall.

Hearing the commotion in the rooms below, the young maid glanced worriedly to her unconscious mistress. Eileen lay curled in a tiny ball upon the bed, her thick hair escaping from its pins and falling about her face, her gown spread in a puddle of wrinkles across the mattress. The maid wished desperately to be told what to do, but, lacking instructions, she did what she thought the lady would do. She grabbed up the heavy ebony writing box and took a position behind the door.

Edmund never knew what hit him. The strong arm of the young village girl swung a blow her mistress would never have been able to wield. She caught him fully on the back of the head, sending him sprawling across the uncarpeted floor.

She screamed in dismay as she saw what she had done, but Lord Sherbourne scarcely gave his stricken cousin a second look as he flew through the open door and discovered his wife's lifeless form upon the bed. In two strides he was across the room and lifting her in his arms. Shouts from below went unregarded as Drake swung around and encountered the terrified gaze of the nursemaid.

"Go to the children. Have someone send a physician, quickly."

The curt words escaped Drake's stiff lips with difficulty. Eileen was no weight at all in his arms, and he could not feel her breathing. Panic began to replace rationality. The first faint whiffs of smoke from the kitchen made no impression on his senses. He held his life in his hands, and anger took the place of thought.

The men in the hallway hurriedly escorted the maid from the room, creating a path for Drake and his frail burden. The need for revenge had disappeared with the pure terror of uncertainty. Drake stepped over Edmund's unconscious body without a second thought.

Michael met him as Drake crossed the door step into the freshness of the cold night air. His anxious gaze glanced from the lifeless figure in Drake's arms to his friend's frozen features.

"Is she . . . ?" He couldn't say the words.

"I don't know." That simple phrase sounded an anguished cry from the heart. Drake hesitated no longer, but took long strides toward the warmth and protection of the gypsy encampment.

Michael's shout behind him halted Drake's progress with its urgency. He turned and saw what Michael raced toward. A small flame licked the roof beside the chimney, and for the first time he noticed the odor of burning wood.

Even as he watched, a wall of flame discovered the open stairwell and soared upward. Frantically Drake screamed for Michael to halt. The last of the band of men in the yard heard his words and caught Michael before he could go farther. The small group backed away from the awesome sight. The old wood in the deserted lodge caught like kindling, sending showers of sparks across the roof and lawn.

Gradually Drake's friends drifted to his side, pushing him away, turning him around, leading him toward the dark grove of trees ahead.

Even those who knew a man lay in the upstairs room said nothing as they retreated from the blaze. Edmund Neville died in a hell of his own creation.

Chapter XXXII

The patter of an early spring rain on the wooden roof first stirred Eileen from her slumber. The scent of wood smoke and bacon frying awakened memories of a cozy kitchen and warmth, and she snuggled deeper into the stack of comforters. It was raining. She did not need to go out today.

Sunlight poured in the room's only window when next she woke, and physical discomfort slowly forced her to recognize the need to rise. She pushed awkwardly at the comforters practically burying her before realizing she had no idea where she was. She had been dreaming of Dulcie and the village, but Dulcie did not have these luxurious covers on her bed. Eileen had not even had a bed in those days.

The lodge hadn't been so well provided, either. Eileen stretched and opened her eyes sleepily. Just the bed at Sherbourne had been as large as this room. Puzzled, she stared at the planked roof overhead, then let her gaze wander over the brightly painted walls with their odd ornamentations. A table and chair sat at the far end, and a blanket roll lay neatly upon the floor beside her. She recognized none of these things, and she rose up on her elbow to take a better look.

The comforter fell from her shoulders, exposing her arms to the unheated chill of the room. She realized she wore nothing but her chemise, and her glance went hastily to search for her clothing. Where was she?

A door at the far end opened, and Eileen snatched up the covers.

Drake stepped into the room, his golden hair gleaming in the morning sun, his loose shirt unfastened at the throat and covered only by a woolen jerkin. His glance quickly noted Eileen's wakefulness, but whatever he felt he kept carefully hidden.

"The physician said your head may hurt for a little while. He left some powders on the table. Shall I bring you some water?"

The first waves of relief quickly faltered beneath Drake's noncommittal tone. Eileen held the covers tighter to keep from shivering. "I need my clothes," she replied cautiously, testing her uncertain tongue.

"These will be more comfortable." Drake indicated a stack of neatly folded clothes on the chair. "We will not be seeing anyone, so you need not worry how you look. I'll be back with your breakfast shortly."

Was she mistaken, or was there some hesitation in his glance, in his movement, before he turned to depart? She understood none of this. What had she done to cause this icy gap of formality between them? What had happened? The brief flickering memories of that last terrifying night shocked her into action. Richard! Where was Richard? Flinging the covers aside, Eileen leapt from the bed and raced to the door.

Drake crouched beside a small fire and looked up, startled, as his chemise-clad wife came flying out the wagon door, auburn hair streaming down her back.

"Richard? Where is Richard?" she screamed, fully awake and utterly terrified.

Drake stood and caught her by the shoulders. "He's safe. Don't worry. Go back inside and dress before you catch a chill."

When she hesitated, searching his face for truth, he

swung her up in his arms and abruptly returned her to
the wagon. As he set her down inside, he said once
more, "He is safe. I promise." Then he closed the
door and left her alone.

Eileen shivered, cold to the bone though the heat of
Drake's fingers still burned against her skin where he
had touched her. For one brief moment he had held
her, but it was as if he had been holding a stranger.
She did not understand, but suddenly she was very,
very frightened.

Her stiff fingers found the woolen clothes neatly
pressed and waiting for her. She did not recognize
them, but the full skirt of heavy chocolate-brown wool
wrapped warmly about her legs. The thick satin shirt
of gold was chilly against her skin, yet the green knit-
ted vest that went over it kept out the draft. She
pulled on the woolen stockings to warm her legs and
considered the forest-green cloak, but decided against
it. The sun had been shining brightly and the wind had
more of spring in it than winter. She would not need
the cloak.

She looked around for something resembling a mirror, finding a small shaving glass over the washbowl.
She inspected her face carefully, discovering her eyes
looked slightly feverish but clear and the dark circles
of illness had completely gone. She felt stronger than
she had in months, but her breasts ached for her son
and daughter. Why had Drake brought her here?

With nothing to hold her hair other than the bright
red scarf flung carelessly beside the washbowl, Eileen
pulled her hair behind her ears and knotted it in the
scarf. The bright colors made her face look pale and
she pinched her cheeks for color. Seldom had she
given thought to her appearance, but Drake's strange
behavior made her reach desperately for explanations.
Perhaps she had grown ugly to him.

The possibility that the fire between them had somehow died caused irrational panic. It had been so terri-

bly long since she had shared his bed . . . What if he had found someone else while he was in London? Some aristocratic lady that better suited his tastes and needs? And here she was, looking like the gypsy she truly was, and her heart sank to her knees. She could never win him back like this.

She had blithely accepted their separations before, knowing she had no claim on Drake, that each moment with him was a moment stolen from fate. But his words, his promises, this ring on her finger—Eileen raised her hand to be certain she had not dreamed it—had bolstered her confidence. She had begun to believe that the fairy tale could come true, that Drake would always be there, and she would have a home and a love of her own at last. Had she been so wrong?

Eileen fought off the tears that threatened to well up in her eyes. She would not let him see her terror. Let him think that she was strong, invincible. She would not be one of those weak, helpless creatures who could not exist without a man. She was her own person and could stand on her own. But heaven help her, she did not want to.

If she wished to appear strong and resilient, she failed miserably. Drake watched as Eileen stepped gracefully from the wagon and disappeared into the bushes, and his heart lurched at the sight of her small white face with those enormous eyes wide with some emotion he did not dare explore. The layers of clothes several sizes too big for her made her seem no larger than a child, and he almost called a halt to his plans. Only his memory of the woman he knew her to be kept him crouching by the fire, turning the layers of fatty meat in the blackened pan.

When Eileen returned, Drake handed her a plate with well-done bacon and toast and an egg that seemed to have taken on the black grease of the pan. Too ravenous to care, Eileen drank thirstily of the strong tea offered, then silently tackled her food.

They sat side by side on a blanket Drake had spread on the ground. Eileen concentrated on her food, trying studiously to ignore the man staring into the fire beside her. It was a difficult task. His greater size protected her from the stinging edge of the wind, allowing her to bask in the full warmth of the sun. The sunlight glistened along the hairs on his arm, the only part of him she could see clearly without raising her eyes. The gold ring glittering on his finger was the one she had worn for so many months. His fingers were long and tanned and hard and appeared amazingly competent as they maneuvered the various pots and pans and lifted the mug of tea. She knew what those fingers could do to her if only . . .

But he seemed to have no interest in so much as touching her. Concealing the growing ache inside, Eileen asked wistfully, "Might I see the twins?"

Drake reluctantly turned his gaze to the petite figure beside him, knowing his ability to resist weakened with every look, every touch. But somehow, he had to reach her, had to make her understand, since the passion they had shared had obviously not. He must begin as he meant to go on, but it was damned difficult when gazing into eyes like warm seas.

"Will you mind if it is just us for a few days?"

The low timbre of his voice melted chords along Eileen's spine, but his words startled her into staring up at him. Embarrassed when she saw only the coolness of spring skies in his eyes, she quickly looked away.

"I would not mind, but . . ." She hesitated, her embarrassment carrying over to her words, "they are not weaned yet. It is uncomfortable . . ."

Enlightenment slowly dawned, and a small smile played upon Drake's lips as he read the heightened color in her cheeks. "Then I shall send for Emily."

Eileen looked up quickly. "Why just Emily?"

Drake leaned back on one elbow and stared up into

the shadows and hollows of her lovely face. "Because Richard has grown much too demanding, and I would prefer to spend these days with two females. The nurse you chose seems quite competent to handle him."

She could not match the import of Drake's words with the lack of expression in his voice. With an inquiring lift of her brow, she turned to face him.

"Am I to be told why you prefer to entertain us in the midst of wilderness?" She gestured toward the trees crowding around the small glade where the wagon rested.

"That's a long story. I don't know if I have the words to tell it." His gaze held hers searchingly.

A moment's panic made her heart skip a beat, but he seemed so amazingly calm, Eileen could not believe the tale was unpleasant. "Try," she demanded peremptorily.

A long, lazy grin sprawled across Drake's face as he lay down and crossed his hands behind his head, staring into the intertwining tree branches above as he spoke. "Once upon a time, there was an enchanted princess in a forest . . ."

"Drake!" Eileen protested, twisting to beat a small fist against his broad chest. "I don't want fairy tales! Why are we here? Does it have something to do with Edmund?" She looked momentarily horrified as again some brief scene from that night returned to her. "You haven't killed him, have you?"

The grin slipped away and he caught her by the waist, pulling her down on top of him. "Not that I hadn't thought of it, but no. His death was accidental." That was all he told her. She had no need to know the details, nor would the young nursemaid know that her blow led to Edmund's fiery death. As far as anyone who had been there that night was concerned, Edmund had died of an accident of his own making. That was the truth as far as it went.

Eileen remained silent, listening to the nuances of

Drake's words and absorbing the warm glow of being close to him again. He did nothing more than hold her, but she could hear the beating of his heart beneath her ear and feel his lungs fill with deep breaths as she curled more comfortably against him. Perhaps she did not leave him quite cold as yet.

"Then why are we here?" she insisted.

In one lithe movement Drake twisted to trap her between the ground and his heavy weight. His gaze swept searchingly over the silver of hers, moving downward over frail cheekbones and narrow chin, coming to rest on the delicate, moist corners of her lips.

"Because we have a few things to talk about and you have a few lessons to learn and I can do neither with the incessant interruptions of that madhouse. Do you object greatly?"

Eileen stared up at him uncertainly. She could hear the businesslike marquess speaking, but the light in his eyes had a familiarity she had once known well.

"No," she answered hesitantly, and before she could expound upon the subject, he murmured, "Good," and his lips closed over hers.

Joy pounded suffocatingly in her mind, spreading downward to her chest and the tips of her fingers as his kiss deepened and her nails bit into his shoulders. His tongue as he parted her lips dissolved any barriers she may have erected, and Eileen pressed him closer, wanting him to find what he sought in her and nowhere else.

The kiss ended too soon, and she moaned weakly as Drake lifted his weight from her. His hand moved to caress her cheek, to brush a strand of hair from her throat, to touch and know he had the right to touch. When his fingers came to rest on the smoothness of the satin skin over her breast, her eyes flew open, and Drake met her gaze frankly.

"I had meant to wait, to make you understand that you are my wife now, that you do not need to do every thing yourself, but I cannot talk for wanting you. Tell me you will never run away again, and I will believe you."

Drake's voice was hoarse and filled with longing, and Eileen nearly cried with the joy of his words. The promise his hand played upon her breast as his fingers slid along the low neckline of her shirt took her breath away, but she could not tell him what she did not understand.

She brought her hand up to cover his, swiftly untying her shirt and slipping his hand inside so that she could feel his warmth against her skin. Her nipple rose hard and firm against his palm, and she gasped with pleasure as he stroked it sensually.

"Your son and your daughter belong at Sherbourne. Why should I run away?"

"You did not wait for me but ran after our son when Edmund came. You ran away when our children were born. You were running from the convent where I left you when your uncle found you. You have run away from every home you have ever known, Eileen. How can I make you stay in the one I offer you?"

The plea in Drake's voice was plain enough, but she could not answer it with words she did not possess. She touched her fingers to the vulnerable curve of his lips she loved so well, traced the hard line of the jaw muscle tightening now with his anger and despair. How could she tell him what she knew without words or logic? There were so many things between them they had yet to resolve, so many obstacles to darken their futures, how could she make promises she might never keep?

Instead of promises, she spoke her heart. "I never ran away from anything, Drake. I've been running after you for as long as I can remember. Sometimes I have to step ahead of you to make you notice, that is all."

A smile slowly kindled behind Drake's eyes as he

absorbed the truth of her words and read the love in eyes no longer mirrored and unfathomable, but deep and warm and welcoming. He bent his head to kiss her brow, her cheek, the corner of her mouth, and lingered on the lobe of her ear.

"A veritable leprechaun you must be, princess," he murmured, "but I am slowly learning your tricks. Will you mind very much when you are well and truly caught?"

"If you catch a leprechaun, he will lead you to the gold at the end of the rainbow," Eileen whispered hoarsely as Drake's kisses strayed from her ear down her throat.

"It's not gold but you I want." He buried his lips in the hollow of her throat as his hand stroked downward from the curve of her breast to the narrow valley of her waist and beyond.

Then he raised his head to meet her eyes again, deliberately withholding the contact they both wanted. "I cannot demand all of you, all of the time, Eileen. You've been a free spirit for too long and I would not take that from you. But I want to know that you will be there when I come home to you. I want to know you will share your burdens with me and not try to solve them all yourself. You are my wife now, Eileen; let me be your husband."

His voice was harsh, his expression both angry and anguished. It had never occurred to Eileen that she could hurt him, but she had. Her fingers reached out to caress his face, to erase the lines that did not belong there. She would return laughter to his eyes. That would be her wedding gift to him.

"I do not know what you see in me. I have no manners, no breeding, no education. But I love you, I have always loved you, and if that is enough to make you happy, I will never leave."

Drake knew what she was saying, understood the fears behind the words as he had always understood what she did not say. She had spent too many years of uncertainty, too many years as an oddity to be totally comfortable with the life he wished her to live now. But she would soon learn he had servants to manage the household, tutors to teach the children, and guests that entertained themselves. He needed only her quickness of wit, her deep understanding, and her love. No amount of education or breeding could give him that.

It would take time to build the confidence and trust a marriage needed, but they had the rest of their lives for that. For now, what counted was their love. Drake bent and tasted the sweet willingness of her kiss.

"I will make you so much a part of me that you cannot leave," Drake answered roughly, and his kiss deepened until Eileen's arms flew about his neck and her body arched into his.

Sunlight licked their skins as Drake's tongue penetrated the honey of her lips, demanding—and receiving—the answer he sought. Eileen responded vibrantly as his fingers shoved aside oversized shirt and frothy chemise to fill with the heavy weight of her breast. When he turned his kiss to this sensitive peak, Eileen shuddered and held him closer, molding her body into his until she could feel the heat of his desire.

After long, languorous moments, Drake found the hem of her skirt and pushed it upward, his hand trailing over the soft juncture of her legs until Eileen moaned. Releasing himself from the confinement of his clothing, Drake moved possessively over her. And within the circle of greening trees, beneath the sun's blessing, they came together hungrily, with the rush of desire too long restrained. The ground beneath them trembled as their bodies rose and fell and found the pinnacle where they could be one again.

Afterward, when the breeze blew against their heated flesh, Drake lifted his wife in his arms and carried her to the wagon's small bed. This time they undressed slowly and came into each other's arms for warmth.

The rough golden hairs of Drake's chest brushed against the sensitive tips of her breasts, and Eileen sighed happily as his arms closed around her. Her fingers smoothed the hard contours of his chest, and she could feel the heat of Drake's maleness rising against her again. She kissed the strong curve of his shoulder.

"Drake?"

Head resting against the wildflower-scented softness of her hair, Drake managed only a contented "Hmmm?"

"How many children do you want?"

Drake dragged himself up on one elbow and stared at her warily. "Why?"

Having captured his attention, which was all she wanted, Eileen smiled contentedly. "Do we have to have twins this time?"

Drake grinned and stretched his long length beside her and sliding his arm to her narrow waist, pulled her tight against him. "I think that may be the only way to slow you down, tied to the cradle. But one at a time from now on, please. I don't think I can stand the strain of two again."

"One it shall be, then," she murmured wickedly, moving provocatively against him until he had no choice but to shove her back against the mattress and capture her once more.

Epilogue

—— 🖤 ——

Sherbourne
August, 1747

Sitting in the window seat of the nursery with sketch pad and charcoal in hand, Eileen glanced up with delight as her husband's tall frame filled the doorway. Hands on hips, he watched the activities of the three toddlers on the floor with amusement.

At ten months, George was already pulling himself to his feet and making his first tentative steps. He set his distinctly Neville jaw determinedly as he relinquished the safety of a table leg and strode boldly out into the room's center, where Richard was crawling.

Emily sat at Eileen's feet staring in bemusement at a red ball that rolled from her hand each time she touched it. The ball had kept her occupied for some minutes with total disregard of her playmates. Richard evidently meant to put an end to that.

His body long and wiry in comparison with George's plump chunkiness, Richard scuttled at a rapid rate across the uncarpeted floor, his goal obviously the bright object that kept his sister fascinated. Not quite possessing the ability to capture the ball, he did succeed in knocking it from Emily's reach. Emily glanced up in surprise, her wide blue eyes staring in dismay at this ungentlemanly theft, though she made no cry of protest.

Reaching for the rolling ball, George sat abruptly

on his diapered rear, unable to coordinate walking and reaching at the same time. The surprised look on his face as he fell brought a giggle to Eileen's lips, but she motioned Drake to remain still until George recovered his equilibrium. He still clutched the ball, and his gaze now circled to find his cousins.

Richard had already lost interest in the toy and had set off in pursuit of a moth fluttering against the dresser. Gingerly, George pulled himself to his feet again, still clutching the ball in his chubby hand. Then, with unexpected gallantry, he waddled the few remaining steps to Emily, dropping the ball at her feet. Emily's face lit with amazement, not so much at the ball, but at George's acrobatic feat. Within seconds, she was pulling at her mother's skirts in an attempt to right herself as George had done.

Drake's laughing gaze met Eileen's as he strode into the room and swept his daughter into his arms. Over his daughter's red curls, he noted Eileen's expression and grinned.

"Don't be matchmaking already. George is just blinded by her beauty. She'll make mincemeat of him in a few years."

Emily laughed with glee from the safety of her father's arms and reached to grab a wisp of golden hair escaping from Drake's riband. Drake tickled her, sending her into gales of delight beneath Eileen's satisfied gaze.

"Oh, I daresay there will be fights enough to come, but I think George is turning into a very gallant gentleman. He has an adventuresome turn of mind, mayhap, but you shall be proud of him someday."

Drake deposited his daughter on the floor and swept aside Eileen's skirts so he might join her on the seat. Propping one hand behind her, he gazed down at the sketch she had been making. He pointed at the likeness of Richard.

"And what do you foresee for our son, enchantress? Will he marry a princess? Destroy giants?"

Eileen smiled. "He is a dreamer. He may invent flying horses or gamble your fortune away. I hope he will inherit his father's talent. If you will not put your dreams to paper, perhaps he will."

Drake removed the pad from her hands and set it aside. Then, producing a package in paper and yellow ribbons from his coat pocket, he held it out of her reach. "And what would you give to see my brilliant tales in print?" he inquired laughingly.

Eileen's eyes widened in wonder as she read the truth behind his merriment. Eagerly, she reached for the package, but Drake caught her waist and held her tightly against him, his hand sliding knowingly upward to the curve of her breast.

"Your forfeit, madam?"

Willingly, Eileen turned into his embrace, circling her arms about his neck and plying his mouth with eager kisses. Until his book-laden hand came down to press her closer, and she swiftly turned and snatched the package from his grasp.

"That was wicked, princess!" Drake protested laughingly as she tore the paper into shreds to reach the contents.

Eileen ignored his complaint as her hands lovingly caressed the leather bound volume of Children's Fantasies. Opening the cover, she discovered the dedication, "To my wife, my love, my silver enchantress," and her cheeks flushed with pink.

"The whole world will see this," she whispered in delight and embarrassment. The rumors about their marriage had captured the scandalized attention of half of London last spring. Drake had pinned the cartoons and posters above his desk with amusement, but she still had difficulty fielding the prying questions of his aristocratic friends.

Drake laughed at this estimate of the book's sales.

"Perhaps just the English speaking portion," he conceded.

"When did you have time?" Fascinated, Eileen turned the pages one by one, finding the tales of the leprechaun army and the enchanted princess on every page.

"Last winter, when I could not be with you and had to bide in London until the court declared my innocence. I could find no better way to fill my idle time."

Drake watched her with more apprehension than he cared to admit. A grown man writing fairy tales seemed laughable, but if he had her approval, he could withstand the jests of all others. The love and awestruck admiration in Eileen's eyes as she lifted them to him answered his fears. He took the book from her hands and wrapped her securely in his arms.

"You could not have given me a better gift," she murmured before Drake's kiss sealed her lips. His mouth held hers tenderly, speaking his love, promising passion in the moments when they would be alone again. Her heart swelled with the knowledge his laughing words had given her. In all those hours when they were apart, he had not turned to his former pursuits or mistresses, but had remained faithful to her. It was a reassurance she needed.

Reluctantly Drake's kiss moved to caress her brow, and he settled her more comfortably against his shoulder, his hand stroking the underside of her breast as he willed his body to peace. The babies crawling about the floor did not object to their lovemaking, but the nursery was a favorite gathering place and had little privacy.

Impatiently he muttered, "Where are their bloody nursemaids? Why are you the only one inside on a day like this?"

The sun shone gloriously through the window behind them, accenting the coppers and golds of Eileen's hair and melting into the rich yellow of her low-cut gown. In honor of the day's warmth, she had worn no neckerchief, and only the tiny frill of chemise lace hid the valley between her breasts. Drake stared longingly at the rise and fall of her bodice and fought the urge to reach for the tempting ribbon holding it in place.

"Gertrude will be in shortly to take them for a walk. And Hannah will be in by feeding time. You forget, this is her day off, and if I do not mistake, it is also Quigley's." The heat of Drake's hand where it rested beneath her breast kept Eileen distracted, but she concentrated carefully on her words, knowing their importance, if not to her, to others.

Sir John had been persuaded to part with Quigley's services shortly after Drake had restored his family to the safety of Sherbourne last spring. Eileen had become accustomed to Quigley's nonintrusive presence and did not resent his constant companionship as she would another's. But this mention of the village nursemaid in the same breath caused Drake's eyebrows to lift slightly. The girl admittedly had behaved well under pressure and had been rewarded for her quickness of thought in protecting Eileen, but he had hired her as a wet nurse only. In a few months, her services would no longer be needed.

"And what does Quigley have to do with this?" Drake demanded, knowing she only waited for him to ask.

Eileen glanced over her shoulder to the garden below. "You need only use your eyes to discover that. She will be good for him. He's not been himself since Ainsley's housemaid rejected him in favor of the butler. Hannah will make him see sense."

Drake frowned as he followed her gaze to the couple walking hand in hand below. "Can you not limit your matchmaking to the family? We will have servants multiplying like rabbits and just as useless if you make a practice of this. I thought she was married. She's had a child," he reminded her.

"The child died. That's why she came to us as wet

nurse," Eileen chided him gently. "And she was not married. The boy ran off when he learned she was pregnant. I will not hold that against her if Quigley does not. It happens to the best of us."

That touched home, and Drake had to grin at the serious look on his wife's heart-shaped face. "Perhaps this household is not safe for unmarried females. We should hire only toothless old hags. Speaking of which, where is Diane?"

Eileen attempted to appear indignant, but Drake's carefree indolence made it impossible to be serious with him. She settled for insinuating her hand into the snug waistband of his breeches. Her fingers could do no more than slide along the shirt covering his taut abdomen, but Drake sucked in his breath with a gasp of pleasure.

She abruptly tugged the linen of his shirt sharply downward nearly strangling him with his cravat. "Diane is resting as ordered. You must remember you told me Michael needed a compliant wife. I think Diane suits him admirably."

"Which is damned well convenient since they lost no time in proposing to expand the nursery," Drake muttered irritably. "Compliant, you call it? To whom, may I ask? She's always done damned well as she pleased when I was around. I don't blame Michael for this madness. Diane put him up to it, I'm certain."

Eileen giggled at this continuance of Drake's aggrieved reaction to his sister's marriage. The wedding had been in June and the bride had announced her pregnancy at the reception. Drake had nearly fallen into his soup, and Michael had looked as smug as a new father could be. The two men had both wound up roaring drunk by evening's end, however, and the battle had been fought with damage only to the punch bowl.

Boldly she slid his shirt free from his breeches so she could touch the flesh beneath. Drake muttered wicked words in her ears, but Eileen ignored them. "You need a lesson or two, my lord, if you believe Diane solely responsible for her condition. Next, you will be blaming me when there aren't enough cradles around. How was your meeting with the duke? Is there any chance you will be able to persuade him to back the Catholic bill?"

Drake's breath caught in his lungs and his eyes narrowed suspiciously, and not just because his loving wife had succeeded in half undressing him and now played taunting games along his ribs. He knew her too well, and what she carefully didn't say gained more importance than what she did.

"And just how many cradles are we going to need, my love? Surely Diane isn't expecting twins, too?" Completely ignoring her insouciant reference to his trip to London, he settled on the more enigmatic statement preceding it.

Unfortunately, George chose that moment to fall over Richard and both infants set up a wail that brought hurried steps from down the hall. Drake hastily attempted to remedy his state of undress while Eileen leapt to the rescue. In another instant Gertrude and another maid had entered to busily set things to rights.

Deciding he had seen enough of his children without having to watch the process of diapering, Drake swept down upon his wife and carried her off, her protests falling on deaf ears.

The door to their chambers had been fitted with a new lock, and Drake secured it firmly as he deposited Eileen on the floor. The mischievous look she sent him as she scurried from his reach set small blazes smoldering in his blood. He stalked her patiently, cornering her between bed and washstand.

"Now, wench, what is it you are trying so hard not to tell me that it fairly dances from your eyes? Does Diane's doctor say twins? Must I force Quigley to marry our Hannah? Or is it Auguste? My God, I know he's been chasing after the little Maurice girl, but she's just a child . . ."

Her laughter left Eileen helpless to fight off Drake's hold as he flung her to the bed and proceeded to rip open the ribbons that had so tantalized him earlier, She could make no reply to his questions for gasping for breath, and his reckless disregard for her dress did not make it easier. With the bodice opened, Drake untied the strings of her chemise, and her breasts spilled out for his amusement. Since the peaks were already erect and eager for his touch, he was satisfied, and he bent to sample her lips more fully than before.

"I will not let you go until you tell me," Drake murmured against her mouth, drinking deeply of the honey he found there. The perfume of her hair filled his nostrils, and his hands sought the soft purchases he had uncovered.

"But dinner will be ready shortly," Eileen gasped, turning her head from his magnetic kiss so she might speak the words. "Cook has prepared something special for your return . . ." But she knew it was useless. Her bones had turned to jelly and her whole body flamed with the heat of his caresses. She felt the fastenings of her skirt give way beneath his practiced hands, and she could not fight them.

"Then you had better tell me quickly, hadn't you?" In truth, Drake had nearly forgotten the question in the heat of the chase. He wanted the woman more than the answer, and his kisses prevented further conversation.

As their clothes fell in growing piles upon the floor, Eileen ran her hands over the sculpted planes of Drake's chest with satisfaction. She had no doubt of her place in his heart any longer. She had come home.

Her body arched hungrily to meet his thrust, and all thought fled in the heated tumble that ensued. A week's abstinence was not easily assuaged, and it was more than a few minutes before they collapsed in the shambles they had made of the bed.

Naked and sweating and in each other's arms, they paused for breath and to bask in the pleasure they found there. Still not believing the effect this tiny temptress had on him, Drake began a slow exploration of her slender curves. Her breasts were fuller than when they first married due to the twins, but her waist had already returned to a circumference he could easily span with both hands. As his palms drifted downward to the curve of her hip and the soft swell of her abdomen, Drake remembered the question and his breath caught in his throat.

He turned, pinning Eileen's shoulder to the mattress as his gaze sought hers. She smiled languorously up at him, the gray of her eyes still smoky with pleasure.

"How many cradles is the nursery going to need?" he demanded.

Eileen's lips curved in a sultry smile. "Is this a test? My math is not very good, I fear."

"Try it this way, then. How many more cradles will the nursery need?"

Eileen wrinkled her brow in thought. "Well, I suppose George will be a year old before Diane has hers so perhaps he can be moved to a bed." She brought her fingers up behind his back and began to count them off. "And the twins will be more than a year old by February so perhaps instead of adding a cradle, we could take one away. Unless, of course, but you promised one at a time . . ."

Drake's hand shook as it followed his gaze and traced a path from her breasts to the slight mound of her stomach. His brow puckered into a frown of concern as he met her eyes again. "My God, princess, you are not telling me . . ."

She laughed, a gay trill that put the birds to shame as she circled his broad shoulder with her slender arms. "No, I am not telling you. You will have to figure it out for yourself. Will you love me still when I'm old and gray?"

"I will love you still when I am old and gray. That should be this time next year." Drake buried his lips in the curve of her throat and gave himself up to this wayward enchantress he had caught for his own.

Life might not be any simpler with her around, but it would never be dull.

About the Author

Patricia Rice was born in Newburgh, New York, and attended the University of Kentucky. She now lives in Mayfield, Kentucky, with her husband and her two children, Corinna and Derek, in a rambling Tudor house. Ms. Rice has a degree in accounting and her hobbies include history, travel and antique collecting.

Buy them at your local

bookstore or use coupon

on next page for ordering.

There's an epidemic with 27 million victims. And no visible symptoms.

It's an epidemic of people who can't read.

Believe it or not, 27 million Americans are functionally illiterate, about one adult in five.

The solution to this problem is you... when you join the fight against illiteracy. So call the Coalition for Literacy at toll-free **1-800-228-8813** and volunteer.

Volunteer Against Illiteracy. The only degree you need is a degree of caring.